The Heresy

Stephen Marley

The Heresy

Stephen Marley

Originally published by Musa Publishing, July 2013

This e-book is a work of fiction. While references may be made to actual places or events, the names, characters, incidents, and locations within are from the author's imagination and are not a resemblance to actual living or dead persons, businesses, or events. Any similarity is coincidental.

ISBN-10: 1517387973

ISBN-13: 978-1517387976

For Anita, who kept faith.

And my mother and father, who gave me faith.

ACKNOWLEDGMENTS

Thanks to the following, for too many reasons:

Celina Summers, Ella Kennen, Kerry Mand, Dominique Eastwick, Brigitte Delorme, Deborah Beale, Martin Bodenham, David Dew, Neil Dodwell and Martin Wong.

Most of all, a salute to my readers, without whom this book would not be possible, and my parents, without whom I would not be possible.

PREFACE

The Collyridian religion, or heresy, was a real historical faith in the early Christian era that spread from southern Russia and Bulgaria to Arabia. The Collyridians may well have inspired the cult of the Virgin Mary that was officially established at the Council of Ephesus in 431 AD. The historian Geoffrey Ashe has suggested that the Collyridians can be traced back directly to the Virgin Mary herself.

The necropolis beneath Vatican City, which plays a major role in the novel, and to date is largely unexcavated, is a real location. The ancient church of Santa Maria in Trastevere (the oldest church in Rome) is also real.

And a minor point: although I'm British I wrote this novel in American English as my original publisher was in the United States and three of the fictional protagonists were American. I only mention this in case my fellow Brits think I've forgotten how to spell such words as 'colour' and 'ampoule'!

Prologue

Rome, September 28, 1978

The Virgin Mary, nailed to a cross, hung high above her altar.

Mother Hypatia, head of the Dormition Order, knelt before the image in the candlelit shrine, gaze fixed on the Virgin Mary crucifix suspended above the tabernacle. Dense incense clouded the blue-robed figure of Mary's nailed body, its contours inconstant in a shadow play of sputtering candles, the Virgin's face streaked with blood from a crown of roses and thorns.

"*Maria Virgine,*" the nun intoned. "*Mater Dolorosa... Maria-*"

The rattle of the chapel door and the groan of old hinges halted Hypatia in mid-prayer. Footfalls sounded from the dark beyond the candles. Wincing at the stiffness in her joints, she stood to observe a tall figure advance down the aisle into the dithery aura of candlelight.

"Father Cosmas," she greeted coolly, her lined features compressed into a scowl.

The young priest raised a hand in token apology. "Forgive the intrusion. The Vatican has decided to dispose of its pope."

Mother Hypatia frowned at the death-knell note in his voice and slowly folded her arms, tucking arthritic hands in wide sleeves. "When?"

"Tonight."

Agitated fingers drummed a devil's tattoo on St. Peter's crossed keys embossed on a bank ledger.

The thrumming of fingertips was the only sound in the spacious office within the *Instituto per le Opere di Religione*, otherwise known as the Vatican Bank. Outside the locked office door, the voices of bank employees were as muffled as a church congregation, muted by the impending crisis.

The bishop's fingers continued their rhythmic tapping of the Vatican bank ledger.

The new pope, just thirty-three days in office, had begun an investigation of the Vatican Bank. Bishop Paul Marcinkus, as head of that bank, would be exposed. From Prince of the Church to pariah crook. A Luciferian fall.

His eyes strayed back to the note lying beside his ledger. It taunted him, a last testament to his downfall, a condemnation in code:

THE KNIGHT

THE SHARK

THE GORILLA

THE PUPPET MASTER

Bishop Marcinkus slumped back in his chair.

"John Paul the First will be the death of me."

Pope Paul was dead, and a very different man sat in his place. The conclave of cardinals had voted for Albino Luciani, former Patriarch of Venice, now John Paul I.

He stared again at the note, delivered three hours ago by his contact in the Apostolic Penitentiary. The note spelt out his fate in block capitals:

THE KNIGHT: Roberto Calvi, international banker and Marcinkus's business partner. THE SHARK: Michele Sindona, Mafia wheeler-dealer. THE GORILLA... He scowled at the nickname he'd earned in Vatican City: Paul Marcinkus himself. THE PUPPET MASTER: Licio Gelli, head of the Masonic lodge of P2, *Propaganda Due*, the man who pulled everyone's strings.

Unwise to antagonize P2, the secret lodge that was represented at every level of Italy's government and had the attentive ear of Prime Minister Giulio Andreotti.

John Paul knew it all. Four names in a single package, tied up nice and neat, ready to be mailed to the Italian police. That threat must be countered. Plans already formulated would be jump-started into action. None of his business.

He grabbed the note and crumpled it in his fist.

"My hands are clean."

His customary poise tested to the limit, Father Cosmas sat alone in the front pew of the chapel facing the crucified image of Mary. What was keeping Mother Hypatia? He touched the small Virgin crucifix hanging on a silver chain about his neck and whispered the salutation of the Dormition Order:

"Mary abides."

"Mary abides," responded Mother Hypatia as she sat down beside him.

He hid his surprise. "How do you do that, popping up out of nowhere? Some spiritual accomplishment?"

"Halfway to heaven, that's me." A momentary pause. "Ironic, isn't it? We attempt to save the Holy Father from his own servants. I've sent one of the sisters to warn the pope."

He masked his annoyance. "You should have discussed this with me first. Father Thomas Chen could—"

"Father Thomas is in Ephesus. I made alternative arrangements. Father Ignatio will meet with Sister Annunciata when she reaches the Vatican."

He took a slow breath. "*Annunciata*. Why her?"

"Should I have sent someone less able for whom you had less care?" The compassion in her eyes belied the hard tone.

"Of course not. It's just... she's very young."

She nodded her understanding. "Young, and proficient—Mark."

With a forced smile at her unaccustomed use of his first name, Father Mark Cosmas shifted impatiently in his seat. "You shouldn't have sent her." His mouth hardened into a bitter line. "Better a pope dies than her."

Father Mark looked up to the image of the crucified Mary, high above the altar, her brow encircled with thorny roses. His fingernails dug into his palms. "Marked by the thorn."

Sister Annunciata sat on a wooden stool in a Vatican storeroom, surrounded by empty crates and discarded statues. A bare light bulb supplemented what scant daylight infiltrated a tiny, barred window set high in the wall.

A single thought circled inside her head: *have I walked into a trap?* She was out of her depth, drowning in a broth of Roman politics.

She was from *Idaho*, for heaven's sake. Nine years ago, before the God bug bit, she was Sarah Maitland, a cheerleader at Idaho Falls High School. Yellow outfit and red pom-poms and rah-rah and jocks and furtive beers at the local hangout— the whole shebang. Right now she felt like a cheerleader dressed up as a nun, playing at undercover games.

"Divine inspiration would be welcome," she addressed a three-foot-high Blessed Virgin statue perched on a nearby crate. The request was met with blank silence.

She glanced at the red digits of her watch. 7:12 p.m. An hour since she'd entered Vatican City. Her designated contact, Father Ignatio, wasn't there to greet her. Instead she'd been met by a tall young priest who whispered "Welcome, Annunciata," in her ear. The priest, after introducing himself as Father Benoit, escorted her through archways and narrow corridors to the passage that skirted the Court of St. Damasus. Father Ignatio, it appeared, was under surveillance by the Holy Office so Benoit had taken his place. Twenty minutes at most and Benoit would escort her to John Paul's private study. In the meantime, sit quiet as a mouse. Since then, Benoit's promised twenty minutes had stretched to twice that length.

He had sounded plausible at the time. True, Benoit wore the distinctive gold crucifix ring of the Sodality of Petrus Pontifex, a brotherhood favored by some members of Conclave, an exclusive Vatican coterie that operated outside papal authority. But not all who wore that ring were loyal to that covert network: at least three Shrine members also belonged to the sodality. It spoke volumes of Conclave's mentality that it adopted the same name as the conclave of cardinals in a papal election. Conclave, derived from the Latin for a locked room.

Locked room.

She darted a look at the heavy, unvarnished door of the storeroom, then turned to the Virgin Mary statue. "Perhaps we've both been discarded."

Her mentor, Mark, who went under the name of Father Cosmas, had trained her to be proactive in hazardous situations. Make some kind of move...

Annunciata's hand moved to her chest and pressed the contours of the Virgin crucifix, hidden under the disguise of her black Dominican habit. "Mary abides."

Benoit had urged her to be quiet as a mouse. Too bad. This little mouse scented a trap, a trap that had snapped shut.

A few paces took her to the door. Sucking in a deep breath, she grasped the door handle and pulled. And pulled again.

The door didn't budge. Locked tight.

Bishop Marcinkus tried to ignore the clock. From time to time he managed to keep his eyes off the antique clock face for as much as a minute. But whether or not he watched the remorseless cycle of the minute-hand, the clock's brassy ticktock tracked him, step for step, as he paced around the study in his home in the Villa Stritch. The ticking of the clock marked more than the mundane passage of time. It was a countdown, ticking off the seconds to the Final Judgment.

The sudden alarm of the telephone gave him a jolt. The orange panel on the console showed the incoming call was on his private line.

Expelling a sharp breath, he lifted the receiver. "Yes?"

"The Knight." The voice was instantly recognizable as Roberto Calvi, head of the Banco Ambrosiano.

"No need for P2 Lodge code words, Roberto. And to be blunt, this call is not welcome."

"I am not to blame for what is happening," Calvi insisted, verging on the shrill. "You will say this, yes?"

"You are no more to blame than I am."

Marcinkus listened to a brief silence. Then came Calvi's angry torrent: "Is that a vindication of me, of my bank? No, no it is not. Am I the fall guy here? If I am indicted, I will name others also. We are tied together."

"Be careful you're not cut loose."

"Is that a threat? You think you and the others in the Lodge are so high and mighty, above the law. If you can get away with killing a pope, you can get away with kill—"

Marcinkus slammed the phone down, cutting the voice dead. He glared at the phone for a protracted minute. It stayed silent.

Gradually, the tick of the clock resumed the character of a countdown. The hour crept up to nine. John Paul would have finished his supper. Another thirty minutes and he would retire for the night.

If they do it, they will do it tonight. But I have no part in it.

The stress of the day started to manifest itself in a queasy sensation, the onset of a dull ache in his abdomen. The old trouble had flared up again: the elevation of Albino Luciani from cardinal to pope had been the very devil for his digestion.

He sat, slid open a desk drawer, and extracted a bottle of Milk of Magnesia. After giving the contents a shake, he took a gulp straight from the bottle. Leaning back in the padded chair, eyes closed, he let the medicine do its work. Within minutes his stomach settled and his hefty frame relaxed, just a tad.

He opened his eyes and studied the medicine bottle. It contained nothing but a standard medicine, available from any drugstore. Quite harmless. He held up the bottle, and in the blue glass he dimly discerned his own reflection staring back at him as if in accusation.

The hand that held the medicine bottle trembled.

"My hands are clean."

Albino Luciani, Pope John Paul I, settled back on the pillows plumped up against the headboard and prepared to take his nightly medicine.

He reached for the bedside table and picked up a dark red bottle of Effortil, a vasoconstrictor that corrected his low blood pressure. Every night for the past three years he went through the same routine, a sip of Effortil before sleep. Regular as clockwork. Carefully, Luciani poured the liquid into a teaspoon, almost to the brim, and swallowed the syrupy contents. Returning bottle and spoon to the table, he registered the time on his alarm clock. 9:41.

His thoughts gravitated, as so often during moments of reflection, far north of the sultry heat of Rome. North, to the foot of the Tyrolean Alps and the village of his birth, Canale d'Agordo. The air was cleaner, crisper there, and the people expansive of heart. They possessed a simple goodness that counted for nothing in the calculations of the powerful, whether commissar, count, or cardinal. They were the little people.

"Well, I'm one of the little people."

Wearily, he returned to the notes he'd been working on: a list of dismissals, effective as of noon tomorrow. It was a long list, with Bishop Marcinkus at the very top. High-ranking members of the Curia were hand in hand with P2, a Masonic lodge that bore the patent stamp of fascism and whose list of elite members read like a *Who's Who* of Italian society.

Tomorrow the entire network would be exposed. And Conclave, that insidious cabal, must be brought into line: its power and influence had expanded too far under Paul VI, even placing itself beyond papal jurisdiction. Tomorrow, Vatican City would be shaken from crypt to domed crown.

Administrative directives signed, he picked up a beige folder. Inside were photostats of an ancient codex from the most secure area of the Vatican Secret Archives. Clipped to the folder was a note he'd scribbled an hour ago.

"The seventy-ninth heresy," he murmured, noting key references in his jottings. "The Collyridians. Silentium. Chamber of the Dormition."

Luciani turned his attention to the topmost photostat, a copy of the first page of the text known as the Apocryphon Mariæ: the secret book of the Virgin Mary, with an Italian translation attached of the original Koiné Greek, lingua franca of the Roman empire. The original, a codex comprising over three hundred papyrus sheets, was secure in its locked metal box by his bed. He had it removed from the Vatican Secret Archives this morning. He had decided that it belonged to the world.

"The seventy-ninth heresy," he declared, "is *not* a heresy...*Ad Jesum per Mariam.*"

Meditating on Mary's apocryphon, his thoughts meandered back through the centuries to the elusive predawn of the Christian era and the lost science and philosophy of the Great Library of Alexandria, buried with the downfall of the Greco-Roman world.

And as for the tomb reputed to lie within the Dormition chamber in the Vatican necropolis, it was time, after sixteen centuries, to verify its existence.

"A gateway to the unseen," he whispered.

A slight twinge in his chest... He waited a few seconds. The sensation wasn't repeated. He shrugged it off.

Luciani scanned the first lines of the Apocryphon Mariæ codex, as inspired on second reading as at first sight:

I, Mary of Bethlehem, mother of Jesus, was a witness to the beginning, and will be a witness to the end. We are alone in the universe, but the universe is not alone.

A key rattled in a lock. Annunciata sprang to her feet.

Father Benoit strode into the storeroom, flanked by two men in anonymous gray suits, immaculate white shirts, and gray silk ties. They had the look and build of bodyguards.

One of the men locked the door and pocketed the key.

"We heard you knocking the past hour," said Benoit. "Nobody else did. Vatican City contains over ten thousand rooms. Numerous empty rooms, unvisited corridors." He held up a dark red bottle, labeled Effortil. "This came from the pope's bedroom." A contrary meld of resentment and remorse flared in his eyes. "I switched his medicine for an identical substitute— with an extra ingredient. The guilt is on his own head. He should have stayed in Venice."

With an unsteady hand, Father Benoit drew out a holy water bottle from inside his cassock. "Digitalis," he said, exposing the bottle to the naked light bulb, "is colorless and tasteless, like water. There could be, let's say, fifty milligrams of digitalis in a teaspoonful of Effortil, death ensuing within two hours." His fingertip tapped the inlaid cross on the bottle. "There is rather more than fifty milligrams in here." He signaled to the men at her back, then unscrewed the lid of the holy-water bottle. "Father Ignatio has already received a dose of this. You shouldn't have interfered. I'm sorry."

A slab of a hand covered her eyes and nose. Other hands clamped down on her arms.

Choking, she writhed and kicked for all she was worth, reduced to a panicked animal, struggling against the fluid in her throat. The survival instinct betrayed her. An involuntary swallow, a response to the drowning sensation, and she gulped down the poison.

"Finito," the priest declared. He paced slowly across the room, arms folded. "The dose was considerable but will take a while. Time to receive absolution for your sins."

Her sins? He had betrayed his own faith. If she read the man right, the enormity of his crime had unhinged him.

Benoit's manner bordered on the apologetic. "Once your system has absorbed the liquid, you'll be released. I urge you to make an act of contrition. Duty forced me to commit this most mortal sin. Never was a necessary evil more necessary or more evil." He smiled awkwardly, his expression an unsettled mixture of pain, sorrow and... benevolence? "Be reconciled with God, even if I never am."

The pope, vaguely aware that the bedroom lights were still on, subsided into a troubled doze, fractured images of the past intruding into fitful dreams. Some memories were sharp, and cut deep.

His mother, Bertola, looming out of his childhood and lighting votive candles in the holy dark of a Marian shrine in Canale d'Agordo.

The day of his ordination and the tolling of Roman bells.

A train departing. A handkerchief waving. *Andiamo...*

Venice. A gauze of mist making a phantom of St.Mark's basilica.

A record revolving. *Cavalleria Rusticana.*

A black gondola glided out of diaphanous fog on the Grand Canal, steered by a masked gondolier...

Andante...

The gondolier held out a skeletal hand. Luciani proffered two Roman coins.

"Just one coin, Luciani. Special ferry price tonight."

He dropped a coin engraved with the image of Augustus Caesar into the waiting hand.

The gondolier flipped the coin and caught it in his bony palm. The image of Augustus landed uppermost. "You lose."

Luciani stepped into the gondola and the craft slid into the mist to the sober knell of a hidden bell and the slow, solemn beat of a drum.

Lento...

Annunciata gently prodded her stomach with her fingertips. It seemed incongruous that such a lethal liquid didn't burn like sulfuric acid. A gulp of water would have tasted no different.

Her executioners stood over her, arms folded, inhumanly patient.

Minutes left of my life, she told herself. Then, what? Revelation? Oblivion? The concept was abstract.

She pictured Mark the last time she sat on his bed watching him sleep, his mop of hair spread like a black halo on the pillow. She had kissed the thorn-shaped birthmark at the back of his neck, whispering: "Where there's a thorn, there's a rose." The priest who went under the name of Father Cosmas had made a joke of the purple mark: "Marked by the thorn."

She would never see Mark again. Never. There was the sting of death, in that single word: Never.

Father Benoit laid a hand on her shoulder. "You don't understand, do you? You don't understand the challenges we face: the behemoth of soviet communism, the insidious spread of secular relativism. Others— others may be motivated by Mammon, by balance sheets and bank accounts. I am not. I am the servant of a divine institution that has survived two thousand years. His Holiness is in possession of a heretical codex that imperils the Church. Before sunrise the book of heresy will be destroyed."

A new expression stole into his features, the look of one inspired of a lofty purpose. "Are you familiar with the description of the Catholic Church given by the historian Baron Macaulay, a Protestant?" He closed his eyes, rapt in some inner world. "This is what Macaulay wrote of the Catholic Church." He recited with a calm, measured authority:

"...She was great and respected before the Saxon had set foot on Britain, before the Frank had passed the Rhine, when Grecian eloquence still flourished in Antioch, when idols were still worshipped in the temple of Mecca..."

Annunciata felt an ache in her breast, a sudden pain. It felt, for all the world, like the broken heart of a lover.

"...and she may still exist in undiminished vigor when some traveler from New Zealand shall, in the midst of a vast solitude, take his stand on a broken arch of London Bridge to sketch the ruins of St.Paul's."

Annunciata scarcely registered the words.

A throbbing inside her ears. No, a drumming.

Hammering.

But the hammering wasn't in her head.

Her heart—

Mark, goodbye.

She doubled up as a sledgehammer pain hit her chest.

The pope jolted up in his bed, breath whooshing from his lungs at the pile driver in his chest.

Another blow to his heart slammed him back down as a flurry of notes and folders spilled to the carpet. His stomach heaved, the contents staining the pillow and sheets as he slid onto the floor. What was happening? What—

He struggled up into a crouch and jabbed the alarm button beside the headboard. Silence. He pressed again. Silence.

He tried to shout for help, but the pain shrank the cry to a strangled whimper. The pain was tyrannical. It brought him to his knees.

Stomach heaving once more, he crawled to the open door of the bathroom. He crawled less than a yard across the bathroom's tiled floor before his limbs gave out and he was left slumped and stranded, a puppet with snapped strings. Albino's heart had turned against him. Helpless, he sprawled on cold tiles as the remorseless pounding beat him down into the dark.

His flickering awareness strained to reach beyond that dark, seeking childhood figures of faith, luminous in the night.

Jesu Criste... Maria Virgine...

There was a moment, a fleeting moment... a glimpse... A woman in a white woolen robe, face hooded, sat at the mouth of a cave before a sea of ancient time...

I remember...

The image faded. The night closed in.

Then there was neither night nor day.

"Mary..."

Bent double, Annunciata staggered across the bare boards of the storeroom, her heartstrings on the rack. She fought a losing battle for breath, her heart beating a brutal percussion. Arms wrapped tight around her ribcage to stop her heart bursting from her chest, she tottered to the center of the room.

My heart is breaking me.

Vision swirling, she searched beyond the pain for the image, the icon of salvation...

And then she saw the apparition, in white and blue, arms outstretched in invitation, open to embrace.

"Mary..."

Ad Jesum per Mariam. To Jesus through Mary.

She reeled toward the apparition, arms reaching to the Virgin Mother. Fell into the arms of Mary.

And Mary rocked on her pedestal.

The apparition diminished into a pious, brittle statue, all plaster and paint.

She tumbled to the floor as the statue toppled from its perch.

The Virgin statue and Annunciata crashed to the floorboards in unison, Mary smashing into fragments, the nun crumpling into her final pose, limbs spread-eagled.

Annunciata's life slipped away with the ghost of a breath:

"Ave, Maria."

London: June 18, 1982

Roberto Calvi, head of the Banco Ambrosiano, business partner of Archbishop Marcinkus, rotated in the hangman's noose where he dangled under the north arch of Blackfriars Bridge.

Standing on the bank of the Thames under the bridge arch, Father Benoit swiveled the gold crucifix ring on his index finger as he nodded approval to the Mafiosi in the small launch positioned under the hanged body. They had made swift work of stringing up the banker on the bridge scaffolding.

The launch departed quietly as Benoit backed away with slow steps, his eyes focused on the dangling figure of Roberto Calvi. In death, Calvi served as an object lesson: what Conclave chose to hide must remain hidden, be it financial accounts or the Apocryphon Mariæ.

All traces of the Apocryphon Mariæ had been obliterated, burned by Benoit's own hand. All plans to excavate the Dormition burial chamber in the Vatican necropolis abandoned. Case closed.

Father Benoit continued to back away, his vision trained on the bridge arch as it slowly receded and the hanged man merged with the night.

"Finito."

Present Day

Part One

"Tell me where all past years are"

John Donne

Chapter 1

Carlingford Lough, Ireland

Somewhere over the Irish Sea thunder mumbled below the horizon, a remote rumor of a storm happening someplace else to someone else.

Gulls swooped and circled with a lament above the sweep of the sea, the troubled waves gray under a November dawn.

The sea and the sky were larger than he remembered, in the kind of nonsense sense that he felt smaller since he'd come back home, a transitory speck on the landscape. The immensity reminded him how his life had shrunk - and how he'd shrunk to fit it.

He mouthed a line from a favorite poem: "And hear the mighty waters rolling evermore..."

Dominic Quinn's gaze swerved from the wide Irish Sea to the narrow plot of freshly dug soil at his feet. Beneath the humped soil was his parents' cramped resting-place, a tucked-in-the-earth bed, a headstone for a headboard.

The dedications on the headstone were simple and direct:

MARGARET QUINN
Beloved Wife and Mother
BRIAN QUINN
Devoted Husband and Father

Brian Quinn's inscribed name stood out fresh and raw compared to the slight weathering and ingrained dirt of his wife's inscription. After twenty years of separation, husband and wife were reunited.

Eight days since the death notice, four days since the funeral, and still the passing of his father hadn't squeezed his heart with sorrow, let alone wrung it with grief. When he flew back to the States tomorrow, it would be without regrets.

Swaying in a sudden gust from the sea, he pulled up the collar of his field jacket against the light drizzle that so often passed for rain in Ireland and ran his fingers through his damp hair, barely disturbing the spiky locks his ex-girlfriend had disparaged as "trampled hedgehog." He was dressed for anything the weather could hurl at him. His olive-green field jacket, courtesy of the U.S. Army Navy store, was a match for any blustery gale; his black denims were durable; and the Timberland hiking boots damn near weatherproof.

His gaze wandered from headstone to headstone in the cemetery, its death's little acre overlooked by the dark mountain of Sliabh Foy. A movement at the corner of his eye switched his attention to the squat, pebble-dashed church of St. Bartholomew and its adjoining presbytery on the far side of the graves. In a downstairs window a velvet drape gave a classic twitch.

Uh-huh. So Father Kinsella was keeping watch on saintly Brian Quinn's apostate son, fresh from America and soaked in its heathen ways. What with his father leaving all his worldly possessions to St. Bartholomew's and not a cent to Dominic, he'd hoped the priest would cut him some slack.

He fixed his stare on the window to let Kinsella know he'd been caught out in mid-snoop. A long, level stare, unblinking. The drape twitched once, then twitched no more. Point made, he turned his back on the presbytery and took in the solemn majesty of the lough and the Mountains of Mourne overlording its shores.

Little had changed in the two decades since he last stood on Sliabh Foy as a thirteen-year-old boy saying goodbye to Ireland and all the saints, sinners, hurt, happiness, strong tea, and soda bread that went with it. The Irish landscape had a way with it, a way of underscoring mortality. We come this way but once, affecting the soil little more than the passing of a cloud shadow.

With the merest hint of a smile, he recited the last lines of a century-old ballad in a cadence attuned to the patter of rain:

"So I'll wait for the wild rose that's waiting for me
Where the Mountains of Mourne sweep down to the sea."

The smile, slight as it was, vanished. The murmur, soft as it was, gave way to the faintest whisper:

"I remember."

Through a gap in the brown velvet drapes of his study, Father Daigh Kinsella kept watch on the young man in the cemetery, the minutes of the vigil marked by the clunky pulse of a brass clock.

Sagging cheeks still flushed from the embarrassment of being caught spying on the Quinn boy, Father Kinsella struggled to regain his dignity.

The young man by the grave didn't come across as intimidating, at first glance. There was nothing in the easy stance of his athletic figure to suggest the criminal aggression beneath. He could have passed for a Hollywood version of a romantic poet despite the military field jacket. But the priest knew what was under the mask.

That look Dominic had given him a minute ago said it all. That look. Some of the girls in Carlingford, who couldn't see past the skin, doted on the returning native, one adolescent gushing about how Dominic had "eyes like melting chocolate drops."

Kinsella vented a snort of exasperation. The women of this town... *Melting chocolate drops*... Tell that to Father Tierney, Dominic's first victim...

What they couldn't see was that Dominic was a fallen angel, one of those lost souls that had deserted the Church but never forgot the resonance of the consecration bell and the sacramental hymns.

He tensed as Dominic wheeled around and headed in the direction of the presbytery. The priest jutted his jaw in a determined set. "If you're coming, I'm ready."

Chapter 2

London

The Tube carriage, crammed with Monday morning rush hour passengers, kept up its shake, rattle, and roll as the District Line train trundled into Westminster Underground station.

Rachel Gurevich, ensconced in the seat eagerly claimed at the Earls Court stop, made a supreme effort to maintain an adamantine composure as the man to her right elbowed her ribs for the zillionth time in his exploration of each and every page of his newspaper.

The doors swished open and the carriage disgorged a flood of Monday morning commuters onto the platform. Vacated seats were filled in the twitch of an eyelid.

Snug in her burgundy bomber jacket and gray denims, Toshiba Ultrabook balanced precariously on her knees, she frowned as she painstakingly deleted scores of previously downloaded spam e-mails...

Your Loan Request is confirmed
Delete.
VIAa/gra...
Delete.
P/en*is

Had her spam filter gone to sleep?
Delete delete delete delete delete...
Oh, hell!

The delete action was so ingrained that she'd consigned a kosher e-mail to the deleted folder. She restored the e-mail and read the curt message:

Re your request for information on covert Vatican activities, I can assist. Meet north end Blackfriars Bridge. 1 p.m. today.
    Yours, D

Well, it was to the point. The fact that "D" was evidently a person of few words compared favorably with the usual rambling, obsessive replies to the e-mail address she'd left on a number of Vatican-related websites.

She checked when the e-mail was sent. An hour ago— at the yawn of dawn. Arranging a meeting just four hours ahead might be judged presumptuous, but what the hell...

Okay, D, it's a date.

She replied with an equally curt *Will meet as arranged*, ready to send when she resurfaced at street level. Then she glanced at the desktop image on her computer, a photo of the family dog back in LA, a boxer by the proud name of Bonkers, staring bug-eyed into the camera with his expression of perpetual astonishment.

She fondly traced the outline of the boxer's snout. He'd be asleep right now...

Jogged from her reverie by another dig in the ribs from the man with the newspaper and the energetic elbows, Rachel peered out the window as the next station sign glided into sight: TEMPLE.

Huh? What? Huh? Already? She suppressed a sigh. For all her twenty-eight years, she often displayed the diligence of a twitchy teen first thing in the morning. Although, this particular morning, she could be forgiven a degree of distraction. She was on her way to a publisher that had disappeared into the ether.

Only four months ago, a Brit by the name of Simon Dray and with a voice like Alan Rickman's had phoned offering a commission to write a book on the Vatican secret service. A twenty-five-thousand dollar advance, no less. Seems a couple of her lecturers from her UCLA days had recommended her, even though her MA thesis on international relations never touched on the Vatican. So why choose her? She told him she was descended from a long line of Jewish atheists and he'd replied that he couldn't think of a better qualification. He was nuts, but who was she to argue? Her job at Caltrans was hardly her lifetime's ambition: she resigned a day after the phone call.

Everything had gone fine. The money appeared in her account. She came up with a working title— *Vatican Shadows*— and got down to serious research. Two weeks ago, a plane ticket appeared in the mailbox along with an invite to the London Concordat Publishing offices. Smooth sailing.

Then came the e-mail. Project canceled. Trip to London canceled. No explanation. No reply to the dozens of queries she sent off.

Maybe London Concordat Publishing had gone bust but the website was still up and running and the phone rang, although nobody answered. Sure, she had the money, but that wasn't the point. Once she started a job, she finished it. Plus, she had to admit, there was a tinge of intrigue to the whole business.

She put the airplane ticket to good use. It had been a long flight. Next stop, Simon's office on Pudding Lane.

She brought up one of the files on the laptop on the principle that a girl revises until the last minute if she wants to impress. The text from "D" had brought to mind a major strand in *Vatican Shadows*: the Vatican Bank scandal. Blackfriars Bridge was where Roberto Calvi, associate of Bishop Marcinkus, was hanged, just one in a long line of executions following the suspicious death of John Paul I. She scanned down the death list:

September 29, 1978: John Paul I found dead in the papal apartments. Cardinal Villot issues false statements to the press about the circumstances surrounding the death and removes the medicine bottle of Effortil from John Paul's room, along with other evidence. He orders the body to be embalmed immediately without an autopsy.

January 21, 1979: Murder of Judge Emilio Alessandrini, the Milan magistrate investigating the activities of Roberto Calvi.

July 13, 1979: Murder of Lieutenant Colonel Antonio Varisco, head of the Rome security service, during his investigation of P2 and the Vatican Bank.

August 2, 1980: Bologna railroad station bombed under the direction of P2, resulting in 85 deaths and over 200 wounded.

June 17, 1982: Graziella Corrocher, Calvi's secretary, dead of a fall from the fourth floor of the Banco Ambrosiano.

June 18, 1982: Roberto Calvi found hanged under Blackfriars Bridge. The following inquest in London delivers a verdict of suicide, to the derision of the Italian press.

October 2, 1982: Giuseppe Dellacha, executive at Banco Ambrosiano, dead of a fall from a window of the Banco Ambrosiano...

The screen toppled as an elbow jabbed her arm and she twisted instinctively, dislodging the laptop. A last-instant grab saved it from tipping over. Laptop secured, she gripped it with both hands.

"I hope you don't blame me for that."

She turned to the owner of the voice: Elbow Man, a dapper city gent from the cut of his graying hair to the sharp-pressed pants of his elegant gray suit. Newspaper resting on knees, he fingered the knot of his gray silk tie and studied her in an unsettling meld of subtle distaste and frank sexual interest. The skin of his narrow face had a pronounced oily sheen as if he'd indulged in a Brylcreem facial.

"You should take more care," he admonished.

"I suppose so," she muttered. Oh boy, did she want to get away from this guy.

A moment's strained silence.

"Let me guess," he said, "you have an Irish look about you but, hmm, I wonder..."

Her mouth twitched in an automatic smile. Ho-hum and here we go again.

One predatory male glance and the average male predator had her tagged as a girl from the Emerald Isle. The straight, red-gold hair hanging loose to her shoulders, the big green eyes, the whiter-shade-of-pale skin with a faint sprinkling of freckles, they all added up to the full Irish colleen ensemble— to anyone who'd never heard of Russian Jews. Ashkenazy, all the way down the line from Minsk to Ellis Island.

"American," she mumbled, countering any further advances by shoving the laptop into her canvas carryall. "I get out at the next stop."

His eyebrow arched. "Good manners cost nothing, young lady."

She searched for a feisty, Dorothy Parker riposte. And heard herself mutter, "Oh yeah, well, that's— that's right, yeah, um..."

Leaving him reeling from that devastating one-liner, she headed for the doors and leaned against a side-panel, hand hovering over the door button. As the train rumbled into Monument station she prepared for a rapid, smooth exit. Didn't work out. The entire car-load of commuters was on its feet and determined to crush her against the door. The doors slid open and she was propelled onto the platform by the press of the passengers, tumbled to her knees and all but dropped the carryall.

She scrambled to her feet and adjusted her remaining tatters of self-respect. All things considered, the day could have started better.

Deacon folded his newspaper and kept watch on Rachel's departing figure, a mere flicker in the jostling crowds of Temple Station. Perhaps he shouldn't have toyed with the girl, but he couldn't resist it.

He glanced at Phil Craig, a shaven-headed, thickset man in neck-to-ankle pale-blue denim, camera phone raised as he took another snapshot of the girl. When Craig lowered his phone

Deacon gave him a nod. His sidekick nodded in response and made a quick exit from the carriage, following in Rachel's tracks.

Leaving Craig to shadow the Gurevich girl, Deacon leaned back in the seat and slipped a BlackBerry from an inside pocket. He accessed the received e-mails and once again studied the latest image: a neo-Gothic church, St. Mary's. And with the photo, a brief message:

Father Jonathan Taylor. Type 1 Diabetic.

He returned the phone to an inside pocket where it nestled alongside three ampules of insulin. Diabetics had been known to take an accidental overdose.

Accidents will happen.

Chapter 3

Carlingford Lough

Gravel scrunched under his feet as Dominic approached the presbytery that stood to one side of the cemetery gate. As he drew nearer he spotted a slight movement behind a chink in a velvet drape.

Was Kinsella *still* spying on him? Had he nothing better to do?

He had planned to pay a courtesy call on Kinsella before starting on his trek. A polite, if strained, hello and goodbye. That now struck him as a bad idea. Besides, he intended to reach Colin O'Hanlon's house before his friend set off to work. That was the original plan: drop in on Colin, then head on up the slopes of Sliabh Foy. Forget Kinsella.

He turned away from the presbytery, swung the wrought-iron cemetery gate shut behind him, and headed down a trail that meandered along the lower slopes to the village of Omeath. As he walked he fell into the old tempo of his childhood rambling days, his stride lengthening and negotiating each hummock with ease, sure-footed as a veritable mountain goat. A lot had changed in his twenty-year absence. Miles had been converted to kilometers. The medieval town of Carlingford, once dour and down-at-the-heel, had spruced itself up for the tourists. And friends had moved out.

So many changes. And so little forgotten, not least that incident with Father Tierney in St. Bartholomew's. The muffled wake, stilted funeral, and evasive eyes had underlined the general unease at his return. At the conclusion of the funeral, Father Kinsella had shaken his hand as if Dominic had a plague-bearing rat on the end of his arm. It was there, in the priest's eyes, the accusation: attempted murder, desecration.

Twenty years over the water was a long time, but obviously not long enough. Dominic had left Carlingford under a cloud, a big black storm cloud. Perhaps Kinsella believed he'd brought the storm back with him.

Distant thunder mumbled at his back, far out to sea. A hint of wry humor tweaked his lips. It vanished as the strains of a Mozart sonata issued from inside his field jacket. He fished out his phone and silenced the ring tone. A text appeared on the screen, and he started to frown as he read the brief message:

Your father kept a journal. I have it. Long Woman's Grave. 4 p.m. today.
    A friend

"You're kidding."

Had to be a hoax. Sure, his father's house had been burglarized a few days back, but who'd want to steal a journal? Unless... maybe it was wishful thinking... unless it was of special value to Dominic and the thief was aware of that. Could it contain, just possibly, a reference to another will? Chance in a thousand. He smiled at his grasping at straws. Had to be a hoax. But still...

He looked up at Sliabh Foy's clouded peak. The Long Woman's Grave— it was a Neolithic tomb hidden in a hollow far up the mountain.

A vaporous arm slipped down from the cloud as though beckoning, challenging him to climb into the high mist.

A hand encrusted with gold rings enclosed the distant speck that was Dominic Quinn. All a matter of perspective. Framed between thumb and forefinger, Quinn's figure was a mere fifth of an inch in size. From his lofty vantage point on Sliabh Foy, arm held out straight, the observer, a precise judge, made a fine adjustment: make that a sixth of an inch. Tiny, tiny speck of an insect, crawling west along the lough.

Slowly, thumb and forefinger closed, pressed, squeezed tight.

Father Kinsella studied Dominic from his bedroom window, keeping watch as the figure dwindled into the distance.

So he'd read the lad's intention wrong. Dominic hadn't come to confront him. But it was hardly credible that he'd visited the cemetery solely to pay respects to his father's memory. The day he arrived from America, Dominic had stood over Brian Quinn's open coffin and stared down at his father with nary a flicker of the eye. Cold. Impassive.

Dominic's sole reaction was an enigmatic, toneless: "He knew."

The priest sat down on the bed, rubbing his plump leg. Bloody sciatica playing up again. As he tried to ease the pain, his gaze wandered the room with its faded wallpaper displaying wilting roses drowning in sour cream. He gave up on rubbing his leg, eased himself onto the mattress, and flopped his head on the pillow.

As he stared at the webbed cracks in the ceiling, his thoughts returned to the Quinn boy. Kinsella had taken over as parish priest from Father Tierney two weeks after the shocking incident in the church and a week after Dominic left the country.

Sitting beside Brian Quinn by Father Tierney's bed in the casualty ward, he had listened as Brian quietly recounted the outrage committed by his son. Tierney, holy soul that he was, refused to condemn the boy and ensured the whole matter was hushed-up. Dominic was packed off to his aunt Deirdre in America before the end of school term.

And now he was back.

Dominic was planning to contest the will, Kinsella was sure of it. Bernard Quinn's will that bequeathed his entire estate to the parish of St. Bartholomew, perhaps to atone for the sins of his son.

Dominic, for all that he would have been sole heir, should respect that. But a cathedral to a candle he bloody well wouldn't.

And maybe he'd already started to lay claim to the property. There had been a burglary the night after the reading of the will. Certain items were stolen, not least Brian Quinn's journal. Dominic was top of his list of suspects.

Ah, to heck with it. He'd brooded on that boy too long. A busy day stretched ahead. Maybe catch a quick snooze. His eyelids slowly closed.

Downstairs, the doorbell chimed the notes of "Lord of the Dance."

"Oh, God."

With a soulful sigh he heaved himself off the bed and padded down the stairs into the hallway. He opened the door to find an unsmiling stranger standing on the welcome mat.

The visitor was a man of middle-height, mid- to late-thirties, lean as a whippet, sweptback black hair plastered snug to the scalp with curls protruding under the ears. His deeply-tanned face, narrow and angular, was devoid of expression. The tight garish clothes didn't belong to an Irish autumn pushing winter: a flimsy, powder-blue jacket; a red silk shirt; iridescent blue slacks; soft leather tan shoes. And the fingers of both his hands were adorned in thick gold rings.

"Ah, it's— it's very early." Father Kinsella was surprised at the tremor in his voice. "Who might you be?"

"Jones."

As he spoke, a tall woman stepped into view to the left of the doorway. He was confronted by a raw-boned lady, her gray-streaked hair raked back into a severe bun. She reminded him of a stern headmistress or music teacher, minus the pince-nez.

The voice— more bluegrass than Bach, a nasal twang— belied the appearance

"I'm Alice."

"Ah," the priest mumbled, "as I say, it's very early. If you two come back later..."

"Now is good," Jones responded.

The statement— was the accent Spanish?— was delivered in a monotone that was intimidating in its impersonality.

Kinsella started to close the door. "Sorry, but... later. Come back later..."

The stranger placed a finger on the door and halted it in mid-swing despite all the pressure Kinsella could bring to bear.

"Now is good."

Chapter 4

The wind, like the sea, came in waves as Dominic trudged up the steep Wee Road, a lane that wound and unwound its way on the slopes that swept up to the sky above the loughside village of Omeath. An involuntary shiver told him this bracing weather with its robust gusts was getting a little too healthy for his health.

He spotted Colin O'Hanlon's bungalow where the lane veered sharply to the left. The house was clean and unpretentious, instantly recognizable from the images Colin had e-mailed him a few months back.

The car in the forecourt was equally modest. A dark gray four-door saloon. And sitting in the driving seat...

He broke into a run as the engine started to rev. "Hey, Colin!"

The car was out of the front gate before it screeched to a halt.

Colin jumped out onto the grass verge and, with a mouthful of toothy grin, gave Dominic a piston-thumping handshake. "The wild rover returns!"

"More like a bad penny always turning up." Colin was much as he remembered him: slim, finely-featured with a mop of light brown hair, a quick smile, and unassuming manner. The sensible suit and serviceable shoes completed the understated ensemble.

"You've grown," Colin observed, tilting his head.

"No, you've shrunk." Dominic glanced at the car. "You're off to work... guess I should have phoned."

Colin's grin downgraded to a rueful smile. "Yes, off to school, still not recovered from a frenetic Paris school trip. Where have you been staying— your dad's house?"

"No, only went there for the wake. I got a room in the Emerald Glory guest house."

"Ah— I heard about your dad leaving all his worldly goods to the parish. Talk about injustice..." He shifted his feet. "How long are you here?"

"I'm flying back to the States tomorrow. Wanted to catch you first."

"Glad you did. So, what's new? That latest girl of yours, what's her name?"

Dominic made a wince of a smile. "Kathy. She up and left six weeks ago for a guy who sells inflatable swimming pools."

"Seriously?"

"Seriously. Can't blame her. Money problems. We struggled to keep the werewolf from the door and lived in a poky basement. She had her mind set on higher things, like the first floor."

"Ah, well," Colin said, "the right girl will come along some day."

"The right girl's already come and gone, years ago." Dominic's mouth bent into an awkward smile. "I left my heart in San Francisco."

"I left my heart in San Francisco..." Colin declaimed theatrically. "Wasn't meant to be, that one. You said it lasted only a week. And didn't Tim, your college roommate, put you straight about that girl? You should've forgotten her by now."

"Maybe." Even to his own ears, the tone lacked conviction.

"I give in. As for money problems, there must be something you can do with a PhD in, what was it— early concepts of atomism in ancient civilizations?"

"PhDs in history are a dime a dozen. Why else would I end up as a high school substitute teacher in Brooklyn?"

"And what, may I ask, is wrong with teaching?" Colin looked at him askance. "You're not thinking of rejoining the U.S. Rangers, by any chance?"

Dominic gave a firm shake of the head. "Four years running up and down mountains on the Afghan-Pakistan border was plenty for me. I'm happy enough teaching high school— don't have to dodge quite so many bullets."

"And you the boy who once nurtured skyscraper ambitions..."

"These days my aspirations are more bungalow than skyscraper."

"Hmm..." His friend wore his best dubious face, complete with lofted eyebrows.

"I'll bounce back," Dominic put in quickly. "If you're wondering, I wasn't too surprised I was left out the will, the way my father kept calling me a thorn in his side and a 'child of sin, marked from birth.' But he could have spared something for my aunt for taking me in instead of passing on every last penny to the parish."

A sideways glance. "Sorry I wasn't here for the funeral. The school trip, you know..."

"Oh, that... forget it. A lot of people didn't show, my wastrel uncle included."

"Even if I'd been here..." Colin's gaze lowered. "Well, I go to mass at St. Laurence's. The thought of walking into St. Bartholomew's again, well— you know."

"I know. Deep waters. Let's stay in the shallow end."

"But your father must have known what was going on— about Tierney— about all of it."

Dominic gave a curt nod. "He knew. Let it go."

"But I should have said something. Your father packed you off to your Aunt Deirdre in America even though he *knew*."

"We were both very young. Seriously, let it go."

"If you say so." Colin glanced at his watch. "Er..."

Dominic laughed. "I caught that subtle hint, Mr. O'Hanlon. Away with you and teach those children the ways of the Lord. Oh, by the way, has anyone around here mentioned my father's journal? I never knew he kept one, but I got this text..."

"No, heard nothing about a journal. Is it important?"

"Probably not. See you later, perhaps?"

"For sure." Colin shut the gate and stepped into the car. "I'll be back in Carlingford before six. Maybe meet you by the Tholsel Gate some time after that?"

"You bet. Let's make it six-o-clock, okay?"

"Grand." He triggered the ignition. "We'll catch up on old times."

"See you," Dominic called out as the car moved away and gathered speed down the lane. Colin responded with a quick wave as the vehicle disappeared around a bend.

Colin lowered his hand after bidding farewell and steered the car around each familiar curve in the Wee Road until he reached the loughside road and made a sharp right.

In minutes Omeath was a fair ways at his back and he was well on the way to Carlingford town. He eased back in the seat and mulled over his encounter with Dominic.

What with Dominic signing up with the U.S. Rangers a year after finishing his PhD, he'd expected more of a gung ho hardcase. On the contrary, his manner was reserved. But then, Dominic had been much the same as a boy, more retiring than forward, more bookish than boisterous. And the years had been easy on him; he looked closer to twenty than thirty.

Nearing Carlingford he eased up on the accelerator and spared a quick sideways glance at the church on the hill. St. Bartholomew's. After all these years, he...

A warble sounded from his phone, dispelling unwelcome memories. He drew the car to a stop and pressed receive. "Hello?"

The answering voice was low, melodic, American, and just this side of sultry. "Hi there. My name's Martha. We have a friend in common— Monsignor Aylesbury."

He smiled. "Monsignor Aylesbury. I haven't seen him in years."

"The Monsignor wanted me to pass on a message. Dominic Quinn is in danger and any friend of his may also be in danger."

He sat in silence, staring at the phone. "Uh— *what?*"

"I'm in the Quinn house. Come on up. We need to talk."

Chapter 5

Jones shut the trellised gate behind him with a swift, precise action and paced along the concrete path that bisected the overgrown garden of the Quinn property, a dour three-storied Victorian house on the lower slopes of Sliabh Foy.

He glided up the four marble steps to the front porch and slid a key into the door, which opened with a faint squeak of hinges and closed with barely a sound. With silent steps he ascended the stairs, his peripheral awareness permanently on the alert for a dissonant sound, an incongruous scent.

On the top floor he angled left to an oak door, turned the brass doorknob, and stepped into the room, gaze instantly focused on the figure by the far wall.

A black woman in a long, dark brown leather overcoat and tight, black canvas jeans sprawled across a window bench, nursing a cup of coffee in her gloved hands, her profile framed by a mullioned window and a view of fir trees.

He made an instant assessment: she appeared to be in her late-twenties but was closer to late-thirties, five foot nine with the slim, athletic build acquired by regular exercise. The medium-cropped Afro hairstyle implied that she marched to her own drumbeat, heedless of fashion. Her facial features were elegant and the composed set of her expression, free of makeup, conveyed the self-confidence of a strong personality.

Noting the graceful arch of her neck, he calculated that he could cover the intervening distance and snap her cervical vertebrae within four seconds. Yes, four seconds, easy.

She gave him a nod as he shut the door. "Jones."

"Martha." Her execution could wait for another day. No rush.

She took a sip of coffee. "Nice of you to drop by. I got you here to warn you. You're not to harm Dominic Quinn."

He analyzed her accent, and figured it to be northern Illinois, most likely Chicago. But there was an overlay, probably Italian. Chances were she'd lived in Italy for at least five years. Pretty soon, he'd have her all sized up. Before the phone call from the Vatican three days ago, he'd never heard of her. The priest at the other end of the phone had made him a generous offer, generous enough to make him to take on an urgent commission and act like he was this woman's equal. Sure, equal, for now— but not subordinate.

"You giving me orders?" he said. "Your orders I don't take."

"You sound like a South American android, Jones." She paused. "Which is a quasi-weird analogy, now that I think about it. But I digress. Stay clear of Dominic."

"The way Rome tells it, I have carte blanche on Quinn and anyone close to him."

"Then I'm muddying your carte blanche. Hands off, right?"

"Gotta have authority for that. Where's the Monsignor?"

Her hand circled idly. "Away for the day. I speak for him."

Jones considered a moment, then executed a brusque nod. "So what's with Brian Quinn's journal?"

A rueful shake of her head. "No sign of it. We've searched this house from attic to basement and made discreet inquiries in the locality. Nada."

"What about Kinsella? He read the journal. Could be he passed it on to someone else."

"Have you talked to Kinsella?"

He made a mental note that she avoided the question. "I introduced myself. Said hi. Nice and friendly. Friend of mine is keeping him company until I get back."

"Leave Kinsella to me. He's a blundering innocent in this. Not the sharpest scalpel on the surgical tray. He takes a look at the journal, scribbles down a few lines that grab his attention, then strolls back to his home and leaves the damn thing here to get stolen. It's a miracle he managed to e-mail Father Dieter the few lines he wrote down." She fixed her stare on Jones. "You've introduced yourself to Kinsella. Leave it at that, okay? Keep an eye on him, but that's all, got that?"

"You're not the boss of me, lady."

"Beg to differ. No rough stuff, understand?"

Disdaining an answer, he turned on his heel and left.

"Hey!" she called out. "You hear me? No rough—"

"—stuff," Martha concluded with a sardonic twist of the lips as she watched the door swing shut. Jones had even stamped his signature on the closing of a door. Quick and methodical.

A few days ago Jones had been foisted on the Monsignor by Cardinal Chavet in Rome on the pretext that someone from a more— unconventional— background was needed to root out a missing journal. Never was a foisting more unwelcome or the word "unconventional" more understated.

She listened as his soft footfalls receded down the stairs. He was as light on his feet as on his speech. An exercise in economy, no flourishes, no frills. Everything about the man's character was reduced to the basics. Bargain basement.

"He has a minimalist soul," she murmured.

She downed the dregs of coffee and swung her long legs off the window bench. Tapping her booted feet on the threadbare Persian carpet, she hummed a few bars of "Wonderful Copenhagen."

Then she turned to the door of an adjoining room. "You can come out now."

The door opened and Colin O'Hanlon emerged.

"So," she said, "have you heard enough?"

He folded his arms and leaned against the wall. "Who is this Jones?"

"He's a legend— the kind that comes out of the Black Forest. And— and don't you think he talks like an android?"

"Just noticed his accent, sort of Spanish. Didn't fit the name."

"Yeah... *Jones*. Like I'm supposed to believe that's his *real* name. The rumor is he's Paraguayan but he could be from anywhere south of the Panama Canal. Forget him."

"Forget him?" Colin snorted. "You get me up here, and... I mean— what the hell's going on?"

She spread her palms. "I've told you all can. There may be something in Brian Quinn's journal that puts Dominic and anyone close to him in jeopardy. Jones and his accomplices are prepared to carry out that threat. Isn't that sufficient?"

"In a word, no. Listen, I accept you're genuine. The FBI badge looked real enough..."

She nodded slowly. Damn right the badge should look real; it had cost her three hundred bucks.

"...although you're out of your jurisdiction here," he continued. "But you're asking a lot for giving so little."

"I know I'm asking you to take a lot on faith. But it's in your interest, and Dominic's."

He paced slowly about the room, gaze fixed on the floor. She judged that he was on the verge of acceptance. A little push...

"Colin, all I'm asking is you serve as my introduction to Dominic as the Monsignor's name was my introduction to you. He doesn't know me from Cleopatra. Just keep to the meeting you arranged with him and then make for that marina apartment I mentioned. I'll give it twenty minutes or so before I make an appearance. Agreed?"

He halted his pacing. "Agreed," he sighed. "But this better be in Dominic's interest. If not..."

"Implied threat received and understood." She extracted a key from her pocket and held it out. "For the marina apartment. Now you'd better get along to school before the kids run rampant."

He took the key and headed for the door. As he swung the door open, he glanced over his shoulder. "I just wish you'd trust me to tell me everything."

The door clicked shut and she listened to his footsteps descending the stairs.

Martha leaned back and murmured softly, "If I told you everything, you'd have to go hide in another continent the rest of your life." Her voice sank even lower. "And if the Monsignor is right about Dominic, then Dominic will be on his way to Rome in just a few hours."

Jones drew to a halt under the cover of ranked firs two hundred yards from the Quinn house and placed a phone to his ear.

"Benoit," he voice-dialed.

After a single ring: "Yes?"

"Still waiting for a Crypt profile on Dominic Quinn."

"Ah, yes." A short interlude. "Sending now. There's nothing significant. He's an ex-academic. Presently a substitute teacher in Brooklyn. He presents no threat."

"This verified by Substratum?"

"Some days ago, so the intelligence is reliable."

So it should be, coming from Substratum. Some ten years ago he'd learned about the covert listening post in Cesano, north of Vatican City. Substratum, the Catholic Church's ear on the world, had been cooperating for decades with the Anglo-American surveillance and intel-gathering network, codenamed Echelon.

"So," Jones said, "this Quinn guy, his profile doesn't add up to three hundred words and reads kinda bland. You sure it's complete? What if he's a tougher case than it makes out?"

"Unlikely. Quinn has led a sheltered life. But if he proves difficult, use that friend of his, O'Hanlon, to teach him an object lesson in compliance."

"Got it." Jones ended the call and dialed a new number. "Carson— you've got the green light. Give Quinn the full treatment... No, he won't put up much of a fight— he's a pussy teacher. Find out what he knows."

He cut the connection and pocketed the phone.

So much for Dominic Quinn.

Chapter 6

London

Blue flames.

They shone with a steady light, reflected in the priest's dark eyes.

Monsignor Aylesbury stared into the flames of the votive candles as he snapped his lighter shut and slipped it into his overcoat pocket. "*Introibo ad altare Dei*," he murmured. "*Ad Deum qui laetificat juventutem meam.*"

I will go unto the altar of God. To God, who giveth joy to my youth.

A draft skimmed down the Lady Chapel and shivered the candle flames. He looked up at the cool light filtered through the Gothic windows of the Shrine of Mary, bathing the blue and white statue of the Virgin Mary with morning radiance in its alcove above the tabernacle of the altar. He tilted his face to the biblical rainbow of the stained glass.

"My youth was a long time ago." The whisper was followed by a ghost of a whisper. "Annunciata."

His gaze returned to the two candles he'd lit in the empty church of St. Mary's, buried in the heart of London. The candles should last an hour. Two flames for two people, united in destiny.

The Monsignor moved back from the altar and sat in the front pew beside an old priest with tousled hair and a rumpled cassock. Ignoring the priest, he closed his eyes and released a slow breath that sounded like a sigh of mourning in the tall, arched chapel.

Whatever morning business and busyness London was up to outside, not an echo penetrated the silence of the church.

After a long moment he reopened his eyes and turned to the priest at his side who sat with his eyes fixed straight ahead. In the man's left hand was a rolled sheet of paper, clasped tight. The Monsignor placed a hand on the priest's arm. "I'm sorry how things turned out, Jonathan."

He stepped into the aisle and walked to the arch leading to the main body of the church. He paused on entering the long and lofty nave and surveyed its Gothic Revival architecture. To the Monsignor's mind, the Pugin-designed church had been officially vandalized by the diocesan authorities. This church had once been a dark, cool sanctuary that led the spirit one step beyond the mundane, into the numinous.

Now the bare walls glared brashly in the broad light flooding from the new transparent swing doors. Statues had been extracted and discarded like bad teeth. The finely wrought chancel screen had been torn down to allow a modernist altar to thrust aggressively a quarter of the way down the nave. It was a desecration perpetrated by clerical philistines committed to a fad that had passed even as they indulged it.

He scowled at the vandalism. "They raced to catch up with the times and ended up missing the boat."

The Church had become a shell and no pearl remained within to cast before anyone, let alone swine. And if the Church was a shell, it could be easily shattered.

However, what was done could be undone. Mystery could be restored, the lost pearl regained.

That was something of a preoccupation in the Crypt these days.

Instinctively the Monsignor swiveled the gold crucifix ring on his right forefinger and, with the barest movement of the lips, recited in a hushed voice:

"We are alone in the universe but the universe is not alone."

He stood in reflection for a short space, then returned to the Lady Chapel and resumed his seat beside the priest. "I'm back," he said absently.

The flame on one of his votive candles jumped and flickered in a sudden draught. For an instant it threatened to expire, then recovered its little dance of fire.

"You almost became a cliché," the Monsignor observed wryly. He glanced at the sacristy door, locked tight, and ran fingers through his gray hair. "Perhaps a symbolic gesture is in order."

He turned to his companion and grasped the paper in the man's stiff grip. "Pardon me, Jonathan." He took the sheet and unrolled it.

Four words were scrawled in black fiber-tip on the crumpled paper:

MENE MENE TEKEL UPHARSIN

"Ah," he sighed, glancing at Father Jonathan. "The writing on the wall."

Father Jonathan Taylor sat unresponsive as a bloated fly crawled over his open mouth.

The Monsignor looked again at the sacristy door. Then rose and approached the candle rack, taking a candle and angling it to drip molten wax on the back of the paper. Before the wax solidified he hastened to the sacristy door and pressed the sheet onto the unvarnished wood. Retreating a few paces, he perused his handiwork.

According to the Old Testament Book of Daniel, four words appeared on the palace wall at King Belshazzar's feast. Father Jonathan had chosen those same four words.

He approached the priest and rested his hand on a slumped shoulder. "I get the message."

Father Jonathan sat silent, inert. The fly still dawdled on his lips. The old priest, who had a full two decades on the Monsignor, had been murdered in the short time since they'd spoken on the phone.

Way back, in October, 1950, Father Jonathan Taylor had been present at the Transitus excavations in the Vatican necropolis. With Jonathan's murder, the surviving link to that excavation had been severed. And the vision he witnessed before the Transitus Wall, last confided to John Paul I, was now a lost secret.

An empty hypodermic lay on the bench beside Jonathan. The Monsignor, familiar with the ways of the Crypt, knew the executioners would have used the priest's diabetic condition against him. Insulin overdose. Accidental death.

But before Jonathan lapsed into coma he managed to scribble a cryptic little note. The last act of his life was somehow typical of Jonathan.

The Monsignor returned his attention to the note on the sacristy door.

"Mene, Mene, Tekel, Upharsin," he murmured.

Literally translated, the Aramaic words read "It has been counted and counted, weighed and divided." The prophet Daniel's interpretation of the writing on the wall was that King Belshazzar's deeds had been judged and his kingdom surrendered to the Medes and the Persians.

The Monsignor's gaze lingered on the note.

"For those who can read the signs of the times."

Chapter 7

Carlingford Lough

Over the hills and far away...

The fir trees closed in once more when he came within a mile of the neolithic Clontygora Court Tomb at the foot of the Cooley hills.

Dominic had been rambling along a sheep trail at a leisurely pace for over an hour and the landscape was having its way with him, transmuting care to carefree, a slow and easy alchemy. He'd already decided to climb up to the Long Woman's Grave later on and meet the anonymous sender of the "Your Father Kept a Journal" text message. Couldn't hurt.

He peered up at the bulbous clouds that scudded over the summit of Sliabh Foy. In a few hours he'd be on the mountain, walking up into that sky. Over the hills and far—

The sky tilted abruptly. The ground shot up and smacked him in the face before he realized he'd tripped over a tree root.

"Watch your step, idiot," he muttered, straightening up and brushing himself down.

That'll teach you to wander lonely as a cloud.

After checking that he hadn't broken the sore bridge of his nose, he peered ahead and spotted a small gray stone building crowned with a dome. It peeked between the trees several yards off the path, one of the many wayside shrines scattered liberally across Ireland. What was its name... the Sepulcher Chapel? He had some dim recollection of composing a quasi-Yeatsian poem in there when he was twelve going on thirteen.

Well, he was in no hurry. This path was Memory Lane so he might as well pay his respects to the landmarks along the way. He veered off the trail and entered the chapel by its single open archway as the mild drizzle intensified, accompanied by intermittent glimpses of a smeared sun.

He pulled to a halt, feeling like a clumsy intruder. An old nun knelt before the shrine's stone slab in watery sunlight and ghost shadow. She appeared unaware of his presence, her lips moving in unspoken prayer.

After a momentary hesitation at the chapel's threshold, he crept quietly inside and sat on a low bench, studying the slab which was now just a slab, bereft of religious imagery. The shrine had once contained a life-size statue of the dead Christ cradled in the mourning embrace of Mary. The Pietà. Madonna and son after the crucifixion on Golgotha.

On the base of the stone dais was an inscription he remembered, a quote from Dante:

VERGINE MADRE, FIGLIA DEL TUO FIGLIO.

Virgin mother, daughter of your son.

But the statues had been removed; their sole testament bent metal rods protruding from the stone slab. The Sepulcher Chapel was an empty shrine. A negative space had replaced the hallowed effigies.

The nun knelt in devotion before that negative space, arthritic fingers clasped tight around a rosary. Whatever otherness she saw in that absence of imagery, that gap in the sacred air, only she could tell, and for now her lips were sealed in silent prayer.

What he saw, in a sun-flash of memory, was the white silhouette of the Virgin Mary. A blank white image on paper where the June sun glared over Brooklyn and down into his art class at St. Francis High, back in ninth grade.

The art teacher, Miss Cavazos, had instructed his group to sketch the negative space around a subject, the subject being a foot-high statue of the Virgin. Not the statue itself, she'd been at pains to explain, but the shaded spaces around the statue. The task had been straightforward, accomplished in minutes, but then both sketches and the Virgin Mary were removed from sight and a fresh sheet was placed in front of him.

The teacher then told them to shade in those negative spaces from memory alone. Shadows around the memory of Mary.

As his pencil covered in the surrounding spaces, it came to him that the empty area at the center of the sheet was the true negative space. He was drawing the environment of an absence.

That same image had sparked in his mind when he stood before the grave, thinking of his mother, Margaret. His father, big on the fists and the prayers, cast a giant shadow. But his mother was small in memory as in life, dwarfed by her husband almost to the microscopic. Diminutive, joyless, absorbed in household chores, she seemed indifferent to her son. But then, the eyes of youth had a blind spot when turned on adults. Surely he remembered her as less than she was.

"Rest in peace."

A Mozart sonata suddenly issued from his pocket, sounding like an alarm in the hushed chapel. He hurriedly pulled out his phone and backed out the doorway, away from the kneeling nun. "Sorry," he muttered, wincing. "Sorry."

Without turning, the nun acknowledged the apology with an unexpected thumbs-up sign.

He walked several paces from the chapel and held the phone to his ear.

The voice was small and fretful. "Are you there?" His Aunt Deirdre, his mother's sister and his mother in all but name, still with a trace of Dublin underlying her Brooklyn accent.

"Hi, Mom. Caught me at an awkward moment. How are you?"

He could picture her sitting in the family apartment in Brooklyn, perched on the stool in the cramped kitchen, twisting an outmoded phone cord in a nervous hand.

"What toes have you been treading on?" The anxiety was sharp in her tone.

"Huh?"

"I had a visit late last night," she said. "I would have called you then if not for the time difference. I've been up all night. They asked me about you."

"They?"

"Two men, well-dressed but with rough manners. They said they were from Immigration. They started by asking about your background, place of birth, name of parents. Regular questions. Then they wanted to know what you did at Stanford University, who you met there, and whether you'd ever been to Rome."

Dominic frowned. "Rome? Like— why? Did you check their ID?"

"No. They seemed so genuine at first. And they didn't stay long. After I told them about your friends at Stanford, they just got up and marched out the door."

"Listen, I'll fly back tomorrow," he said in a reassuring tone, concerned that she'd fret herself into another heart attack. "Maybe it's something to do with my time in the Rangers."

"They didn't ask about that. They didn't seem to know."

"Whatever, I'll be back tomorrow evening. I promise. Take it easy. Get some sleep."

"I will, son. Bye."

"Oh, I didn't mean—"

The connection had terminated.

He gave the phone a wry smile. "Goodbye."

Chapter 8

London

Rachel stared up again at the name above the glass entrance: FUEGO. She had first caught sight of it the best part of three hours ago. Fuego's was Pudding Lane's solitary tapas bar. And it had the same address as the Concordat Publishing Company. At least, that was the address listed on the Concordat website. No mention of a tapas bar there.

The owner of the bar had been here for years. He knew the area like the back of a tapas. He even served a fair number of the offices that dominated the lane. There was no London Concordat Publishing. Never had been. Simon Dray? Never heard of him.

She couldn't accept it at first. Didn't want to. If the publishing company didn't exist, why would some hoaxer hand her a project and, more to the point, twenty-five grand? The wrong address must have been posted on the website. She undertook a long trudge up and down the lane and up and down again and again, pressing buzzers, making enquiries, feeling increasingly like a total dork. Same message, every time: Concordat-what? Simon-who?

On the upside, she discovered why the name Pudding Lane rang a bell: it was where the first spark was lit that resulted in the Great Fire of London in 1666. Oh wow, wasn't it worth crossing the Atlantic to be reminded of that little nugget?

Now she'd finished up where she started, at first sight staring at a sign in disbelief, now in glum acceptance. What to do next? The sensible course was to see more of London's sights and fly back home. But maybe something could be salvaged. And it galled to leave a job half-done. Would another publisher be interested? And maybe "D" would come up with the goods, some shattering revelation of the Catholic Church's hidden face.

But how to set about finding a new publisher— not to mention all the knotty contractual details?

"I'll jump off that bridge when I come to it."

She stood in one of the bays protruding from the near-thousand-foot span of Blackfriars Bridge and leaned on the parapet, gazing upriver to Waterloo Bridge and the Strand with its theatres and wall-to-wall crowds.

Blackfriars Bridge, named after the Black Friars of a medieval Dominican priory nearby, was a mordant choice for a rendezvous. Back in 1982 Roberto Calvi was hanged directly under the spot where she stood. "D" exhibited a dark sense of humor. Why she didn't just e-mail back and call the whole thing off she wasn't sure. Simple curiosity, maybe.

Still simmering from the Pudding Land debacle, she checked her watch again. Only 12:40? She was way early for the meeting, and the minutes were crawling.

She opened the Ultrabook and brought up her Overview01 file. Passing the time by tapping her toes didn't strike her as too clever. And if D was the real article, she wanted to come across as at least semi-knowledgeable. Keeping half an eye open for any likely candidate for the mysterious D, she sifted through her notes...

Book needs an angle, like David Yallop's In God's Name where he accused P2 of poisoning John Paul I. Coppola used Yallop as the source for Godfather 3. Mario Puzo got rich. One can dream.

Possible angle: Vatican City arguably the most secretive state on the planet yet the only one that denies operating a secret service. Vatican City one giant secret service in itself, with every diocese in the world a potential intelligence-gathering post. No special

Vatican Department X overseen by Cardinal Y or Z— not secret enough. Not so much a structured service as interconnecting webs, informal contacts, unspoken agreements.

Fact: The Kremlin was so enraged by covert Vatican activity that it masterminded the attempted assassination of John Paul II in St Peter's Square in 1981 via the Gray Wolves society in Turkey and its proxy, Mehmet Ali Ağça

Fact: John Paul II in not-so-secret meeting with President Reagan in the Vatican Library, June 7, 1982. After that meeting the Vatican escalated covert anti-soviet action, chiefly though the Russicum college in Rome's Via Carlino Cattaneo.

Cool fact: One of the bullets the assassin Mehmet Ali Ağça fired into John Paul II was later inserted into the crown of the Virgin Mary statue in Fatima.

Fact: The Jesuits, presently twenty-thousand strong, served as papal spies down through the centuries. Still active?

Unconfirmed rumor: the Cesano annex of Vatican Radio is part of the Echelon global surveillance network.

Unconfirmed rumor: insider name for the Vatican secret service is "the Crypt"

Recognizing that she had all this down pat and was just filling in time, she opened another file that contained the one puzzle she hadn't been able to get a handle on. Simon had sent a request at the very beginning of her research. She still didn't see how it fitted into any covert Vatican agencies.

Once again, she read the request, trying to figure out what was behind it:

Investigate the seventy-ninth heresy. Eighty heresies were condemned by Epiphanius of Salamis in the fourth century. The Collyridians were the seventy-ninth.

Aside from some preliminary checking, she'd put the whole seventy-ninth heresy thing pretty much on hold. Just how relevant was some obscure cult from sixteen centuries ago? But then, you never knew what you might find. Maybe she should have spent more than a couple of minutes on Google before letting it drop. She was on the verge of starting a thorough online search when an icon flashed up incoming mail. She clicked open the e-mail, then read the message with a deepening frown.

Rachel,

Please return home immediately, I beg you. Your life is at great risk. But if you persist, then head for the location attached as a last resort. You will be contacted there.

Regards,
Simon Dray

"Is this a joke?"

She opened the attachment and was presented with a jpeg image. A picture postcard of a church fronted by a spacious square with a raised fountain.

"Okay, pretty. But— who— what..."

She wheeled around, wits whirling, and blankly viewed the eastern reach of the Thames, past the truncated legs of the former railroad bridge pillars to the spindly Millennium Bridge and the seventeenth-century dome of St. Paul's.

"If it's a joke, it isn't funny."

She leaned against the parapet, then straightened up at the sight of a tall, dapper man bearing down on her. His narrow face wore a wide grin. It didn't fit. It was Elbow Man, scourge of Underground passengers.

"Hello, Rachel," he greeted, thrusting out a hand. "Not been waiting long, I hope?"

She performed a double take. "You're..."

"I'm D. As in D for Deacon. Excuse the subterfuge on the train. Just thought I'd strike up a conversation and then introduce myself." A laugh, slightly off-key. "Made a hash of it." He indicated the stairs leading down to the north bank. "Shall we talk?"

Rachel found she was doing most of the talking.

For the best part of twenty minutes Deacon had said very little. Nor was she too crazy about the location, right under the arch where Roberto Calvi was hanged; it smacked of cheap theatrics.

Nor had D— Deacon— convincingly explained his presence on the train. He claimed to have access to a "Vatican tracing program" that enabled him to follow her from her Hammersmith hotel. None of it quite added up but she decided to find out what insider knowledge Deacon might possess. Then get the hell away from this guy. She had enough on her plate with the crazy message from Simon.

As for Deacon, smooth he was, svelte he was, from his slick hair and gray silk tie to his polished toecaps, but there was a granite ego under the urbane façade. Besides, no way could she trust a man whose face looked like he moisturized with Brylcreem. Even the man's accent and phraseology were slightly awry: a parody of the posh English gent replete with jolly-this and Dear Lord-that. She didn't buy it.

She allowed a pause to lengthen as he tapped his Gucci-heeled foot. Or maybe the shoes were Armani. Something ending in i.

"So," he said finally. "Fill me in on this London Concordat Publishing company. Can't actually say I've heard of it."

"Since you're the one who e-mailed me about covert Vatican activities, how about you supply me some info on the Crypt? Isn't that what the Vatican secret service is called?"

He blithely ignored her attempt at fishing. "Have you been contacted by an old priest, by any chance? A priest by the name of Father Jonathan Taylor?"

"Er, no. Is he someone I should meet?"

His mouth twitched in a suggestion of a smile. "If you haven't met him yet, you never will." He angled his head like a curious fox. "Father Thomas Chen... Heard that name?"

"No, I haven't."

"Sister Annunciata?"

"No."

He gave a slow nod. "Hmm...just one more question. Has anyone ever mentioned the seventy-ninth heresy?"

Somehow, she kept a deadpan expression. An instinct told her to act dumb. It also told her to make a quick getaway. "Means nothing to me. Listen, what I'm after is the big picture, so if you don't know anything I might as well—"

"The big picture," he broke in. "Dear Lord, that's an epic symphony. Requires more than a quick burst on the jolly old banjo." He polished his manicured fingernails on his lapel. His tone was bland. "If I may say so, I find you massively ignorant. But in your case, ignorance is bliss."

His eyes twinkled and his lips bent into a gradual smile. Then, just as gradually, the stare hardened to granite and the smile fossilized. The mask was off.

He spun around and walked to the river's edge. "You need to be taught a lesson. I have one all prepared. Come and see."

Discretion urged her to vamoose, but there were plenty of sightseers strolling along the embankment and— a blessed sight— a policewoman within yelling distance. Surrendering to curiosity, she approached Deacon.

He pointed to where the bridge arch met the river. "There's where it happened, Calvi's hanging." He held up a digital camera whose lens pointed directly at the scene of the crime, LCD screen flipped open at the side. "Look and learn."

The viewfinder screen came to life as he pressed a button.

And Rachel's family appeared on the screen. Herself and her mom and dad and younger sister and brother, seated around a

Thanksgiving dinner table with Bonkers sitting in his basket in the corner. They looked up at the camera, her parents grinning, her siblings pulling faces and the boxer dog, as usual, looking astounded. A neighbor had taken that photo a year ago almost to the day and her dad had posted it on his blog site.

Before she could comment the image was replaced by another to the accompaniment of a faint click from the playback button. She saw herself as a baby in a bassinet, also an image posted on her dad's blog. And another image took its place: Rachel toddling her first shaky steps on a mercifully thick carpet. Then Rachel in fifth grade, wide smile showing off her wire braces in their full orthodontic glory. After that came her UCLA dorm room, where she sat on the bed in her flared jeans and made a doomed effort to look cool.

Every image had been taken from the web, but witnessing them displayed on a stranger's camera amounted to personal intrusion. She was about to voice this thought when Deacon pressed playback again.

And she saw, on the screen, herself, dressed in bomber jacket and gray denims, laptop tucked underarm, leaving her hotel in Hammersmith— just five hours ago. Another click of the playback. The interior of a crowded underground train, Rachel leaning over her Ultrabook, Deacon sitting beside her, his glance slyly slanted to the laptop's screen.

The image stayed visible for several seconds. Then the button clicked again.

And it seemed that the screen had switched from playback to viewfinder, showing her present location from her precise viewpoint. She was looking at the northern arch of Blackfriars Bridge as seen through the camera lens.

A rope dangled on the underside of the bridge. On the end of the rope, neck constricted in a noose, hung a red-haired woman dressed in a bomber jacket and gray denims. Despite the contorted features, the swollen, unseeing eyes, the protruding purple tongue, she instantly identified her own face.

Her blood froze to red ice.

Deacon lowered the camera, revealing the site of her portrayed death under the bridge arch, the ghostly afterimage of her hanged body superimposed on the scene.

Deacon moved in front of her, smiling a scimitar smile. "Don't you just love Photoshop?"

Rachel struggled for breath, unable to respond. The painstaking effort that had gone into the fabrication was almost as daunting as the image. No idle threat.

He sniffed airily. "Consider yourself warned. You're a little girl who wants to play with the big boys. That's a game you'll lose. If you're planning to head for Rome— don't. That's a trip you won't return from." He brushed idly at his lapel. "Go back to Los Angeles— *now*. Your ignorance has saved you."

She didn't know whom she hated most at that moment, Deacon or herself. She hated him because he had shrunk her into insignificance. And she hated herself for letting him do it.

Walk away.

"I'm going," she said meekly, retreating from his advance. "Going home, like you said."

"Now there's a good girl." He all but patted her on the head. "Run along."

Rachel headed for the stairway, already questioning her decision but determined to see it through.

One thing was sure: she wasn't running home.

Chapter 9

Carlingford Lough

"Over the hills and far away."

Dominic hardly heard the words even as he spoke them.

He was nearing the top of the Windy Gap, a deep fold in Sliabh Foy that curved up to a bowl in the mountain's lap, a bowl of silence known as the Long Woman's Grave. It was four p.m. but no sign yet of the text message "friend."

Ascending the Windy Gap at an easy pace, he soon reached his destination, a natural amphitheatre on whose far side, through a gap in the southern banks, the peak of Clough Patrick raised its rounded head. From this vantage point, it was easy to imagine that the southern pathway led to not just one summit, but to peak behind peak, a world of Sidhe hills and Druid stones and narrow paths winding up into tiered clouds.

Some stratum of his soul was attuned to this land. After all, he had maybe three hundred generations of Irish ancestors receding into a primeval vanishing point. It brought to mind a line of the poet John Donne:

Tell me where all past years are.

The line led him to a well-beaten track of thought. Where were all those ancestors? Did they still live in the past, which for them was another now, all times coexistent? The past, according to the block time of mathematical physics, still existed, but what was demonstrated by equations eluded the imagination. Where *is* the past? Did the Stone Age hunters still wield their axes, the Bronze

Age warriors brandish their spears, the Iron Age armies wage their wars?

Was it possible, with a sidestep of the spirit, a momentary straying from his path in time, to greet those lost ancestors, himself a fleeting ghost from the future?

He smiled at the wild speculation. The silence and isolation of the Long Woman's Grave had definitely got to him. No harm in that; when he got back home to Brooklyn, it would make a fine old whale of a tale, suitably embroidered, while recounted over a bottle of Guinness in Doyle's Bar with Enya supplying the backing track.

Back home to the States...

His hand almost strayed to the air ticket in his breast pocket. An open return.

A wistful smile. "I left my heart in San Francisco."

His gaze wandered up Sliabh Foy to the turbulent clouds that persisted in masking the summit. With the dying of the wind, the mist was sneaking down to blanket the middle slopes.

In fact, the fog *had* covered the middle ridges. As he watched, the cloud descended the mountain, a slow phantasmal avalanche.

The hollow gradually lost its sharp definition as the mist sank into it. The sense of isolation was total and the silence absolute. The wraparound fog cocooned the deep bowl in the mountain.

A sudden mumble of distant thunder only accentuated his impression of solitude.

The low murmur faded for a moment, then resumed its remote complaint.

The mumble lengthened, gradually rising in volume. Broadening in pitch.

As he listened, the sound expanded to a rumble that reverberated in the encircling banks, approaching from the north. The rumble continued to expand. Stronger, fuller...

Louder, closer... A deep-throated roar.

Dominic whirled around to the curtain of mist in the amphitheatre's breach.

Christ!

A black motorbike blasted from the fog, the bellow of its engine bouncing around the hollow.

Instinct flung him aside as the front tire thudded into the soil right in front of him. He hit the ground with a jarring thump and lay sprawled until survival instinct kicked in and launched him back on his feet. The rider, mounted on a brute of a Harley-Davidson, swerved in a wide arc, pulling to a halt with the front wheel aimed straight at Dominic.

The man, clad in garish red-and-white motorcycle gear and reflective visor helmet, flexed his bulky shoulders. Then revved the engine and raised his left arm, brandishing a baseball bat in a gloved fist. After a couple of beats the motorcycle advanced, at full charge.

He stood motionless, waiting until the last second to dodge. The oncoming motorbike was almost on top of him, the baseball bat hefted to crack his skull. He had seen enough enemy combatants to know when a man was out to kill him.

He feinted to the right. Then leaped to the left, splashed by a copious spray of mud as the wheels sped past. Before the biker had time to recover, Dominic was on his feet and sprinting to the far side of the hollow. The encircling mist and surrounding silence made the thunderous confrontation all the more unreal.

He reached the nearest bank and clambered up the incline. He had to gain the high ground. At the approaching growl of the Harley he halted, planting his feet wide. The biker was streaking in a straight line toward him, mounting the slope.

As the wheels devoured the distance, his feet itched to jump.

The rider opened the throttle further and the bike accelerated up the remaining few yards.

Hold on... hold on...

Then Dominic jumped. Up high. Feet first, spine arched back, he leaped over the wide handlebars. His feet smashed into the biker's face, the impact snapping the man's head back and lifting him clean off the seat.

Dominic ignored the shock of the impact, twisting to the left and doubling-up. It seemed as though he was airborne for a painfully long, slow-motion time.

Then he was back to earth with a thud. Mercifully his feet hit the slope first and he rolled down the bank to end up near the floor of the hollow with life and limb intact.

Sparing a couple of deep breaths, he sat on the ground, testing for injuries. Aside from a numb sensation in his calves and right arm that promised impressive bruises by evening, he'd gotten off pretty lightly. The rider, who'd slid down past him, was in a less healthy state.

Dominic cast a look at the slope... just in time to witness the Harley tumbling back down, aiming straight for him as if to avenge its master. He hopped sideways and watched the metal monster skid by, slow down, and topple.

The biker, prostrate on the ground, emitted a grunt and wrested the helmet from his head, revealing bloated, middle-aged features and a near-skinhead scalp dyed an acid yellow.

Dominic walked up and put his foot on the man's bull neck, pushing his head back down. The rank smell of sweat from the blubbery body— all two yards of it, and then some— didn't improve the situation.

"That was invigorating," Dominic said. "So who the hell are you?"

The only reaction was open scorn in the man's pale blue eyes and a slow sneer.

Okay, be that way. He pressed the toe of his hiking boot harder into the rider's neck, extracting a sharp gasp. The man bit his lip as if to seal in the invective that pressured to burst out.

"Let's try again. Who are you? Why did you get me up here with that text message— that *was* you, right?"

"Was it a fluke, that fancy jump you made?" the man growled.

Ah, it talks... Dominic glanced at the Harley. "Oh, that. That's thanks to the Sergeant Wong and the Rangers."

The man's eyes narrowed in equal measure to the drop of his jaw. "U.S. Rangers? Special Forces? You were a Ranger?"

"Uh-huh. What's it to you?"

Hot anger suffused the man's face. "That fuckin' spic *liar*. Some pussy teacher you turned out to be."

"And who might the 'spic' liar be?"

The biker's expression phased from anger to shiftiness. "I ain't saying no more."

Dominic figured that was no empty boast. The man had been caught off-guard but was getting himself together. He was attempting to sit up, his glare homicidal.

"Behave yourself," Dominic reprimanded, stepping over to the Harley. "Stay put."

He grabbed the handlebars and, after a moment's maneuvering, heaved the bike up. The prostrate biker, suddenly catching on, struggled to scramble away as Dominic lowered the Harley toward him as far as possible until his muscles protested. With a foot to spare, he let go.

The heavy motorbike impacted the bulging belly. Breath whooshed from the gaping oval of his mouth. Trapped beneath his Harley, the man planted gloved hands under the bike and pushed. He gained a few inches of space before it fell back, extracting another pained gasp.

Dominic sat down beside him. "Now... let's talk."

Chapter 10

Father Daigh Kinsella sat in front of the old ThinkPad laptop planted on his desk, glowering at the seemingly limitless inventory of the Quinn estate displayed on the LCD screen.

Anything was better than looking at Mr. Jones. Whoever or whatever Jones was, the man who had pushed his way into the presbytery and acted as if he owned the feckin' place had thoroughly rattled him as surely as if he'd found himself sharing a room with a grouchy panther. The twenty minutes Jones had gone off somewhere would have been a relief if it weren't for the equally unnerving Alice. At least when Jones returned, he was spared the presence of that psychotic-looking woman who was apparently off on some errand for her boss for the past hour.

He would have made a run for it when he had the chance if the man's credentials weren't so impressive. Alongside the laptop lay a letter that was undeniably from Vatican City, the crossed-keys-headed page clearly bearing the insignia of the Congregation for the Doctrine of the Faith and signed by none other than Cardinal Chavet.

At first it was difficult to take in the contents of the letter. The Holy Office was "under strict orders from the Apostolic Palace" and he, Kinsella, should "obey directives from authorities higher than the archdiocesan level." The gist of it was that he supply the bearer of the letter every assistance. Despite appearances, Jones was some sort of Vatican emissary.

A low whirr made him glance up at a wall clock showing the hands at four o'clock. The clock was designed to imitate the façade of St. Peter's Basilica with a greatly enlarged papal balcony. A plastic image of Pope John Paul II popped out of a little window onto the balcony, right arm creaking upward in unison with the pope's taped voice: *"In nomine Patri, et Filii, et Spiritu Sancti."* The hour duly marked, the pope retreated from the balcony and the window clicked shut.

The miniature St. Peter's was blocked out by the figure of Jones as he slipped into sight, silent as a ghost.

"You've had enough time, Father. What's the verdict?"

Kinsella stretched his stiff shoulders. "Three apparently missing items from the inventory seem to have been misfiled. So the only item actually stolen was Brian Quinn's journal."

"That figures. Okay, fill me in on how all this started."

"I've already gone through this with the Monsignor."

"Go through it again."

Kinsella made an effort to preserve a calm façade. "Well now, after the will was read out, I went up to the Quinn house to start on the inventory. I came across the journal, skimmed through some pages, then locked it back in the desk." His head sank. "How was I supposed to know the house would be burgled that same night? And anyways, who'd expect anyone to steal a journal?"

"Tell me all you remember of it."

"Everything? Ah— well now, I skimmed through it, as I said. That's when I came across the entries about John Paul the First's death. I scribbled a few of those lines down and e-mailed them to the Holy Office."

"I saw the e-mail," said Jones. "It was nothing special, except for a single sentence: 'Sometimes I pray that Sarah renounced the seventy-ninth heresy and the Apocryphon Mariæ, even as she breathed her last.' Have you ever heard of the seventy-ninth heresy or the Apocryphon Mariæ?"

Jones's stare was glacial. Kinsella began to feel like an ice statue, with Jones seeing right through him. "No. Any reason I should?"

The moment stretched and stretched, close to snapping.

Jones turned away, releasing Kinsella from the cold scrutiny.

"John Paul the First's death was no big deal, Father. Conspiracy theories of his murder are all over the web. It's history." Jones paced slowly to the window. "Those unusual words and phrases you saw when you glanced through the book— make a list of them."

"But you must be familiar with them. I told the Monsignor everything I remember."

"Easy to miss something. Write them down. Might jog your memory."

Kinsella sucked in a lungful of air. There was no contradicting this man: he exuded the authority of menace. He took out a sheet from the printer and a pencil from the desk drawer, completed the list in a couple of minutes, studied it for another minute, then spread his palms. "That's it— that's everything."

He glanced again at the scribbled words:

Marked by the thorn

I have eaten the bitter bread of silence

Annunciata

Brother, you have made offering to Diana of the Ephesians

Went to the Proleek dolmen today but heard no voices

Epiphanius

A vagabond made of rain is tapping at my window

Santa Maria in Trastevere

Chamber of the Dormition

Who is she who looks forth with the dawn?

Jones scooped up the sheet and scanned its contents. He looked across at Kinsella. "There's an item here I haven't seen before."

"That's the full list I gave the Monsignor, truly," Kinsella protested.

"That so?" He returned to the sheet and spoke in a low voice: "Annunciata. Now why would the Monsignor leave that one out?" He flipped open a phone, pressed a single key, and spoke in a low voice: "Alice... seems the Monsignor's been playing his own game... No, I'm just about done here. Come on in."

Barely a minute passed before Kinsella heard the front door open and close and the soft tread of approaching footsteps.

"Alice," Jones acknowledged as the woman walked into the study. "Are the men on their way?"

"Be here real soon." The accent might or might not be Kentucky. "You want me to go through the priest's stuff now or wait a while?"

"I guess the journal's someplace else but it's worth a look around here once we get rid of the priest. I had Quinn down as the guy who took it but now I've got the Monsignor on radar."

She cast a disdainful look at Kinsella. "So the priest here is baggage. Dump him in the lake?"

Jones nodded. "They call it a lough around here, but yeah, get a couple of the boys to drop him in there later. Try Calabrese and Felici— they know how to cover their tracks."

Father Kinsella gripped the sides of his chair, thunderstruck. *Dump him in the lough?* Had he heard right? Were these people actually discussing his execution as if it were a trifling chore, blind to the fact that he was right there in the room with them?

But— this couldn't be happening. Could it?

Run.

No, it was a sick joke. They couldn't mean it. Could they?

RUN!

Oh God, they *did* mean it...

As Jones moved toward the window, Kinsella launched his heavy frame out of the chair in a wild bid for the hallway, the front door, open air.

He scarcely reached the study door before he was yanked off his feet by the scruff of his neck. The hand at his collar rotated him to face the expressionless Jones, holding him aloft from a straight arm as though he were disposing of a kitten. Quite apart from his phenomenal speed in crossing the room, the wiry Jones must have the strength of an Olympic weightlifter. In sheer panic, Kinsella kicked and punched his tormentor, landing solid blows. No reaction. Not so much as a change in expression.

"Take a look at where you're going," Jones said in a flat tone as he strolled to the window, upraised arm never wavering from stair-rod straight, still oblivious to the barrage of fists and feet. "Look out there, past the graveyard. Deep, deep waters. Maybe you can feed five thousand fishes."

Kinsella sensed the powerful grip being released and then he was falling. He barely felt the impact on the thick carpet.

Jones, ever impassive, looked down at him. "Now you're where you belong. Beneath me." He drew back his fist, each finger decorated with a chunky gold ring.

The next instant a detonation shattered Kinsella's jaw and reverberated in the dome of his skull.

Wits dulled, he heard a voice from some out-there-ness. "Let you off real light, Father." Jones's face swam into focus, up close. "Hey, Father, you're giving me dirty looks. Don't look at me. Look the other way."

He felt a pressure each side of his head: fingers gripping, the touch of cold metal.

And then there was...

Alice looked down at the priest's body, the neck snapped, the head twisted around to stare blindly over one shoulder.

"That was quick."

Jones gave a minuscule shrug. "He was nobody special. Didn't deserve a special send-off. But, you know, it had some kind of style. These priests, they're like these authority figures above you. And then, topsy-turvy. Me topsy and him turvy. And as for the boys taking him on a boat trip— wait until dark."

She caught his questioning glance. Was this another of his movie references? Yeah, it had to be. She gave a snort. "I don't get it."

"No? Well... there's this cool guy from Scarsdale—"

The trill of a ring tone severed his sentence. Jones pulled a phone from an inside pocket, glanced at the caller display on the screen, then spoke in a low tone:

"What's the news? Did he talk?" He waited a brief space. "What's the problem?" A longer pause. "I don't know what the fuck that means." His shoulders tightened a fraction. "I'll be coming. Count on it."

Alice frowned at her boss. Ten years since he'd turned up at her door in Louisville, and not once had he showed a sliver of emotion. But now, if she didn't know better, she'd say his expression betrayed a hint of anger.

He thrust the phone back into his pocket and stared at her for several long seconds. "Someone just challenged me."

She experienced mild shock. "Challenged *you*? You gotta be kidding."

He moved to the door. "Deal with Kinsella. We'll meet up later."

He strode lightly out of the study and into the hall. Soft footfalls sounded in the hallway. The gentle creak of an opened door. A loud bang as it slammed shut.

Fifteen minutes-plus and Dominic hadn't extracted a single word from the rider pinned under the Harley. He had prompted, threatened, cajoled. Not a word in response.

But he could see how far bluffing got him.

The baseball bat lay a few yards up the slope. He swept it up and strode down to the rider whose eyes betrayed more than a hint of apprehension. Dominic stood over him and hefted the club. The weight and balance of the weapon suggested a lead filling.

"Let's try a different tack," he said.

The man averted his face, still sneering defiance.

Dominic prepared to deliver a mild blow, then spotted a name written on the bat in red Magic Marker: *ROBERT CARSON*

So, he likely had the man's name. He noted an inordinate amount of stains on its surface...He'd seen stains like these before, too often. Oxidized blood.

"Well, Robert Carson, you're not a man to wash away the evidence, are you?"

Maybe it was the utterance of his name, but the man finally reacted. He spat out a string of saliva and grinned. "Done a bit of enforcing in my time. Grew out of it and left the gang. But our lads could show you fuckin' GI Joes what real fighting's about, so we could. Street-wise, you know?"

Dominic smiled contemptuously. "Street-wise, world-foolish." It went right against the grain to hit a helpless man but it wouldn't be long before this behemoth was up and about again, hot for havoc. "Either you talk about the journal or bones will crack. And who's the Hispanic that sent you?"

Carson snorted. "I've said all I'm gonna say."

Dominic made a careful study of the man's expression. "I believe you."

He swung the bat at Carson's skull. The man emitted a surprised grunt, eyes wide, then his head flopped to one side, out cold.

"You'll wake with just a headache," Dominic muttered, heaving the bike off the man and wheeling it upright. "If you were on top, you'd treat me like a jellyfish in a steam press."

He knelt down and unzipped Carson's biker suit, then gave his pockets a thorough examination. After a couple of minutes all he found of interest was a Motorola phone and a British passport confirming the man's identity as Robert Carson. He threw the passport aside and brought up the phone's menu. A minute's experimentation and he found the list of calls. The only name on the list was Jones. Not overly Hispanic.

Dominic pressed to dial Jones in a forlorn hope. He'd pretty much given up on the journal, but still...

The phone trilled a few times. A voice answered:

"What's the news? Did he talk?"

Did he talk? Interesting expression.

Was that accent faintly Hispanic? Dominic hung on, instinctively holding his breath.

"What's the problem?" the voice asked sharply.

Hispanic. Probably. Enough to risk a challenge...

"Hello, Jones. I turned up but your errand boy didn't deliver the goods. Do you have a journal handy by any chance?"

The answer was silence. An eloquent silence. No real doubt about it, this man had sent Carson.

"I don't know what the fuck that means," the voice said at last.

Dominic let Jones stew a while. When he spoke, he kept it quiet and cool. "The name's Dominic Quinn but I suppose you guessed that. Carson can't make it to the phone right now— he's indisposed. Next time, do your own dirty work. Come for me yourself, you little prick."

This time the pause was brief. "I'll be coming. Count on it."

Dominic heard a terminal click as the connection was cut.

He threw the phone beside the prone Carson and gazed around the Long Woman's Grave, its rounded margins still hazy with fog. Someone called Jones had sent Carson. Which begged the question: why?

And the answer was: he didn't greatly care, despite the macho exchange on the phone. Why look for trouble? He was leaving tomorrow, so they could all go to hell. Stretching bruised limbs, he prepared for the long trek back to Carlingford, then looked at the Harley.

"I think I'll borrow something of yours," he declared, hurling Carson's baseball bat into a swath of long grass behind a low mound. "You can walk."

He swung onto the seat of the motorbike and turned the ignition key, sparking the powerful engine into rumbling life. He eased on the clutch and opened the throttle, swerving the bike around, then gunned the Harley and accelerated into the mist.

Chapter 11

"Twilight"

Seated on Brian Quinn's deathbed, Martha slanted a look at the Monsignor. "So you just said."

Monsignor Aylesbury dumped his overnight bag and turned from the window of Brian Quinn's former bedroom. "Ireland has a gently mournful twilight, quite unique."

Martha's brow contracted at the Monsignor's subdued response. He'd been preoccupied since they arrived in Carlingford over a week ago. And in the five minutes since he returned from his overnight trip to London, he'd been uncharacteristically taciturn.

She observed his tall, stately figure draped in the customary black cashmere overcoat. His silvery mane of backswept hair, which he was wont to call "leonine," was paler than usual in the fading light and his posture, habitually erect, was slouched. He looked his real age— the morgue side of sixty. Not since that time in Holland had he looked so... burdened.

"Lighten up," she said. "We've survived worse."

He regarded her with those deep brown eyes of his. "Worse...?"

"When you were Amsterdamned and Eurotrashed.'

"Oh, that. Water under the canal bridge."

"Right, right. So how did London work out?"

"Not well." He paused. "Jonathan's intimations of mortality proved accurate. Someone got to him before I did. Insulin overdose."

"Oh, no..." Her head sank slowly. "So whatever he witnessed, back in 1950..."

"Is a lost secret. If I'd got to him in time, I believe he'd finally have revealed what he saw."

"Maybe so. Anyway, I did what you wanted. Colin O'Hanlon will introduce me to Dominic. But I vote we get Colin the hell out of Ireland and let me approach Dominic directly."

He compressed his lips. "Dominic trusts Colin. Colin will help him trust you."

"I still don't like it. Oh, and by the way— there's been no sign of Father Kinsella since this morning. I think maybe Jones silenced him."

"I suspect so, but not of his own volition. Jones is acting under orders."

"Martin, we're on our own, and that isn't good. You have to get Il Gesù back on our side. Monsignor Ortega is technically mission director; won't he help?"

He winced at the mention of Il Gesù in Rome, mother-house of the Society of Jesus and headquarters of the Sodality of Loyola, the Jesuit intelligence network.

"I'm not exactly flavor of the month with my fellow Jesuits, even Ortega. We'll get no help from that quarter." He expelled a slow breath. "Jones is no fool. He might have worked out by now that I stole the journal. We must leave for Rome tonight. Head for Santa Maria in Trastevere— by separate ways. I've notified Thomas Chen."

She eyed him warily. "Separate ways...why separate ways? You're not planning another of your long-shot throws of the dice, are you? What are you up to?"

"Nothing you don't know about. A mission to fulfill. Debts to pay. I owe it to Annunciata."

"Promises to keep?"

"And miles to go." He crossed the room and sagged into the bedside chair. "I confess to a slight touch of exhaustion, which I trust will pass." He glanced around. "You scanned the appropriate pages and copied them to a memory stick, yes? And you burned the journal?"

"Of course I burned it." Her mouth formed a crooked slant. "The way things are going, we might as well have jumped into the flames with it."

Carson awoke by degrees in the Long Woman's Grave, blearily discerning his phone lying beside him in the wet grass.

"What..." He struggled to his feet. Then remembered what Dominic Quinn had done to him. And then realized that Quinn had stolen his motorbike. The rage seeped into him with each breath of the foggy air. Dominic Quinn: that Yank had gone to the top of his hate list. Scrub that: he'd replaced the whole list.

His baseball bat was gone. Another strike against Quinn. With an axe, maybe.

A few unsteady paces through the long grass, then he slipped on a loose object. Anger transformed to delight as he saw a baseball bat skip out of the grass. "Yeah!"

He grabbed the bat and wielded it, stronger with the weapon in his grip. He could've searched the entire hollow and never found the weapon before dark. It was a sign from God.

He'd learned to watch for signs since Jones first hired him as backup for a hit in Newry. The hit turned out to be a Protestant lawyer. Protestant, Catholic, it was all the same. As a youth he'd followed the July 12th drum with the best of them, shouting, "No Popery!" loud enough to deafen God, but he'd wised up with age. First it was the Loyalist cause, then it was the money. With Jones, he'd found both a cause and money. He was God's warrior, with a healthy bank balance.

He staggered to the northern gap in the mountain hollow, his pace slowing as the outlines of a car gradually became visible. It was Jones' SUV. Carson pulled open the passenger door and sank into the seat. Jones stared straight ahead, expressionless.

Carson frowned. "How long was I lying out there?"

"Half an hour. Time for you to recover. Time for me to think."

"You just left me there?"

"Yeah. You screwed up. But at least we know Quinn doesn't have the journal. He called me on your phone and asked if I had it. He wasn't playing games."

Carson shifted in his seat, resentment at full boil. "Yeah, well, some pussy teacher he turned out to be. You got bad intel. He was in the U.S. Rangers."

"That a fact? Seems someone's been messing with Substratum's files. Reckon I can guess who. I'll call Benoit. Quinn's profile needs updating."

"Whatever," snorted Carson. "I want me some vengeance for Quinn. An eye for an eye."

"And I want justice. An eye for an eye is vengeance: two eyes for an eye is justice."

"Uh-huh... so where do we start?"

"You want to hurt a man, hurt his friends first. Drive him crazy." Jones started the car. "There's a teacher's cottage on a little lane. Cute, huh? Let's make ourselves at home."

Chapter 12

He had delayed his visit to the church but couldn't put it off any longer. With a sidelong glance at the graveyard, Dominic passed under St. Bartholomew's Gothic archway into the glass-fronted narthex and pushed open a swing door into the nave. The dimly lit church was empty at this betwixt and between hour.

He looked to one side, to the prayer bench in front of a statue of Our Lady of Mercy. His mouth curved in a smile. "Mary abides." The smile faded as he headed down the aisle to the altar, barely registering the red sanctuary lamp that signified the real presence of Christ in the silver tabernacle.

This was the place. This was where he'd almost killed a priest. He expected a tidal wave of memories, stark images. Nothing came. It was as though the whole event had occurred to some other Dominic, enacted in a scratchy old movie, faintly recalled.

He moved from the altar to the arched entrance of the sacristy. The sacristy walls had been repainted the same cream gloss coating as that night when he'd walked into the vestry, drawn by Colin's loud sobs, wondering what was wrong...

The past pounced into the present...

...Father Tierney's semi-nude body, the scrawny buttocks flexing, pushing against Colin who was bent over the vestment table, naked from the waist down, with the priest's left hand forcing him flat against the polished surface. And that look on Colin's face. That look. Desecrated. Desouled.

"*Jesus...*" he breathed hoarsely.

He sat down in a pew and leaned back, gaze vacantly scanning the timbered roof, the altar table, the Stations of the Cross on the white gloss of the walls.

"Jesus."

He remembered charging at Tierney... Tierney running out the vestry... Then nothing. Nothing until he found himself with his back to the altar, its crucifix at his feet, the tabernacle dislodged from its niche and the communion wafers scattered on the carpet. And blood on his trembling fists as he stood over the battered priest.

If a single incident marked his loss of Catholic faith, it was that moment. The fall from grace had come that night.

He straightened up at the *clack* of a latch from inside the sacristy arch. He recognized that particular click, resonant with guilt, from childhood. It was the door to the confessional booth, the odor of its penitential varnish permeating his soul.

A middle-aged woman emerged from the archway and darted him a smile. "If you're waiting for confession, the priest doesn't seem to be here. Been talking to myself the last minute."

He essayed a smile. "It's okay. I'm not here for confession."

As the woman left the church, he headed back up the aisle. At the door he turned to the right, to the statue of Our Lady of Mercy on a plinth of Connemara marble, her image fronted by ranks of candlelight. This was why he'd come, to stand at this one special spot. Here was the one place in St. Bartholomew's that remained sacred.

A candle on the lowest row of the candle rack had blown out. He relit it with the flame of its companion, then stepped back and gazed in silence. His focus wasn't on the mediocre statue of the Virgin Mary, but the small prayer bench at its feet. The empty bench was expressive of the shape that once occupied it, the silence eloquent of the prayer once heard.

She had knelt there, when he was five, maybe six, back in a winter morning of his life. Not a girl he knew. Not a girl he loved at first sight. Not a girl he ever encountered again. But a small girl who saw something that wasn't in the statue, or the church, or the county, or the world. And because she saw, she was transfigured.

He could recall only two words of her mumbled prayer:

"Mary abides."

When darkness fell that day, long ago, he had taken a candle from the church, walked out into a night silent with God, and reached up to light a candle from a star.

Chapter 13

Six-o-clock gone and still no sign of Colin. Dominic paced slowly back and forth as he waited by the Tholsel Gate, the archway of a fifteenth-century tollhouse in the medieval walls of Carlingford town.

The streetlights were on, highlighting the lines of houses with painted cement façades. O'Hares, otherwise known as the Anchor Bar, would be stirring into action, its staff busy stacking the oysters and gearing up for the night's entertainment. The pub would resound with traditional music and the *bodhrain* would receive a suitable bashing. And there was always the pub leprechaun displayed in its glass container, just in case any tourists had forgotten they were in Ireland.

Wincing at a spreading soreness from his tumble after kicking Carson from his bike, Dominic checked his watch. "Hurry up, Colin." At that precise moment a young couple appeared around the arch. Caught talking to himself, he instantly converted the mutter to an ostentatious yawn. Their knowing looks showed he wasn't fooling anyone.

"Dominic!"

Colin emerged from behind a car, hand raised in greeting, then eyed Dominic's mud-stained clothes and mud-caked hiking boots. "You have the same pride in your appearance as in the old days, I see."

"Oh, yeah. Sliabh Foy. Steep, slippery slopes. But nobody in O'Hares will care what I look like. Sound all right to you?"

"I'm not so sure. Even if your outfit were clean, it wouldn't pass muster in the couture department."

He shrugged. "I'm a dedicated bucker of fashion."

"Right... um..." Colin glanced around, nodding vaguely. "Truth is, I think you should meet someone. There's an apartment close by. I'll explain when we get there. Something's going on, and it involves a woman called Martha and a man by the name of Jones."

"Jones..."

Colin looked at him askance. "Does that name mean something to you?"

The apartment was strictly 80s retro, complete with black leather chairs riddled with steel tubing, the legs sunk deep into a black carpet. At least the wide window— which resembled a pane extracted from an Amtrak railroad car— afforded an expansive view of the marina. Yachts and launches and small speedboats bobbed on the lough under a sky phasing from twilight to night, backgrounded by the black silhouette of the Mourne Mountains.

Dominic took a grateful gulp of a rich African blend of tea, then parked the mug on a glass-topped coffee table.

"Didn't realize how thirsty I was," he said, glancing across the table at Colin. "As for that story of yours— Martha the FBI agent, the monotone Jones, imminent danger etcetera— to be honest, I'm past caring. How about we head for your place and chat about the good old bad old days over a peat fire?"

"Um, well, I promised Martha." Colin shuffled his feet. "She shouldn't be long. Apart from anything else, she's a friend of Monsignor Aylesbury, and I owe him. Almost as much as I owe you. You attacked Tierney for my sake and got packed off to America for it."

"Hardly a jail sentence. Aylesbury... that name never came up in your e-mails."

"He asked me to keep it to myself. The first time I saw him was the year after you left. He restored the faith I thought I'd lost with Tierney." His mouth formed an awkward slant. "I guess that night in St. Bartholomew's killed your faith."

"You think so?" Dominic reflected a moment. "Not entirely. I'm all for the rituals and mysteries, Gregorian chant in venerable monasteries, Palestrina in baroque basilicas, incense in midnight chapels."

Tongue in cheek, Colin remarked: "Those are the trappings of religion. The luxuries."

"It's the luxuries I need. The necessities I can do without."

Colin broke into a laugh. "Hey, that quick-fire retort *ricocheted*."

"It wasn't aimed at you. And, there's the old chestnut: more people have been killed in the name of religion..."

"And you a historian! If it's Christianity you have in mind, here's a fact: in the space of five centuries all the inquisitions combined resulted in the deaths of some twenty thousand souls. In the short span of the twentieth century, atheist states murdered over a hundred million of their own people."

"Oh... yes. That'll teach me to spout clichés. Thank God I'm agnostic." He paused, uncertain whether to dip a toe into the deep waters. "Then there are priests— priests like Tierney..."

Colin's gaze dropped to his feet. "Priests like Tierney, that's the singer, not the song. I believe in the song. Tierney's dead, the song goes on. But what about you? What do you believe in?"

Now there was a question with no easy answer. "When someone dies," he finally began, still ordering his thoughts, "they leave a negative space. Not the negative space of formal art composition but more like— an absence at the center that's only given shape by the shading of the surrounding canvas. The notion that death will turn everyone I know into nothing— negative space— I find unbearable. I want to believe that existence has a purpose, that our lives border on eternity. I'm with the Church on that one." He summoned a smile. "Besides, Catholicism is unfashionable— that's always a plus."

"Spoken like a reluctant believer." Colin's mouth formed a lopsided grin. "Am I getting preachy? Should I lighten the tone?"

Dominic mirrored the grin. "Gets my vote."

"I was wondering how your folks took the news about the parish getting every last bean from your dad's estate. You do have *some* relatives somewhere?"

"Apart from Aunt Deirdre, just a wastrel uncle— as my father called him— no-one else to speak of. In many ways, the Rangers were my family. I miss those guys."

"You never said a word about Afghanistan in your e-mails. What was it like?"

"It had its moments, some of which I'm trying to forget."

Colin's expression was contrite. "Did I tread on a landmine there?"

"Not even an eggshell."

"That's good. It's just that I never imagined you signing up. To be honest, I wondered if you were overcompensating. You know, the Irish immigrant trying to be more American than the Yanks, saluting Old Glory, eager to belong."

Dominic leaned back in the chair. "That's uncomfortably perceptive of you, Mister O'Hanlon."

Colin evinced a mock wince. "Well hey, you *are* wearing a national flag on your sleeve," he said, indicating the Stars and Stripes patch.

Any response was silenced by the chimes of the doorbell.

"Ah," Colin muttered. "Martha has landed." He got up and disappeared into the hallway. He returned with a tall, strikingly attractive woman in a brown leather overcoat. She dropped into an armchair and crossed her booted legs, gracing Dominic with a languid wave.

"Hi. I'm Martha." The voice was low and husky.

"Hello, Martha."

The newcomer took out a folded note and looked up at Colin hovering by her side. "Change of plan. You need to leave right away. Don't go home. Drive straight to Ballinasloe. There's a farm outside the town where you can lie low. Here are the directions."

Colin ignored the proffered note. "The agreement was I introduce you to Dominic then leave you two alone for maybe half an hour. Now— *Ballinasloe*?"

Martha shrugged an apology. "The game has just gotten very rough and you're best out of it tout de suite. Genuinely sorry."

"Is that a fact?" He turned to Dominic. "I'll go get dinner ready. See you in half an hour, how's that sound?"

"Colin," Martha said with marked intensity as the teacher moved to the hallway. "Do-not-go-home."

He kept his back turned on her. "See you in a while, Dominic."

"Colin!" Martha called out, but he'd already passed into the hallway. "Colin!" Seconds later there was a thunk as the street door swung shut.

Martha subsided into her chair. "*Damn*. But can't say I blame him." She curved an unexpectedly gentle smile. "Did he tell you I was FBI? Bit of a fib. I'm from a more shadowy world. And that world of shadows is closing in on you. It's almost here. Bit of a bolt from the blue, huh?"

"I've known a few bolts from the blue in my time. One more can't hurt."

She tilted her head. "How about a dozen?"

"Fire away."

"I will, but first, did you come across anything unusual today?"

"A brute from the paddling end of the gene pool named Carson and a guy called Jones. Now you."

She straightened up, then slumped back in the chair. "Oh, not good. You'd better fill me in."

He studied her, and noticed she was studying him right back. And he trusted what he saw in Martha's eyes. Unusual candor was evident there, inner strength. And despite her peremptory treatment of Colin, he also liked her at first sight— but maybe that was sexual allure.

"Fine," he said. "I'll fill you in. But who are you?"

"I was a nun once upon a time, way back before the Fall. Long story. *Ben-Hur* length."

"Give me the trailer."

She flung up a hand. "Oh, if you insist... Born in Chicago. Got religion. Joined a Carmelite Order in New York State. Left the convent in search of adventure in Europe. Met an unusual priest in Rome. Went back to the States. Now I'm in Europe again. End of story." Her smile was winsome. "Okay then, tell me what happened to you today, pretty please?"

Chapter 14

In the gathering dark the saloon car glided smoothly along the loughside road. As Colin drove homeward he questioned his decision to introduce Martha to Dominic. But then, Dominic could surely handle anyone.

After he'd finished directing the school play rehearsal he raced to a supermarket in Dundalk and stocked up on all the items for a Chinese meal. For good measure, he added a magnum of champagne— a magnum of thanks for all he owed Dominic.

It had taken him years to recover from Tierney's violation and Monsignor Aylesbury had been a help, but it was Dominic who ended the assaults when he kicked hell's bells out of Father Tierney. Set against all that, a magnum of champagne seemed small beer.

Sliabh Foy crawled by as the kilometers clocked up. Soon he was turning onto the Wee Road, taking its bends at a moderate pace until he drew to a halt in front of his gate.

A minute later, he'd parked the car in the forecourt and unloaded the shopping. Crammed shopping bags hefted under each arm, he stepped into the dark interior.

The lights came on before he even moved to the switch.

A stranger sat in his fireside chair. A slim, gaudily-dressed man in a powder-blue jacket and red silk shirt, his expressionless face thin and angular and crowned with black hair swept back tight to the scalp.

The stranger's voice was toneless, void of emotion. A voice he recognized. "Hello, teacher."

The slam of the door behind him made Colin swing around. A hulk of a man in a red-and-white biker suit stood behind him, a vacuous grin on his flabby face, baseball bat in double-grip.

The grin widened. "Time someone was taught a lesson."

Martha tapped her boot heels together and stared out the apartment window.

"Mm..." she murmured softly, mulling over Dominic's account. "You've certainly riled Carson. And challenging Jones isn't a recipe for a healthy life, or any kind of life."

Dominic glanced pointedly at his watch.

"Okay, okay," she sighed. "Cutting to chase... Everything that's happened to you today is connected to the Catholic Church. You've been caught up in history. It will probably kill you."

"Ah— right," he said cautiously. "You've got my attention."

"I thought I might. Let me state my position. For me, the Catholic Church performs a vital political function: cultural cohesion. That's not some sophomoric issue of right versus left. I'm liberal in my conservatism— give me women priests and Latin, that's what I say. In my book, secularism is dandy— I'm a fan. But when it becomes an end in itself, it can degenerate into nihilism, easy prey to violent, fanatical creeds. Where there's a vacuum at the center, civilizations implode. Christianity may be a bitch, but she's a bitch with a heart. Your turn. What's your take on Christianity?"

He reflected for a brief spell. "I believe Judeo-Christianity and many other religions stand for something essential, the conviction that human existence has a meaning beyond itself, that we're not the accidental by-product of a cosmological quirk. And I'm not too crazy about death. I don't believe that anyone deserves to be snuffed out like a used candle. In the Church, for all its faults, the flame still burns."

Martha angled her chin. "So— is that all of it?"

"No. There's a mystery, a hidden wonder to life that points beyond this world. I guess a few lines from a poem convey the idea:

'...Though inland far we be,
Our souls have sight of that immortal sea
Which brought us hither.'"

Martha's pensive gaze shifted past him to the window framing the lough. "You've heard of Gilgamesh, king of Sumeria, yes? Then you'll know he went in quest of immortality, failed in the quest, and consoled himself that our deeds live on after we cease to exist."

"I was never at home on Cold Comfort Farm."

Her smile was wafer thin. "Me neither. The approval of posterity is cold comfort indeed."

"Given your background, I'd have thought you'd have mentioned God by now."

She shrugged. "As for the nature of God, who knows? He moves in so many mysterious ways he's got me so I don't know which way to turn."

"Have nuns, even ex-nuns, changed since I was a good Catholic boy or are you a little off-center of mainstream?"

"Huh? Oh— I'm an intelligence officer on temporary assignment to the Vatican. After I returned to the States I moved to Langley and joined the CIA. I'm a secret agent. Don't tell anyone. If you do I'll have to— I'll have to scold you."

He couldn't resist a smile. "No, seriously."

"Yes, seriously. I was trained by the CIA and then I became a ghost."

"You became... a ghost..."

"Ghosts are agents who work in a Catholic undercover world known as the Crypt."

"Now it's *Tales from the Crypt*."

She smiled indulgently. "Ah, yes... that joke gets funnier each time I hear it." Her expression sobered. "The name Crypt is shorthand for certain sections in the Catholic Church that deal in intel gathering and covert ops. The network is dispersed all over the world although the Il Gesù office in Rome, Jesuit headquarters, plays a major role, second only to the Vatican. Pretty dull work, most of the time. We don't even carry weapons. It's a kind of protocol in the Crypt, established in the late eighteenth century. No weapons, no hardware escalation. Also, we're spared all those interminable car chases and silly explosions."

"And just how do I come into all this?"

"Your father's journal. On the upside, the Monsignor staged a break-in at the Quinn house and got hold of it before Father Kinsella had a chance to study it properly. On the downside, Kinsella e-mailed a few incriminating phrases to one Father Dieter in Vatican City. In those phrases were hints that your father was privy to dangerous secrets. He might have passed them on, to his one and only son. That turns the Vatican searchlight on you."

She extracted a folded paper from her overcoat and handed it to him. "I scanned some passages from the journal before destroying it." She paused, gave a low sigh. "The latest news is that Father Dieter was abducted on his way home from the Vatican."

He unfolded the sheet and perused the contents, recognizing his father's stilted handwriting:

For three decades I have remained devoted to the True Faith and sought restitution for the sins of my youth. I have eaten the bitter bread of silence. I have bowed down before the Dormition idol. I have knelt before the altar of Santa Maria in Trastevere.

I have prayed for you, Annunciata. I have prayed that you do not endure everlasting punishment for succumbing to the heresy of the Collyridians.

We are alone in the universe, but the universe is not alone." Is it true that she wrote those words in the Apocryphon Mariæ so long ago?

"And this is what all the fuss is about?" he muttered. "The Apocryphon Mariæ... Who's supposed to have written it?"

"The Virgin Mary."

"The secret book of the Virgin Mary?" He shook his head. "Strains belief."

"Granted, the apocryphon's authorship is disputed. Mary may have written parts of it but other contributors were Simon Magus and Helena of Tyre."

"Still not taking this seriously."

"Whatever. Later additions to the apocryphon, classified as the Ephesian *Transitus Mariæ*, were composed in the first and second centuries. And, as you're so cynical, you can reference them online, along with other Marian scriptures. Go google *Transitus Mariæ* and you'll get thousands and thousands of hits. And if you're really lazy, just type Assumption of Mary in Wikipedia."

He raised a hand in submission. "Okay, got it. So where can I read this apocryphon?"

"It was destroyed over thirty years ago. Only second-hand fragments remain." She settled back into the armchair and stretched her legs. "Here goes... from the first century there existed a religion known as Silentium, the Silence. The Catholic Church and modern scholarship have it listed as the seventy-ninth heresy. That religion's bible is the Apocryphon Mariæ. According to legend, it was written by Mary during her last days in the city of Ephesus in the province of Lydia."

She paused for several seconds, a shade embarrassed, scrabbling for words. "Mary's apocryphon, begun circa 26AD, is partly an account of her life, but it's also a repository of lost science of the ancient Greeks, expounding theories of the nature of consciousness, multidimensional space-time, an infinite ensemble of universes." She paused again. "And aside from the apocryphon, there's a sarcophagus in the Vatican necropolis, unseen for sixteen centuries. The sarcophagus is in a vault known as the Chamber of the Dormition." She made an awkward attempt at a smile. "Otherwise known as the tomb of the Virgin Mary, hidden behind the stones of the Transitus wall."

He gave a cynical glance. "Imaginary tombs, so that's what this is all about."

"Not imaginary. In October 1950 the Transitus wall was discovered in excavations of the pre-Constantine necropolis beneath St. Peter's. Pius XII ordered the wall to be left intact and the entranceway sealed. But three months ago it was rediscovered by an archeological team. In a matter of days, that wall will be breached."

She drew a deep breath, then spoke in a muted tone. "The *Transitus Mariæ* documents state that there's something in the sarcophagus— a presence— a presence that transcends time and space, a portal to another world. And that, Dominic, is what this is all about."

Chapter 15

Jones took a swig of O'Hanlon's champagne and studied the teacher as he hopped on his right leg around the room, the left leg trailing, its kneecap shattered. O'Hanlon's initial scream had been quickly stifled by Carson shoving his motorcycle glove into the man's gaping mouth, followed by the application of masking tape.

Jones settled back in the fireside chair, refilled his champagne glass from the magnum, and watched with professional interest as Carson tracked the terrified teacher, swinging the reinforced baseball bat with perfect timing and accuracy on the man's ribcage, fracturing a rib here, a rib there.

O'Hanlon stumbled into the wall and cracked his nose, much to the amusement of Carson, who drove the tip of the bat into his lower back. The teacher spun away from the wall, useless arms flapping about, the elbows stunned from two well-timed strikes.

Jones took another gulp of champagne. It was an inferior vintage.

The teacher had nothing to tell, that was obvious after the first minute of punishment. This was no longer an exercise in interrogation, but the creation of a scenario. He knew O'Hanlon's history; therefore he knew what would break him. And breaking the teacher would throw Quinn into a rage. A man in rage loses control. A man who loses control loses the battle.

"Whoa!" whooped Carson as O'Hanlon tripped and crashed to the floor. His skull jarred in the fall and he lay there, face turned toward Jones. The man was clearly close to asphyxiation from the heavily padded glove strapped inside his mouth. His face was bloated and suffused with a ruddy glow from the uprush of blood to his head.

And, in the Irishman's eyes, pain without limit.

Yes, Jones liked that look. He lifted his camera and took a shot to add the eight he'd already taken.

One more would deliver the coup de grace.

"Remove the glove," he ordered Carson.

Jones knelt beside the teacher and held up a printout of a little girl, dressed as an elf, standing onstage in front of a canvas backdrop portraying forest scenery.

"Fionulla," Jones announced. "According to the class files on your computer, she's ten years old and excels in drama classes. Want her to succeed in acting where you maybe failed? Well, me and Carson are gonna pay her a visit..."

Jones leaned close to the printout and slid out his tongue. In a lascivious motion, the tongue glided over the image of Fionulla, licking her from head to toe.

Jones winked at O'Hanlon. "Get the picture?"

Carson giggled.

"You want to me to spell it out, teacher? What a priest did to you as a boy, we'll do to her, except— we'll be using a baseball bat."

"Don't hurt her, please. *Please.* I've told you what I know. I swear to God."

Jones held up his hands. "Hey, man, I believe you. Trouble is, you don't know *enough.*" He thrust the girl's image back into O'Hanlon's face. "Think about how she'll *feel*. It'll kill her soul before her body goes cold. And you know what— it'll be *your* fault. You didn't know enough to keep us sweet."

Jones observed O'Hanlon's expression with professional detachment. The prospect of a sexual assault on an innocent killed something in O'Hanlon. This was rape by proxy, psychological violation.

Ah yeah, there it was, in O'Hanlon's eyes. That look. The look he was after.

He grabbed the camera and took the final shot.

Neat.

He e-mailed them off to Dominic Quinn along with a pre-written message:

"Wish you were here."

He signaled Carson. "We go."

"Huh? Is that it?"

Jones took a last swig of champagne. "This isn't about O'Hanlon."

He knelt beside the prone teacher and caught him by the hair. "Gonna do you a favor. Big, big favor. The little girl— Fionulla – we'll not go near her— on two conditions." He held up a finger. "*First*, when the police ask questions, you tell them you surprised three teenagers breaking into the house. *Second*, you tell Quinn what happened here, every detail. If you don't, we do the girl. And if Quinn repeats any of this to the police, we do the girl. Got that?"

O'Hanlon forced hoarse words from his throat. "Understood."

"Say 'I'll do as I'm told, Mr. Jones.'"

"I'll— I'll do as I'm told, Mr. Jones."

Jones patted him on the head. "Good boy."

Martha fidgeted in her chair, awaiting Dominic's response.

He finally broke the silence. "I'm speechless— and that's saying something."

Her mouth tightened a fraction. "It sounds crazy, I know."

"It's insane. What has a two-thousand-year-old manuscript got to do with me? As for the magical tomb under the Vatican, that belongs in the Twilight Zone."

She expelled a sharp breath. "Okay, okay, forget about the tomb. Stick with the Apocryphon Mariæ. Pope John Paul I was ready to make the apocryphon public knowledge. A priest by the name of Father Mark Cosmas discovered a plot to murder the pope and reported the conspiracy to one Mother Hypatia, who sent a nun to warn the pontiff. That nun was Annunciata— remember— the name in your father's scribblings? Her mission failed and her body was found on Rome's Janiculum Hill."

"I still don't see how this links to me."

"Because Brian Quinn's journal revealed inside knowledge of the Apocryphon Mariæ. That knowledge would have gotten him killed if he wasn't already dead. He might have passed on that knowledge. You're next in the firing line."

"The Vatican does not go around killing people," he said flatly.

"Of course it doesn't! We're talking about one man, the same man who poisoned John Paul I and burned the apocryphon, a priest who rose to the rank of cardinal, a cardinal by the name of Auguste Chavet, Crypt codename— Benoit."

"Just one man…"

Martha rolled her eyes. "That's all it takes. Cardinal Chavet is the de facto head of Conclave, a covert and effectively independent limb of the Vatican Curia. Popes come and go. Conclave remains. Chavet has access to all Conclave channels of information. He has a blank check from the Vatican Bank. In the short term he can do pretty much what he wants so long as he appears to stay within Conclave rules."

His gaze strayed to the wide window and across the dark lough to the Mountains of Mourne, their contours almost dissolved in night. His shadowy reflection was a ghost superimposed on the window. He recalled a line from an epistle of St. Paul. "Through a looking glass, darkly."

Martha's faint ghost in the glass inclined its head. "I think you're getting the picture. Now you have one of two choices."

He gave her a wry glance. "Only two?"

"Only two. One, you take the next flight to JFK and from there I'll drive you to Iowa and a new life under a new identity."

"Like *that's* going to happen. And the second option?"

Her voice was subdued. "You walk out of here on your own and up to your old house. You'll find the front door unlocked and the study door open."

He waited for her to continue. She didn't.

"A little light on the exposition," he remarked.

"Necessarily so. If you go through that study door, you'll never be the same person again."

"Isn't that a tad melodramatic?" He reached for his phone. "I'll think about what you said, but not until I've had dinner with Colin. Give me your number and I'll call you later."

Ignoring her protests, he brought up Colin's number on the phone. He was on the verge of sending a be-there-in-a-minute text when an incoming message caught his attention.

"Wish you were here..." he read out loud. Then he opened the attachment.

For an instant the column of jpegs didn't register. Then they impacted like a blow to the skull.

Colin. Colin hopping on one leg, a wad of padded leather in his mouth.

And the last picture in the column. Colin lying on the floor, gag removed, mouth wide open...

His face. Violated. Desouled.

Dominic stormed out the room, pushing past Martha as she sprang to her feet.

"What is it?" she exclaimed, running after him down the hallway. "Dominic..."

"It's Colin."

She grabbed his arm. "If we're racing the clock, my car's right outside."

He wrenched open the door. "Let's go."

Chapter 16

Dominic propped up Colin on the sofa as the first distant wail of the ambulance siren sounded down the lough.

His friend had described everything Jones and Carson had done. Everything, down to the graphic warning about Fionulla.

At the sound of the siren Colin raised his head, suppressing a wince. "Took them a while, or is that just me?"

Dominic settled Colin's head back on a cushion. "They'll be here soon."

"So will the police." He wheezed from his damaged ribcage. "You and Martha, you should go..." His gaze roved the room. "Where is she? She mustn't repeat..."

"She went to wait in the car. She won't repeat anything, don't worry. This is because of me. Christ, I'm so sorry."

"Don't be sorry, be smart. Get away before the ambulance arrives. Don't want the medics mentioning you to the Garda. And take this..." He pulled a folded sheet from his jacket pocket. It was a stained printout showing a little girl dressed as an elf.

"Just in case you feel tempted to repeat any of this," Colin said, a shade apologetic. "I'm sure you won't but..."

Dominic took in the charming innocence of the girl, her shy smile at the camera. "I'll keep it as a reminder of what kind of man— what kind of reptile— Jones is."

"He wasn't bluffing about what he'd do to her. He meant it. He'll do it."

"If he lives that long."

Colin cocked his head. "What did you say?"

"Nothing. Don't worry. Nobody's going to harm Fionulla."

"Best leave now. And don't fret, you hear? My bones will mend." His voice faltered. "But Jones broke me, inside. He broke me."

Dominic reached down and held his friend's shoulder. "That'll mend too."

"Yeah, sure it will." He frowned at the rising note of the ambulance. "You've got to go."

Dominic backed away. "The medics will look after you— you'll be fine." He raised a hand in farewell. "Be seeing you."

Colin lifted his hand in response. "Keep the faith."

The road to Carlingford town sped under the Range Rover's wheels. Dominic and Martha sat in silence, underscored by the hum of the engine. At length he broke the silence.

"Why did they do that to him?"

Martha tightened her grip on the steering wheel. "They were sending a message. If you're unlucky, you'll learn what it means."

"Let's hope I'm unlucky."

She shook her head. "You're out of your depth."

He released a slow breath. "The world has spun out of orbit."

"Know the feeling. As for those options, they still stand. Take the first option. Start a new life in Iowa. We have a nice little safe house there, close to a river, surrounded by forest. You'll be employed at a lumber mill under an assumed identity. It'll be like living inside a Grant Wood painting."

"How about I drop off the planet?"

"Bit radical. Iowa's not that bad. Otherwise... you walk up to your father's house and into the study. But there's no way back from that path. Don't take it."

He stared out at the night surface of the lough. "If I go up to the house, I'll never be the same person again, isn't that what you said?" His gaze remained fixed on the lough. "The first option is not an option."

She lifted a hand in defeat. "Okay then, go on up to the house. You're not going to like what you find."

"Only one way to find out."

Chapter 17

London

See Naples and die.

That familiar phrase kept going round and round in Rachel's head like murderers dancing in a ring, hand in hand.

She sat in the Starbucks café at London Heathrow's Terminal 4, nursing a cooling latte and studying her open laptop. From time to time she looked up, searching for a glimpse of Deacon and praying she wouldn't catch one.

The temptation to quit and run kept nagging away. After all, why risk her life on some wild enterprise? The reason, she admitted, was that she'd been a dog-at-a-bone character since childhood. Dogged from birth.

She returned her attention to the laptop screen, seeking some clue why she was suddenly a target of a shadow world. Simon Dray's e-mail referring to the seventy-ninth heresy had stood out as singular, coming from left field. Then Deacon had used the same phrase. Reason enough to research it in greater depth. Entering "seventy-ninth heresy" on Google produced few hits; "Collyridian" brought up a whole lot more.

Highlighted text from one of those Collyridian pages was displayed on her laptop. The article told of a religion that flourished in the early centuries of the Christian era, a religion condemned as heresy by Epiphanius of Salamis, the seventy-ninth in his list of eighty. The Collyridians were devotees of the Virgin Mary, whom they acclaimed as Mother of God and Queen of Heaven at a time when those terms were blasphemous to all

Christians, being titles accorded to N't, the mother of the Egyptian sun god Ra, and Isis, goddess-sister of Osiris. Virgin Mother was likewise a pagan title.

The geographical range of the Collyridian religion was impressive: from Upper Scythia— modern day Russia— to Arabia. A cult or religion that extended that far was a major league faith. The article disclosed that Muhammad believed the Christian Trinity was comprised of the Father, the Son, and the Virgin Mary: pretty clear evidence that the heresy was still thriving in seventh-century Arabia, so the range in time was as striking as the compass in space.

What was notable about Mary's devotees was their belief that she was greater than her son Jesus. Collyridians made Catholics look like Protestants.

She shut her laptop, preparing to head for the check-in counter.

This was the irrevocable step, onto the first rung or over the brink. She brought up an e-mail, the last message from Simon showing her where to go as a last resort: the location portrayed on the picture postcard, a spacious square with a raised fountain in front of a church.

And on the lower border of the postcard, a simple caption:

Santa Maria in Trastevere, Roma

"See Rome and die."

Chapter 18

Carlingford Lough

Dominic trudged up the muddy trail to where six late-Victorian houses huddled together as though for warmth and company. Set apart from the cluster was a turn-of-the-century neo-Gothic house, tall, thin, gray and angular, encircled by overgrown shrubbery. After a backward glance at Martha's Range Rover down the trail, he stopped at the garden gate.

His home, or what used to be his home. The façade stared blankly into the night, blind to his presence. He pushed open the trellised garden gate and walked down the concrete path to the front door.

If you go through that study door, you'll never be the same person again.

"*Que será, sera,*" he murmured. At a push, the door swung open. A few paces down the hallway brought him to the study door, yawning wide and radiating a ruddy glow of lamplight.

"Do come in," invited a baritone voice.

Dominic stopped in his tracks.

A man stood on the far side of his father's large teak desk. A tall, elegant man in a long black overcoat, the clerical collar just visible above the lapels.

"Hello, Dominic," the man said. "I'm the Monsignor."

He was sure he hadn't seen the priest before, but something about him was familiar. A familiar stranger.

The Monsignor sat down in his father's leather chair, indicating a seat in front of the desk. Dominic crossed the threadbare carpet and sank into the chair. Close up, the priest conveyed an impression of authority, lightly worn. His liver-spotted hands, one of which bore an elaborate gold crucifix ring, rested on a beige folder planted on the desk surface.

The Monsignor produced a wisp of a smile. "I knew you'd come." He slipped a small, creased photo from the folder. "I suggest you take a look at this."

Again, that twinge of strange familiarity, evoked this time more by the voice than the appearance. "How about telling me who you are? The Monsignor isn't much of a name."

"Haven't you guessed? I haven't seen you since you were six months old and I share few features with my brother, but still..."

Dominic leaned forward as light dawned. "You're my uncle..."

"No doubt your father referred to me as your *wastrel* uncle. He wasn't my biggest fan."

Despite himself, Dominic eased into a tentative smile. "He wasn't too crazy about me either. He used to call me the 'child of sin' when he was in full flood of rage. 'A thorn in his side, marked from birth.'"

"How typical of him." The priest pushed the photo toward Dominic. "Now perhaps you'd look at this?"

He picked up the photo. It showed, in faded colors, a teenage girl dressed in a yellow cheerleader outfit, beaming at the camera as she brandished red pom-poms. She possessed a singular bright, kind beauty with rich brown eyes in an oval face framed by a black bob of hair.

He flipped the photo over and saw that words had been stenciled on the back:

SARAH, IDAHO FALLS, FALL OF '68

"Sarah," he murmured.

The Monsignor extracted another photo from the folder and slid it across the desk. "Her full name was Sarah Anne Maitland."

This next photo showed an older Sarah, mid-twenties perhaps. She had lost none of the freshness of her teenage years, and her warm beauty was, if possible, more striking. And she wore the habit of a nun.

He turned the photo over and saw the name on the back:

ANNUNCIATA, ROME, '77

He felt as though a phantom had kissed the base of his neck, at that place where he bore a purple, thorn-shaped birthmark. *Marked from birth...*

"Annunciata," he said in a whisper. He glanced up at the Monsignor. "Martha mentioned her. Annunciata was the one who tried to save John Paul the First."

"Indeed she did." The Monsignor made a show of studying his fingernails. "More to the point, she's your mother."

Seated in a Nissan X-Trail parked close to O'Hares pub on Tholsel Street, Jones lifted the phone to his ear and voice-dialed.

Benoit's voice issued from the receiver. "Report the situation."

"Quinn kicked Carson's ass but I'm sure he didn't steal the journal. Now he's up in his old man's house— with the Monsignor. Martha's skulking close by. Oh yeah, and we gave O'Hanlon a bit of a workout. He won't be dancing no Irish jigs, but he'll live."

"You were warned about collateral damage. An assault on O'Hanlon was the worst possible course of action. According to his updated profile, Quinn will go on a rampage."

The truth was that Jones wanted Quinn on a rampage. Nothing more satisfying than a man who comes looking for you— then wishes he hadn't.

"I hear you," he drawled. "Now hear me. That Rachel Gurevich chick made a fool of Deacon. He should have grabbed her while he could. Let's not make the same mistake. The way I figure it, the Monsignor stole the journal. To protect Quinn. He's hiding something from us. I say bring them in: Quinn, the Monsignor, Martha."

A long silence. "Yes, agreed. Haul them in. Keep the Crypt out of this. Use outsourced operatives only. No ghosts."

"Yeah, yeah, sure." Jones pocketed the phone. It would take under fifteen minutes to cover the mountain trail and join his men in the trees above the Quinn house. And less than a minute to storm the place.

He stared at the Monsignor. And went on staring.

"That's— impossible..." he heard himself say. It came out as a croak.

"Why impossible? You noticed it, didn't you, the family resemblance?"

The photo of Sister Annunciata fell from Dominic's hand, landing beside the picture of the younger Sarah Maitland. "No, Margaret's my mother. She gave birth to me in Dublin, moved here when I was three. It's in the records."

The Monsignor leaned forward. "Margaret gave birth to a boy, that's true, but he died before his first birthday. You replaced him. You bear his name. Your original name was Mark, named after me, in fact, although these days I go under the name of Martin Aylesbury."

Dominic's head swam. The room was reeling. "No. No way. Margaret's my mother. I was born in Dublin..."

The more he said it, the less he believed it. Margaret Quinn, distant, indifferent, as though he didn't belong to her. Sarah Maitland, her features almost a mirror of his own.

Monsignor Martin's voice seemed to echo from a great distance:

"You weren't born in Ireland, Dominic. You were born in Rome."

Dominic slumped back in his chair. It was impossible, but the photographic evidence was in front of him. He felt he belonged to the woman in the photo, that she belonged to him. He and

Margaret had nothing in common, not even antipathy. There was nothing there. Now he understood why.

Annunciata. Sarah Maitland. She was his mother.

"It's true," he heard himself murmur. Someplace, deep below memory, there was an absence only the image of Sarah Maitland could fill.

He looked at the concerned face of Monsignor Martin. "I'm sorry, it's— it's a lot to take in," Dominic murmured. "Uh— Martha told me— about Annunciata— her murder."

The priest inclined his head. "I'm sorry."

"Tell me," Dominic mumbled. "Tell me what happened— back then."

"It's a long story and we're short on time. You have enemies, I'm afraid. They'll be closing in and we're packed and ready to leave."

"Just— tell me."

"Very well, but I must be brief." Monsignor Martin leaned his elbows on the desk, fingers steepled. "I was a priest working in the Vatican diplomatic service when your father came to Rome back in 1977. Brian was soon attracted to Sarah, who'd taken vows as a nun under the name Sister Annunciata. They became lovers and, after a short while, you were conceived." He paused a moment. "This was not your usual order of Catholic nuns but a Silentium order that has no binding vow of chastity. That said, Brian acted abominably when Annunciata told him of her pregnancy. He reverted to the self-righteous mindset of his childhood and denounced her as an infernal heretic and declared you the 'child of sin.'"

A wistful smile brushed the Monsignor's lips. "The first time I set eyes on you was two weeks after your birth. I noticed the purple birthmark, shaped like a thorn, at the back of your neck. I made an unforgivably feeble joke: 'marked by the thorn.' Your name was Mark then, you see? Ah, yes, a feeble joke... She would kiss you on that birthmark when you were asleep, and she'd whisper: 'where there's a thorn, there's a rose.'" The smile faded. "Back in the days when I went by the name of Father Mark

Cosmas, I discovered a plot to poison the pope. Your mother was sent to warn His Holiness. In the event, both died."

Dominic felt curiously calm now. Calm and quiet and cold.

They took her from me. I never knew her.

"Who murdered her?"

"A cardinal by the name of Auguste Chavet murdered the pope, that's certain. As for your mother, I can't be sure. That trail has gone cold." He checked his watch. "Time is against us. Chavet, with all the resources he commands, may well have identified you as Annunciata's son by now. If he sets Jones on you... well, you don't want to meet Jones. You have two choices. You can hide in America— highly recommended. Or you can be the latest recruit to the Crypt— a near-suicidal option."

Dominic picked up the two photos and gazed from one to the other. Teenage Sarah. Twenty-something Annunciata.

"My mother's younger than me."

The Monsignor nodded his understanding. "There is no option. I know that." He rose to his feet. "And we must go."

"Rome is where I'm going."

"Of course. The scene of the crime. But you must travel with Martha, not me." He strode to the door. "Run down to Martha's car. Hurry. I'm leaving by another route. See you in Rome."

Bewildered by the race of events, Dominic rose slowly from the chair. "This is a bad dream. And I'm still in the dark."

The Monsignor looked over his shoulder, mouth bent in the bitterest of smiles.

"Welcome to the Crypt."

Part Two

"O God,
If there is a God,
Save my soul,
If I have a soul."

Ernest Renan

Chapter 19

Rome

There are cat cities and dog cities: that was Rachel's simple taxonomy. Her second day in Rome and she already had it tagged as a cat city. London was a dog city, bluff, blunt, and busy. National icons notwithstanding, more of a bull terrier than a bulldog. Rome was a cat city, svelte and lax, still redolent of *la dolce vita* and exuding a feline scent of *amore*.

Rachel suppressed a shiver at the nippy mid-morning air as she sat under a trattoria's blue-and-white-striped awning and sipped from her glass of *amarone* wine as she took in the sights of the Piazza Navona.

She was starting to get a feel for Rome. It was a city that brought out the best and the worst in people. Bland it was not. If she'd come here under different circumstances she would probably have been in full retro mode by now, acting out as a young Sophia Loren while humming a couple of Dean Martin songs with *amore* and *volare* in their titles.

She had taken the subway from Fiumicino two nights ago and booked into a modest little *pensione* on the Esquiline Hill, three spear throws from the Colosseum. Sleep hadn't come easy. When it finally came, it stayed. She woke deep into the afternoon, glue-eyed. And thought immediately of Deacon, holding a photo under Blackfriars Bridge.

If you're planning to head for Rome— don't. That's a trip you won't return from.

She did her best to push the image away as she forced herself out of bed. Fixing her mind on her destination helped— a little.

By the time she'd freshened up, eaten, sorted out a tourist map, and navigated the maze of streets, the daylight was already failing. It was evening by the time she reached the church of Santa Maria in Trastevere— only to find it locked for the night.

This morning she had woken early, sharp and ready to renew her mission.

She stood up from the table, dropped a ten-euro bill on the side plate, and hoisted a canvas carryall over her shoulder. From the northern end of the baroque square, she looked down the long stretch of the Piazza Navona. The piazza frothed with humanity and fizzed with vitality.

She meandered through the crowds of tourists, interspersed with talented buskers, skilled quick-draw artists, and mimes who were slightly less ludicrous than their Venice Beach counterparts back home.

She made her way out of the square and onto a main road crammed with manic traffic and harassed pedestrians. She soon quitted it for the relative calm of the Ghetto, an area of narrow, twisting alleyways known as *vicolos*.

As she traversed the fan-patterned paving stones, passing manhole covers embossed with the acronym SPQR, she reflected on the history of the church she was heading toward.

Santa Maria in Trastevere was probably the oldest church in an old city. The granite pillars flanking the aisles had been transported from the Temple of Isis and portrayed female deities on their capitals. Like numerous churches in Rome and elsewhere, pagan and Christian went hand in hand.

So far, so moderately interesting. Basic guidebook material. What caught her attention was that the original building was known as the *titulus Calixtus* after Pope Calixtus, martyred in 222AD. Its unofficial dedication to the Blessed Virgin seemed to have followed soon after. From what she'd gleaned online, Mary was a relatively minor figure in the early Church. Which begged the question, were the Collyridians behind the early dedication of Santa Maria in Trastevere to the Madonna?

She smiled ruefully. "Where's a historian when you need one?"

The Ponte Fabricio, a bridge constructed before Julius Caesar crossed the Rubicon, was up ahead. Ah, the grandeur that was Rome...

Traversing the bridge she alighted on the island of the Isola Tiberina, then crossed the Ponte Cestio, built about the time Julius Caesar was assassinated, and continued on to the *rione* of Trastevere, a region that in imperial Rome lay outside the city walls. The *Trasterverini* still regarded themselves as a people set apart from the decadence of the modern city. Something of that isolationism had stamped itself onto the very look of the buildings. Ochre-painted houses standing windowed eyeball to eyeball was the dominant theme.

As she threaded through the crooked labyrinth of vicolos and minor vias, inadvertently sidetracking into cramped courtyards festooned with washing lines like ship's rigging, she reminded herself that Trastevere— literally, "beyond the Tiber"— had its dark side. One sign of that was an unkempt man of indeterminate age slumped against a wall, head sunken, knees pulled to his chest, arms tight around the knees, enclosed in his own hunched body. Beside him lay an empty hypodermic like a discarded popsicle stick.

She walked past him, turned a corner and there it was, in the heart of the Trastevere *rione*, the Piazza di Santa Maria. The seven-stepped fountain in the center of the piazza played forlorn water music to its near-deserted square. On the far side of the square was the church of Santa Maria in Trastevere, instantly recognizable, in daylight, from Simon's e-mailed postcard.

I'm here. Now what?

Making a beeline for the church door, she glanced at the mosaics on the upper façade depicting the Virgin Mary flanked by wise maidens on the left and unwise maidens on the right.

"No prizes for guessing which side I'm on," she muttered.

She stopped at the church door, drew a deep breath, then pushed the door open. The interior was brimming with darkness and the silence of the sacrosanct. Hesitantly, she stepped in.

"Here goes..."

Chapter 20

Lyon, France

Mother Hypatia descended the eroded stone steps of the open stairwell in the eighteenth-century tenement, her hand brushing the less-than-reliable protection of the rusted iron railing, her heart sinking a little further with each step of the descent.

The nun reached the small inner courtyard and passed through the oak gate onto the Quai Gailleton which faced the black Alpine rush of the river Rhône. Sleety rain greeted her, provoking an involuntary shiver. Wheeling around, she gazed at the tenement she'd just left. It reared tall and narrow, its drab gray façade relieved only marginally by a smattering of ornate window-gardens in tiny windows. Her own window, up on the fifth floor, was shuttered and barred against the world.

She resumed her journey, enduring the bouts of rain and sleet and winds more customary in spring than autumn, weather the locals dubbed the *giboulée*.

As she traversed the gritty surface of the eighteenth-century Place Bellecour, her keen sight missed nothing as it scanned the edges and corners of one of the largest squares in Europe.

The nun spared a glance at the *cheval de bronze* statue of Louis XIV on horseback: some Jean-Luc Godard devotee had spray-painted the slogan CINEMARXISME in bold red letters at its base. A blue ball bounced through the rain and rebounded off the statue, rolling back to the cracked shoes of the tramp that had kicked it. The tramp stared at it as if it were a dog that refused to go away.

Hypatia halted at the sound of a Vivaldi ringtone and took out her iPhone. She started to smile at the round, bespectacled face on the screen. "Nice to see you again, Father Thomas, but this is not a good time. An hour from now, perhaps?"

Thomas Chen made a weak effort to mirror her smile. "Just a quick call. Have you heard from Monsignor Martin at all?"

"Hasn't he contacted you yet?"

"He has not. Chavet will make his move very soon. Martin is supposed to be a move ahead of him, not several moves behind."

She shrugged. "You know what Martin's like. Plans within plans, usually kept to himself."

"I know. If he contacts you, please inform me."

"Of course." She hesitated. "Is Maria there?"

"Ah, Maria," he sighed fondly. "She's out walking somewhere."

"In Trastevere? Isn't that dangerous? If she's who you believe her to be, you should be keeping her safe from the world."

He gave a light laugh. "If you'd met her, you would know better. I'd be more concerned in keeping the world safe from her. Maria is..." His voice faltered. "Well, she is what she is."

"As you say, but for now I must go. I'm late for a meeting. I'll call you soon."

"Look forward to it. Goodbye."

She pocketed the iPhone and, after a moment's reflection, resumed her journey. The sky underwent another fey mood and unleashed a torrent of hailstones that stampeded commuters and sightseers alike. The hail scourged the vast square with Old Testament ferocity but she was scarcely conscious of the deluge as she neared the Pont Bonaparte, its arches spanning the leisurely currents of the Saône, the little sister to the Rhône's boisterous big brother.

The hail relented and gave way to heavy rain as she crossed the bridge. Up ahead on the western bank, veiled by rainfall, the hill of Fourvière rose above the medieval streets.

Almost there.

The puppet show carried on in the rain as though for the sole entertainment of the two remaining onlookers huddled under a single umbrella.

The glove puppets, passable reproductions of characters from the Théâtre de Guignol, played out their tiny drama inside a gaudy booth in the square of Place St. Jean, overlooked by the Gothic and Romanesque façade of St. Jean Cathedral. Guignol, a puppet with a silly, innocent face crowned by an eccentric hat, made exaggerated overtures to his shrewish wife, Madelon. She spurned him with a swerve of her body and a swish of her arms. Bulbous-nosed Gnafron, Guignol's drinking partner, jeered from the wings.

Martha leaned closer to her partner under the umbrella. "I'm getting rained on from this side."

Dominic tilted the umbrella to adjust for the wind change and his gaze wandered across the deserted Place St. Jean with its drumming rain and effervescent puddles to where blurred faces peered through the steamed-up windows of crammed cafés.

She gave him a sly look. "Looking for trouble? Look for it and it will come, sure as eggs are *oeufs*. Oh— it's over."

Guignol and company were taking their bows. Martha bowed right back at the puppets, then nudged his arm. "Let's shelter under the church entrance."

He hesitated. "We should hang around to tip the puppeteers."

"Puppeteers never show their faces."

"They do when the show's over," he said, clapping his applause as two slender young men exited the booth, a leather bag in each hand.

Martha's face expressed mild surprise as she joined in the applause. "I imagined grandfatherly figures with stooped shoulders and white hair and optional clay pipe. Look at them— they're so young."

"Not much younger than me," he observed.

"Like I said, they're so young." She approached the two performers and thrust a twenty-euro bill into each of the astonished men's palms.

Dominic felt obliged to follow suit and added a couple more twenties to the men's takings. Not too much of a hardship as Martha had stuffed his wallet with Euros. The men's astonishment doubled and they mumbled profuse thanks.

"It's nothing, really," Martha said in fluent French. "Covered by expenses. Vatican spy expenses. But don't tell anyone or I'll have to— I'll have to lock myself in the toilet and burst into tears."

They responded with shrugs and baffled grins. The woman was obviously crazy.

"We'll be gone a half-hour. Please, wait inside until the rain eases off," invited one of the men, indicating the booth as he moved away. "There are stools inside."

She clapped him on the back. "Hey, we'll do just that." Her eyebrows shot up as the melody of the "Port of Amsterdam" suddenly warbled from her overcoat pocket. "Excuse *moi*." She waved the performers goodbye as she fished out her phone and checked the screen. "About time," she muttered, frowning. The frown deepened. "What the hell does that mean?"

Dominic leaned in close. "What does what mean?"

She showed him the screen. "It's from Martin— the Monsignor."

The screen showed a terse message:

Am near the Apostolic Palace. All may soon be well.

"I should have known," she groaned. "*Separate ways.* We go to Rome by separate ways. I should have known he was up to something. He's trying to win with one throw of the dice. 'All may soon be well' my ass."

"What do you think he's doing?"

"Making a deal; it must be that." She simmered down. "Probably to get you off the hook. You mean a lot to him. He often talks about you. Hey, let's get out of this rain." She pulled back the booth's side-cover and ducked inside.

Dominic took a breath, folded up the umbrella, and followed her lead. The interior was roomier than he expected and there was ample space to move about, despite two stools and an empty wooden box.

"Cool, huh?" Martha grinned.

"This isn't some Vatican drop-off point, by any chance?" He sat on a stool and eyed the stony ground. "I almost expected a manhole cover leading to a secret rendezvous passage."

"Very funny." She opened the curtains a fraction and peered out. "Shouldn't be long. It's not as if she'll charge past."

Dominic gave a vague nod, reflecting on the imminent meeting and still slightly dazed from the rush of events.

He felt he hadn't so much traveled to Lyon as teleported here. The precipitate drive from Carlingford, the flight to France, the hotel in le Vieux Lyon, had been a whirlwind succession of evanescent images, unreal.

Yesterday he'd strolled with Martha through the mixture of medieval and Renaissance streets of le Vieux Lyon as they explored the city's unique *traboules,* narrow passageways and tiny courtyards linking the main thoroughfares. There was no shortage of tourist sights in Lyon, birthplace of the Roman emperor Claudius and capital of Gaul when Paris was a fishing village on the Seine. With her guided tour, Martha had deliberately distracted him from brooding. She'd given him time to adjust. And he was starting to adjust, thanks to her.

In the short time he'd known her they had already struck up a brother-sister relationship, an easy understanding. And she'd taken care of everything, including calling Aunt Deirdre with a cock-and-bull story about loopholes in his father's will that required extended investigation and even managing to lay her mind to rest over the bogus immigration officers who were either Jones's men or ghosts from the nebulous Crypt.

But despite her efforts it was difficult to accept the existence of the Crypt. Intellectually he recognized there was such a creature as a Vatican secret agent, but— *Vatican secret agent—* the term had a fantastical ring to it. Equally he knew that men walked on the Moon before he was born, but Apollo 11 still felt one step short of science fiction.

Yet here he was, sitting inside a puppet booth in the middle of France, waiting to meet a nun from this secret world. And in a few hours they'd be driving to Rome.

"This could take a while." Martha tapped her foot as she kept watch. "How about another quick quiz? I'll take your emphatic shake of the head as a yes. Now let's see if I can stump that overrated brain of yours." She glanced down at him. "Who invented the steam engine, and when?"

"Trick question. Some say Savery at the end of the seventeenth century, others say Newcomen at the beginning of the eighteenth. It's neither. The steam engine was invented by Heron of Alexandria in the first century AD. He called it an *aeolipile*, a wind ball. The steam was converted to rotate a sphere at about fifteen hundred rpm. In fact, it may have been invented even earlier, by Ctesibius and Vitruvius. And how long before I pass the test?"

"Huh?" She was all exaggerated innocence, mouth agape, eyes big as CDs, not even attempting a convincing performance.

"You've been quizzing me on the history of science since we got on the plane."

Martha huffed. "Half a dozen questions over a couple of days. Hardly a test."

"Make that two dozen, and then some. And almost all connected with Alexandria. What's the subtext here— the reputed science in the Apocryphon Mariæ?"

"Well, yes. The Monsignor wanted me to test whether you were up to speed on ancient science before he tells you what's known of the theories in the apocryphon."

"Doesn't the apocryphon also cover Mary's life story?"

"Uh-huh. So?"

"I'd be interested to hear it."

She flashed a disarming smile. "Time enough for all that in Rome."

"Why not give me an outline, or just the beginning?"

Martha stiffened to an alert pose, stare fixed on the south side of the square. "She's coming."

Dominic peered through the curtain and spotted her instantly. So that was Mother Hypatia. At first sight of her face, he was uncharitably reminded of a crab apple.

Martha parted the curtains wide. "She'll give a sign. We follow a minute later."

The nun darted a look in their direction, performed a double take, then tapped her swollen-jointed hand twice to her breast and arced away toward the street named Montée du Gourguillon.

"It's the house past the Café du Soleil," Martha observed. "It's her favorite of the three rendezvous points." She smiled across at him and parted the booth's side-cover. "Come on, she has quite a tale to tell."

Chapter 21

Rome

The white and gold papal flag fluttered on the hood of the black Mercedes as the vehicle slid under the shadow of the Leonine Walls of Vatican City, gliding down the empty stretch of the Viale Vaticano in the light rain of late morning.

Monsignor Martin Aylesbury reclined in the back seat, arms crossed, as the vehicle followed the medieval wall toward the Porta Sant'Anna, one of six entrances to Vatican City. As the car neared the gate, the Monsignor uncrossed his arms and reread the message he'd sent to Martha. He knew what Martha would say if she were here: *Don't go.*

But he had Father Burgholzer's assurance of safe conduct, the backing, albeit reluctant, of the Jesuits, and the security of meeting in the Apostolic Palace where even Cardinal Chavet wouldn't dare lay hand on him. One bold throw of the dice and Dominic and Rachel would be safe.

"All may soon be well."

He stared through the tinted windows at the Swiss Guards who dutifully saluted as the car swung into Porta Sant'Anna. The dark blue uniforms of the Vigilanza, the papal gendarmerie armed with Beretta sub-machine guns, were nowhere in evidence. The tourist guides that dwelt so glowingly on the haughty, taller-than-thou Swiss Guards rarely mentioned the military-style gendarmes.

The Mercedes swept past the Swiss Guard barracks and the *l'Osservatore Romano* building, home of the Vatican's international newspaper, and the Monsignor caught his first sight of the Vigilanza. Two policemen were waiting for the car as it reached the junction of Via San Pio X and the entrance to the Apostolic Palace. So, Chavet had provided an armed escort.

Here, in a sovereign state planted right at the heart of Italy's capital, spreading across 109 acres and staffed by 800 full-time employees, resided the center of authority for 1.2 billion Catholics, a religious empire presided over by Francis I, latest in a line of 266 popes stretching back to Peter. Everywhere in Vatican City were echoes of the Roman empire, not least in the Catholic title of pontiff, derived from pontifex, a pagan priest of ancient Rome.

The Monsignor squinted up at the angular bulk of the Apostolic Palace and stepped out of the car onto the paving stones, nodding his thanks to the chauffeur and heading into the outer courtyard. Flanked by two machine-gun toting policemen, he wasn't sure whether to feel like a dignitary or a political prisoner.

Entering the Vatican was akin to being swallowed by a landlocked Leviathan. Stair after stair, corridor after corridor, hall after hall, the Vatican displayed its baroque grandeur.

The passages were mostly deserted; what footsteps there were echoing eerily in the vast silence. He'd forgotten the oppressive magnificence but now he recalled the shrinkage of the ego as he felt the historic weight of politics, religion, and architecture bearing down on him. The building was operatic in its aspirations: grand opera, histrionic and florid.

The escort took a couple of abrupt turns and he found himself in one of the public sections, close to the formidable double doors of the Sistine Chapel.

The Vigilanza spun on their heels and left him to his own devices.

Monsignor watched them go through narrowed eyes. *I've just been given the grand tour.*

Adopting a nonchalant air, he walked into the imposing hall of the Sistine Chapel, thronged with sightseers. Near the far end of the chapel, he spotted the priest. He was hard to miss, standing under Michelangelo's *Last Judgment*, tall and thin in a black cassock, a lightning rod to God: Cardinal Auguste Chavet, the nearest thing Conclave had to a controller-in-chief since the last ailing days of John Paul II.

"Auguste," the Monsignor greeted with a show of amiability, sauntering up to the unsmiling, gray-haired cleric. "I was conducted here via the scenic route. If the aim was to impress, I'd say you gilded the lily with an entire can of liquid gold." He glanced around. "Where's Burgholzer?"

Chavet's gaunt features, a meal short of emaciation, were unresponsive. "Follow me." He swept down the chapel, not looking to see if the Monsignor kept pace. Chavet always *swept* out of any location, be it box room or basilica.

He matched the Frenchman's long, rapid paces stride for stride out of the chapel and down a corridor of veined marble. By the time they neared an arched entrance to the Apostolic Palace, its door flanked by Swiss Guards, he'd drawn alongside. And side by side, they threaded the corridors of the Apostolic Palace until Chavet turned into a tight side passage and opened a door fronted with panes of frosted glass.

Inside was a small, spartan room containing little more than a desk, a laptop, and three uncomfortable-looking chairs. The cardinal sat behind the desk and clicked on the computer, attention fixed on the screen.

The Monsignor's unease mounted. "When is Burgholzer joining us?"

"Patience. There are matters that require attention."

"Yes, indeed. Such as the nature of— what shall I call it— the Indwelling?"

That induced a degree of heat in the cardinal's sang-froid. Did the Monsignor detect a slight flicker of an eyelid?

"What are you talking about?" Chavet snapped, still focused on the computer screen.

"Your imminent breaching of the Transitus wall, without the pope's permission."

Chavet's eyelid flickered on full twitch. Satisfying when a shot in the dark scored a bull's-eye.

The cardinal pursed his lips. "His Holiness Pope Francis, unlike Pius XII, may believe the Transitus wall hides nothing but the tombs of nondescript Romans but some members of Conclave are more— cautious. Conclave has left the matter of the Transitus wall to me. His Holiness will be kept in the dark."

"No surprise there, what with Pope Francis still finding his pontifical feet and Benedict out of the picture. I'm more concerned with the arrangement made with Burgholzer. You call off your attack dogs from Dominic and Rachel and you and I, along with Burgholzer, work together on discovering what's beyond the Transitus wall. Opposing purposes, but a common aim."

The cardinal finally looked away from the screen and leaned forward, his hooked beak of a nose resembling an eagle's, scenting prey. "Opposing purposes, that's for sure."

"Auguste— is there a deal, or have you made a fool of me?"

"You've been extremely foolish," the cardinal said in an arch tone of reproach. "Your previous service to Conclave would normally grant you immunity. Nor would we lightly risk retaliation from Il Gesù but your fellow Jesuits are equally exasperated by your double-dealing."

"I still have some influence."

"Your influence is past tense." The cardinal studied the Monsignor over steepled fingers. "I knew you'd come at the prospect of joining forces."

"Are you implying that I'm gullible?"

"Allow me to quote from your great hero, Julius Caesar: 'What we wish, we readily believe, and what we ourselves think, we imagine others think also.'"

"So much more insightful than 'veni, vidi, vici.'"

Chavet shrugged. "I convinced Burgholzer and my other Conclave associates that I have no intention of destroying the sarcophagus. Only you know otherwise. Even if I let you go, you couldn't prove it."

The Monsignor glanced at the door. Surely even Chavet hadn't the nerve to detain him in the Apostolic Palace? "What's to stop me walking out of here?"

Disdaining an answer, the cardinal slid his elbows off the desk and swiveled the plasma screen around. The screen showed images of Dominic and Annunciata, placed side by side, the resemblance impossible to miss. "I discovered, some days ago," said Chavet, "that this is a family affair." He was close to purring. "Just look at those two. One might say, peas in a pod." A studied pause. "The autopsy on Annunciata showed she'd given birth a few months earlier. That fits with Quinn's age."

The Monsignor retained an appearance of composure. "Hmm... interesting."

Chavet brought up another image. "Almost as interesting as this." The screen displayed a photo of the Monsignor, aged twenty. "A parallel investigation revealed that the Martin Aylesbury of your date and place of birth in England did indeed exist— until his death, aged fifteen. Substratum uncovered the truth— you're Mark Quinn, born 17 July, 1944 in Ballinasloe, County Galway, brother of Brian Quinn, uncle of Dominic Quinn."

"And if I deny it?"

"Don't be ridiculous. Brian Quinn possessed inside knowledge of Silentium. His son was conceived by Annunciata. That son is your nephew. These facts you have concealed for decades. The pattern— conspiracy. Conspiracy to hide and perpetuate a heresy that could split the Church in two. I wondered why you so eagerly volunteered to investigate the case of Brian Quinn's journal. Your eagerness made me suspicious. My suspicions led me to uncover your subterfuge."

The Monsignor straightened up in his chair. "As I said, Auguste, I still have influence. And what's to stop me walking right out of here?"

I informed Burgholzer of your deception two hours ago. He washed his hands of you. How much influence do you have now?" He pressed a buzzer. "As for you walking out of here, I think I'll let Mister Jones escort you to your new premises."

The door opened and a slim man of medium height sauntered in, his fingers encrusted with gold rings.

"Hi, Monsignor." Jones drew a hypodermic from his pocket. "One jab from this and you won't know up from down. You'll be hauled out the back way like some drunk."

The cardinal waved a dismissive hand at the Monsignor. "I'll see you in the Benedictus House."

As the needle penetrated his neck the Monsignor slumped in despair. He had nothing left to bargain with. He'd come to save Dominic and Rachel and unwittingly delivered them to the *Domini canes*— the Hounds of the Lord.

Chapter 22

Lyon

Dominic kept pace with Martha as they walked past the Café du Soleil up the Fourvière hill. Martha jabbed a finger at a narrow house up ahead. "There, the one without a window box."

They crossed the slick cobblestones to the tall, thin house that squeezed between its neighbors like a skinny wallflower in a beauty line-up. Martha pressed a buzzer, pronounced "Introibo," and was rewarded with a click of the latch. Dominic followed her down a narrow passage and up a series of zigzagging stairs to the top floor with its solitary door.

She halted and touched his shoulder. "What happened to Annunciata— it wasn't Hypatia's fault. Don't take it out on her."

"Don't worry, I won't. Hypatia... unusual name. Was she named after the philosopher in ancient Alexandria?"

"None other, although she was more of a mathematician than a philosopher. Big hero of the Collyridians, down the ages."

She pushed open the door and they entered a converted attic with bare floorboards and a large dormer window. There was little in the way of furnishings: a table, a small sofa, and a couple of ancient armchairs.

The old nun was seated in one of the armchairs, elbows tight to her sides, gnarled fingers interlaced below a silver pectoral crucifix. "Hello, Martha, Dominic," she greeted in English with a hint of an Italian accent.

"Hi there Hypatia," Martha responded, plumping herself on the sofa. "Or should I call you Sister Teresa these days? How's the move to France working out?"

"Well enough, although I miss Bologna. Tell me— have you heard from Martin recently?"

"Just a brief text saying 'All may soon be well.'" She shrugged. "Let's hope he's right."

"Indeed, let's hope." Hypatia glanced up at Dominic, who remained standing. "You have your mother's looks."

Dominic sat, meeting the woman's probing gaze. Her angular face, webbed with lines, and the intensity of her clear gray eyes, bore the stamp of suffering not so much endured but overcome. Her resonant voice belied her age which, according to Martha, was ninety-plus.

"You want answers," she said, staring directly at Dominic.

He nodded. "About my mother, yes."

"First permit me to provide a brief history of the Shrine."

"Go ahead."

She kept her gaze on him as she began: "The original Shrine— the Shrine of the Dormition— was built in Rome in 226AD on the site of a second-century villa, the meeting place of a community of Collyridians. Within its walls they communed with the spirit of Siopi— Silence. According to the Collyridians, Silence, along with Grace and Wisdom, is one of the divine aspects of Mary. Not the mere absence of noise, but a silence greater than any sound, the silence of the soul. From then on the religion of Mary became known as Silentium, with the Shrine its spiritual center until its decline and final abandonment in 392. Not until sixteen centuries later was it restored, in 1972." She paused. "Have you heard of the apparitions in Zeitoun, Egypt?"

"Can't say I'm familiar with them."

"Zeitoun is a district on the outskirts of Cairo. From 1968 to 1971, the image of Mary frequently appeared there as a moving being of light above a Coptic church. The apparitions were witnessed by millions over the three-year period. They were photographed, televised."

"You can find the images on the web," Martha interjected.

"I saw her with my own eyes on the dome of that church," Hypatia stated. "I was in Egypt with your uncle on assignment for Il Gesù in concert with Father Thomas Chen, who was engaged in exploring Marian sites in Ephesus." She paused. "With your academic background, I suppose you'll know that the city of Ephesus, remarkably well preserved from Greco-Roman times, was once the site of one of the wonders of the ancient world, the Temple of Artemis, the biblical Diana of the Ephesians, a goddess with whom Our Lady was later identified by many Christians."

"I didn't know about the Artemis connection," he admitted.

"Ephesus contains, to this day, the house that Mary lived in and, four hundred years after her passing, the Church of Mary. That church was raised after the First Council of Ephesus where Mary was proclaimed the Mother of God and Queen of Heaven. When the Ephesians heard the council's proclamation, they danced in the streets in celebration of the return of Artemis, whose temple had long been destroyed but whose spirit lived on— in the Virgin Mary."

"Hypatia," he broke in. "I understand this history means a great deal to you, but..."

Her mouth curved in a gentle smile. "Your mother...you want to hear about your mother, Sarah."

"Well, yes."

"Of course. Let's leap over the centuries...We set about the restoration of the Shrine in its original location in Trastevere. By 1976 the renascent Shrine had attracted hundreds of Christians and non-Christians who were disaffected with the loss of mystery, the death of transcendence in the modern world. Sarah, a twenty-two-year-old fresh from Idaho, arrived in Rome and met the Monsignor, who introduced her to the Shrine. Sarah was one of those souls who never forget that whisper over the shoulder: 'Remember thou art mortal.' She hoped to find answers in the Shrine. She adopted the name Annunciata and joined the Dormition order, an informal sisterhood. A few months later she became pregnant by Brian, who reverted to his fundamentalist origins when he discovered she was carrying his child. Apparently he blamed her for the pregnancy, then he blamed his brother— the

Monsignor— for enticing him into a nest of heretics and away from the True Faith. Blamed everyone except himself, ranting about sin and damnation right up to the night of your birth. And the birth proved— difficult— for her, and for you. I don't know the details— something about an undiagnosed heart defect— but, soon after the initial contractions— she almost died. But, by the grace of Mary, she survived, and you were safely delivered."

Dominic sensed a false note— no— a skipped note in the narrative. "The grace of Mary?"

She smiled, her eyes clouding with memory. "She said the Virgin Mary indwelt in her."

"What does that mean, some sort of benign possession?"

"Hard to explain. It's known in Collyridian scriptures as the Indwelling. For Sarah, it lasted only an hour or so, until the moment you were born, but the memory stayed with her the following months until— the end. You could call it a miracle."

With revelations coming one on top of the other, he was hard-pressed to retain focus. A miracle? Belief in miracles belonged to his childhood. That age of magic was lost. Sure enough, he wanted it to be true, but the wanting was no proof.

"I used to believe in miracles, way back when, but..."

"What matters," she insisted, "is that you're on a path your mother once took, except you're much closer to the goal. Everything leads to the pre-Constantinian necropolis underneath St. Peter's basilica."

"That's hardly some dark, mysterious place. Tourists have been on conducted tours of those streets of the dead for decades. The Scavi Tour. It's no big secret."

"No, it isn't. But it contains a secret. The sarcophagus of the Virgin Mary. Mary's sarcophagus encloses... a miracle. Your mother dreamed of that miracle revealed to the world. The Monsignor believes you'll realize her dream."

"Hypatia, that's all it is— a dream."

The nun sank back and heaved a gradual sigh. "Time will tell, in its own time."

Silence filled the room, wall-to-wall and bone-deep. Dominic glanced across at Martha who reacted with a don't-ask-me shrug.

He was tempted to respond in kind. Hypatia's belief in Virgin Mary possession was even more outlandish than the science fiction tomb under the Vatican.

He held Hypatia's gaze. "Did Chavet kill my mother?"

"I don't know," she answered without hesitation. "There's no hard evidence. That trail is too cold, I fear."

She rose slowly to her feet. "Ah, well. I've said my piece." She shuffled to the door, patting him on the shoulder as she passed by. "Must be on my way." At the door she gave a backward look. "The Shrine we created was abandoned after Annunciata's death. Some say it was a failed experiment. But its story isn't over. You're part of it, Dominic."

She hesitated a moment, then took out a large crucifix from inside her habit and held it up on its slender chain, almost obscuring the silver pectoral cross at her breast.

The cross she held up was the familiar shape, two limbs of varnished wood. But the figure on the cross was not what he expected. The Virgin Mary, clad in a blue robe, was nailed to the wood, her head crowned with a circlet of thorny roses.

"This," Hypatia declared, "is our symbol. Perhaps one day it will be yours."

He found the image both striking and slightly disconcerting. "Is that a Silentium article of belief— that Mary was crucified?"

"In the Apocryphon Mariæ, Mary reveals that the cross of Jesus was a sword to her heart. The theme is echoed in the gospels of Luke and John. There are later legends of a bond between Mary and her son, a bond so strong that the stigmata of Christ's wounds appeared in her flesh. Above all, Mary is a co-Redeemer with Christ, her suffering a symbolic cross. *Ad Jesum per Mariam.*" She raised her hand. "Goodbye, Dominic, Martha, and may Our Lady protect you both."

"Goodbye," they chorused as the nun left the room.

Dominic glanced at Martha. "*Ad Jesum per Mariam*...To Jesus through Mary. Isn't that a saying among conservative Catholics?"

"It's older than them. Centuries older."

"And a Virgin Crucifix. That's... unusual."

Martha eyed him knowingly. "It certainly is. And you think Hypatia is full of tall tales."

"About the supernatural— the tallest." He glanced at his watch. "So— now what?"

Martha stretched her arms. "In a minute or so we'll head out. Then we eat. It's a long drive to Rome."

"I'll do my share of the driving— it won't be too bad. Have you booked a hotel?"

She shook her head. "No hotel, not in Rome. Too damn risky. We'll be staying in an apartment. In Trastevere."

Marking the emphasis she placed on the final word, he gave her a quizzical look. "Is there something special in Trastevere?"

Hands cupped behind her head, she leaned back in the sofa. "Just an old church."

Chapter 23

Rome

The candle flame stood straight and slender in the quiet air. Rachel wasn't certain why she'd lit it— perhaps it was the primordial light in the darkness theme, older than Abraham or Moses.

Fitting enough in a church dark as this.

She turned away from the candle-rack and returned to her seat in the front pew.

Two hours since she'd entered Santa Maria in Trastevere and already the ancient church had worked its slow spell. At first it had welcomed her with a sense of sanctuary. Then as time passed, a hint of a sacred presence, beyond the altar, this side of breath, brought a peace that exorcised anxiety.

Not that she'd wallowed in the unburdening of her spirit. She had checked with the church's sacristan about Simon Dray. Did he know anyone of that name? Had anyone of that name left a message? A polite no to both questions. It was beginning to look like a wild goose chase. All the same, she couldn't let go just yet.

Thanks to the helpful sacristan, she knew a lot more of the church's history than when she first crept into its murky interior. She'd learned that somewhere around 225AD local Christians had requested the use of an assembly hall as a place of worship and the Emperor Alexander Severus, no Christian himself, offered them a *taberna meritoria*, a former rest home for retired legionaries. Then in 340 Pope Julius I ordered a basilica constructed in place of the assembly hall, a basilica modified in the ninth century and reconstructed in the twelfth.

By any standards, this church, through its three incarnations, was old. As in *old*.

She raised her eyes to the golden mosaics of the semicircular apse high above the altar, the hieratic images dimly discernible in the murk. A medieval mosaic depicted Mary's coronation as Queen of Heaven, her exalted figure seated beside Christ and flanked by prophets, popes, and saints. Below the Virgin's coronation in heaven ranged six panels recounting her life from birth to her mysterious quasi-death, known as the Dormition, the Falling Asleep.

Rachel's memory summoned a verse from the Song of Songs, aware that the verse from Hebrew scripture was later ascribed by Christians to Mary:

Who is she who looks forth with the dawn,
Fair as the moon,
Bright as the sun,
Terrible as an army with banners?

For all the hardcore atheism hardwired into Rachel from infancy, it was impossible to ignore the weight of awe in this shadowy sanctuary. Maybe when she got back home she'd break the habit of a lifetime and start attending the local synagogue. Couldn't hurt.

But, for now, she had to leave this sanctuary. The sacristan had told her the church would be closed from noon to 1 p.m., and the time was a couple minutes short of noon. She shrugged her carryall onto her shoulder and reluctantly made her way up the aisle.

Each corner she turned in Trastevere, Rachel discovered a minor architectural wonder. Threading the twisting vicolos, taking in the variety of charming little shops, she was starting to feel at home in the Eternal City. For all its defects, Rome had a warm heart.

Still feeling full from taking lunch in one of the less busy cafés, she slowly wandered around the weekday stalls in the vicinity of the *Porta Portese* market, mixing with the tourists, until, at a glance at her watch, she decided to head back to the Piazza di Santa Maria.

The number of tourists increased as she made her way onto the Viale di Trastevere, from where, if map and memory served, she would find a relatively straight route to the Santa Maria church.

She was about to turn into a side lane when she noticed a man some thirty yards ahead, standing with his back to her. For some reason, he stood out from the crowds.

An instant later Rachel grasped why. The sleek, gray suit. The tall, athletic build. The arrogant stance.

He turned around, his head sweeping to-and-fro.

It was Deacon.

The illusion of security vanished. Rome's heart went cold.

He was staring right at her.

See Rome and die.

Resisting the temptation to run, praying he hadn't spotted her, she walked the few steps to the street corner, head bowed.

After agonizingly protracted seconds, she turned the corner. Against her flight instinct she forced herself to maintain a steady walk until she was out of Deacon's line of sight— presuming he hadn't come after her.

She risked a backward glance. And there was Deacon. He was strolling along the Via di Trastevere and if he as much as glanced down the empty lane, he couldn't fail to spot her.

Please, God. Please...

Moments later, he passed out of view.

Rachel ran like hell.

Chapter 24

"She's here, in Rome." Jones leaned on the statue-adorned parapet of the Ponte Sant'Angelo and stared at the turbid currents of the Tiber. "Gurevich is here."

Deacon, facing in the opposite direction to his companion, elbows propped back against the parapet, nodded his agreement. "I walked my legs off in Trastevere without seeing the bitch, but she's got to be here. Benoit should have let me grab her while she was within arm's length." He glanced sidelong at Jones. "But your man disappeared from under your nose."

Jones maintained his scrutiny of the Tiber. "If Quinn's not here yet, he'll be here soon. And you talk to me— you talk with respect. I lead, you follow. And spare me that fake Brit accent. It'll take more than a phony voice and face job to hide a Boston hit man."

Deacon bristled but knew better than to risk a challenge, especially with Robert Carson hulking at the end of the bridge in front of the Castel San'Angelo. Okay, so his own man, Phil Craig— dressed in his customary pale blue denim— was at Carson's side, seemingly striking up a conversation, but if internal rivalry ever broke out he rated both his own and Craig's survival as near zero.

This was the first time Deacon had dealt with the legend known as Jones face-to-face and the experience was more than a little intimidating. According to criminal underworld fable, this was a man born without a soul, who never went bad because there was no trace of good to go bad. It was said that Jones believed the Earth was hollow— that odd belief was a sure fit with his character.

Deacon found he was instinctively stroking his gray silk tie and instantly dropped his hand. "I meant no disrespect. Did Benoit order you off Quinn?"

"Benoit changed the rules. Or rather, Cardinal Chavet. Found out Benoit's real name yesterday. When he connected the Monsignor to Quinn, I was told to bring them both in. Stormed the Quinn house ten minutes too late. So now— no more screwing around. We go after our targets as a single unit." He drew back from the parapet. "Time we made a move."

Deacon pulled himself up straight. "Where to?"

"Place called the Benedictus House. Only ten minutes' walk. Father Dieter, the Holy Office flunky that passed Kinsella's e-mail on to Chavet, has a secure little room there."

"And you're going to start... work on him?"

"I've already started to work on him. Time to finish the job." He walked toward the Castel Sant'Angelo, beckoning Deacon. "Watch and learn."

The grounds of the eighteenth-century Benedictus House, thirty paces by thirty paces square, were walled high and secure by solid masonry, surmounted by razor wire. Originally a Conclave property, the house currently served as a makeshift prison, with Chavet its custodian.

Monsignor Martin, hands thrust in his overcoat pockets against the chill, paced over the uneven lawn, back and forth. Chavet, indifferent to the late autumn cold, sat on a garden bench, motionless.

The Monsignor debated his next move. Chavet had, so far, kept his prisoner in relatively comfortable accommodation. Which was more than could be said for Father Dieter; that luckless functionary was confined to the cellar.

"Whenever you're ready." Chavet's voice brought his pacing to a halt.

He strolled up to Chavet and stood close to the bench, raising his gaze to the sullen gray clouds. "Jones seems to be taking over. How long do you expect to deceive your Conclave associates? You can't lead curial cardinals around by the dog collar forever."

"*Jones*," muttered the cardinal. "Hired from necessity. There is none better at annihilating obstacles, obliterating opposition. Necessary— and evil. But, I grant you, a necessary evil is still evil. There are times, in the service of God, that we must make a deal with the devil."

"Tell that to your friends in Conclave."

"Don't be obtuse. You know what Conclave wishes to avoid. If Silentium returns in full flood, it will crack the Rock of Peter. The Church will be split asunder, divided between followers of Christ and Mary."

"And your allies among the ayatollahs and imams and mullahs will have no need of you," the Monsignor observed cynically. "Your goal of carving up the world between Catholics and Muslims is, at best, naive. As Wahabi-funded mosques proliferate in Europe, church attendances decline. When critical mass is achieved, a radicalized Islam will inherit the wreckage of Christianity. Your unholy alliance with Islamists will be redundant."

Chavet's eyes flashed. "Unholy? You dare use that word to me? Fundamentalist Islam— the *authentic* Islam— is our strongest ally against the secular materialism of the West."

"Still playing that old tune? Turning the Church into an anti-Agincourt where we imitate the action of an ostrich?" He shook his head. "Your diagnosis is false. You deliver poison in the guise of medicine."

Chavet glanced up sharply at the pointed reference. His response was subdued. "On that topic, let us remember that I'm not alone in guilt."

The Monsignor studied the cardinal's tense, conflicted expression. The subtle signs of Chavet's gradual loss of sanity, year on year, were apparent to one who knew where to look, *how* to look. It was an insanity that could pass as stoic fortitude. He perceived it for what it was: controlled psychosis.

"You've never really understood your own faith, have you, Auguste? All those reported visions, real or imagined, down through the centuries, are they visions of Christ? Rarely. It's Mary that haunts the visionaries. Have you never wondered why?"

"Superstition. Stop playing for time. Where do Quinn and Gurevich fit into this?"

The Monsignor shrugged, feigning resignation. "Any role Dominic was to perform is now defunct and Rachel was merely a red herring to put you off the scent."

"A red herring?" Chavet seethed. "Do you take me for a fool?" Following the outburst, lines puzzled his narrow forehead. "Could it be that you're hiding the truth in the wrong box? Could it be that the red herring is not the girl, but Quinn?"

"Your paranoia is running away with you."

Chavet stood up from the bench. "We'll see when Jones brings in Gurevich. You're out of time. Tomorrow you'll be talking to Jones."

With that, the cardinal strode across the lawn to the locked door of the house. The Monsignor kept pace with him.

Chavet gave his companion a look of reproach. "We were on the same side once. You, I can't forgive. Let's not forget what you forced me to do."

"You damned yourself, Auguste. Your choice. And fail to keep Jones on a leash and God himself won't stop the entire Crypt from crashing on your head."

"Once my mission is accomplished, the whole world can crash down on my head." He unlocked the door and opened it wide. "I will pray for you, Aylesbury. I hope you do the same for me."

The Monsignor considered a moment, then nodded. "I'll pray for you." He took a step into the doorway. "I'll pray you go to hell."

The reply was toneless: "I'm already there."

Deacon stumbled out of the cellar of the Benedictus House and into the tiled lobby, desperate to reach the bathroom before he threw up his lunch.

His stomach rebelled before he took a single step. Dropping to his knees, he vomited semi-digested pasta and wine onto the tiles. Trembling between violent spasms, he voided the full contents of his meal, then continued to dry heave.

What he'd seen down in the cellar, what Jones had done...

A redhead. A nervous giggle rose up in his throat. Redhead. That word would never sound the same again.

Father Dieter, the luckless recipient of Father Kinsella's e-mail, was chained to a metal chair down in that cellar. Up to the neck, he was just another man in a black suit and clerical collar. Above the neck...

Deacon had killed four women and raped many more but Jones made him feel like a preschooler in crime, stuck in kindergarten.

Jones had set about work with a cheese shredder, its serrated surface peeling off the priest's graying hair in ragged ribbons. Strip by clumsy strip, Jones skinned the head of its outer layer.

Redhead.

Carson, scratching his beer belly, had observed Jones with doglike devotion. Phil Craig watched with an excitement that verged on the sexual, heightened when Jones switched the shredder for a sheet of sandpaper.

In the nimble fingers of Jones, the sandpaper scraped the priest's exposed nerves, tendering the flesh.

"This is the real art," Jones said between Dieter's howls. "Teasing. Tormenting. Making it last.' He leaned over his victim. "Feel *that*? Oh yes, you do. And *that*..."

It was then that Deacon experienced the first upsurge of bile, swallowed with difficulty. Jones's exhaustive torture of the priest struck him as a horrible form of love: no effort was too much, no painstaking attention to detail too demanding, no touch of malice too petty to overlook.

Jones stepped back for a moment and, with a flourish of the hand, the soul of showmanship, picked a salt cellar from the table. "And while we polish off our work with fine sandpaper, we rub a little salt into the wound." Another flourish and the man's head was sprinkled with a steady stream of salt. After the best part of a minute, Jones put the salt cellar aside. "I think that's enough seasoning. Now, before we start to scrape parts of the flesh down to the bone, we get our hands dirty. Rub the salt well in."

Jones gripped the howling head in both hands as he stroked and massaged.

That was when Deacon's stomach got the better of him and he raced up the stone steps and into the lobby.

Kneeling, he squatted for several hundred breaths, each a fraction slower.

He flinched as the door opened and Jones emerged. His expressionless eyes surveyed the vomit-stained floor.

Deacon unsteadily regained his feet and manufactured what he hoped was an apologetic smile. "Sorry about all this. A bit too... extreme... for my taste."

"*Extreme?*" For an instant, a monstrous abstraction looked out of Jones's eyes. "You don't know *extreme.*"

Deacon backed away, rattled to the core. "Ah, no. I suppose not. Did he— did he talk?"

"No. Now he'll never talk. Go put him in the ground."

"Oh, yes, of course. So, is this the usual modus operandi? Is this the sort of treatment Quinn will get?"

Jones shook his head. "Different every time. Quinn's going to die like a rat."

Chapter 25

Fréjus Tunnel, French-Italian border

The odometer on the Toyota hatchback had clocked up 260 kilometers on the journey from Lyon. And that was just the first stage in a long drive. Dominic, taking over the wheel from Martha, drove away from the French tollbooth and into the mouth of the thirteen-kilometer Frèjus Tunnel. The Trans-Alpine traffic flow was heavy but hadn't yet ground to a halt.

As the tunnel walls closed in and the Alpine panorama was shut out Martha flexed her shoulders, working away some of the muscle stiffness from driving the first leg of the journey to Rome.

"Traffic's slowing down," he observed.

"Damn traffic."

He smiled. "You're not the most patient person in the world, are you?"

She folded her arms. "I am patient— so long as everything happens very quickly."

"Well, it's going to be a long trip..."

"So let's not waste the time." She stroked a finger across her lips. "Now that you know something of your situation, has it occurred to you that all those birthday and Christmas gifts from your uncle were... singularly appropriate?"

"What with all the excitement I haven't thought about it, but, yeah... My aunt just passed them on and said Uncle Mark was busy but would find time to fly over one day. The gifts were all books, and all the books were on ancient science. I was a bit pissed off, at first, then got into it in a big way."

"Your uncle can fairly be described as manipulative."

He grimaced. "So even back then, I was being primed? He wanted me to take up history?"

"No, he wanted you to be a theoretical physicist, but we can't have everything." She threw a sidelong glance. "How familiar are you with ancient Greek science?"

"I majored in the history of science."

"At SUNY and Stanford. Now, if you were a Yale alumnus like me... I jest. No, I don't. It's been a while since you were in the halls of academe. Regarding Mary's apocryphon, it would help if you brushed up on Greek science, especially related to the Great Library of Alexandria." She stretched out. "Go on, impress me."

He shrugged. "Okay. A while back I mentioned the first-century genius, Heron of Alexandria. Apart from inventing the steam engine, he also created an ingenious array of automata operated by analogue programming. As well as fully automated puppet theatres and automatic doors, Heron constructed coin-operated vending machines. But he was just one of many geniuses connected with Alexandria."

"And what about the Great Library of Alexandria itself? How much can you tell me about it?"

"It was a combination of university, several libraries, a museum and a temple, containing up to half a million different books at its height in the first century BC. The Library went into a decline after the murder of the mathematician Hypatia and was eventually destroyed with the Muslim conquest of Egypt in 640."

"A hell of a loss," she remarked.

He nodded. "Of the vast collection of volumes, virtually nothing survives intact, and a tiny percent in later, adulterated versions. What scraps of information filtered down, second- or third-hand, are tantalizing. Democritus, in the fifth century BC, co-created the atomic theory of matter with his mentor Leucippus, and also propounded the thesis of many worlds in an infinite cosmos. Epicurus said much the same thing a century later: 'There are infinite worlds both like and unlike this world of ours.'"

"You sound like a lecturer."

"I was one, part-time, for a couple of semesters. I'm back in the zone."

She raised an apologetic hand. "Sorry to interrupt. Do go on."

"Aristarchus, in the fourth century BC, proposed that the earth and moon orbited the sun and calculated the size of the moon within twenty percent accuracy. He said the stars were 'infinitely' far way, beyond any known measurement. Eratosthenes, writing in the third century BC, calculated the circumference of the earth within an accuracy of five percent."

"You certainly remember your stuff. How great a loss would you count the destruction of the Great Library?"

Dominic thought that one over. Many scientific advances of the twentieth century were prefigured in the Library's archives. And if the twentieth century had been prefigured, why not the twenty-first?

"Trouble is," he said, "mere scraps of that ancient knowledge survive in any form, even adulterated. Odds are that some of the lost texts contained speculative theories regarding matter and energy, time and space, equal to or possibly more advanced than our own. Alternative universes, definitely. Democritus and others came up with that idea. Block time, the idea that space-time is a single, unchanging entity— they conceived of that for sure. Space as composed of a hierarchy of dimensions far beyond the three we experience, again, within their ability to conceive. Basically, they could theorize on anything amenable to thought experiment. It's worth remembering that's Einstein's theory of relativity was the result of a thought experiment." He slipped a look at Martha. "And this is feeling one-sided. Surely you can reveal one little theory from the Apocryphon Mariæ."

"Okay, okay. I guess it won't break the bank." She pondered a few seconds. "Right... you mentioned block time. The apocryphon is big on block time. It compares a human lifespan to the pages of a book. The book doesn't disappear when you finish it— it's a solid block, all the pages intact. We 'read' time— scan it, if you will— from the *outside* just as a reader is outside a book. Therefore the seat of consciousness lies outside of time and can't vanish when the last page is read. Hence, death is a 'deception of the senses.'

After the last line is read the non-temporal observer reverts to the first line and reads the book through again. We relive the same life an infinite number of times. As it says in the apocryphon: 'The soul has no memory.'"

"Now there's a double-edged sword. What about those people whose life is hell?"

"What indeed?" she said. "But this form of bounded immortality is what the apocryphon calls the sleep of time. It reminds me of those lines of Wordsworth in his 'Ode on the Intimations of Immortality': 'Our birth is but a sleep and a forgetting.'" A diffident smile. "I happen to know that's your favorite poem. And before I stray from the point... the apocryphon states that it's possible to awake from the sleep of time, to skip to an earlier page, so to speak, with full awareness of all that succeeded it. But that brings in the whole multiverse, multi-timeline thing, and that's not my specialty. Mary, like all those others before her, believed in a multiverse. An infinite number of universes in which whatever can happen does happen, an infinite number of times. And you'll have to wait until you meet Thomas Chen if you want to learn more. He's the expert. My area is more the early history of Silentium."

Dominic braked the car to a stop as the Audi in front drew to a halt. "Silentium's early history... is much known about that?"

She gave a yes-no side-to-side shake of the hand. "Bits and pieces. The watershed was reached in the early fifth century at the Council of Ephesus where the Catholic Church proclaimed that Mary was the *Theotokos*, the Mother of God, along with other exalted titles, all drawn from Collyridian sources. The Church and the Collyridians soon parted ways but provisionally reunited when Islamic armies conquered half the Christian world. Christendom had barely been born and already it was being crucified. Christ and Mary followers fought side by side in the year 732 at the Battle of Tours, a battle that began the long fightback. Despite what Conclave believes, Marianists are as Catholic as any cardinal. Subvert Christianity, and you won't establish a liberal secular utopia on earth. Instead there'll be a religious vacuum. Another religion will fill the gap. And Mary diminishes."

"What makes you think secular societies are so insecure? Do we really need any religion?"

"The disenchantment of the world has starved the soul. The world hungers for wonder. A re-enchantment of the world." She eyed him with distinct affection. "Everything will be made clear, soon. By the way, you're way more ready for this than the Monsignor expected."

"Careful with the compliments," he warned. "You might strain something." He peered ahead. "Traffic's still gridlocked. Let's hope the road's clearer south of Turin."

"We'll be in Rome soon enough."

He cast a sidelong look. "Not impatient any more?"

Her face was somber. "Not now that I think of our destination. Where all roads lead."

Chapter 26

Rome

Rachel had Santa Maria in Trastevere all to herself, a cool, hushed sanctuary from dapper London gents who used psychological terror under a London bridge and stalked the Roman streets.

The bastard was out there somewhere, and his sudden appearance was beyond coincidence. How did he know she was in Trastevere? The very sight of him pumped fear into her pulse.

He's making me small, damnit. He's making me *small*.

So do unto others as they do unto you. Make Deacon small. Shrink him by viewing the vista of the past. See the grand design. Her gaze roved the church interior: the rows of granite columns that had once graced the Temple of Isis in imperial Rome, the numerous paintings and mosaics, the deep orange of dusk in the small windows. And above all, the mosaic panel in the apse and its depiction of Mary's mystical death/sleep. The Dormition. According to Catholic and Eastern Orthodox traditions, that wasn't the end of the Virgin Mary's story, but a new beginning.

Gradually, her thoughts gravitated back through the ages. "Older than the Anastasia."

Browsing the web she'd discovered that the official cult of Mary began in Constantinople in 379 where a hall was christened the Anastasia, Greek for the Resurrection. It was in the Anastasia that the tide turned in the Christian mainstream until Mary was launched from a compliant virgin to the status of Mother of God and Queen of Heaven. A goddess in all but name.

But was it possible that Mary was first adored here, in Santa Maria in Trastevere? She smiled as she discovered that Deacon had shrunk in her mind, small and getting smaller, dwarfed by Mary. She pulled out the laptop from her carryall and reread a passage that described a church founded on the site of the Anastasia in the early fifth century. The historian Sozomen, writing soon after, gave a strange account of that ancient church. Squinting in the dimming light, she scanned a few lines from his chronicle:

A divine power was there manifested, and was helpful both in waking visions and in dreams, often for the relief of many diseases and for those afflicted by some sudden transmutation in their affairs. The power was attributed to Mary, the Mother of God, the holy Virgin, for she does manifest herself in this way.

Divine power, waking visions, and dreams from the time of Byzantium. And that majestic title: Mother of God. It was as if she'd caught an archaic echo of an era when goddesses still held sway, under whatever thinly-veiled Christian title. In the twilight of Rome and the predawn of Europe, Isis, Artemis, and Cybele still cast their spell under the blue mantle of Mary.

"What have we lost?" she murmured, looking up at the mosaic of Mary enthroned in glory. "Do we know what we've lost?"

"Legend's soul," said a low, melodic voice at her back.

Startled, she spun around. A tall, slender young woman stood in the aisle, hands buried in the pockets of a long, navy blue raincoat, straight black hair spilling over her shoulders and framing her oval face. And that face— not merely beautiful but... Rachel wasn't sure a word existed for what she saw in the woman's dark, impenetrable gaze. Abruptly aware that she was gawping, she fumbled for speech:

"Uh— ah... hi!"

"Hi. Mind if I sit with you a moment?"

Rachel shuffled over a couple of feet. "You're welcome. I'm— ah— Rachel."

"I'm Maria."

Maria slipped gracefully into the vacated space on the pew and stretched out her long legs clad in narrow black denims and scuffed gray sneakers.

Entranced and disconcerted in equal parts, Rachel shifted uneasily. "So, er, are you a tourist?"

The woman's smile was slanted, her expression enigmatic. "I'm something of a traveler."

"Uh-huh? Can't quite place your accent." In truth, Maria had the most elusive accent she'd ever encountered.

"I've picked up a lot of accents in my travels."

Rachel nodded sagely, none the wiser. She pointed to the small, eight-pointed silver star brooch on the woman's raincoat lapel. "New Age?"

"Old Age." The woman's unusual leftward slant of a smile became pensive as she gazed up at the mosaic of Mary's coronation as Queen of Heaven. "That mosaic... inspired by the Byzantine school," she murmured. "Rome and Byzantium, so long ago. Rome kept its broad feet planted firmly on the earth. Byzantium stood on tiptoe, reaching for the heavens."

Rachel struggled to form a response. "I guess so. I don't know much about Byzantium, or Constantinople— whichever name the city went under."

"Byzantium is the original name," Maria said, gaze still focused on the mosaics above the altar. "The flag of Byzantium bore the image of the crescent moon, symbol of Artemis, patron goddess of the city. When its residents embraced Christianity, the eight-pointed star of the Virgin Mary was added to the crescent moon. Moon and star— the Byzantines reached for the heavens."

Maria lapsed into a thoughtful silence, then leaned toward Rachel. "You're here to meet someone."

Rachel's eyes widened. Maybe it should have clicked earlier, but she'd been expecting a more direct approach. "Simon sent you?"

"No, a priest called Thomas Chen."

Hadn't Deacon mentioned that name? "Who's he? Does he know Simon?"

"In a manner of speaking. Listen, Rachel, nowhere in Rome is safe for you. I know you're on a mystery hunt. Let it go. If you don't leave Rome, you'll die."

Rachel's heart did a double-skip. "I'll *die*? Who are you? How do you know all this?"

"I'm just a traveler. And I just know."

Was Maria telling the truth? Something about the woman precluded doubt. Emotions warred in her: concern for her own life, a desire to know more, an instinct to flee.

"I can't let it go," she said finally. "Not unless you give me a reason."

Maria looked up at the golden mosaics of the apse. "Mene, Mene, Tekel, Upharsin."

Rachel waited several seconds. "Belshazzar's feast? That's an answer? I need the writing on the wall spelled out."

Maria lowered her gaze. "The West is undermining its foundations. Lacking integrity, fracture lines spread. When the edifice shatters, enemies will grab the spoils. 2001 didn't begin with a space odyssey to the strains of a Strauss waltz: the century was ushered in to the thunder of toppling towers."

Rachel waited for further exposition. "That's it? Did you major in cryptic?"

"It's sufficient." Maria leaned over and gave Rachel's hand a fond squeeze. "I'm not here to give a lecture. Just help. You should go home."

Rachel heaved her shoulders. "If I do that, I'll spend the rest of my life with a bunch of whys and what-ifs. But... I'll think about it."

Maria stepped out into the aisle. "Good enough. The sacristan will be locking up any minute. Permit me to give you a ride?"

"No, thanks. I'll walk."

"Out there, people are looking for you. Safer to go with me." Maria tilted her head with a winsome smile. "So— you coming?"

The red Vespa scooter tore a hazardous path through the dense traffic of the Via Claudia, the eroded walls of the Colosseum receding rapidly in its wake. Rachel, thighs clenched to the scooter's pillion seat, clung to Maria's waist for precious life.

"You'll miss the turn!" she shouted at Maria. "Via Marco Aurelio."

Maria swerved the scooter into the tightest of turns. Throttle wide open, she charged the vehicle up the road.

"Here!" Rachel yelled out. "Here!"

The Vespa screeched to a stop directly outside the *pensione*. Maria turned as Rachel dismounted. "You'd best get inside. Stay in tonight and take an early flight out tomorrow. Promise me you'll do that."

"It goes against the grain to run away— can't make any promises."

"Oh, well," Maria sighed. "I tried."

Rachel spread her palms. "Truth to tell, I'm going to give it a few days before I head off home. Stubborn as a mule, you know?"

"I understand. Can't leave the mysteries alone. I'm much the same. The path of stones and the sea of stars." In the space of a breath, her expression mellowed into a blend of wistfulness and composure that escaped definition. Eve, perhaps, dreaming of lost Eden. Then her face enlivened with a smile that was nothing short of enchanting. "I'll watch out for you."

She gave a wink, opened the throttle, and sped off at a breakneck pace.

Rachel watched the rider race off into the night. Watched her speed around a corner. And continued to stand there, staring at the empty corner.

"Wow."

Chapter 27

His ghostly reflection stared back at him, superimposed on the midnight of Rome. Outside the car's passenger window, lightly misted by his breath, Dominic watched the buildings give way to the black stretch of the Tiber as Martha steered the Toyota onto a bridge.

He smiled across at her. "Feeling near the edge?"

"After thirteen hours on the road, I'm halfway down the cliff. Also, I'm dying for a pee."

He brandished the iPad she'd supplied him with. "And I'm going blind researching Marian cult history." His fingers kneaded the back of his neck. "There's something I've been wondering."

"Uh-huh?"

"That Crypt protocol, about not carrying weapons..."

"Oh, no," she groaned. "Not again. They're *verboten*. You know the old saying: any fool can pull a trigger. The system works. Sort of. Live with it."

He shrugged in resignation. "Okay, it's your world. Ghosts don't carry guns."

They had left the bridge behind and were speeding alongside the Tiber. After passing a couple of narrow side streets, Martha turned the car into an even narrower lane and took a sharp right under a low arch into a tiny courtyard.

She pulled to a halt, turned off the engine, and sagged back. "Thank *God*. Now let's get the luggage out the trunk real quick."

He got out and retrieved his bags, then waited as she opened a solid oak door that boasted two hefty locks and a keypad. He followed her up a series of sharply angled stairs whose walls were so close that his shoulders kept brushing the painted plaster.

"It's right at the top," she said. "A view of the street below and not much else."

After five flights they came to a formidable door with no fewer than three manual locks and another keypad.

"Tight on the security," Dominic observed.

"Always," she replied, preoccupied with the rigmarole of unlocking. "Always." She opened the door. "Make yourself comfy. I'm heading for the bathroom." With that she switched on a light and darted out of sight.

The medium-sized, high-ceilinged living room, with its solitary shuttered window, was simply but comfortably furnished in a mixture of thrown-together styles. An old, compact hi-fi sat in one corner under a soaring rubber plant. The plain white walls were decorated with two pastoral watercolors and a poster of Buffy the Vampire Slayer. On a small table by the window sat a foot-high antique hourglass in a mahogany stand inscribed TEMPUS FUGIT.

He deposited his bags and walked across the tiled floor to sink with gratitude into a snug velour armchair. Slowly, he straightened his legs out under a stained coffee table.

On the other side of the room was a set of slightly cockeyed shelves crammed with a rank-on-rank rabble army of dog-eared books. It reminded him of his own book collection back in his Brooklyn basement.

He closed his eyes. And saw an endless autostrada rolling relentlessly toward him. His eyes sprang open and his head flopped back.

Martha strolled back into the room. "That was a relief. Bathroom's all yours."

He flicked a hand. "I'm good. But I'll take a shower later if that's okay."

"Of course it is. Want some tea? Bit late for coffee."

"Tea's fine, but shouldn't we unpack our stuff first?"

She brushed the suggestion aside. "It can wait. Unpack yours by all means." She pointed to the opposite door. "Through there, first on the right, there's a box room with a camp bed. Which— heck— means you've no excuse to share my double bed."

The remark, laden with geological layers of undertones, came out the blue and threw him off base. He'd gotten so used to a brother-sister relationship that the abrupt change in ground rules demanded a moment's reorientation.

She produced a pronounced wince. "Pretend I didn't say that. I'm out of my skull with fatigue."

"We're both tired," he said, making light of the moment. "I'll probably be babbling jabberwocky before the hour's up."

"Right, then," she said, a trace of awkwardness remaining. "Tea's on its way. There's a spare laptop over by the bookcase. Consider it yours. Click on the desktop Word doc named Santa Maria in Trastevere."

As she left, he detached the laptop from its power cable and switched it on. It was still firing up when Martha returned carrying a tray bearing two large mugs and a metal teapot.

"Changed my mind." He put the computer to one side. "Sorry, but I'll leave this for tomorrow. I'm whacked."

"I didn't mean you should read it now," she sniffed, placing the tea tray on the coffee table. "Tomorrow's fine."

"Oh. Right. So, I guess that Santa Maria in Trastevere is associated with Silentium in some way?"

"Yep, although remember that the name of Silentium is lost to history. Historically, Silentium is known as the Collyridian religion, the nickname Epiphanius gave them after the Greek for a bread roll: *kollyris*."

He took a gulp of tea that was an oasis to his parched mouth. "I didn't find anything online linking Santa Maria in Trastevere to Silentium— the Collyridians."

"No surprise there. Few are aware that the church was the first in the world to be dedicated to the Virgin Mary."

"Really? According to the websites I came across, the original church was dedicated to Pope St. Callixtus, way back in 225. The pope was martyred three years earlier— thrown out of an upper window into a well. Must have been a hell of a good shot."

"Nobody's arguing about the Callixtus dedication, but as minor a figure as Mary was in the third-century Christian pantheon, she outranked Callixtus by several heavens. There's nothing strange in the idea that Mary gradually supplanted Callixtus as the church patron. Church dedications weren't official in those times, after all."

He conceded the argument with a lift of the shoulder. "So... how is the Santa Maria church bound up with the Collyridians?"

"The Collyridians— Silentium— whatever — comprised a large percentage of the church's congregation. Somewhere around the year 250 they dedicated the building to the Virgin Mary. More than that, they transformed it into a place of worship of Mary above all others. As such, it attracted many pagans, especially devotees of Isis and Cybele. And— I'm tired."

He raised a hand. "Sorry for keeping you up."

Martha rubbed her eyes. "All those miles from Lyon to Rome have just hit me, a bullet between the eyes. I'll take my shower first and then crash into bed; that fine with you? A few minutes and the shower's all yours."

"Go ahead." He downed the tea in one gulp, then gathered his belongings as she made for the door.

In turn, he headed for the opposite door. "First on the right?"

"First on the right." She gave him a wiggly finger wave. "Nighty night."

"Sweet dreams." He pushed open the door and entered a stub of a passageway. At the far end— all of three paces— was an open door displaying a wide bed draped in a patchwork quilt. None of his business. Out of bounds. But— maybe tomorrow if she was of a mind. It wasn't as if the thought hadn't already occurred to him— more than once— back in Lyon. He opened the door to his right and walked into a box room, most of whose space was taken up by a camp bed with a Scooby-Doo sleeping bag.

He sat on the bed and leaned against the wall. And found his eyes closing. He forced them open. Might as well skim the Word doc while the shower was occupied— it was one way to stay awake. He planted the laptop on the mattress, then opened the Santa Maria document. As he scrolled down the pages, a passage caught his eye, a quotation from the fourth-century bishop Epiphanius of Salamis:

St. John tells us in the Apocalypse that the dragon hastened against the woman who had brought forth the man-child and there were given to her the wings of an eagle, and she was taken into the desert that the dragon might not seize her. This then may have been fulfilled in Mary. However I do not decide, nor say that she remained immortal; neither will I vouch that she died.

He placed the laptop on the floor. Then he sprawled out on the bed and his head hit the pillow, his sleep-starved brain barely aware of the pad of Martha's feet past his room, the soft *thunk* of her bedroom door as it closed.

The day closed with it as his eyes shut and he sank into the dark.

Inches to go before I sleep...

A scrap of text drifted down with him.

...nor say that she remained immortal; neither will I vouch that she died

It was the fatigue, must be the fatigue, but he thought he glimpsed a shore of ancient time, and a hooded woman in a sea cave.

Chapter 28

Martha struggled awake to the strains of Jacques Brel's "Port of Amsterdam". For a fleeting instant, she wondered where the hell she was. Then it all rushed back. Trastevere. Her apartment, infrequently visited. Since the new excavations in the necropolis had galvanized the Monsignor into action, she'd spent hardly a month here in total. It still didn't feel like home.

Failing to locate the remote, she stretched out and jabbed off the alarm button on the old hi-fi. Then her glance descended to the small drawer in the bedside stand. Instinctively, her hand reached to the drawer.

"No, you can't," she snapped, pulling her hand back. "Damn it."

Instead she picked up her phone and checked for messages. After she'd run through the menus, her brow contracted in frustration. No message icon.

Jesus, Martin, I've called you eight times. What's going on?

Since the Monsignor's cryptic text yesterday— nothing. She selected his name from the directory and pressed for call. A brief silence. Then a voice announced that the number was not recognized.

Her head flopped on the pillow and she heaved a heartfelt sigh. Without the Monsignor she was left working blind and Dominic was left high and dry. With the hounds of Conclave tracking them down, they had as much chance of survival as celluloid cats in hell pursued by asbestos dogs.

She was angry more on Dominic's behalf than her own. In the past few days she'd developed a strong affection and admiration for the man who was six years her junior, although his natural maturity made it easy to forget the age difference. Sometimes too easy to forget. As early as that first night in Lyon she had lain in her hotel bed, separated from Dominic's room by a single wall, toying with speculations of what it might be like to have him lying next to her.

It wasn't merely that he was easy on the eye— plenty of men were, and too many of those smugly aware of it. He was surprisingly gentle, at variance with most of the entries in the file the Jesuits had compiled on him. Of one piece with the gentleness was vulnerability, the vulnerability of the wounded, hidden under an insouciant veneer.

Most of all she discerned an intriguing mismatch in him. Difficult to pin down, but although his feet were planted firmly on the earth there was another side to him that was slightly off-balance, or maybe seeking equilibrium in a world, a universe, several imaginations away.

How to sum that up? Dominic's center of gravity was a little off-center? A man afflicted by divine discontent? Too trite.

And she shouldn't be wasting her time daydreaming.

Glancing back at the phone, she vented a snort of frustration. Martin had performed a disappearing act and left her and Dominic dangling.

"You're driving me up the wall, Martin."

She turned over in the bed and eyed the drawer once more.

After long seconds, her hand slowly returned to it. Equally slowly, she pulled the drawer open. Her fingers fished inside, then drew out a packet of Marlboros and a disposable lighter. The packet contained precisely nineteen cigarettes. She remembered that fact with clarity from four months past when she swore off the cursed things.

"Damn you, Martin."

She extracted a cigarette, planted it between her lips, hesitated a second, then snapped the lighter and drew in a deep breath of smoke. She experienced the simultaneous onset of relief and depression. Expelling the smoke in a blue plume, she watched it curl in the air.

Four months' abstention gone up in smoke.

"Now look what you've made me do."

A splash of cold water in the face shocked Dominic further awake. He straightened up from the wash bowl, toweled the water from his eyes, and turned to face the muted morning light filtering through the pebbled glass.

He really had lost it last night, allowing his numbed wits to wander down archaic labyrinths, following the mud-brick road and constantly losing the thread.

The habit of early morning wake-up he'd acquired in the Rangers had kicked in and bounced him out of muddled dreams well short of seven a.m. With the sleep debt he'd incurred since Monday, five hours was three hours too little.

He turned off the faucet and slipped out the open door— almost colliding with Martha in the passage. Looking downright homely in her oversized bed shirt and fluffy slippers, she acknowledged him with a robotic wave as she shuffled through the kitchen doorway.

"Morning," he said. "Sleep well?"

"Slept well. Woke badly. Need coffee. Need shower. Talk later."

"Say no more." He headed down the passage into the living room and, settling back in the armchair, resumed making notes on the iPad. In the hour since he'd woken, he hadn't made much progress.

He broke off at the sound of Martha's return as she walked into the room, bearing coffee and toast on a silver tray. She sagged into an armchair and waved vaguely in the direction of the mugs and plates. "Take what you want."

"Thanks, I will."

After a minute's silence she nodded toward the laptop. "Been doing your homework?"

"On and off. There seems a good case for a Marian religion dating from the time of Mary right down to the rise of Islam. Six hundred years. Yes, I buy it. And I'd lay long odds it persisted well past the time of Muhammad."

"Oh yes, it did."

"And one thing in particular I noticed. Epiphanius constantly refers to Mary's mysterious death, or rather non-death. Although as an orthodox bishop he's hostile to the Collyridians, he clearly shares some of their credo. The Collyridians believed that Mary had, in some sense, not died. For all his pussyfooting, it seems that Epiphanius believed the same thing. When he writes of Mary's ultimate fate, he states that the gospels conceal it deliberately to avoid confusing the faithful with what he calls an 'exceeding great marvel.' Frustratingly, he refuses to reveal the nature of the marvel. 'I do not dare say it,' he writes, 'but thinking about it preserve silence.'"

Martha, sipping her coffee, regarded him over the rim of the mug. "Your point being?"

"It's possible that Epiphanius gave a hint of the real name of the Collyridians. The clue is in the phrase: 'thinking about it preserve silence.' In the original Greek text 'Siopin asko'— preserve or maintain silence. It could mean that he's preserving a mystery or religion whose *name* is silence: Siopi in Greek, in Latin, Silentium. He was against the Collyridians' deification of Mary but, equally, he viewed her as unique among humans. Silence was one of the attributes sometimes ascribed to Our Lady. Although he was opposed to the Collyridians he still believed they possessed a secret about Mary, one best hidden behind a derisive nickname to avert hostile attention." He shrugged. "It's a stretch, I know."

Her smile was a lethal overdose of sugary sweetness. "Did no one ever tell you nobody likes a smartass?" She consulted her watch. "We have more than an hour before we're due to meet Martin, but I'd prefer to get there early. Although— still haven't heard from him. 'All may be well,' like hell."

"Well, he turns up or he doesn't. In the meantime, how about giving me an idea of what's in the Apocryphon Mariæ, about Mary herself? Her story."

"Won't it keep?"

"You said on the way here you'd leave it until today. Now it's today. And we've an hour to spare."

"I don't have an hour. I need to get ready, think things through." She inhaled a slow breath, released it even more slowly. "I suppose it won't do any harm to cover some of Mary's story. But five minutes, max, agreed?"

"Sure."

She paused a moment for a sip of coffee. When she spoke, the tone was uncharacteristic, delivered in formal recitation mode:

"According to the Apocryphon, Mary was born in Bethlehem to Hannah and Joachim of Bethany in 17 BC. Joachim had no love for Mary, his sole offspring. He wanted a son, not a daughter, so he named her Mariam, meaning Bitterness, the bitterness of brine. She was only three years old when Joachim, an importer of silks and recipient of royal patronage, was requested to introduce Mary to Herod the Great, appointed ruler of Judaea by Augustus Caesar. Herod was obsessed with the memory of the wife he executed, Mariamme, whom he adored in his curious fashion, and who he believed would one day be reborn. When he set eyes on Mary, who bore the same name as Mariamme, it seems he saw a resemblance to his late wife, despite the girl's tender years. The seeds of a new obsession were sown. He promised to marry her when she was of age. She refused. Ever quick to vindictive rage, Herod responded by confiscating Joachim's property and banishing the family from Judaea.

"They moved to Alexandria, which contained a substantial Jewish quarter, larger than the entire population of Jerusalem. It was in cosmopolitan Alexandria, cultural and intellectual capital of the Roman empire, that Mary grew up under the tutelage of her nurse, Esther, a pagan Jewish woman from Athens who frequented the great Library of Alexandria and mixed with its philosophers and scientists. Esther, Mary's nurse and mentor, became more of a mother to Mary than Hannah ever was."

Martha took another sip of coffee, leaned back her head.

"Well, a time came when Herod demanded to see Mary again on her twelfth birthday. The family returned to Judaea. It seems her parents died soon after, circumstances unknown, leaving Mary alone, scarcely out of childhood. When Herod saw the near fully-grown Mary he became besotted with her, acclaiming her as Mariamme reborn as some sort of Virgin Mother of pagan myth. He was convinced that an offspring of Mary would be a god, destined to rule the world. He wanted to be the father of that god. She managed to escape from Herod's palace and found her way to the vehemently anti-Herodian village of Nazareth. It was in Nazareth, in the home of Salome of Magdala, a prostitute, that Mary hid from Herod's spies. Soon after, she became pregnant, scarcely thirteen years old. All we know of that event is a reference to a somewhat menacing angel Gabriel that steps out of a dream and an unexplained 'sea of stars.' No mention of paternity.

"Whatever the circumstances of the pregnancy, Mary then married a builder, Joseph, and gave birth to her son in Bethlehem during the feast of Passover when Jerusalem and the surrounding district were swollen with pilgrims. Herod had recently died and his deranged son Archelaus inherited his throne. He also inherited Herod's obsession with Mary. Mary wrote that Herod went mad with age but Archelaus was born mad. At the Passover that saw the birth of Jesus, Archelaus ordered a massacre of the pilgrims gathered in the Temple. The slaughter spread well beyond Jerusalem, certainly as far as Bethlehem. In all, three thousand were killed, according to the first-century Jewish historian Josephus.

"Mary fled to Alexandria and stayed there nine years until Archelaus was deposed. She came back to Nazareth in 6AD at the tail end of an abortive uprising led by Judas of Gamala against a Roman census imposed for taxation purposes. Hundreds of rebels were crucified on the hills north of Nazareth. Mary records that Judas of Gamala's cross bore a *titulus* at its crown with the plaque bearing the mocking inscription: Judas of Galilee, King of the Jews. It so happens Salome of Magdala, Mary's surrogate mother, had a son by the rebel leader, and named the baby after him, Judas. This son was later acclaimed as Judas Sicarius by the rebel army of the *Sicarii*, the 'dagger men' that took up the cause of his crucified father. Judas Sicarius, who appears in the New Testament as Judas Iscariot. Mary, keeping the identity of both

Jesus and Judas secret, brought them up as brothers in her Nazareth home. As time passed, Nazareth became less friendly to Mary. The villagers called her Mary the Egyptian, Mary the Pagan, Mary the Whore. She was treated as an outsider. She was different. She didn't belong.

"And that," Martha said, flexing her arms, "is all you're getting for now. Any questions?"

Dominic didn't know which question to pose first. Out of the historical drama of demented rulers, imperial conquest and rebel armies, the figure of Mary shone through in a different light from the meek image painted in the New Testament.

If Martha's account was to be believed, from the age of twelve Mary had enemies on all sides, not least the Herodian dynasty. From what he'd read of Herod's palace, it was *I, Claudius* meets *The Lion in Winter*. In a twist on the traditional nativity story, it was not Jesus that Herod sought out, but Mary.

"Assuming that any of that story's true, she was— remarkable," he concluded lamely.

Martha flashed a smile. "She was that. I'll go get myself ready and we'll head out in thirty minutes or so." She got up, coffee mug in hand, and trudged toward her bedroom.

When she passed out of sight he expelled a slow breath. Martha had given him a lot of information to absorb. He needed to order his thoughts. And with that in mind, he picked up the iPad and reread to some of the notes he made earlier:

Epiphanius describes Mary's final fate as manifesting some "marvel."

The Council of Ephesus: 431

Mary acclaimed Mother of God and Queen of Heaven and virtual Co-Redemptrix with Christ. Evidence the Church adopted elements from the Collyridians without crediting the source.

Rome: 1940

Excavations under St. Peter's papal altar uncover a 2nd century necropolis. NB: First stage of excavations completed October 1950

Rome: 1950

The Doctrine of the Assumption, the belief that Mary was translated bodily into heaven at the point of death, was announced by Pius XII from the balcony of St. Peter's on November 1: Last Catholic dogma to be accorded the status of papal infallibility. Why? Earliest mention of Mary's passing involves the Dormition, her mystical falling asleep, not the bodily assumption into heaven of Catholic doctrine. Possible link... necropolis?

These snippets, along with others, supplied tantalizing bits and pieces of a pattern, like isolated tesserae of a shattered mosaic, but the big picture eluded him, the design resistant to reconstruction.

He was still trying to assemble the fragments when the bustling entrance of Martha in her leather overcoat made him look up from the screen.

"Homework's over," she declared. "Forget your scholastic pursuits in SUNY and Stanford. Think Army Rangers. The tan beret."

He shrugged on his olive field jacket. "I'll keep that in mind."

"Okay, then," she said, heading for the door, "to war."

Chapter 29

Deacon scowled at the gawking tourists in the Piazza Mercanti as they poured enthusiastically into the church of Santa Cecilia in Trastevere in the western section of the old *rione*.

He shuddered in the chill air and turned up the collar of his overcoat. December was just around the corner, but granting the lateness of the year the cold was objectionably unseasonal, underlined by wisps of mist from the Tiber a hundred paces down the Via del Porto.

Deacon wasn't best pleased with the task allotted him by Jones: scour the entire Trastevere *rione* for Gurevich, focusing on the churches.

The team was just too thinly stretched. Aside from the wasted observer on the Via Venezian, keeping watch on the bricked-in and plastered former entrance to the Shrine, just ten searchers spread across central Rome. And it rankled that Jones had warned him off hunting Quinn or Martha. Deacon had put better adversaries than those two in the ground since he'd given up bodyguarding half-brained celebrities a decade past for the more lucrative occupation of freelance enforcer.

Expelling an exasperated breath, he headed for Santa Cecilia. Fifteen minutes, at most, searching out a face in the crowds. Then on to the Piazza Mastai for the briefest of recons.

After that, Santa Maria in Trastevere.

It was going to be a long day.

When the candle burned down, her time would be up.

Rachel watched the candle she'd lit by the side-chapel, observed the dance of the flame and the dripping wax that pooled in the holder. She'd given herself a candle's-length of time to reach a final decision. That decision had pretty much been made: when the wax burned down and the flame was out, she was up and away from Santa Maria in Trastevere. Out of here and straight to the Vatican: what better place to look for evidence of the Crypt?

This morning, seconds after waking, she was haunted by the memory of Santa Maria in Trastevere, its sacrosanct silence, its golden mosaics half-hidden in the dark. And, equally haunting, the presence of Maria. Maria had warned her to go home. Deacon, although in stark contrast, had said the same— go back to LA. Shouldn't she do just that?

Over a soggy ciabata at breakfast, she'd shifted halfway to a decision. Make her way over to the church in Trastevere, sit in a corner pew behind a pillar, away from the hub of visitors, and go over the pros and cons of poking her nose into Vatican City.

She looked up at the apse mosaic of Mary's coronation as Queen of Heaven.

Help me out here. After all, you're a Jewish girl too. And I will start going to synagogue, that's a promise.

Not surprisingly, answer came there none. The august icon of the Queen of Heaven remained immutable in her celestial realm, presiding over her church of shadows and candles.

Rachel glanced again at the candle. It had melted a quarter of its length. Another half hour or so, then off to Vatican City, unless she could come up with a cast-iron reason not to.

The candle sputtered, then resumed its steady decline.

Glum drizzle from a drab canopy of cloud cleared some of the strollers from the Via della Pelliccia as Dominic and Martha walked down the narrow street. A couple of blatant pickpockets sidled up to them and, on closer inspection, thought better of it and scuttled away.

"We must look real heavy," Martha observed.

She swerved into a twisting slit of an alleyway that gloried, and glorified itself, in the name of the Via della Fonte d'Olio. After a few dozen paces they turned a corner and the piazza opened out, displaying an impressive, seven-stepped fountain that gurgled quietly to itself. In the far corner, Santa Maria in Trastevere.

Some local entertainer had set up a temporary booth to the right of the basilica. The audience, all children, could be counted on one hand.

"Puppets again," Martha remarked, nodding at the tiny stage where a doll danced on strings.

"Well at least it's a variation on a theme," he said. "This time it's a marionette."

"Marionette? Enough of the French. Bambolina."

"Huh?"

"We're in Italy now," she said. "They call puppets bambolinas."

He watched the puppet performance out the corner of his eye as they skirted the fountain and approached the basilica.

Gazing upward, he studied the twelfth-century mosaics surmounting the portico. "The Blessed Virgin flanked by the five wise and the five foolish virgins. The wise virgins stayed awake and kept their lamps lit. The foolish ones slept and allowed their lamps to go out."

"I was a nun once. I know the parable, and the moral."

"The moral is you can stay awake with the wise virgins or sleep with the foolish ones."

She pursed her lips. "Some jokes mature with age. That isn't one of them."

He pushed open the door into the church. And almost squinted in the unexpected darkness. A moment later his attention was drawn to the lofty apse mosaic at the far end of the shadowy nave. He'd seen it before online, but that was with the lights turned up full. In the dim illumination that congregations centuries ago would have beheld the hieratic imagery, the impact was profound.

Martha drew alongside him. "The photos don't come close, do they? You're lucky— no gawkers to spoil the ambience. And they haven't turned the lights on. Doubly lucky, atmospherically speaking." She sat down in a back pew. "A first-timer should explore this place alone. Go ahead."

He walked down the aisle, instinctively keeping his footsteps muffled. He was already familiar with the architecture and décor from web-browsing. What was absent online was the overwhelming *presence* of the basilica or, perhaps, a presence *within* its quiet walls. He'd long ceased to be a believer in dogma but he hadn't given up on reaching out to a sacred mystery behind the world, a mystery that was its own answer.

He approached the *baldacchino*-framed altar with slowing paces and finally came to a halt, gazing high above the altar to the mosaic portraying Mary enthroned as Queen of Heaven. There was more than Christian hagiology behind that august figure. She was the goddess Astarte of Phoenicia, Anath of Canaan, Isis of the Upper and Lower Kingdoms of the Nile. And in later ages she was *Stella Maris*, the Star of the Sea.

The first-century Galilean woman had undergone an apotheosis, from earthbound to heavenward. In ancient Byzantium, and in the Orthodox Churches of Greece and Russia, Mary was acclaimed as "the dawn of the mysterious day," the living portent of another world. This was the woman who blazed in glory from the twelfth chapter of the Book of Revelations:

And a great sign appeared in heaven,
A woman clothed with the sun,
With the moon under her feet,
And on her head a crown of twelve stars.

"Mary abides," he murmured, just above a breath.

He stood a few moments longer, then skirted the altar toward the Altemps chapel. Then realized he wasn't alone. In the shadow behind a column sat the indistinct figure of a woman, her body angled away from him, facing a rack of votive candles.

Careful to avoid disturbing her, he trod softly as he neared the chapel. He slowed down when she eased around in her seat.

She cast a glance at him. And froze.

He took a pace toward her, and pulled to a stop.

For several seconds, motionless, they stared at one another.

Her eyes were big with astonishment, her voice small and hesitant. "Dominic?"

He went on staring, his entire world focused on those large green eyes, the overgrown bob of red hair, that willowy figure. "Rachel?"

For a fleeting instant his memory replayed an old lyric:

I left my heart in San Francisco

And he mouthed his affectionate term for her:

Wild rose

Chapter 30

Martha stomped into the living room, bearing a tray laden with a teapot, a jar of milk, and three empty mugs. She plonked the tray on the coffee table and plumped herself beside Rachel on the sofa. Then stared across the table at Dominic, seated in an armchair.

"Well," she said, "this is a hell of a thing."

"I guess it's a pretty bizarre story," Rachel admitted with a weak smile. "Hard to believe, I know. I, um, could go through it again in more detail if you like. Not sure a few minutes were enough to get it across." She turned to Dominic. "I'm not making this up. London Concordat Publishing... Deacon... Maria... it's all true."

"Nobody's doubting the truth of it," he assured her, still marveling that Rachel was right here, almost within touching distance. "The point is our stories seem to converge."

Martha was frowning and shaking her head. "He didn't tell me. He didn't tell me you two knew each other. Bastard."

Dominic leaned forward. "Who didn't? The Monsignor?"

"None other. I don't know this Maria, but if Thomas Chen sent her, you can trust her." She glanced at her watch. "I need to be in Santa Maria just in case the Monsignor shows up." She sprang to her feet. "In the meantime, you two stay here. I'll be back within an hour, whatever happens. Before I go..." She turned to Rachel. "I want you to know I wasn't in on that publishing house setup. It has the Monsignor's fingerprints all over it." She snorted. "Simon Dray... he hasn't used that alias in years."

Rachel appeared little the wiser. "You're saying this Monsignor person set it up? And he's one of the *good* guys?"

Martha opened the door and looked over her shoulder. "One thing's certain. The Monsignor was drawing you into the same net Dominic got caught up in. It must have something to do with you two being— what— friends?" She gave them both a shrewd glance. "Back soon."

The door clicked shut and Dominic was left alone with Rachel and a shared silence. The silence persisted as he poured out the tea and milk, his mind frothing with speculations.

Rachel tapped her foot for a few beats, then pointed at the poster showing Buffy flanked by Willow the witch and the vampire Spike. "You a fan?"

"Huh?" Well, the question was as good a start as any. "Uh, yes, I am. But it's not my poster. This is Martha's apartment. I'm just staying over." He essayed a smile. "We're friends."

"Right." She nodded, her mouth mimicking his weak smile. "Right."

"Met her four days ago."

"Right."

The silence returned and Dominic found his gaze wandering around the apartment, occasionally glancing back at Rachel.

She pointed to the tall hourglass. "*Tempus Fugit.* Does that thing make time fly?"

"Ah, if only. If only."

After a long pause, she made a show of brushing an invisible speck from the thigh of her jeans. "I still think about San Francisco."

"You were there only a week." He made another dismal attempt at a smile. "Shame you had to go back to LA so soon. Er... how are things with Lee?"

"I left him. Years ago. How are things with Jane?"

He ran that last sentence through his head a couple of times and it still came up enigmatic. "Jane who?"

"You know, Jane. Your roommate Tim told me about her. You left Stanford and got hitched with a girl called Jane back in New York. I— I came back to San Francisco to see you but you'd gone." Her hand performed an exaggerated flourish. "It's okay— no big."

He was dumbfounded. "Rachel— there was no Jane. Where did you get that from? I had to quit the semester early and fly home because my aunt was in hospital."

"You— huh? Tim told me you'd got engaged— that's why you went back to New York."

He fell back in his chair, trying to take it in. "Tim's a damn liar."

"I thought he was a friend of yours."

"Roommates doesn't mean we were bosom-buddies. Far from it. In fact—" Light began to dawn. "He had a thing about you."

He could tell the light was beginning to dawn on her too. She leaned forward, her eyes brightening. "Dominic, he *did* make a pass but I laughed it off. So— you didn't go with anyone else?"

"No way. Ask my friends in Manhattan. I've talked about you all the— I've mentioned you from time to time."

"And I was thinking about you yesterday, as in 'where's a historian when you need one?'"

"But Lee... I thought— you and he..."

She shook her head. "I went back because he needed me. Then I realized he needed me like a glutton needs lunch. And I kept thinking about you. After a couple of weeks I left him, came back to San Francisco to see you. Missed you by two days."

"Days," he echoed. "Two days."

Rachel slumped in the sofa. "Oh God." She shut her eyes. "Oh-my-God."

"Amen." He leaned back his head. "Talk about bad luck. We had it in spades."

Her eyes opened slowly. "I never forgot you. And— I'm not with anyone."

"Neither am I..."

Suddenly they were both smiling at each other, speech redundant. They'd lost a few years, but there were plenty to go.

Soon, they'd have to get down to the immediate business of figuring out what the hell had burst into their lives since last Monday. Soon, but not this precise moment. The rest of it could wait a while: Thrones, Dominions, Principalities and Powers, they could wait.

"Dominic," Rachel said at last, a blush enlivening her cheeks, "would it be okay if we just sit on the sofa and hold each other until Martha gets back? Just rest in each other's arms and be quiet with each other? Be still. Is that okay?"

Brimming with a happiness that threatened to bubble over into the whole wide world, he hastened to the sofa. "Once you're in my arms, I can't promise I'll let go."

Her face lit up. "Works for me."

Santa Maria in Trastevere had its fair share of sightseers. One look at Martha and they gave her a wide berth as she paced the walls like a confined panther.

What the hell was the Monsignor up to? He'd gone too far this time— way, way too far.

What really steamed her was Martin's manipulation of Rachel. Even by his standards, that was beyond the pale. He had lured the woman into the fringes of the Crypt and exposed her to extreme danger. It was different for Dominic: he was born into this masquerade of shadows. Rachel was a bystander brought in from the warmth.

Halting her restless pacing, she consulted her watch. 11:30. Thirty minutes late was the height of tardy for the punctiliously punctual monsignor. No point hanging around.

She marched up the left aisle to the narthex door. It swung open and a sharply-dressed man stepped through.

Smart gray suit. Sleek gray silk tie.

He froze at the same instant as she.

Deacon.

Martha, he mouthed, his eyes large with shock.

The instant passed. They acted in unison, Martha making a leap for him, Deacon beating a rapid retreat. Legs pumping, Martha sprinted out into the piazza. She cursed as she slipped in a puddle, allowing her quarry to gain a couple of yards on the ten he already had.

He veered to the right into the pedestrian-clogged alleyway, pulling a phone from his pocket. Martha's heart thumped with alarm. If Deacon reported this location...

He ran into a tiny piazza, then disappeared down a narrow vicolo. She raced around the corner after him— straight into a small boy that backed directly into her path. She jumped clean over his head and hit the ground running.

She raced to a corner and skidded to a stop, looking left and right. No sign of Deacon.

Praying for luck she ran in the direction of the Tiber, darting glances to and fro at each little lane in this medieval warren. Street after street, and no glimpse of Deacon.

Her morale had hit rock bottom by the time she reached the Ponte Garibaldi. By now he would have had time to call Jones or whomever five times over.

Gulping deep breaths, she leaned forward, hands resting on thighs. She'd blown it.

Now the enemy knew where to look.

Chapter 31

Rachel's head rested on his shoulder as the Intermezzo from Mascagni's *Cavalleria Rusticana* reached its dying fall. The small talk had long since petered out.

He stroked her red-gold hair and, eyes closed, she smiled a leisurely, lazy smile. To him, the smile was beatific. At first, side by side on the sofa, the simple holding had been just that, a mutual easing of isolation, arms enfolding. Then came the kissing, slow and easy.

Never, even in their brief romance in San Francisco, had he experienced such a quiet longing, a vibrant peace. If he had a faith, it was Rachel. He was a believer.

Whatever troubles came before, whatever tribulation followed after, this had been their time. Time itself had abandoned its linear flow, had broadened into a pool, a temporal oasis.

She nestled still closer and opened her eyes. He'd forgotten their precise hue of soft green tinged with brown. He wouldn't forget again.

He continued to stroke her hair, that red hair that inspired his pet name for her: "Wild rose." He ran his fingers through the shoulder-length strands. "I'll wait for the wild rose that's waiting for me."

Her smile widened as she responded: "Where the Mountains of Mourne sweep down to the sea." Her fingers brushed his mouth. "You remembered."

"I remembered."

"You'll show me Carlingford? The Mountains of Mourne?"

He nodded. "A promise is a promise, however late it's kept."

Rachel ruffled his hair. "Robin Hood. That's who you are." A shy smile. "I had my own private image of a dark, dashing outlaw in Sherwood Forest when I was still wearing braces and pigtails. You fit the image."

"Well, that's flattering. But how long am I supposed to keep that up? Men who start out looking like Robin Hood end up looking like Friar Tuck."

She quivered with mirth. "Either I'm madly in love or that was pretty funny."

"It wasn't that funny, so..."

Her mirth subsided. A slight frown puzzled her brow as she peered around the room. "Is it me, or is it getting dark in here?"

He glanced at the graying panes of the window. She was right, the light was dimming. "It's not you." For a crazy moment he wondered if they'd lain in each other's arms all day.

"Darkness at noon," she said ominously, her eyes rolling theatrically.

"I'll take a look." On the verge of rising he suddenly thumped his forehead. "Martha! What was I thinking? She should have been back by now."

Rachel sat up and, in unspoken accord, they reluctantly disengaged from each other. He walked to the window and pressed up to the glass, misting the surface with his breath. For a moment, he had the illusion that the breath mist was spreading down the entire window. Then the exterior view slipped into focus and he realized the mist was outside, descending in plumes and whorls.

"Fog," he remarked. "River fog maybe."

"Fog in Rome? But I guess as it's late November... Ah well, should make myself useful. Coffee? Tea?"

He threw a backward look. "Tea would be great, thanks. I'll do the next round."

"You bet you will," she responded with a wink as she headed for the kitchen.

He gazed back out the window down the narrow vicolo, whose pavement seemed fairly clear of fog. "Correction, not from the Tiber," he called out. "It isn't rolling along the ground."

He peered up at the slice of sky visible above the rooftops. The sky was dense with cloud, a solemn presence. As he watched, the cloud came down to earth. It stroked the roof tiles, caressed the eaves.

Within a minute, the rooftops were ghosts in the fog, the houses opposite insubstantial silhouettes. The surging mist sank down to street level, transmuting house fronts and shop fronts to impressionistic daubs and smears. The fog, having assumed dominion of the ground, executed a curious rise and fall, distorting perspective and making an uneasy phantom of the street.

At that moment, a specter entered the street, gliding along the far wall. It halted almost directly opposite the window and looked up. The specter was a young woman with black hair draping her shoulders, dressed in a long dark blue raincoat and black jeans.

"Maria."

His heart skipped a beat. Rachel had moved up to the window. He'd forgotten how quietly she stepped around indoors.

"Maria," she repeated, squinting down at the woman. "It's her. The one I met. She must know I'm here." There was more than a trace of fascination in Rachel's expression.

"How would she know that?"

Rachel smiled awkwardly. "She's an unusual woman."

As Rachel spoke, Maria pulled out an apple from a pocket and took a bite. She remained fixed in position, looking up at the window as she munched the apple.

"She's unusual, I'll give you that," he conceded. "What does she want, an invitation?"

"Apparently not," Rachel observed as the woman turned on her heel and departed the way she came. In a few moments she disappeared into the fog.

He stepped back from the window and moved over to the sofa. Rachel followed his lead and they sat down together, meeting each other's gaze.

"Any idea what that was about?" he asked.

She shrugged. "Your guess is as good as mine."

He gave a vague nod. "Well, maybe we'll find out— sometime." It was a vacuous response, and they both knew it. The mood had changed.

He still felt blessed that Rachel was back in his life, sitting right beside him, after six years' separation. But the temporal oasis they'd briefly enjoyed was slipping away. To bask in it any longer was an indulgence. Enemies were on the hunt out there in the Roman fog.

"Back to business?" Rachel queried.

He smiled thinly. "Afraid so. Time-out has just timed-out."

"Okay," she sighed. "So tell me how you fit into all this."

He leaned back in the sofa. "Right. Early Monday morning I got this text message..."

As he went through his account, the fog outside the window gradually thickened until the room was in semi-darkness.

By the time he concluded with his arrival at Santa Maria in Trastevere a full thirty minutes had passed.

Rachel sat motionless, hands resting on her lap, her face a portrait of bewilderment.

"Wow," she said finally.

"That adequately sums it up," he said with an attempt at a smile.

She shook her head in bemusement. "And I thought my story got A-plus for extraordinary. How did you cope with it all? I mean, your mother especially."

"I don't know. Just go with the flow I suppose, even if it turns into a cataract. But, Rachel, I need to know what happened to you in a little more detail. Then we can compare notes."

She nodded assent and went through her story, blow-by-blow.

When she finished he sat in silence for a while, piecing together what elements he could. The pattern that was beginning to emerge was disturbing. In a quantum leap, or more of a quantum stumble, he realized he was able to fill in some of the blanks.

"My uncle used the book commission to draw you into the Crypt, into the whole Apocryphon Mariæ mystery. My guess is he aimed to bring us together, but the journal messed things up.

That's why he canceled the project at the last minute. It had gotten too dangerous. He wanted to keep you out of it."

"Then why send me that picture of the Santa Maria church?"

"He knew you were in London; he must have. Maybe he thought you'd go on digging and get deeper into trouble so he reverted to the original plan— meet up in the church. Last resort."

"I *was* getting into trouble," she admitted. "Deacon..."

"Yeah. Chavet hired Deacon to warn you off and Jones to finish me off. It was easy for Chavet to trace me. As for you— I reckon they got your name from my Aunt Deirdre a few days ago— the so-called Immigration officers. The moment Chavet discovered you were researching the Vatican secret service, of all things, alarms would have gone off."

"I suppose it adds up, as far as it goes," she agreed half-heartedly. "This world of the Crypt, it's a labyrinth with shifting walls."

"And full of ghosts. All the more reason you should leave. The Monsignor has been pulling both our strings. Time to cut and run."

She rested her hand on his. "What about you?"

He tried to smile. *What about me? Four days ago I was just an ex-soldier and former scholar with no plans beyond looking for my next job. Then I saw my mother's photo...*

"I'm... I'm part of all this," he began. "Born into it, you might say. I have to see it through."

"Then I'm staying," she said resolutely.

He prepared for a long, intense dispute, marshaling every argument he could think of. "Rachel, if you stay you'll be putting both of—"

The pad of footsteps on the stairs cut off the sentence in its prime. He stood up as the door swung open and Martha breezed in, leather overcoat billowing. "The idiot's gotten himself captured," she stormed, ignoring Dominic's gesture of welcome. "Walked straight into the Apostolic Palace." She fell into an armchair, simmering. "Now we're left high and dry."

He resumed his seat. "We're talking about my uncle, right?"

"Well— *duh*."

"How did you find out?"

"A phone call from Thomas Chen." She flung back her head and exhaled sharply. "I ran into Deacon in Santa Maria. He got away. Now Jones and co will be scouring Trastevere. All in all, I'd say things could have gone better." She leaned forward and alternated her gaze between Dominic and Rachel. "Have you two had a good chat?"

Rachel glanced at Dominic. "He was about to come up with a string of reasons why I should go home, but that's not even an issue."

Martha flopped back and groaned. "What do you think this is, some female empowerment movie? You live too near Hollywood, that's your trouble. Goddamn La-La-Land. You were tricked into this and you don't belong here. You're going home on the next flight, three hours from now. I've already booked the ticket. Fiumicino's clear of fog— I checked."

Rachel shook her head, her expression obstinate. "I'm staying with Dominic."

Martha squared up to her. "You have a thing about Dominic, I respect that." Her tone resembled sharp steel scraped on silk. "But stay here and it's us that will have to watch your back until you get us all killed."

Rachel folded her arms. "I don't accept that."

"Well, you'd better accept it because the only place you're going is home." Martha glanced at Dominic. "Would you mind leaving us alone for a minute, let us talk woman-to-woman?"

Dominic found that a no-brainer. Pressure had been building in his bladder for some time but he'd delayed the inevitable bathroom visit. Before he started playing the diplomatic interlocutor he figured he needed his mind on the job and not on crossing his legs.

"Back in a few minutes," he said, rising to his feet. "Don't start a fight without me."

As though a temporary truce had been declared, the two women lapsed into silence while he made his way to the bathroom. The interchange resumed when he closed the bathroom door, although the tenor of the conversation seemed to have softened. The voices, a distant murmur, were muted.

He stood in front of the toilet and gratefully relieved himself, going over in his mind just how to persuade Rachel to fly back to LA. The truth was, if he were in her place, he would also insist on staying. The more he deliberated, the more he suspected there was only one way: they leave together. And if that meant letting the mysteries in Rome lie there, unsolved to the end of his days, so be it. Rachel was more important.

By the time he washed his hands the decision was made. Unless Martha could somehow bring Rachel round, he'd fly out with her.

After draping the towel over the rack, he moved to the door and out into the passage. Judging from the low volume of the conversation, they hadn't come to blows yet. His impression was confirmed when he entered the living room and saw Martha smiling broadly and Rachel wearing a sheepish grin.

In a short space the atmosphere had changed in the room. All was calm accord.

"I'm a dope," Rachel confessed as he sat beside her. "Martha spelled it out for me. I didn't want to admit it but I knew she was right. There's nothing I can do to help, just hinder. And I *could* get us all killed." She paused. "Dominic, just promise me— we'll see each other again when this is all over."

He put his arm around her, torn between relief that she was bound for safety and sorrow at saying goodbye so soon after finding her again. "We'll see each other again."

"Sorry to butt in, you two, but we haven't much time." Martha was already on her feet and moving to the door. "We have to pick up Rachel's stuff at the *pensione* and with all this fog and Roman traffic southbound, three hours is cutting it razorblade thin."

Dominic stood up. "You're right. We'd better make a move."

Rachel rested a hand on his shoulder. "Not you, just me and Martha. An airport farewell is too much for me to take. You understand?"

The reality of her imminent departure from his life hit him full on. He wanted her safe but— he also *wanted* her. And despite his promise, the chances of him surviving to join her in America were not good. He did his utmost to mask his feelings as he kissed her on the cheek.

"Sure, I understand." He begrudged the loss of another couple of hours with her— the prospect of it induced something close to physical pain— but he recognized that was plain selfishness. "Take care of yourself."

She picked up her bag and planted a kiss on his lips. "You too. Take a *lot* of care."

"Dominic," Martha called out. "You'll hear the rest of Mary's story. That's a promise."

With that, she hovered by the open door, glancing at her watch, the soul of indiscretion. Rachel shuffled reluctantly to her side, tracked by Dominic, step for step.

While Martha stared at the ceiling he hugged Rachel close, not wanting to let go.

Just one moment more.

One more.

One more.

And then somehow they were standing apart, and Martha was starting to close the door.

"I can't think of anything to say," Rachel mumbled.

He made it half way to a smile. "How about 'till we meet again?'"

She forced a grin. "Till we meet again."

Then she turned away and Martha shut the door. He stared at its blank wooden face as he listened to the receding footfalls. When they faded into silence he crossed the room and sat on the sofa, the indentation on the cushion next to him manifesting the absence of Rachel.

At least she was safe. At least one thing had turned out right.

Weaving a hazardous path through fog and impetuous traffic, Martha steered the Toyota onto the Ponte Garibaldi.

Rachel stared dully out the window at the befogged Tiber. "I have to do this."

Martha's voice was thick with self-reproach. "You don't have to put your neck on the line. I mean, you really don't. The more I think about it, the more I'm inclined to drive you to the airport after all."

They were traveling in the direction of the Roman Forum. Martha's talk about Fiumicino airport had been a smokescreen for Dominic's benefit.

Rachel had been prepared to stay at Dominic's side against all odds. When he was out of the room, Martha shattered that resolve. Thomas Chen had earlier phoned Martha with the news that two men, one an occasional enforcer for Jones, had placed Rachel's family home under surveillance in the last twenty-four hours.

During Dominic's brief absence Martha mentioned the possibility of a trade: Rachel for the Monsignor. His captors knew he'd never talk, but a woman, closely linked to Dominic, might open up to interrogation. With Rachel in the enemy's hands, her family would be left alone.

That was enough for her to make the decision. Added to that was Martha's admission that the Monsignor, for all his recent foolhardiness, was Dominic's sole hope of deliverance from the trap that was closing in. He held the key to the mysteries; he knew which doors to unlock.

Informing Dominic of the trade was out of the question. He would never agree. Most likely he would have stormed off to Vatican City and the trap would snap shut on him.

Rachel heaved a sigh. "See Rome and die."

Martha looked across at her. "If you go through with it, you won't be harmed. Conclave has ground rules forbidding injury to civilians. Once they catch on that you're an unlucky bystander they'll release you. No need to brood on the 'See Rome and Die' theme."

"I wasn't thinking of myself." She met Martha's gaze. "Those ground rules, they don't apply to Dominic, do they? They don't regard him as a civilian."

Martha fixed her eyes on the road, refusing a reply. For Rachel, that was answer enough.

Chapter 32

From the summit of the Capitoline Hill, beside the sixth-century church of Santa Maria in Aracoeli erected on the site of the Temple of Juno, there was a clear view over the Roman Forum, all the way along the Via Sacra to the walls of the Colosseum. A clear view, on a clear day.

Martha, standing beside a shivering Rachel, blew on her frozen hands and peered into the fog, barely discerning the remaining eight Ionic columns of the Temple of Saturn directly below, which rose from the mist like the petrified fingers of a Titan.

Beyond the Temple of Saturn, the fog held sway. The jagged ruins of ancient Rome were hidden as though in the mists of history before the valleys were raised and the hills brought low. The city of the Caesars was diminished to a staccato silhouette and wraiths in the fog.

Here they were, in the middle of that wide-open family squabble known as the nation of Italy, and hardly a soul was in sight.

Rachel hugged herself for warmth, eyeing the ruins, phantasmal in the haze. "This is the most haunted place I've ever seen."

Martha made an attempt to lighten the girl's mood. "Exchanging hostages in the fog. We should be wearing trench coats."

Rachel's mouth came close to a smile. "You sound like some cool secret agent."

"I am some cool secret agent. But don't tell anyone or I'll have to— oh, never mind."

They shared a moment of silence, then Martha spoke quietly. "Once I've gotten the Monsignor safe, I'll move the seven hills of Rome to set you free."

Rachel's smile widened, then died on her lips. "They're coming."

"I see them." Martha frowned. "The text message from Chavet promised no more than two representatives from his side. We're not off to a good start."

Three figures walked abreast past the Temple of Saturn with a brisk, purposeful stride that marked them out from casual sightseers. They halted in unison. And waited.

"Come on," prompted Martha. "Let's go say hi to these goons. And remember the code word— Jesuits."

"Jesuits. Got it."

They descended the steep slope and were soon within kicking distance of the three men.

"Hi, Carson," Martha greeted blithely, acknowledging the towering Irishman with a swish of the hand. "Fallen off any motorbikes recently?"

Carson seethed, then bellowed over his shoulder: "Bring him here!"

Three more men materialized from the swirling vapors. In moments, she discerned the Monsignor's figure. Flanked by Jones and Deacon.

"You're very sure of yourself, lady," Carson remarked as the men approached. "Five to one, not counting that elf you've got there." He looked at Rachel and sniggered.

"I'm sure of my people in position around here," Martha lied smoothly. "Two on the Palatine Hill. Two more on the Capitol. Crypt agents, not street rats like you. There's an old Crypt saying— don't screw with the Jesuits."

She didn't turn to check if Rachel was starting to move back at the verbal signal. The woman was smart, she'd follow the plan.

"Hi, Martha." Jones had reached the group, his hand gripped tight on the Monsignor's forearm. "You're not—" He broke off, glaring over her shoulder.

"She's making a run for it!" roared Carson, launching into a charge.

Martha whirled around, and rejoiced when she saw nothing but billowing vapor. Rachel had skedaddled with aplomb.

"Leave her!" Jones ordered Carson. He turned to Martha. "I get the scenario. You've shown us the girl and it's down to business. So how you want to play this?"

"The Monsignor walks to the Piazza Venezia. The rest of us stay here. Five minutes after he leaves, Rachel will return. In the meantime, I'm your hostage. And play nice, I've got the Sodality of Loyola watching my back."

"Jesuit ghosts in the mist?" drawled Jones. "Wasn't born yesterday, lady. There's nothing to stop me taking you and the Monsignor both."

As he spoke she caught a glimpse of a shadow in the fog. A slender dark blue silhouette high on the Palatine Hill. The figure descended a few paces down the slope and was revealed as a woman in a dark blue raincoat, blurred by mantillas of mist. Even at this distance there was a still presence about her, an embodied silence.

Jones looked in the direction of her stare. "Who the fuck is that?"

She wasn't about to pass on a free gift. "A friend."

He clicked his fingers. "Felici, Calabrese... Go fetch."

The men sprang into action. As they raced toward the woman, she receded into the mist.

Jones watched his trackers, then gave a shrug. "Okay, you can have your Monsignor. But that girl better be back here or they'll have to invent new words for what I do to you."

"Whatever." She strolled over to the Monsignor and whispered in his ear. "She's inside Santa Maria in Aracoeli. I'll meet up with you in Il Gesù. By the way, you're a fool."

"Perhaps more than you think," he whispered. "Conclave knows nothing of this. Chavet is operating solo. The rules don't apply."

Her heart turned to lead and sank. What the hell should she do? If the Monsignor stayed, Jones would take them both and then either hunt down Rachel and/or punish her family. But she couldn't let Rachel fall into their hands...

She had scant seconds to make a decision. "You have to go. Warn her to get away."

He gave a heavy nod. "I will. And I'll make sure Il Gesù comes looking for you. See you soon."

She stared at his retreating figure, wondering if she could make a break for it. Start with a few casual paces. One pace. Two...

Three men closed in on her.

"Going somewhere?" Jones queried. "Another step and I break your legs."

"Twitchy, aren't you? I'll stand stock-still if that makes you happy."

Jones studied her a moment, then stepped back and began speaking into his phone in a low voice. She didn't catch a word of it, but it was probably a progress report to Chavet.

Seconds after he concluded the call, Rachel appeared from the mist.

"Rachel!" Martha yelled at full volume. "Get out of here! *Run!*"

Rachel halted a moment, then kept on coming.

"No! Run away! Your life's in danger!"

She shook her head as she approached. "I don't care."

Deacon and Carson jumped forward and grabbed the girl roughly by the arms.

Jones gave an approving nod. "We're done." He turned to Martha. "And you're coming along. Two for the price of one." He glanced over her shoulder. "Hello, Alice."

She spun around and saw three newcomers emerge from the fog, a woman and two men, who might have been tourists with their polyester parkas and dinky backpacks but who bore the stamp of mercenaries on their unforgiving features. None more so than the Alice that Jones greeted, a skinny, sharp-featured woman with graying hair pulled back tight to a bun like an old-time spinster, but with eyes of liquid helium.

Even as her heart upped its tempo, Martha realized Jones had made a small slip: he'd momentarily taken his eyes off her. She launched into a sprint, sidestepping a wild lunge from Carson. "I'll come for you, Rachel," she called out as she raced over the bumpy paving.

Jones's toneless voice pursued her: "You won't live that long."

She covered the level ground in seconds and then it was sharply uphill. Her wits raced as fast as her feet. They would think she was heading for the illusory safety of the Piazza Venezia and her parked car. So use the fog and what cover the hill provided to encourage that illusion.

She veered left at Santa Maria in Aracoeli and ran for all she was worth downslope, away from the piazza. As she hoped, the fog, hugging lower ground, intensified with each step of the descent. A backward glance. Swirling fog. No sign of pursuit.

She kept up a relentless pace to the bottom of the hill and down a bend in the road, startling the occasional pedestrian. Nearing the Tiber, she slowed to a stop and leaned forward, hands on thighs as she gasped for breath. Running in fog was a killer. Her legs were wobbly and her muscles protested at full volume.

Still breathing heavily, she resumed her run, dodging traffic in true Roman style as she crossed over to the river. The weather had transformed Rome into a city of cars, hardly a human to be seen. She soon caught sight of the Ponte Fabricio and, moments later, she started to traverse the ancient bridge to the island of Isola Tiberina.

At the midpoint of the bridge, she pulled to a halt.

One of the Italians from the Forum emerged from the island, his hand slipping a phone into his pocket. He'd called in. Now Jones knew where she was, just as he'd known to post his men on the nearest bridges to Trastevere.

Her mind flashed back to Jones talking on his phone. He must have called off his men from hunting the mysterious woman on the Palatine and ordered them to the two likely crossing points to Trastevere. Jones, always thinking ahead, damn him.

The Italian hurtled toward her, as athletic in action as in physique.

She sprang forward, bending her leg to knee him in the stomach. He showed his reflexes by landing a kick bang in the hollow of her right knee. An electric shock darted up her leg and it folded, almost plunging her into a headlong fall. Arms outspread to regain equilibrium, she swiveled around on her left leg, arms raised to block a blow, only fractionally in time to fend off a ferocious uppercut.

She replied with a head-butt that sent him reeling. With a quick shake of his head, he collected his wits and was back in business, eyes hot with rage.

Hopping back on one leg, trying to ignore the red alarm signals from her incapacitated knee, she watched for his next move, sizing him up. He was quick, quick as a cobra. If she didn't take the initiative she was done for.

She hopped backwards, moving away from the island and toward the middle of the bridge and fetched up against the parapet, the stone ledge digging into her back.

He paused for an instant, then lunged. At the last instant she saw his right hand clench. He was preparing to punch into her upper body. His arm twitched...

At that moment she dropped to her knee and lowered her head. His arm swung at empty air and his body slumped over her, off balance. She pushed her shoulders between his legs and, ignoring the bolt of pain in her knee, jack-knifed her body upward, carrying the attacker with her.

One last heave...

She fell back against the parapet, the stone jarring her spine. Her adversary had nothing to break his fall. He flew off her shoulders and over the parapet.

It was two or three seconds before she heard the crunch of bone on hard rock. He'd hit the stones surrounding the bridge's central pylon, probably head first. Unlucky. For him.

Leaning over the parapet, she looked down. The body was splayed on the rocks around the bridge pylon, head haloed by a spreading crimson pool.

On the verge of literally hopping away she sighted a woman approaching, her plain dress phasing from gray to green as she emerged from the fog. She'd seen or heard something, judging from her apprehensive expression. She glanced warily at Martha, then peered down at the river. Her jaw fell in concert with her widening eyes. "*Jesu Criste!*"

"Help me!" Martha yelled hoarsely, stretching out a hand.

The woman gave her a last frightened look, then fled, vanishing into the smog as she yelled out: "*Polizia!*"

Martha almost smiled. The police were the least of her worries.

Using the parapet for support, pushing herself to the limit, she made painful but steady progress across the Ponte Fabricio. She figured three minutes at most before she reached the Trastevere bank. She was almost at the island and in sight of the Ponte Cestio when she caught the pad of pursuing feet.

She looked over her shoulder, groaning inwardly. Enemy troops had arrived.

The other Italian, Felici? Calabrese? was at the forefront, followed by the two fake tourists that had tracked her in the Forum, then Carson, baseball bat in hand. Jones was stepping out of a saloon car, a shoulder bag in tow. As he mounted the sidewalk the car sped off.

She found herself encircled, her arms grabbed tight, no opportunity to scramble over the parapet. Carson, his flabby mouth revolving around a wad of chewing gum, studied her as though she were a technical project, taking note of her right leg, its heel raised off the ground. He leaned into a slugger pose, bat hefted for a base hit.

Another chew of gum inside his blubbery chops. And the bat slammed into her left kneecap. The rap of the club and the crack of bone were as one. The agony was an eruption, a detonation. She tumbled to the ground, teeth biting through her lower lip. She wasn't going out screaming, she wouldn't give them that.

Jones strolled into view and waved the woman over. "You do the honors, Alice."

Alice strode up to Martha and stood over her, booted foot upraised. Her thin lips spat out a single word of accusation. "*Apostate.*"

The boot stomped like a pile-driver into Martha's stomach. It felt as though her insides exploded. The lights started to switch off in her skull.

The foot rose, and fell again. Rose and fell.

The dark expanded with the pain.

Rose and fell.

Martha's consciousness flickered, a tiny candle flame. Then a last breath blew it out and the world went away, taking the pain with it.

"That's enough."

Alice withdrew her foot from Martha's stomach and gave Jones a baffled look. "She ain't dead yet."

"I don't want her dead, yet. Empty her pockets."

As she complied he scanned the Isola Tiberina and spotted Calabrese move into position near a stretch of shrubbery. It was time.

He unzipped the shoulder bag and pulled out a coil of polyester cord, one end looped into a noose. Kneeling down beside Martha's inert body, its eyes open and blind, he slid the noose over her head and fixed it about the neck, allowing for an inch or two of slack.

Satisfied, he stood up. "Carson, put her over the side."

Carson lifted the limp form effortlessly and pushed it over the parapet, transferring his grip to the cord. Leaning back to take the woman's weight, he slid the cord through his hands for several yards, then held tight.

Jones signaled Calabrese to begin taking shots with his camera. The Italian set to work, recording the image of a hanged woman on the bridge of Ponte Fabricio. The Judas image, to be transmitted to Chavet.

Far off, muffled in fog, the wail of a siren keened.

Carson angled his head. "Carabinieri. Better go."

Jones nodded. "Give it another ten seconds, then let her drop." He leaned over the parapet, savoring the sight of Martha dangling like a veritable puppet on a string.

One down, one to go.

Quinn's execution would last a lot longer.

The dead have open eyes.

Martha was dead. Her eyes were open.

So, she reflected, the dead have open eyes.

The river Styx flowed below her where she dangled in air, but she couldn't glimpse its burden of souls, just a mortal on the shore taking snapshots of Hades, and now he was leaving and only the dead remained.

Everything was gray and dim and dismal. This world of the dead was a cramped domain, enclosed by dull, cloudy walls.

Would she hang here forever? Suspended over the river of the dead.

She looked along the riverbank. And saw a woman in the mist.

The woman was tall and slender, and in a world of gray, she wore a long blue coat. She possessed a beauty that had no word in any language, living or dead.

Slowly, the woman uplifted her arm in a sign of blessing.

And then Martha was falling, falling into the river of souls.

And as she fell she wondered...

Do the dead remember, or do the dead forget?

Chapter 33

Cardinal Chavet read the e-mail as he walked between the inner colonnades of St. Peter's Piazza, flanked by two Vigilanza, De Mola and Belucci, the only men he trusted from the ranks of the Vatican's gendarmerie. He closed his eyes for a moment, then read the e-mail once again:

girl secured. memento mori

The message proved Jones's worth. Just as Lucifer misled the virtuous into doing his bidding, so God could find work for wicked hands. *Girl secured...* Rachel Gurevich was safely locked away in the Benedictus House. *Memento mori...* An image soon to be delivered of a hanged Martha as a Judas to her Church. He would pray for her.

St. Peter's Basilica was barely visible in the fog as he approached the Arch of Bells to the left of the mighty edifice. But its presence presided over Rome, unseen. And the faith the church symbolized, its power veiled, guided the destiny of nations.

Below his breath, he recited the words of the historian Macaulay:

"The proudest royal houses are but of yesterday when compared with the line of the Sovereign Pontiffs... She is still confronting hostile kings with the same spirit with which she confronted Attila... She was great and respected before the Saxon had set foot on Britain, before the Frank had passed the Rhine, when Grecian eloquence still flourished in Antioch..."

"Your Eminence?" inquired a voice.

Realizing his recital had progressed above the sub-vocal, he gave a thin smile. "Just musing, De Mola."

They passed under the Arch of Bells and skirted the south side of the basilica to reach the *Ufficio Scavi*, the Office of Excavations, entrance to the necropolis.

He was about to enter when his phone warbled the melody of *Faith of Our Fathers.*

Irritated, he turned away from his companions and placed the phone to his ear. "Yes?"

"Auguste— a brief word." Father Burgholzer's basso profundo, a clogged bassoon of a voice, was instantly recognizable.

"By *phone?*"

"Exigency overrides protocols. His Holiness is preparing to move against you. If he learns that he wasn't consulted concerning the hidden item..."

Chavet prepared to bluff out the exchange. His authority relied on the good will of fewer than a dozen men within Conclave's elusive network. The Austrian priest Burgholzer was one of those men, lower in ecclesiastical rank, but in the protean power structure of Conclave, almost an equal. One false step and Burgholzer would be his superior.

"No evidence will be left for His Holiness to find," he smoothly reassured. "The item will be removed to a secure location in a few days."

"So soon?"

"The archeological team is close to circumventing the wall. It would be unfitting for a secular team to stumble upon any sacred... item."

"Agreed. But a majority of our associates have decided that the item should be researched on site. You are authorized to breach the wall and confirm the existence of the item— no more. It must *not* be moved, it must not be touched."

He tried to preserve a calm, convincing tone despite his accelerating heartbeat. "I will do as our associates direct. To the letter."

"We expect no less. But we have other concerns. A considerable sum has been diverted from the Vatican bank and simply— disappeared. One line of inquiry leads to your office. And

Substratum has raised questions about your extensive use of its facilities over the last ten days."

Chavet considered a lie, then opted for the delaying tactic. "Complex matters, inextricably related. I will explain the intricacies of the situation to the group's full satisfaction at our next conclave on Friday morning."

"I'm sure you will. As for the details of how you should proceed with the necropolis enterprise, we'll discuss those on Friday. This conversation did not occur."

"Of course. Till tomorrow."

Chavet pocketed the phone. *Tomorrow, Burgholzer, will be too late.*

At a nod from Chavet, Officer De Mola unlocked the *Ufficio Scavi* door. Signaling the Vigilanza to stay put, the cardinal entered the *Scavi* office, crossed the reception area and descended the steps of a narrow stairway, sparsely illuminated by small lamps. He soon passed the fourth-century foundations of the first basilica of Constantine and continued down to the second-century level where both the mausolea of pagans and the tomb of St. Peter resided.

He walked down a tunnel for thirty yards, then turned west and followed the path between the brickwork façades of second- and third-century tombs with their stucco decorations and faded frescoes.

Drawing close to St. Peter's tomb, situated directly beneath the basilica's main altar, he turned south and passed through a transparent climate-control door and proceeded down a new tunnel that terminated in a wall adorned with a nondescript fresco.

Only four of the Scavi team were present, one in the process of restoring the fresco, two occupied in the task of forming a passage to the left of the wall, and one, the Scavi director, rising from a study of his laptop. The director, as usual, was dressed sloppily, hairy chest peeking between the unbuttoned flaps of his stained shirt, plump legs sprouting from khaki shorts.

Chavet nodded curtly to the director. "Doctor. Hope all is well. You are requested to ensure your staff quit the premises by eight at the latest. And not to return until noon tomorrow."

Doctor Verecchia gave him a wry look. "Requested, or ordered?"

"Requested, if you accede. If not, ordered."

Verecchia snorted. "Eight o'clock is out of the question. We'll be gone by ten; best I can do."

Irked by the man's obstinacy, Chavet was tempted to have it out with him here and now, witnesses be damned, but controlled himself. The Vigilanza would eject the team by eight p.m. whether or not the director liked it.

"Ten p.m., then," he sighed. "The request has been delivered, let that suffice."

Verecchia's eyes gazed heavenward, mouth grimacing. "Never let it be said I let progress stand in the way of tradition."

Letting the remark pass, the cardinal walked up to the wall, his gaze roving the fresco which showed little of its original imagery despite the ongoing restoration. At the base of the wall an ancient graffito had been inscribed:

TRANSITUS MARIÆ

The archeological team dismissed the inscription as no more than an interesting scribble. He knew better.

He stood in front of the Transitus Wall, immersed in reflection. The location of the wall, first discovered in 1950 by a team including Father Jonathan Taylor, had been expunged from all records by order of Pius XII just as the excavated tunnel to the wall had been filled in. But it was impossible to erase knowledge of the general area. It was equally impossible to silence rumors of Father Taylor's reputed vision of what lay beyond the wall, a vision first confided to Pius XII. Now no one knew, or ever would know, what the priest witnessed. All that remained were the words Father Taylor murmured on his knees before the Transitus Wall: "Mary abides... Mene, mene, tekel, upharsin."

Chavet was convinced that Father Taylor's quote from the Book of Daniel was a warning that the Church would be destroyed if the secrets of Mary were revealed. For six decades that danger had been averted.

Three months ago, everything changed.

The structure was rediscovered in an excavation of a north-south passage leading from the southernmost of the necropolis streets and was immediately identified as a partition wall. Ultrasonographic readings indicated an extensive open space beyond it. A chamber, or a series of chambers close to the foundations of Nero's circus.

The wall, its core composed of *opus caementicium*, ancient Roman concrete, faced with igneous tufa rock and a coating of plaster, bore a barely decipherable fresco that was as uninspiring as it was dilapidated. An unrecognizable bird. A vase. A nude human figure so poorly executed that its gender was beyond guesswork.

The fresco was of no account. The location of the partition wall, however, was of supreme significance. The Transitus Mariæ identified the site of the Virgin Mary's tomb as close to the north wall of Nero's circus, two hundred Roman *pedes* due south of the tomb of Peter, over sixty yards by modern measurement. On the far side of the wall were the foundations of the ancient circus where charioteers once raised their hands to the acclaim of patricians and plebeians. And, beneath those foundations, the Chamber of the Dormition. In a few hours...

It was a pity, he mused, that Monsignor Aylesbury wouldn't be here to witness the final act. Despite becoming enemies, they had once been friends.

Unconsciously, his hand had stretched out to touch the wall as his mind imagined it tumbling before the sledgehammers.

"Your Eminence!"

Retracting his hand, he glanced down apologetically at the young woman engaged in restoring the fresco.

"Excuse, Eminence," she said in a subdued tone, "but you might have blemished it."

He smiled benignly. "Wouldn't that be a shame?"

Chapter 34

After half an hour drifting aimlessly around the apartment, picking up books, dropping them, pointlessly checking for e-mails on the phone, Dominic braced himself to achieve the impossible. Get down to work and put thoughts of Rachel to one side.

Getting down to work wasn't working too well. Relegating Rachel to the cognitive sidelines wasn't working at all. But he persisted, marshaling his thoughts as he organized his notes. Whatever Martha had told him about Silentium, whatever anyone might tell him, he had to reach his own conclusions. After several hours, he was getting there.

Conspiracy theories of history reveled in highly organized secret societies that survived through the ages, plotting for good or ill, but in the real world such cabals would struggle to remain covert for a couple of decades, never mind sixteen centuries. The revamped Marian religion of the Shrine lasted a mere six years from its foundation in 1972. The notion of an underground Silentium coordinated by masterminds down the centuries was right up there with the Bond villain's secret base and the Priory of Sion. It was, simply, ridiculous.

So, where to look for proof of a Marian religion? He leaned back, his stare roving the high ceiling. Aside from its chronicling by Epiphanius, some proof of Collyridian worship must have come to light sometime, somewhere.

And maybe it had, unrecognized.

He picked up the laptop and reviewed a couple of passages he'd jotted down in the morning. The first passage referred to a fragment of a third-century Greek prayer, the *Sub tuum praesidium*. Translated, it read:

Under your protection we take refuge, Mother of God. Heed our supplications: suffer us not to be in adversity, but deliver us from danger.

Two centuries before Mary was acclaimed Mother of God at Ephesus, the unknown composer of the prayer addressed her by that same title. And the wording resembled, all too closely, a line from the Lord's Prayer: "lead us not into temptation, but deliver us from evil." It put Mary in the place of Christ.

The second passage, comprised of brief extracts from a long poem, mysteriously entitled "Thunder, Perfect Mind," was a Coptic translation from the original Greek, most likely from second-century Alexandria. As he reread the extracts, his first impression of the identity of the goddess behind the poem was confirmed:

I was sent forth from the power...
I am the honored and the scorned one.
I am the whore and the holy one.
I am the wife and the virgin...
I am war and peace...
I am the one whose image is exalted in Egypt
and the one who has no image among the barbarians...

Scholars were almost unanimous in identifying the feminine divine power that spoke those lines as Isis. He, however, believed he was looking at a Collyridian declaration. Perhaps the notion that Mary was the female deity in the poem hadn't taken hold because statements such as "I am the whore" and "I am war" clashed head on with the traditional image of the Madonna. But from what little he'd learned of the Apocryphon Mariæ, Mary was a paradox, like the divine voice behind the poem.

He leaned back in the sofa, rubbing the nape of his neck as he began to form an overview.

The triumph of Christianity's male deity in the fourth century hadn't persuaded the people of the late Roman empire to forget the former goddesses, such as the Greek Artemis, worshipped in the Artemiseum of Ephesus, one of the seven wonders of the ancient world. On the borders of the empire and in hidden places at its heart, the Collyridians propagated the image of Mary as a deity, invested with the enchantment of lost female divinities.

By the fifth century, the Church was faced with a Pyrrhic victory: having taken over the Roman imperium, it inherited a falling empire. Disenchanted Christians deserted the Church in droves. The Church elders reached a compromise with their disgruntled flocks. The goddess-shaped hole in their religion had to be filled without obliterating their Christ-centered credo. The "Collyridian" Mary fitted that goddess-shaped vacancy. The First Council of Ephesus in 431, a gathering of Church leaders tasked with defining the nature of Christ and the status of Mary, absorbed what Collyridian elements it could, ascribing divine attributes to Mary, now Virgin Mother of the Christian Church, Mother of God, and Queen of Heaven.

Although second only to God, Mary never sat easily on her subordinate throne. The inclusion of a deified Mary was essentially an attempt to square the triangle of the Trinity. Time and again, her flourishing cult eclipsed that of her son, not least in the Middle Ages when it was to Mary, not Christ, that most supplicants had recourse in time of trouble.

Silentium, after the Council of Ephesus, was more an idea than an organization. That's how it survived the fall of Rome and the rise of Europe. But, in the end, Silentium failed. The Christian religion ingested the Marian religion, with whatever dogmatic indigestion. By the end of the Middle Ages, when popes had the power to enthrone and dethrone secular rulers, the long process of reducing Mary back to her pious, literally virginal role was underway.

He broke off and glanced at the clock. Almost six. Martha should have been back by now. Putting the laptop aside, he walked to the window.

He felt like a dog on a leash. And he wanted to be let slip, preferably to a cry of havoc. Leaning against the glass, he peered down into the fog. The lane was scarcely visible with the density of the mist and the distance to the ground, a twenty-meter-plus drop. The apartment was well-situated to keep intruders out. Unfortunately, it also prevented him from getting back in if he went out onto the streets.

"Martha," he murmured, "hurry back. Let's take the fight to them."

Chapter 35

As prisons go, Rachel conceded, it wasn't the pits, although it was in the basement. She was confined in a former wine cellar, evidenced by several musty-smelling wooden racks in a far corner. A flight of worn stone steps led up to a formidable oak door, triple locked. The sole items of furniture were two chairs on each side of a weathered table. She leaned against the padded backrest of her chair. As prisons went, it could be worse.

The same couldn't be said about the company. She couldn't have found any worse in hell.

Jones sat in the chair opposite, motionless. She saw nothing behind those uneventful eyes. At first she couldn't get a fix on the absence. Then she identified it. There was no soul behind those eyes. No hint of good, but no sense of evil either. Just— no soul.

Deacon had taken up a position directly behind her chair, a claw hammer in his hand.

Just terror tactics, she told herself. I won't let it get to me. The accelerating tempo of her heart disagreed.

"Put your right hand on the table." Jones's voice was devoid of any human quality, not even menace. "I'll flip a coin. Heads, the hand gets the hammer. Tails, we move on. If you keep those arms folded, no flip of the coin. The shoulder gets hit. Bone gets shattered. Your choice."

"You're not going to ask me any questions?" She cursed inwardly at the shake in her voice. And fought the urge to turn and check what Deacon was up to. She could feel his damn breath down the back of her neck.

"Sure. If your hand's on the table. And if I like the answers, I won't flip the coin. You get to keep your fingers. Everybody's happy."

Jones could be bluffing but the man was unreadable. There were rules about harm to Crypt outsiders, but perhaps the rule book had been thrown out. Hadn't Martha warned as much in the Forum?

She shrugged. "Fine, I'll play your game." She planted her hand flat on the rough grain of the table's surface. And that's all it is, a game, she affirmed inwardly, trying to keep her hand from trembling.

"Spread the fingers wide," Jones ordered. "Don't want to mash two at a time. And don't turn around— mustn't spoil Deacon's little surprise if the hammer comes down. If you turn around— got some pliers in my pocket, the right size for your fingernails."

Pulse thudding, she spread her fingers, wide as possible.

"Okay then," he said. "Where's Quinn?"

"No idea."

Jones tossed the coin and caught it in his cupped palm, hidden from her sight. "Remember, girl— don't look round." He glanced above her head and gave Deacon the nod.

She stopped herself looking over her shoulder at the last instant. Shut her eyes tight. The pause lengthened excruciatingly. Finally her eyes opened.

The hammer thudded down. The wood shuddered from top to table leg.

Rachel stifled a scream. Then saw that the hammer had landed two inches from her hand.

"Tails," Jones said. "First time lucky."

Her heart was banging against her ribs. "Lucky me."

"Second chance. Where's Quinn?"

"How can I tell you if I don't know?"

Expressionless, he flipped the coin and gave it a quick glance. He nodded to Deacon.

Another pause, drawn out to make her sweat.

The hammer crashed down. She bit back a cry at the judder of the wood.

But the hammer rested an inch from her hand.

"Tails again. Lucky girl. Wanna try for third time lucky?"

For a moment she was tempted. The moment passed.

"Go fuck yourself, Jones."

He sat quietly for several seconds. Leaned back in the chair.

Then gave a nod.

"Jones!"

Her gaze swerved to the door at the top of the cellar steps. It was ajar, a tall, thin priest standing in the narrow gap. The owner of the imperious voice pushed the door wider. "Young lady, would you accompany me please? I am Cardinal Chavet."

She needed no further bidding to spring up and hasten to the stairs. As she reached the cardinal, he aimed a stern look at her tormentors. "You were warned. One more transgression and your overly generous funds will be curtailed." He bent what she assumed was meant to be a smile. "Miss Gurevich, come with me."

As she followed him out of the basement, Jones's voice tracked her. "You're about to get a change of scenery, girl. You won't like the view."

The door swung shut behind her.

Chapter 36

Doctor Verrecchia dropped the trowel in the toolbox and wiped the sweat from his forehead. It was always warm and stifling in the necropolis. Not hot, not suffocating, and hardly a trace of humidity, but oppressive enough over long periods.

His team, mostly graduates fresh from Rome's Università della Sapienza, had put in long hours on the new excavations. It was little more than a month since they fully uncovered the partition wall. Restoration work on the wall's frescoes had been slow, the images almost obliterated with time, and the task of tunneling around the wall arduous, constantly delayed by unforeseen obstacles, both physical and bureaucratic.

Cardinal Chavet had been a major obstacle all by himself. By rights, the prelate should have no authority over necropolis excavations. According to the Vatican website, Chavet's sphere of influence lay in international diplomacy. But the cardinal had interfered with the excavation from the beginning, forbidding this, demanding that.

But then, he wasn't inclined to argue with a cardinal of the Catholic Church when he was engaged by the Vatican to work beneath the floor of St. Peter's. His team would be gone by the compromise time of ten p.m. and wouldn't resume until the following noon, as ordered.

Interesting, how that strange British priest, Father Thomas Chen, had seemed to expect some such order from Cardinal Chavet, predicting that Chavet would demand the site be cleared of non-Vatican staff at some point in the near future. When that happened, he had agreed to inform Father Thomas immediately.

The priest had done him a favor, almost three months ago, by tipping him off to a new excavation in the necropolis, the potential site of an undiscovered chamber. The archeologist promptly put in a successful bid for the excavation.

He picked up a bottle of mineral water, took a swig, then headed up the passage to the main area of the necropolis, taking care to shut the transparent climate control door securely behind him.

The necropolis was empty of tourists, the Scavi tours long since finished for the day, and he took the opportunity to stroll around the fully excavated passages while he sought a signal from his phone.

No matter how many weeks and months he worked in the necropolis, he could never shake off its somber spell as he could its strong earthy odor. It was, in truth, a city of the dead, and each funeral house he passed reminded him of the fact. Many visitors came expecting cells or caves. What they found were small replica houses lining miniature streets, once open to the air, now buried for sixteen centuries. The two main streets were laid out parallel to one another in an east-west orientation, and the grim brickwork façade of many of the houses contained elaborate stucco decorations, frescoes and mosaics surrounding opulent sarcophagi.

And inside the sarcophagi and humbler tombs and loculi, the remains of the dead resided, either inhumed or cremated from the second to the fourth century. The north street was predominantly proto-Christian, the south chiefly Pagan. Whatever religious disputes had bubbled and frothed in that distant time, the dead in the necropolis had long since arrived at a truce, theological disagreements buried under a weight of years. To Verrecchia's eyes the silent streets housed not simple Pagans and Christians, but Christian Pagans and Pagan Christians. In the tomb of Caetennius Antigonus was an image of a woman drawing water, an image that might be Pagan, might be Christian, might be a meld of both. In the vault of the second-century Julian mausoleum was a fresco of Christ as Helios, sun god, driving a chariot. Not Pagan. Not Christian. Christian Pagan. In Rome, Alexandria, Antioch,

Ephesus, and Corinth, Christianity was born as much from ancient mysteries as from gospel verses.

The doctor left the southern street and threaded one of the alleys that led to the northern corridor and a small piazza flanked by three mausolea, site of the discovery of the reputed bones of St. Peter.

He moved on a few steps and came to a halt inside an ornate, tiny chapel from which, through a round aperture, the *confessio* was visible, the Niche of the Pallium that fronted the main altar of St. Peter's basilica directly above his head. A reverential murmur sifted down from the niche, intimating that a mass was underway.

Mass or no mass, this spot, the only one in the necropolis with open access to the basilica, provided a guaranteed strong signal for his phone.

He held up the phone. Fine, three bars on the screen. He name-dialed Thomas Chen and waited several seconds before a voice answered.

"Thomas Chen speaking. What can I do for you?" The Italian was fluent but with a trace of an English accent.

"It's Doctor Verrecchia. You asked me to call you if Cardinal Chavet ordered us out of the necropolis for any reason. He has. He insisted we leave by eight."

"This is *earlier* than usual?" The tone was subtly amused.

"I've been known to work until midnight," he riposted. "Oh yes, and we're not to return until midday tomorrow. But I told Chavet we'll be here until ten tonight. He went along with it. He had no choice."

"He agreed that you can stay until ten, are you sure?" There was no trace of amusement now but rather a sober deliberation.

"Sure I'm sure. Ten p.m. So— now you know. Mind telling me what this is about?"

"Ah— there are some people I wanted you to meet. Unfortunately, they haven't arrived yet. There's been some difficulty. It may be the plan has to be abandoned."

Verrecchia frowned. "What plan?"

A brief pause. "Barring the unlikely event of my friends turning up very soon, let's just say you should prepare to breach the Transitus Wall well before ten."

"Smash through a fifth-century fresco!" Verrecchia exclaimed in disbelief. "Why the hell would I do that?"

"Because what's beyond the Transitus Wall justifies it. Should my friends make an appearance in time, we'll come to you and I'll answer all your questions."

"The Transitus Wall. Why do you call it that, just because of some old graffito? Don't tell me you're taking the Passing of Mary reference seriously."

Another pause, significantly longer. "In a manner of speaking, yes."

Verrecchia groaned inwardly. With what he'd learned of Father Chen, he should have guessed. He really should have guessed. "In that case, count me out. Listen— I respect your academic qualifications— but you're a priest, and I'm not. I don't believe in magical tombs, nor do I expect to find the Lost Ark or the True Cross or the Seven Sleepers of Ephesus. And— I checked your background. The years you spent searching for the Virgin Mary's sarcophagus, first in Jerusalem, then Ephesus." He drew a breath. "No offense, Father Thomas, but I'm not a believer, just a dull-as-dust archeologist. Whatever's on the other side of the partition wall, we'll locate it soon enough by tunneling around."

The response was hesitant. "Would you, ah, believe me if I told you that Cardinal Chavet is most likely intending to breach the wall tonight?"

"Why would he do that? He's a pain in the ass but that's— ridiculous. And even if that were true, I haven't the authority to stop him."

"No, but you could break through ahead of him."

Verrecchia had physically drawn back a few inches from the phone and mentally distanced himself several miles. "Smash through a fresco because Chavet might do the same thing later... Yeah, that makes sense. Again, no offense, but I have work to do. So, um, *ciao*."

"Doctor, I give you my word... what is beyond that wall will change the world. Please, at least think about it."

"Oh, sure. I'll give it serious thought." *Like hell.* "Must go. I'll be in touch— sometime." He terminated the connection and pocketed the phone.

"Back to work," he muttered to himself as he retraced his steps back to the southern street. Although starting to regret his brusqueness with the priest, he kept to his opinion of the man's gullibility. He had assumed Father Chen had grown out of his youthful follies. A mistaken assumption.

"Back to work," he repeated as he passed through the climate-control door. He plodded down the tunnel to the partition wall, retrieved his trowel, and hunkered down to the task.

Then his glance strayed to the rough inscription on the wall:

TRANSITUS MARIÆ

It was nothing. No real significance. The necropolis was covered in ancient graffiti, vandalism sanctified to religious heritage by the passage of time.

On the other hand, he recalled his initial sensation on discovering the wall. He hesitated to call it dread, too melodramatic a word. But no other word came close.

And, as though that recollection had summoned its inspiration, from nowhere, for no reason he could fathom, he felt that breath of dread again. It was akin to standing on the threshold of a sacred danger: a holy, forbidden place.

I've let Father Chen get to me.

He told himself there was nothing to fear; his fear told him otherwise. A sense of something inviolate, beyond the wall, challenged any desecrator to trespass. Here was no sense of evil, but the menace of divinity.

Grinding his teeth, Doctor Verrecchia set to work on the side tunnel, determined not to let his imagination get the better of him.

Minute by minute, the presentiment abated.

But from time to time, in reflex action, he glanced at the wall, and at the archaic inscription:

TRANSITUS MARIÆ

Part Three

"Our birth is but a sleep and a forgetting:
The soul that rises with us, our life's star,
Hath had elsewhere its setting,
And cometh from afar."

William Wordsworth

Chapter 37

She stood in the tenement's lobby, hands thrust in her navy blue raincoat pockets, at the bottom of a flight of grubby steps leading up through the building's six floors. The grimy walls were barely visible in the low-level illumination of a bare light bulb. The stench of stale urine permeated the air.

"Home sour home."

Maria commenced the climb to the topmost floor, her gray sneakers occasionally squelching in puddles of dubious origin. Six flights later she halted at a door that exhibited more bare wood than blistered paint and a grimy plaque displaying the occupant's name: Moretti.

"A bad goodbye."

She pulled out a hairgrip from the back pocket of her jeans, made short shrift of picking the simple lock, pushed open the door, and strode into the apartment.

The two occupants, a middle-aged man and woman, looked up in astonishment, mouths agape.

Maria gave them a nod. "Hi."

They sat immobile, speechless.

"This is a fine welcome, I must say," Maria remarked, strolling across the red-tiled floor to the couple seated by the table. "A year away and this is all I get?"

The man jumped to his feet. "Bambolina!"

Maria shook her head. "Not any more. I'm nobody's puppet—least of all yours."

He glared raw anger as he sank into his chair. "You leave home and then hitch up with that foreigner Father Thomas Chen. I know what you are." He all but spat out the words: *"Imbecile Madonna."*

"Charmed, I'm sure." Maria turned to the woman. "Vincente here broke up my childhood games and introduced me to his more— adult ones. Is that news to you, Benedetta?"

"She hasn't spoken like that, ever," the woman whispered. "Vincente, our daughter sounds— normal. And— what did she mean— about adult games?"

"She's no longer our daughter!" His fury broke in full flood, launching him to his feet. "She's possessed!" He lurched at Maria with a clumsy swing.

She parried the blow and responded with a kick to the stomach. It hurled him back into his chair, which tipped over and sent him sprawling.

Vincente glared up from the floor, fear slowly ousting anger. "You're possessed..."

She shrugged. "Well, you've got that right."

The woman rose nervously to her feet, her gaze a mixture of fear and hope as she shuffled forward. "Bambolina... Do you know who I am?"

"Of course I do, Benedetta. Mama. And don't call me Bambolina. I told you, I'm no puppet. Nobody pulls my strings anymore."

Benedetta engulfed Maria in a hug. "Maria... God has cured you! You're no longer an imbecile!"

Maria grimaced. "That could have been better phrased. But— thanks, I guess."

Benedetta turned to her husband, eyes shining. "Vincente, our Bambolina, she is no longer backward like a little child." Noticing that he was struggling to rise, she rushed to his side. "Did she hurt you badly?"

"One can but hope," Maria muttered, turning her back on the couple and strolling across the room. She stopped at the mantelpiece, picking up a framed photograph.

The photograph showed a nineteen-year-old woman in a stained dress sitting cross-legged on the tiled floor, blue socks concertinaed around her ankles, mouth dribbling, childlike eyes staring up at the camera in a mixture of fear and incomprehension.

With the tip of her finger, Maria stroked the image of the woman with the mind of a two-year-old. "Poor Maria. So lost in the dark. Midnight's soul. But all's well now. All's well now, Maria."

"Now she talks to her own picture," Vincente muttered. "That is the devil in her."

Maria turned around. "The only devil here is you and your... grown-up games with your Bambolina."

Benedetta drew close to her husband, held his arm tight. "What are you saying, Maria? Vincente would never do anything— bad— to his daughter."

Maria's mouth curved in a humorless smile. "I knew you'd say that."

"Vincente is a good man, he really is."

"No, he really isn't. Sorry, Benedetta, there's no more to say. Don't know why I came." She moved to the door past a scowling but subdued Vincente. "Well, must rush. Things to do. Places to be."

"Where in the world are you going?" Benedetta called out.

"There are many worlds."

Leaving them staring after her in stupefaction, Maria shut the door and descended the stairs to the lobby where her Vespa was chained to the newel post.

She made haste to unlock the chain and prepared to head out. As she'd told her parents upstairs, she was in a rush. Things to do. Places to be.

A world to overturn.

Chapter 38

The music ended.

Dominic stood in silence, staring out the window. The street below was empty. The room felt emptier. Another look at his watch. Almost seven. Why no word from Martha?

He swung away from the window and knelt by the hi-fi, ejecting the Roy Orbison CD, then opting for Allegri's *Miserere*.

As the seventeenth-century motet surged into the room, he moved to the sofa and sank onto the thick cushions. The sleep debt since Monday was catching up with him. His vision periodically unfocused and a low-level hum bedeviled his inner ear. He picked up the phone and dialed Martha's number, an action he'd performed so often in the last hour that he could have accomplished it blindfolded. After a moment, the familiar message sounded in his ear. Unobtainable. The word had a terminal ring.

He was on the verge of dialing again when an incoming e-mail showed up. Eagerly, he downloaded it and read the text in the upper screen:

Forwarding this from Martha. I expect to see you soon.

Best wishes,
Thomas Chen.

And underneath, the original message:

Hi Dominic,

Figure it's time you heard the whole story. Here's something I prepared earlier, just in case. Thomas Chen will contact you with further instructions. There's plenty of food in the kitchen. Don't break anything.

Your adoring fan, Martha

Attached to the message was an mpeg. Mary's apocryphon. Any historian would have given his eyeteeth, and maybe the full set of ivories, to hold what he held in his hand. He downloaded the file, pressed play, and leaned back in the sofa, stifling an involuntary yawn. He was deep into the redeye zone.

Martha's voice issued from the laptop, uncharacteristically formal:

"A summary of the Apocryphon Mariæ drawn from second and third century Greek and Syriac analecta of primary Ephesian source.

"Mary's parents resided in Bethany, outside Jerusalem's east wall, but when her mother, Hannah, went into labor she was in Bethlehem..."

He let the narrative run on until it reached the point where she left off earlier in the day, where it jumped a number of years. Ignoring the demands of sleep, he paid closer attention...

"Some years after Judas joined the *Sicarii*, John the Baptist, or Mad John as Mary refers to him, visited Nazareth, determined to lead Jesus into the holy war between the Sons of Light and the Sons of Darkness. The reference to Sons of Light and Sons of Darkness clearly establishes John as a member of the Essenes, the most puritanical sect in first-century Judaism. Jesus followed his cousin to what John called the 'City of Light,' the settlement now known as Qumran by the Dead Sea. John then instigated armed insurrection against Antipas and Philip, the sons of Herod. Within a year he led an army numbering up to five thousand and set up camp in a desert in the region of Gilead, where Jesus exhorted the followers 'not to eat of the bread of the Herodians'. There was also a secret Essene message involving the numbers of baskets of loaves and fishes eaten by the insurgents. When John was captured by the forces of Antipas and later executed, his former followers acclaimed Jesus as king of the Jews. Mary writes that 'John's mantle became Jesus' shroud.' Faced with leading the army as a warrior Messiah, Jesus escaped the camp at night and literally made for the hills.

"The next three years are even more patchy. It was during Judas' marriage feast at Cana that Mary, Jesus, Simon Magus, and others planned a root and branch reform of the Jewish faith, combining it with Greek and Syrian mystery cults. According to the Gospel of John, Jesus, at the bidding of Mary, changed the water in six amphorae into wine. In the apocryphon, each of these amphorae represented a man or woman as a vessel whose indwelling spirit can be redeemed from its former state. Jesus promised to reveal 'secrets hidden from the creation of the world,' a phrase echoed in Matthew, chapter thirteen, verse thirty-five, and which Mary's apocryphon identifies as theories of time and space from the Library of Alexandria. Simon of Gitta, the historical Simon Magus, for his part, put forward the figure of Wisdom— Sophia in Greek— as a personification of the feminine aspect of God. Wisdom, or Sophia, figured in several books of the Old Testament.

"And a full fifteen centuries after Simon Magus, Michelangelo, in painting the Sistine Chapel ceiling, was to place Sophia on God the Father's left side with his arm embracing her. Essentially, the family group at Cana supplanted the male Yahweh with a matropater, a Mother-Father deity.

"In the second year of Pontius Pilate's rule as praefectus of Judaea, Mary set up her community of friends on Mount Carmel. Soon, news of trouble came from Jerusalem. Mary hurried south only to witness Jesus' crucifixion, which almost unhinged her. In the following days Jesus' followers claimed to have seen their teacher resurrected. Mary, however, never saw him, much as she wanted to believe.

"After the crucifixion, Mary survived less than a year. She left Mount Carmel for the city of Ephesus, joined there by Simon Magus and his future wife Helena of Tyre. It was in a sea-facing cave south of the city that the early parts of the Apocryphon Mariæ were written. And it was in that cave, at the age of forty-five, that Mary died. Extensive additions to the apocryphon were composed some years afterward by Simon Magus and Helena. It's in these later writings that the strange events surrounding Mary's passing are recounted. So— ah— end of summary."

A few seconds later the mpeg terminated.

He lay still for several minutes, legs stretched out on the sofa. Perhaps he'd expected too much from the recording but he'd hoped it would cover Mary's mysterious dormition. He was willing to suspend disbelief, take Martha at her word, at least for a while, but the crux of the story was missing. He was left in limbo, with no signposts. The whole Collyridian case rested on the manner of her passing. What happened *after* Mary died? What was the "exceeding great marvel" that Epiphanius refused to disclose?

Or had he overlooked something?

Chapter 39

The Monsignor fidgeted in a back pew in the church of Il Gesù. How much longer would they keep him waiting?

Expelling a heavy breath, he shifted restlessly in his seat as his vision roved the opulent interior of Il Gesù, the spacious nave designed by Vignola, originally unadorned in the sixteenth century, its plain marble later smothered in gold, gold, and more gold with an abundance of lapis lazuli, overtopped by Baciccio's flamboyant ceiling frescoes. The founder of the Jesuits, St. Ignatius Loyola, would have cast an unfavorable eye on the present church. But then, the saint would be less than enamored of the Monsignor's mission.

The news that he was to be traded for Rachel had come as a harsh blow. The thought of gaining his freedom at the cost of Rachel's was unconscionable.

He sighed in relief at the sight of Monsignor Federico Ortega approaching from the church's side entrance. At last. The stocky, fifty-year-old priest, his hair prematurely chalk white, was dressed in his customary blue jeans and brown leather jacket. His expression, however, was unusually sober.

Ortega walked up to him and indicated the side entrance. "I apologize for the delay. If you'd come with me..." If the Spaniard's expression was sober, his tone was downright solemn.

He rose and followed Ortega to the side door that led to the apartments of St. Ignatius and a busy office complex.

"You don't seem too pleased to see me, Federico."

"You could say that, Martin."

They passed into the St. Ignatius apartments with their *trompe-l'oeil* frescoes, then turned a corner into a carpeted passageway lined with heavily varnished doors. Ortega opened one of the doors and stepped into a small office. The two men settled into leather chairs beside a low table.

"So, you wanted to see the Vicar General," Ortega began without preamble. "What makes you think he'd want to see you?"

"Because the matter is urgent, Federico."

"With you, is it ever anything else?" He cast a disapproving glance at the Monsignor's crucifix ring. "I'm surprised you enter a Jesuit church with a Petrus Pontifex ring on your finger."

"There was a time Conclave was convinced I was on their side. It's not easy playing a double game."

"The trouble with a double game is that it requires a two-faced player. Whose side are you on?"

"My own, ultimately," the Monsignor admitted. "But that almost invariably coincides with Jesuit interests."

"How convenient." The Spaniard made a show of studying the back of his hand. "I heard that you visited London. Why?"

"I got a call from Father Jonathan Taylor. He used code phrases to indicate he was in danger and that it was urgent we meet. I suspected he was willing to pass on his secret— the vision he witnessed before the Transitus wall."

"Jonathan's vision," Ortega groaned. "Jonathan's delusion. If Pope Pius hadn't panicked at seeing an old graffito on a wall and hearing an impressionable priest's so-called secret, the purported wall would have been breached decades ago and the space beyond revealed as just another tomb of some Roman nonentity."

"Well, that's your opinion, frequently expressed. But let's bear in mind that you don't even believe in your own religion."

Ortega frowned. "Of course I believe in it. Catholicism is a political necessity, just as God is a valid hypothesis." He waved a dismissive hand. "Tell me what happened in London. Did you reach Jonathan before Deacon got to him?"

"You know about Deacon?"

"We're Jesuit HQ. We know everything worth knowing."

"Still suffering from delusions of adequacy, I see. No, Deacon got to him first. But Jonathan left a message: a Belshazzar warning."

"Ah, yes, the Belshazzar warning," Ortega murmured. "Mene, mene, tekel, upharsin. I suppose you have a theory about that?"

"As a matter of fact, I do."

Ortega leaned back in his chair. "Then enlighten me."

A red tip of a cigarette flared in the dark, then dropped to the paving stones and was extinguished under a hiking boot.

Carson blew out a plume of smoke that mingled with the fog. Calabrese, squat, bull-necked, and sporting a long ponytail, stood at his side, indifferent to cold and damp. The two men maintained their watch on the church of Il Gesù from the far side of the Piazza del Gesù.

He had phoned Jones the moment he witnessed the Monsignor enter the church. His orders were to report back the instant the priest left. Carson had no intention of following orders. Better to shadow the priest and see if he led them to Quinn. He wanted to send the Yank screaming from the world, personally. Jones would understand.

The somber façade of the church was a phantom behind the mist, the door scarcely visible. He would need to keep his eyes sharp to spot the Monsignor leave. And then, yes, then he would follow.

The Monsignor lapsed into silence as, for a moment, he recalled the silent Lady Chapel of St. Mary's, the morning light streaming through the windows on both walls, crisscrossed beams. And Jonathan's slack body, slumped in the pew.

Ortega inclined his head, waiting for the priest to continue.

The Monsignor inhaled a deep breath. "The Belshazzar message was, in my opinion, a simple warning that the Transitus wall excavations were about to unearth a secret that would shatter the Church into a dozen hostile provinces."

"You, of course, don't agree with Jonathan's assessment."

"I suspect his warning was directed at me— don't penetrate the Transitus wall or schism will result. I don't accept that analysis. Schism is a process already at work. Our own order has a sizeable splinter group of moral relativizers with their blather about situational ethics. In my view, the faith of the Collyridians will renew Christianity in the twenty-first century just as it did in the fifth."

"With Jonathan gone," Ortega said, "you're the only one left who credits the supposed Chamber of the Dormition with— what— otherworldly power? The luminaries of Conclave may believe there's a sarcophagus containing Mary's remains, but— an indwelling presence? Human amphorae to be filled with the wine of divinity? Water to wine, a spiritual equivalent of the marriage feast of Cana? Colorful legends."

"If you wish to disprove what you call legends, then send a team of Sodality agents into the necropolis. Chavet will breach the Transitus wall at ten tonight. If your men go in an hour later, you'll catch Chavet close to the Dormition Chamber, with incontrovertible proof he plans to destroy the sarcophagus, against Conclave's express prohibition. No one will complain about violation of Vatican sovereignty."

Ortega leaned back, arms folded. "If Chavet took such a foolhardy course, his career would be over."

"He doesn't care. He's obsessed."

"Ah— obsessed. You should know all about that. On the wild assumption that the Indwelling legends are true, what makes you think we'd want them revealed? Evidence of Mary as co-equal with Christ would split the Church into Christian and Marian factions, with Islam the ultimate victor. Constantinople has already fallen, its crescent and star flag appropriated by the followers of Allah. Unless we remain vigilant, Rome will be next."

The Monsignor gave a vigorous shake of the head. "The old Islamic threat. Now who's obsessed? We defeated Muslim invasions from the eighth century to the seventeenth. All we need do is recover our soul— the spirit of Mary. It was under her standard that we fought the invaders of the past."

Ortega lifted a silencing hand. "Before you launch into another of your Marian eulogies, understand this— since the Iron Curtain fell, an Iron Veil has been raised. Christianity is under attack, yet again. And this time we have no Charles Martel or Jan Sobieski on our side, instead we have a decadent West that has forgotten its origins, lost its heart. The priority is to ensure the integrity of the Church, which a resurgent Collyridian heresy would fracture."

The ensuing silence was so thick it coagulated.

At length Ortega spoke in a more subdued tone. "We shouldn't be arguing. It's just that— God, the damage you've caused." Ortega's unusual somberness acquired extra gravity. "You had better see this. It was e-mailed to us twenty minutes ago."

He leaned to one side, opened a desk drawer, and withdrew what appeared to be a printout.

The Monsignor took the sheet from Ortega and held it up. The image on the printout was high definition, each detail portrayed with cruel clarity.

Martha, hanged by the neck from a bridge, tongue bulging from her open mouth. Her eyes, too, were open.

Somewhere, on the far side of the world, a man was speaking.

"Martin?"

Martha, hanged...

"Martin?"

Martha...

"Martin!"

He came to with a shudder to witness Ortega leaning over him. "Oh... yes, Federico. I was— I lost track... for a moment."

"It was more like a minute," the Spaniard said gently. "I have some brandy in the cabinet. If you..."

"Brandy? No. No brandy. Just— give me a moment." He placed the printout on the table, very delicately, as if too sudden a motion might hurt it. "Tell me what happened."

Ortega nodded. "The source of the e-mail was the Vatican. From Chavet, obviously. No message, just the photo. At present we're unsure where Martha was taken. We should know soon; our friends in the carabinieri will inform us. Best you stay here and—"

The Monsignor stood up abruptly. "No."

"No?"

"I have to save what I can. Contact Dominic. Find Rachel. Will you help?"

Ortega placed a hand on the Monsignor's arm. "I'm sorry, Martin. I told you— no one here believes the Chamber of the Dormition exists outside of old stories, ancient heresies. Take my advice; let it drop before more people die."

"Then Martha would have died for nothing! I can't let that— I won't..." He pushed away Ortega's hand.

"It's not exactly safe for you out there. You're welcome to stay..."

"No. I must go."

"If you must." Ortega picked up the printout. "I believe this was meant for you."

The Monsignor took the printout and stared at the woman looking out from the photo.

Her open, dead eyes stared back at him in accusation.

Chapter 40

Doctor Croce walked down the olive-green hospital corridor of the Policlínico Humberto Primo to where two gum-chewing carabinieri guarded the door to a private room. He entered the room and viewed the patient, newly transferred from the ER. The Croatian nurse, what was her name? Danijela? was seated by the woman's bedside. The patient, recently taken off life support, was hooked up to a glucose drip.

He had already read through the case records and could scarcely believe the unidentified patient was alive, let alone in the first stage of recovery. Indeed, the initial police report had her down as deceased at the crime scene: not until the ambulance was en route to the hospital were life signs detected.

"Danijela?" he greeted. "It *is* Danijela?"

"Yes, doctor."

"How's Signora Incognita coming along?"

"She shows signs of emerging from coma."

He gazed at the patient, her drawn face crowned by a cropped afro. The woman, perhaps ten years younger than his own forty-five, was beautiful, her features elegant and sculpted, a Nubian Nefertiti. Around her throat, the brand of a cord was red and raw.

The police had located her in the Tiber, deposited in the shallows surrounding the central pylon of the Ponte Fabricio. But they weren't the first to find her. A witness stated there was another woman under the bridge, a young woman in a navy blue raincoat. She had removed the noose on the victim's neck and then stooped over the victim, presumably administering CPR.

Moments before the police arrived, the woman in the blue raincoat had waded across to the Isola Tiberina and disappeared in a stretch of dense shrubbery along the bank. Whoever the mysterious woman was, she had saved the victim's life.

Even so, Signora Incognita should have died from her injuries. Perhaps, before the stranger intervened, she *was* dead for a brief space. The rate of her recovery was astounding.

He leaned over the patient to examine the cord marks on her throat.

As though his proximity triggered a response, her eyelids flickered open. The brown eyes were unfocused. He waved a hand in front of her but elicited no reaction.

After several seconds her mouth opened. A word wheezed out: "Tell Martin that he..."

He glanced up at Danijela, who had moved to the other side of the bed and bent close to listen. "Is that English? Do you understand it?"

She nodded. "Better than Italian." Danijela stroked the woman's hair. "Tell who?"

"Tell Martin... he..."

"Yes?" the nurse encouraged.

The patient fell silent a few moments, then resumed her struggle to speak. Doctor Croce watched as Danijela listened close, straining to catch the words.

At length the patient closed her eyes and lapsed into sleep.

"So," he queried. "What did she say?"

The nurse looked puzzled. "The lady said: 'Tell Martin... he was wrong. She has already risen, harbinger of the storm.'"

Chapter 41

Rachel dogged the cardinal's steps as he escorted her through St. Peter's, the basilica's vast interior deserted since the doors were closed for the night. Behind them walked two Vatican Vigilanza, sub-machine guns at their sides.

"You're about to get a change of scenery. You won't like the view."

It didn't take a genius to figure Jones hadn't been referring to St. Peter's. She was headed someplace else. Relieved as she was at being taken out of the Benedictus House, she wasn't taken in by Chavet. By any other name, this was the good cop/bad cop routine.

Chavet had subjected her to a series of monologues outlining the entire history of the Catholic Church, no less, concluding with veiled references to a "momentous task" to be accomplished tonight. After proffering a lukewarm apology for the "necessary evil" of hiring men such as Jones and Deacon, he told her she was about to take part in the aforementioned "momentous task." The unspoken threat hovered in the air between them: the risk of harm to her family if she failed to cooperate. It was a no-brainer. Besides, this was preferable to Jones and Deacon's coin and hammer game. At the mere thought of it, her fingers automatically curled and tightened.

"This basilica was built on the site of an earlier basilica, erected by the emperor Constantine in 324," Chavet was saying as they neared the main altar surmounted by Bernini's soaring bronze baldacchino. "Pope Julius II laid the foundation stone of the new basilica in 1506. The entire work was finally completed in 1666. One hundred and sixty years— think on that, Miss Gurevich. Some empires have risen and fallen in less time than it took to complete this basilica. The Catholic Church exists, not only in time, but on the edge of eternity, overseeing the passing of centuries. Michelangelo and Raphael were but two among many who put their genius to work in St. Peter's. There are side chapels in this basilica larger than many churches. The Statue of Liberty would fit easily under Michelangelo's dome. But the grandeur of vision, the imposing scale, are but the outward show of an inner power that transcends the ages. It is this power I serve."

Rachel nodded numbly at the rhetoric, unsure of the expected response. She had the feeling that Chavet was attempting to somehow justify his actions in his eulogy of St. Peter's and maybe convert her in the process. For the time being, she played along by playing dumb.

He halted when they reached the high altar and raised his eyes to the massive dome of Peter. "There," he said, "inscribed on a frieze that encircles the lower dome are the words Christ spoke to Peter, the first pope." He declaimed the Latin with quiet reverence: "*Tu es Petrus et super hanc petram aedificibo ecclesiam meam et tibi dabo claves regni caelorum.*" He looked down at Rachel. "That means—"

"You are Peter, and upon this rock I will build my church, and I will give to you the keys of the kingdom of heaven." She had produced the quote, familiar from guidebooks, without thinking. So much for playing dumb. But at least she'd refrained from mentioning that many biblical scholars suspected those words were put in Jesus' mouth by Matthew the evangelist to bolster Peter's authority.

Chavet's thin lips produced something resembling a smile. "Indeed, Miss Gurevich. In my experience, many Jews possess greater knowledge of Christianity's origins than the majority of Christians. Not for nothing were the Jewish people honored as the Chosen Race."

She lifted her shoulders, arms outspread. "Well, you know what we Jews say— why didn't God choose someone else?"

The remark flew straight past him. He lowered his gaze to the expansive recess in front of the altar. "The Niche of the Pallium.

And behind that niche, the tomb of St. Peter, directly below the altar and the apex of the dome. St. Peter is the Rock of Christ, and this church was built upon that rock. And, as Christ promised, the gates of Hell will not prevail against it."

He stood in silence for a moment, then turned on his heel and addressed the Vigilanza. "It's almost eight. We've waited long enough. Eject Doctor Verrecchia and his team from the necropolis. If they protest... well— ignore their protests."

The men nodded and walked briskly to the doors, leaving Rachel alone with the cardinal. He studied her with an air of solicitude.

"Miss Gurevich— *Rachel.* I'm aware of how you must regard me. But I am not capricious or cruel. And I believe you can be trusted to keep your word."

Rachel kept a straight face. *Sure, I'll keep my word. Especially as you have my family under threat.*

"I must leave you for a while," he said. "Please stay here. You can tour the basilica at your leisure. Sit in contemplation if you wish. Or pray if you will."

"I'm agnostic going on atheist."

The cardinal was unfazed. "We're all agnostics. It's merely a matter of degree. My doubts of God's existence are small. Yours are larger. In any event, I advocate prayer."

She watched as he left her and headed to the northeast corner of the basilica, the rustle of his cassock clearly audible in the silent basilica. After he slipped into the shadows, she heard the low reverberation of a door opening and closing.

The basement door that Chavet pushed open was richly veneered, highly polished. Thirty years ago the wood was unvarnished.

He closed the door and stood in the shrine whose tiny window, set high in the wall with a ground level view of the Court of St. Damasus, now bore a stained glass icon of the Virgin Mary. Thirty years ago, that window was of plain glass, crisscrossed with iron bars.

He crossed the floor that was once bare floorboards and was now marble tiles and stood in front of the altar of Our Lady of Sorrows. On the altar, and on ledges newly set around the walls, reared candles in silver holders, their congregated flames transforming the statue of Mary into a chiaroscuro image, shadow and light alternately concealing and revealing mysteries.

Thirty years ago this shrine had been nothing more than a storeroom strewn with crates. A storeroom in which he had locked Sister Annunciata. And in which he dispatched her from life. That storeroom he had converted into a shrine to the Blessed Virgin in her aspect as Our Lady of Sorrows, heart transfixed by seven swords.

He had prayed for Annunciata's soul every night, and with every nightfall he remembered Annunciata's last moments. The nun toppling to the floor in unison with the plaster statue of Mary, the two hitting the floorboards as one, the statue shattering, Annunciata lapsing into her final breath:

"*Ave, Maria.*"

And in that last instant, her head angled toward him on the floor, the look in her face...

He had never seen such a look before, or since. It was a look that belonged to another world. It was pure spirit, vivid as a star. Then her eyelids closed, and the look was gone. But the memory remained, scorched into his soul. Whenever he prayed for her, that memory burned.

He knelt before the altar, head bowed, fingers entwined.

"Holy Mother, Blessed Virgin, Mother of Christ, it is not against you I raise my hand, but against those who would place you on your Son's throne. It would wound your immaculate heart to witness the dethronement of our divine Savior. For my life, and my sins, I throw myself on Christ's mercy. Intercede with your son for my immortal soul. Amen."

Crossing himself, he rose to his feet. He took three steps to the door and then stopped just short of the spot where Annunciata had breathed her last. After a brief pause, he walked carefully around that woman-shaped vacancy as if the empty air still held a living memory.

Chapter 42

Dominic's head sank slowly back on the armrest of the sofa as he listened, once again, to Martha's mpeg.

His dream-deprived brain wasn't submitting to the demands of sleep. Just needed a moment's...

Rest

His eyelids flickered shut.

Not sleeping. Just close my eyes for a moment...

In the distance, somewhere, Martha's voice related the Apocryphon Mariæ for the third— or was it fourth?— time:

"After the crucifixion, Mary survived less than a year..."

The voice receded farther.

"...She left Mount Carmel for the port city of Ephesus..."

Now the voice was at his ear, whispering softly.

"...It was in a sea-facing cave south of the city that early parts of the Apocryphon Mariæ were written..."

A voice... He didn't recognize it...

"...it was in that cave, at the age of forty-five, that Mary died..."

Then, the dark.

Nowhere, no time, no...

Daylight.

The daylight arch of a cave mouth.

He looked down a long tunnel to the cave mouth where a woman in a hooded white robe sat in an iron wheelchair, facing a sand-and-pebble beach and, across the billows of a narrow sea, the rolling contours of an island.

"That's what I thought," he said.

He turned and viewed the interior of the cave. It opened out into a small, circular roller-skating rink thronged with happy couples in top hats and frock coats, straw bonnets and pinafores. Arm in arm, they roller-skated in intricate choreography, never once colliding while an organ-grinder played "I'm Forever Blowing Bubbles."

Martha, in a red T-shirt and blue silk hot pants, appeared from the frolicsome throng and skated down the tunnel to meet him.

"Hi, Martha! I thought you were in Constantinople."

"So are you." She grinned, handing him a baguette. "They're not catching many fish this season."

"Yes, I read that in the news today. The war goes badly."

She pointed to the woman in the wheelchair. "Have you met my friend?"

He felt a profound reluctance to approach the hooded woman. "She won't like me. I'm very ugly and these aren't my pants."

Martha gripped his shoulder in reassurance. "Everyone knows that. It was on television. Come on, I'll introduce you."

She seized his elbow and pulled him toward the cave.

The farther they advanced to the cave mouth, the farther away it moved, shrinking to a tiny peek of light.

Then they were standing in the cave mouth, behind the woman in the white woolen robe.

"Must dash," Martha said, skating back down the tunnel that was now tiled with sea green mosaics and hung with oil paintings in rococo frames.

He wanted to run away. He *had* to run away.

Then he was suddenly paddling a boat down a river.

The river led him to a sea of ancient time.

A hooded woman in white sits in a cave, looking out to sea. She has waited there for him. She has waited there for everyone.

Few come.

He was back in the cave mouth.

He shrank away as the hooded woman stretched out a hand and beckoned.

Her voice was a glissando on a lyre. "It's all a matter of time."

He inched around the wheelchair until he was facing her bowed head, the face hidden in the shadow of the hood. Now that he looked more closely, he saw that her body was contorted by a wasting illness, the hands crooked and knob-knuckled. The iron wheelchair was larger and more majestic than at first sight: its soaring, elaborate backrest dwarfed her, the metal serpent armrests too widely spaced for her reach.

He looked in awe at this mangled monarch on a throne of iron.

"I brought you a baguette," he said. "But I lost it someplace."

"It's the thought that counts."

She threw back her hood with a sudden motion. Her face reminded him of a young Neve Campbell.

"Do you know where Rachel is?" he asked. "I've lost her again."

"She's riding the subway. Don't miss the train."

"I won't," he promised.

Even as he spoke she changed before his eyes. Her body became straight and healthy, her limbs longer and more supple, her arms resting easily on the sides of the wheelchair throne. And her face now wore Rachel's features.

"That's a good trick," he said.

She smiled. "I'm a woman of many faces. Some call me a queen. I've been called a whore. Maybe I'm legend's body. It's all the same to me." She leaned her head to one side. "Are you hungry, thirsty?" She indicated a small cloth spread out on the sand beside the wheelchair. On the cloth reposed a jar and cup and a heap of small bread rolls.

"No, thanks," he said. "I have a cliff to climb and if I get too full I'll fall."

She shrugged. "Everybody falls. I've seen them fall from the living light into forgetful limbo like angels damaged by too much paradise."

"Then I'll swim in the sea."

"It's the wrong sea. You'll sink."

She leaned forward, fire from heaven in her eyes. And with that look, the cave filled up with bright daylight or bright nightlight. Either, both. It was too astounding, too outside the familiar yet known from before birth. A crack was opening in the door of the world.

"It's the vision that makes us fall," she declared in a voice that he'd always known, always forgotten.

His wits whirled. He stumbled backwards, blinded.

And tumbled out of the dream...

To slide off the sofa and hit the floor with a thump.

Ear pressed against the carpet, with a bug's eye view of the apartment, he felt the dream slipping away.

He tried to catch it. It slipped away again. Dreams were the slipperiest of fish.

Something about a woman with a baguette on a beach? And before that, Martha skating? The jumbled images blinked out before he could pin them down. Some sort of sea cave...

Ah, that had been on the audio file he'd been listening to when he fell asleep. Whether it was the Jungian collective unconscious on a full head of steam, bearing encrypted revelations from the dark or merely his mind playing with images summoned from Martha's audio file... flip a coin.

Rubbing moisture from his bleary vision, he checked his watch. Difficult to assess the time he'd fallen asleep, but it couldn't have been more than a half hour.

Martha... Still no sign of Martha.

He sat back on the sofa and tried calling her once more. And again heard the unobtainable message. Stretching his arms, he moved over to the window and was about to peer out when his attention wandered to the Tempus Fugit hourglass. Leaning over, he spotted a recessed switch at the mahogany base. He pressed it— and was mildly surprised at the result.

The black fluid in the bottom of the glass began to drip— upward. Drop by drop, it ascended from the lower lobe to the apex of the upper.

He gave a weak smile as he watched the topsy-turvy hourglass. What was it, some sort of ferrofluid reacting to an electromagnet?

"*Tempus fugit*. If only you made time fly backward."

With a shake of his head, he returned to the sofa and picked up the phone— and almost dropped it at a series of chimes from the door. Moments later he was up and hurrying to open it. Martha, at last?

He pressed the intercom and after a short interval heard a familiar voice. "Dominic? It's Monsignor Martin."

"I thought you... Hang on." He pressed the outer door release for a couple of seconds and waited for the sound of steps on the stairs. When they came near he opened the door and let in the Monsignor, neither speaking a word.

His uncle looked older than he remembered, face etched in lines, shoulders stooped, feet dragging. He subsided into an armchair as though he'd found his last resting-place.

Dominic sat facing him. His uncle had a lot of questions to answer.

Chapter 43

"We've tracked Quinn down. I can taste it."

Carson stood in the cramped courtyard and surveyed the six-storied tenement, barely visible in the dense fog. Carson and Calabrese had tailed the apparently distracted Monsignor from Il Gesù to this corner of Trastevere in the hope he would lead them to Quinn. Instinct told him the gamble had paid off.

Carson pulled back the hood on his padded ski parka and looked down at the foursquare figure of Calabrese standing, arms folded, at his side. "We take this slow and sneaky. Then we give 'em hell."

Calabrese twitched his massive shoulders. "We tell Jones. Jones comes. That is the command."

Carson shrugged at the warning. "We take both of 'em out. Send them to hell. Jones'll be pleased we did the job for him, you'll see." He paused. "Look, someone's coming out— we can slip in."

The Italian raised a club of a fist and grunted a grudging assent.

Carson brandished his baseball bat and grinned as he headed for the doorway. "Playtime."

The Monsignor slumped in the armchair as though drained of life.

Stemming the flood of questions on his lips, Dominic moved to the kitchen. "I'll make you some food. You look like you need it."

The Monsignor shook his head. "I can't face food." He reached into his pocket and extracted a printout. "Be prepared for something of a shock."

Dominic took the printout and glanced at it. The glance froze to a stare. "Oh, God." His depth of field vision went awry, the photo advancing as the room retreated. "Oh, God."

"It was Jones's men," the Monsignor declared in a dead tone, "by order of Cardinal Chavet. Chavet now has Rachel incarcerated. It is my conviction that this same cardinal, while a young priest, murdered not only the pope, but also your mother."

Dominic slowly lowered the printout. Martha. Rachel. His mother's killer. He didn't know where to start. He was in the middle of a mob of questions, each drowning and canceling out the other.

The priest massaged the bridge of his nose with his fingertips. "Let me explain. Four months ago I learned from your Aunt Deirdre that Rachel was the love of your life. You never forgot her. Romeo and Juliet, she called it. I thought Dante and Beatrice more apt. When I was first made aware of the bond between you two, I made plans to induct you both, step-by-step, into the Crypt. You were to be reunited when the time was right— a few months from now. Events, however, dictated otherwise."

Dominic found himself staring at the ascent of the black fluid in the hourglass. Miniature stalactites were forming at the crown of the upper lobe. "Why bring Rachel into this?"

"She was the love of your life. A few children, one in a hundred thousand, a million, a hundred million, are born children of destiny. You were such a child, and your choice of love was an act of fate. It set Rachel apart from other women. Last Monday, in St. Mary's in London, I lit two candles, one for you, one for Rachel. Two flames, but one in destiny." A mirthless smile. "Your candle almost blew out."

Dominic expelled a sharp breath. "I'm no child of destiny."

"But you are. The Virgin Mary's spirit indwelled in your mother at your birth. You were destined to discover the Indwelling in Mary's tomb. And Rachel was destined to be at your side, an amphora for the Indwelling."

"Amphora?"

"A metaphor. When the sarcophagus is opened and its power released, if Mary's spirit were to be made manifest, it would be in a woman. She has a natural affinity with women. Even Rachel's Jewish ancestry might prove a factor, an added affinity. Gender and genetics."

Dominic was having serious doubts of his uncle's sanity. "Let's... let's leave the mysticism to one side. Tell me what happened the last couple of days."

For the next few minutes he listened to the Monsignor's account until it concluded with the exchange in the Roman Forum. Dominic sat silent, absorbing the mass of information. And above all, repressing a maelstrom of emotions.

"Well," he said, "was this obsession with the Indwelling worth Martha's life and the risk to Rachel's?"

Slowly, the Monsignor shook his head. "Since I saw that image of Martha— on the bridge— I've asked myself the same question. The answer is— no."

Dominic barely listened. He pushed aside his anger at the Monsignor and his lunatic theories and instead fixed his mind on Rachel. Martha was dead— he couldn't change that, no matter how grievous the loss. In the situation he was in, emotions could get him killed: they told him to rush out into the fog and track down Rachel. That wasn't the way.

"The Jesuits," he said after a pause, "won't they back us up?"

"They may, possibly— in locating Rachel. Not for anything else. I'll go back to Il Gesù and request help— again. In fact, I should leave soon."

"But if they won't help, we're on our own."

"Yes, we're on our own." The echo was hollow.

Chapter 44

Jones had told her she wouldn't like the view. She didn't.

Rachel stood at the end of a narrow tunnel, facing a frescoed wall that Chavet informed her was a fourth-century concrete core partition known as the Transitus wall. From infancy, she suffered from claustrophobia. Maybe they knew it. They seemed to know pretty much everything else.

The archeological team had been evicted before Chavet conducted her into the necropolis and the spooky underground streets, disturbingly narrow, were deserted, literally quiet as the dead. The men with her had made little more noise. As though walking through the basilica overhead, their footfalls were soft, their demeanor reverent. Two of the men were Vigilanza, minus their guns, the other two, carrying a bulky metal case between them, were burly Italians in work overalls who introduced themselves as Esposito and Fratta.

The workmen, after depositing the metal case inside the transparent door at the tunnel entrance, headed off in another direction, leaving her with the cardinal and the two policemen.

She mopped her brow, sheened with perspiration teased out by the stuffy warmth and half-listened as Chavet continued his lengthy exposition of the Transitus wall's significance. He broke off and smiled at the return of Esposito and Fratta. They advanced down the passage, hefting sledgehammers and pickaxes.

"Ah." Chavet smiled. "Now we start."

One of the Vigilanza pointed at the metal case on the ground. "Shall I open it?"

Chavet pursed his lips. "Not yet. Wait until we're inside."

"What's in the case?" Rachel asked. "More tools?"

"You can't bury a chamber with hand tools. The contents of that case will bring down the roof in seconds."

It took a moment for her to catch on, instantly followed by a speeding pulse. "Dynamite? I'm standing next to a case of dynamite?"

"Plastique," he said. "It's perfectly safe over a wide temperature range. Safe, that is, until the blasting caps are attached and the electronic signal transmitted."

Her pulse was still racing. "You're not planning to blow me up, are you?"

"Of course not; the plan is that you walk free of here, if all goes well."

"Just why am I here anyway? What use am I to you?"

"You serve as a hostage in case Aylesbury persuades his Jesuit friends to interfere."

She tilted her head. "Something tells me there's more to it than that."

Chavet tightened inward, arms rigid at his side. "There's— a legend. It's unlikely to be true, but— caution is always advisable."

"What legend?"

Ignoring her, he nodded at the workmen. "Time to start. Use the hammers."

The two men walked up to the wall, massive sledgehammers in each firm double-grip as they took up position in front of the wall.

"At last," the cardinal breathed softly. "At last I complete the work."

He glanced at the Transitus Mariæ graffito, then signaled the laborers. "Begin."

Chapter 45

Carson stood still and silent on the top floor landing, baseball bat in double grip, glare focused on the heavy, multiple-locked door.

Calabrese, standing by his shoulder, brutes of fists at the ready, was equally patient.

Best case, someone inside opens the door of his own accord. Then he'd blast through the doorway like the wrath of God. Club Quinn and the priest to mashed flesh and smashed bone.

He listened to the conversation beyond the door. Although the words were muffled, Quinn's voice could be easily distinguished.

Quinn was in there, no shade of a doubt.

"Open the door," he hissed under his breath. "Let us in."

Dominic looked his uncle in the eye. "If we're on our own, we need to trust each other. Be straight with me. Tell me how you knew about the plot to poison John Paul the First."

The priest lowered his gaze, brows knitted, silent, and stared into a distance only he could perceive. The seconds ticked by.

"I knew," he said at last, "because I was the one chosen to poison the pope."

Dominic leaned back in the chair, frowning as he absorbed the news. Then, after some moments' reflection, he began to nod. "Yes, yes— I can see how that adds up. But you either changed your mind or you'd infiltrated the ring of conspirators."

The confession had done nothing to unburden his uncle. His bowed frame looked as though it carried the weight of the world. "I had already infiltrated a radical splinter group of Conclave," he said in little more than a mumble. "My allegiance was always to the Shrine. I spied on Conclave on behalf of the Shrine. The order came down for the pope's assassination, to be carried out by a Vatican insider. I was one of the insiders. I tried to warn John Paul and succeeded only in alerting Conclave to my true allegiance. And Chavet was forced to take my place as the pope's assassin. The prospect horrified him. The act unhinged his mind."

The Monsignor lapsed into silence. A faint creak sounded outside the door. Dominic swerved a look at the doorway. The sound wasn't repeated.

He shrugged and returned his attention to the Monsignor. The priest still sagged in the armchair, weighted with guilt. For all his uncle's machinations, Dominic couldn't help feeling sympathy for the man's past regrets, his lost hopes. As for the pope's assassination, over three decades ago, how could he shoulder the blame for that?

"It was my fault," the Monsignor sighed.

"There was nothing more you could do for the pope."

"I was thinking of Sarah, your mother." He heaved another sigh. "I have to leave for Il Gesù. One last effort to gain help."

Dominic eyed the upward drip-drip of the hourglass. *Tempus is fugiting.* "There must be something I can do."

"Not for the present. But you may find some answers from Thomas. The original plan was that we all meet up in Santa Maria in Trastevere and then proceed to the Shrine where Thomas spends much of his time. You should go to him."

After brief deliberation Dominic shrugged assent. "Okay. You go to Il Gesù and call me when you hear anything. We've got to find Rachel."

The Monsignor consulted his watch, then heaved himself up from the chair. "Almost eight-thirty. I must go."

Dominic rose to his feet. "So where is the Shrine?"

"Go to San Callisto, fifty yards south of the Piazza di Santa Maria. You'll find the windows bricked-up— the church is derelict.

Rap on the door, three knocks of three, and Thomas will let you in."

"San Callisto is the Shrine?"

"No, it's the entrance to it, via the well of St. Callixtus preserved inside the church. The Shrine leads to the original site of the Virgin Mary's tomb, directly under Santa Maria in Trastevere, before it was removed to Vatican Hill. The former Dormition Chamber, under the first Marian church in Rome."

Despite his skepticism of the Dormition legends, Dominic felt a touch of awe. "Nobody told me about a connection between the Shrine and Mary's tomb."

"Mary's tomb was the reason for the creation of the original Shrine. And the Shrine's heart is haunted by something more than the memory of a ghost."

Before Dominic could respond the Monsignor buttoned his overcoat and moved to the door. "Can't dawdle any longer. There's precious little time left, for either of us."

He gripped the door handle, then paused. "Go quickly to San Callisto. Goodbye and—" He started to turn the handle. "—Mary abides."

Mary abides. The words revived an old memory. "Mary abides. Is that a common phrase? I heard a little girl say that once, way back. She was kneeling before a Virgin statue. It was— a moment."

The Monsignor dropped his hand from the door handle. "Outside of Silentium, not a common phrase. That little girl, that was just— coincidence." He smiled pensively. "God is in the coincidences."

"Maybe so. Uh— wait a moment. I may as well walk out with you."

He pulled on the field jacket, his gaze moving to the photo of Martha hanging from a bridge. It hit almost as hard at second viewing. He could smell Martha's scent in the room, close as his own breath.

If Jones and his men were watching the Shrine, let them come for him. He'd meet them head-on. He picked up the printout. "For you, Martha."

He took a last look at the room, to the chairs where he and Martha chatted, the sofa where Rachel had held him, and across to where night had painted the window as black as the hourglass fluid in its final ascending droplets.

The Monsignor turned the door handle. "Ready?"

"I've been ready all day."

The door was open a bare inch before it blasted inward, its abrupt swing slamming the priest against the wall.

A storm of brute force burst out the doorway, aimed straight at Dominic.

Chapter 46

A sledgehammer punched a deep dent in the Transitus wall. Plaster and old concrete sprayed in all directions, clouding the tunnel with dust.

Rachel instinctively retreated at the first hammer blow and kept her distance as the workmen established a steady rhythm, their efforts focused on the center of the ancient wall.

Chavet crooked a finger at one of the gendarmes. "De Mola, go and wedge the climate control door open. We'll need as much air circulation in here as we can get. Then stand guard near the necropolis entrance."

The cardinal summoned the other officer as De Mola left. "Belucci, bring the lamps."

Belucci followed in De Mola's wake. Rachel watched him leave and then turned on Chavet. "What if I just walk out of here?"

His narrow frame stiffened, a poker of a priest. "That would be unwise. Think of your family." A hint of guilt showed in his face. "As you know, there are men I've been obliged to employ. Hounds on the loose. If you leave I can't be responsible for what happens."

"You're a real piece of work, Cardinal."

"We do what we must."

For the next minute she stood in silence and watched as sledgehammers smashed chunks of concrete loose and the debris mounted up at the wall's base. As she watched, Belucci returned with a medium-sized crate which he deposited beside the cardinal.

"How many lamps do you have there?" Chavet inquired.

"Twenty."

"Not nearly enough. Bring two more crates."

The policeman gave a subtle shrug and departed on his errand.

After a brief interval, Chavet caught Rachel's gaze. "Beyond that wall," he declared, "is the tomb of the Virgin Mary. A holy relic we should treasure, you might think. Not so. I have read of Mary's life in a codex of papyrus pages and discovered she was not the paragon of obedience and chastity that Church tradition portrays. She was pre-Christian, effectively pagan. And at times she opposed Our Lord, setting herself up as the Messiah. And the very existence of her body in a tomb overthrows one of the basic doctrines of Catholicism, the Dogma of the Assumption."

"Trust the Catholic Church to make a dogma out of an assumption," she mumbled.

"Most droll. The Dogma of the Assumption states that the Virgin Mary, at the point of death, was assumed bodily into heaven. But according to the Collyridians, although Mary lies in her tomb she also walks the earth in some strange, mystical fashion. The doctrine of the assumption countered that bizarre legend."

"You mean you don't believe in it?"

"The doctrine of the assumption is fodder for the masses. Essential fodder, but fodder. Mary died naturally, and by Christ's grace, not her own virtue, was enthroned Queen of Heaven for bearing our Savior. *That* Mary I revere, Mary the handmaid of the Lord, Mary the *Virgin*. The object of superstition beyond that wall, I abhor." He snorted contemptuously. "*Ad Jesum per Mariam...* a saccharine heresy that leads the gullible into darkness."

She was mildly surprised at the open cynicism. "The Vatican can close down any excavation it wants. Why not just do that?"

His mouth hardened to a resolute line. "The Vatican has nothing to do with it. It's my task to prevent what is hidden from coming to light."

A crash of masonry made her jump back. A black hole, wide enough to accommodate a man's head, gaped at the center of the wall. A chunk of concrete had fallen inward.

The workmen who called himself Fratta looked up with a grin. "We're through."

The door banged on its hinges.

The Monsignor rocked on his heels by the doorway, stunned by the sudden invasion.

Dominic had a fleeting impression of Carson's cannonball head bearing down on him. Instinct kicked in and launched him to one side.

He fetched up against the sofa and instantly side-rolled and sprang to his feet, backing into the corner near the window. Two intruders had barged into the room; he preferred to keep his back to the wall in two-to-one combat.

Carson had pulled to a halt in the middle of the floor, reorienting himself. Fast on the charge but slow on the turns.

Over by the door, a shorter, squatter man in a ponytail had the dazed Monsignor by the throat, a boulder of a fist pulled back to land a crushing blow. With no way to cover the ground in time, Dominic grabbed the laptop from the sofa. Ignoring Carson's renewed charge, he launched the laptop spinning across the room to meet the back of the ponytailed head.

But the fist landed on the Monsignor's jaw a fraction before the corner of the laptop cracked into the assailant's skull.

The next thing Dominic saw was a flash of crimson. Then a shock of numbing pain jolted his right shoulder. He instinctively lashed out with his foot and connected with something bony that evoked a gasp from his attacker.

Operating on autopilot, he jumped forward onto the sofa, his vision clearing. Out the corner of his eye he glimpsed the Monsignor crumple to the floor and Ponytail standing on his feet, swaying side to side.

Carson, in a garish ski parka, advanced to the sofa, crouched in a slugger pose with the bat, his face a mixture of rage and glee. "High ground won't save you this time, Quinn." He took another step and swept a God-almighty swing at Dominic's legs.

The most predictable attack he could have chosen.

Dominic leaped upward at the first twitch of Carson's shoulders, knees tight to his chest. The club whisked under his sneakers. He dropped onto the cushion in a low crouch as the Irishman's swing twisted his body, throwing him off-balance. He converted his fall into a jump with the sofa as a springboard, snap-kicking his foot hard into Carson's jaw.

Carson went flying, his broad back meeting the far wall with a thud. The club skittered across the floor. He made a grab for it but his adversary, a couple of feet closer, beat him to the lunge. Carson straightened up and backed away, brandishing the club as much defensively as offensively. As he retreated, he spat blood and tooth fragments from his mouth. He was more wary now, and that wasn't good.

"Come for me, Yank, come for me," Carson goaded.

He didn't rise to the bait. His shoulder throbbed from the first blow of that lead-cored weapon and he was in no hurry to rush into its orbit.

"Twice lucky, Quinn. Third time, dead."

He spared a quick glance over his shoulder. The Monsignor was sprawled on the carpet. Above him, Ponytail was *still* standing, swaying on his feet. The blow from the launched laptop had been potentially lethal. The guy must have the skull of a Neanderthal.

He turned back to Carson, who'd taken a pace forward in the sub-second Dominic checked on the Monsignor's assailant. The bastard didn't miss a trick. Carson retreated a step and put his goading face on again. "Come on, boy. Calabrese's a hard man. He'll be fit to fight in no time at all. Then you're dead for sure."

That, Dominic somberly reflected, may be no idle boast. He circled Carson, staying just out of range of the club, moving close to the window where he could keep an eye on both men.

"Anyone tell you about Martha?" Carson's mashed mouth widened to a mocking grin. "I laid into her good with this bat, heard the cracking of the bones. Then Alice gave her a good stomach stomping, pulped her insides a treat. And ya know what? I hung her at the end, like in the Westerns."

Dominic came within a hair of losing it. Of falling for it. He almost went for Carson, caution be damned. He stayed himself at the last moment. Then wished he hadn't.

The man that Carson called Calabrese came alive as though douched with ice water, spinning on his heels, taking in the scene. An instant later he barged straight into his target. Dominic leapt back, dodging an opportunistic blow of Carson's bat as Calabrese barreled into him off-center. Dominic grabbed the Italian by the collar and swung him round... for Calabrese to receive the full brunt of an injudicious swipe from Carson's club.

Missed your target, pal.

Calabrese grunted in pain but refused to drop. Christ, it would take a pile driver to hammer this man down.

The situation appeared to Dominic in brutal clarity. Two of them. One of him. Preschool arithmetic: subtract one of them from the room. The door wasn't a viable option. That left the window. Outside the window was a sixty-foot-plus drop to paving stones. Not his problem.

He heaved into the unbalanced Calabrese, propelling him to the window. Quickly catching on, the man bellowed in fury, trying to twist free. Dominic wasn't about to let that happen: a last-instant push sent Calabrese headfirst through the glass, his bulky physique all but taking the entire window with him, frame, panes, glazing bars and all.

For a moment he teetered on the brink, crunching glass shards under his feet, spine arched forward, arms flailing. Left to his own devices it could have gone either way. Dominic decided the issue with a kick that launched the Italian out into the fog.

Even as the man's scream shrilled up through the mist, Dominic whirled around to deal with Carson. But not soon enough to prevent the hulking shape from charging like a bull with a roar to match, knocking the stuffing out of him as he was thrown off his feet.

The next thing he felt was a stab in his lower back. A sharp line of pain, punctuated by stings. And above that stabbing line, a sensation of a yawning gap below him.

He glanced to one side: his heart lurched. He was hanging halfway out the window, head tilted back. The remaining glass splinters in the window frame sliced into his flesh. Carson was on top of him, bloated features inflamed with outrage. "You go the same way as Calabrese, Quinn!" he shrieked. "Pray you die when you hit ground. I'll pray you don't."

Carson had positioned himself so that Dominic, dangling above sixty feet of nothing, had no chance of kneeing his opponent over his head. Wasn't going to happen. Carson started to push at Dominic's chest, relishing that his adversary knew he was about to plummet, beyond any hope. At that same moment Carson's eyes widened in realization of his crass mistake:

A man who's about to lose has nothing left to lose. He'll take you with him.

Dominic's hands sprang to Carson's collar even as the hit man's recognition of folly dawned. He pulled the heavy hulk to him and arched backwards. If he was about to die or suffer critical injury, then so was Carson. Make the world a better place as you leave it.

Roaring in rage and fear, his opponent struggled frantically but Dominic hung on like a Rottweiler, committed to the death. A violent kick of the legs and twist of his torso took Dominic into empty air, and Carson with him.

Adrenaline boosting his nervous system, he experienced the fall through the fog in slow motion. His mind was fixed on one objective: keep twisting through the descent.

Carson was on top when they slid off the window ledge. Dominic wanted him underneath. So keep twisting around and hold on tight.

His adversary was too occupied with screaming in terror to grasp what was going on, flailing his limbs as if to fly himself out of his plight.

And with tortuous slowness, as it seemed to Dominic, the two men rotated and leveled out as they plunged through layers of mist.

The hard landing pad of paving stones appeared abruptly through the fog. One last turn and Carson was below him.

So was Calabrese, directly below, where he knelt, knees splayed on the paving, his upper body swaying erect.

In the last instant before they hit street level, comprehension sparked in Carson's eyes: he was crashing to earth, with Dominic on top of him. Dominic had condemned him to death by saving himself.

"*You—*" he screeched.

Then they hit.

Calabrese's head broke Carson's fall. It also broke Carson's spine and Calabrese's neck.

Dominic heard the dull crunch as Carson's bloated body rammed the Italian into the ground. A violent jolt ran through him, despite the expansive cushion of Carson's beer belly.

Carson burst like a sack of wet cement as his ribcage imploded. Blood and fluids bubbled up from the shattered hulk as Dominic slipped off the body and sprawled on the paving stones, stunned into immobility.

Finally he forced his unwilling limbs to crawl a couple of yards, then struggled upright. His legs were foam rubber and every muscle in his back and stomach protested at high pitch.

He took a step that turned into a stagger. As far as he could tell he had cracked a couple of ribs but, fingers crossed, no damage to vital organs.

He took another step. Still upright.

All things considered, it seemed he was very, very lucky.

"Must be a child of destiny after all," he muttered, then toppled to the ground.

For several seconds he lay there, watching windows opening above, then looked across to Calabrese and Carson, conjoined in a macabre flesh sculpture.

Sympathy wasn't high on his list this precise moment.

More windows swung open and a chorus of shouts echoed up and down the street, spreading alarm. He forced himself back to his feet, groaning with the effort. He had to get away before the carabinieri arrived but he couldn't walk the streets covered in someone else's blood. He spared a final look at the ruin that was Carson.

"Street-wise, world-foolish."

He moved away and staggered into the courtyard, praying that the Monsignor had woken up from Calabrese's hammer blow. Slamming his palm on the top floor buzzer, he rested his forehead against the door and waited.

Mercifully, he heard the Monsignor's voice, albeit slurred. "Who is that?"

"It's me. Let me in."

"And those two men?"

"Street pizza."

The entry buzzer sounded and he pushed the door open. By his reckoning he could spare five minutes to clean up and get clear. Hopefully the dense fog would delay the police.

If he got away before the police turned up, his next stop was the Shrine. And, if the Monsignor was to be believed, an encounter with something more than the memory of a ghost.

Chapter 47

Monsignor Federico Ortega sat by the hospital bed and waited for Martha to open her eyes.

After Monsignor Martin left Il Gesù, the news had come in that Martha had been located, not in a morgue, but in a private room in the Policlínico Humberto Primo. Intelligence had been sloppy in tracing her and the police remiss in filing a deceased person's report, but in mitigation Humberto Primo was one of the largest and busiest hospitals in Europe and the police had their hands full with the city chaos created by the fog.

Martha's eyes blinked open. "Getting bored, Federico?" Her voice came out in strained gasp.

He smiled. "I thought you were asleep. I've only been here for-"

"Five minutes. I know. Just collecting my thoughts. Don't want to waste words."

Ortega leaned forward. "Was it Jones?"

"Uh-huh. Jones and his men. And a couple of Deacon's. Chavet's the paymaster. I think he's making his move tonight."

"You mean the Chamber of the Dormition?" He shook his head. "It's a fantasy."

"The Monsignor thinks otherwise."

"The Monsignor..." Ortega muttered. "I'm a monsignor, my subordinate is a monsignor. Only Aylesbury would have the arrogance to call himself *the* Monsignor." He checked himself, his weak smile apologetic. "Sorry. Inconsiderate of me. You're a brave lady. It's a miracle you survived."

"Yes, a miracle. Thanks to a woman."

"The woman who resuscitated you? Who was she?"

Martha's mouth made it to a smile. "Now there's a question... All I can say is, the dead have open eyes." She halted for breath. "Federico, you must send your best agents into the necropolis."

"Can't be done. The Vicar General would never sanction a flagrant incursion into Vatican territory on the strength of an old legend."

"We have a Jesuit pope now. Should count for something."

"A Jesuit pope, with the emphasis on pope.' He shook his head. "Pope Francis severed all links to us the day of his papal accession. No aid from that quarter. I've done what I can, Martha. I contacted Langley about your condition. They expressed sympathy but it was evident they'd written you off some time ago as ex-CIA, a renegade, working in the Crypt."

"They're not wrong," she said. "More of a ghost than a spook."

"Indeed. Regarding your safety, I've pulled more strings than a puppet theatre. Officially you're still listed as deceased."

"Good move. The dead are safe. Which reminds me... Dominic and Rachel. If they survive the night, do what you can to protect them. Use all the Sodality's resources to keep them from harm. Promise me."

"That I can promise. *If* they survive the night." His gaze strayed to the dark beyond the window. "The nurse told me you mentioned something— something about a woman that has risen, a harbinger of the storm."

"Yes. The woman who saved me..." Her eyes strained as if peering into an unfathomable time and distance, or the other side of now. "The woman. She's the one. The Indwelling."

He hoped a skeptical note didn't sound in his tone. "The Virgin Mary?"

"I don't know. I don't what she is. That's sort of the point. I saw her up close. Saw her face. And I saw her in another place, lying in a tomb, but her face was different there. She's one of us, and she's far beyond us. Worlds beyond."

"You'd better rest," he suggested delicately.

She appeared not to hear him. "And when the storm comes, she'll be with us. Through the years of the tempest, we'll hear her voice above the gale, we'll see her star above the sea."

"Martha— rest."

"You think it's the morphine talking? But I know a hawk from a handsaw. Call Martin. Tell him what I said. About the woman. The Indwelling."

Ortega raised his shoulders. "I doubt he'll listen."

"He'll listen. In the end, he'll do the right thing, even if it kills him."

Better a pope dies than her.

The Monsignor recalled his words to Mother Hypatia from thirty years past as he trudged up the Janiculum Hill. He had never told Hypatia of his love for Sarah; why should he? He had never told Sarah either.

And now Sarah's son had been put at great risk— by the Monsignor. At least, at the last minute, he had directed his nephew to the relative safety of the Shrine.

He had been on his way back to Il Gesù when a phone call changed his course.

Martha was alive. Hospitalized, incapacitated, but alive. He all but shouted out his joy. Her presumed death had been a warning from God. Warning delivered, she was restored. As for the mysterious woman she claimed as "the harbinger of the storm," that, surely, was the heavy-duty painkiller talking.

Dominic was out of harm's way. Now he had to rescue Rachel. Which meant turning back from the route to Il Gesù to head instead for Vatican City.

He still felt pride at his nephew's elimination of the two thugs. In peace, he was like his mother. In war, utterly unlike. While Dominic had cleaned up and scrubbed the more obvious bloodstains from his jacket and the Monsignor had removed the glass splinters from his back and applied adhesive bandages, his nephew's relative calm and determination had impressed him. Heading back down the stairs, they heard the first notes of an approaching police siren. They got clear with literally seconds to spare.

He failed to save Sarah, but, belatedly, he helped save her son.

He hadn't told Dominic the whole story. He'd told no one the whole story.

Hypatia was unaware Sarah's mission would fail, but *he* knew. Because of what Conclave considered his defection, they were on the lookout for anyone outside their orbit seeking access to the pope. Sarah had virtually no chance of survival. So...

He winced at the memory. So he phoned Chavet and promised he would prevent anyone from warning the pontiff on condition that Annunciata came to no harm. The pope's life for hers.

Chavet had given his word. And broken it. Not once had he admitted he was responsible for Sarah's poisoning, insisting that others had intercepted her. But over the years, his suspicions of Chavet increased. And now he was near-certain.

By trying to save Sarah, the Monsignor had condemned her to death.

In the ensuing years, by every underhanded method to hand he had bluffed his way back into a modus vivendi with Conclave. All for the sake of a pair of enduring objectives: uncovering Mary's tomb and retribution for Sarah. Now he had one more objective.

"Better I die than Rachel."

Chapter 48

The facade of Santa Maria in Trastevere was floodlit in the fog. By grace of the artificially luminous mist, the Virgin Mary and her attendant virgins were iconic phantoms, hovering in midair.

The few strollers in the piazza cast elongated, shape-shifting shadows on the uneasy fog. It was a preternatural realm, out of this world, out of time.

Dominic, hands thrust deep in his pockets, slipped furtively across the piazza, observing the night walkers for signs of unfriendly eyes. His muscles ached like hell from the fall and the cracked ribs made breathing difficult, but nothing appeared irreparably damaged. He could cope.

San Callisto was about a hundred yards dead ahead. Voices issued from his befogged destination, muffled and displaced, archaic echoes. As he neared his goal, he reflected on his uncle's tales of a haunted Shrine and an ancient sarcophagus, and his skepticism wavered.

He had no difficulty in accepting the speculations of deep physics: an infinity of universes in an overarching superspace, each universe separated by the behavior of a single photon; regions of space where time flowed backward; the phantasmal dance of subatomic quarks and leptons; the mysterious interplay between consciousness and space-time.

The Newtonian notion of mechanistic matter had proved a myth. Modern physics regarded the cosmos as more like a vast thought than a mighty machine. Why was it so incredible that a woman, two thousand years past, with the immense resources of the Library of Alexandria, should have passed beyond the matter myth and bridged the infinite worlds of superspace, each world closer than his own breath?

But if Mary had achieved that goal, it was high irony that frontier physics had come full circle to mingle with ghosts-by-gaslight tales and gaunt shadows in the fog.

Hugging the east side of the square, across from the basilica, he neared the Ristorante Sabatini, its interior bright and busy. The restaurant door slammed open and a woman swept out, face buried in a Fodor's Rome guidebook as she blundered straight into him.

"I'm sorry," he apologized, automatically lapsing into English.

"Oh, hi!" she beamed. "I'm American too!"

"Small world." He stepped back, acutely conscious of the dried bloodstains on his jacket.

"Do you know how to get to the Isola Tiberina?" she asked, squinting at the guide.

"Uh— I think so, if I remember the map right. Turn around that corner back there and go along the Via della Lungaretta. Should be pretty straightforward."

"Well, *thank* you!" she gushed. "You're a fine young gentleman."

"Don't mention it," he said, discreetly backing away. "Have a safe journey."

Instead of following his directions she returned to her study of the guidebook, frowning intently. He gave her a wave and moved off, leaving Santa Maria behind and coming within sight of the tiny Piazza San Callisto, a hazy profile in the mist.

Peering over her Fodor's guidebook, Alice watched him leave.

When Dominic was out of earshot, she lifted a phone to her ear and voice-dialed: "Jones."

After a short wait a voice answered. "Yeah?"

"Quinn's here, in Trastevere, heading for San Callisto."

"Follow him. I'll be with you soon as I can. Traffic's gridlocked."

"Do you want me to call Calabrese or any of the others?" she asked.

"No, I'll do that. I want everyone in on this. Everyone. Unfinished business."

Enfolded in dense fog, Dominic looked up at the church of San Callisto.

The church showed a blank face to the night. The church's windows were blind eyes, sealed with bricks and plaster.

If this building had ever opened outward to the world, those days were long gone. This church looked inward, inside its own walls, unvisited. It conveyed an unmistakable message to any intruder: no trespassing.

The tall door, darkened with age, loomed above Dominic almost half the height of the façade. He hesitated an instant, sensing he was about to cross more than a physical threshold. He'd given up his faith long ago, and he wouldn't run back to it because the night had closed in. But by the same token he wouldn't run away if a new revelation came.

He tapped on the door, three knocks of three.

After a brief silence a bolt was drawn with a prolonged screech and the door slowly opened

Chapter 49

A lump of concrete, brittle with age, fell into what was now a wide, jagged entranceway into the darkness. All that remained of the graffito was the word TRANSITUS on the far left of the wall. The MARLÆ had gone the way of the demolished plaster.

Chavet raised a hand. "Enough. Clear the rubble."

As Esposito and Fratta set to work, the cardinal smiled at Rachel. "You're privileged, Rachel. We are about to enter where none has walked in sixteen centuries."

The workmen freed the entrance of rubble in under two minutes. Task accomplished, they looked up eagerly. The cardinal moved forward, beckoning Rachel to follow. They passed under the gap with ample headroom, flanked by the workmen who had produced flashlights that probed the dark.

A glance over her shoulder showed a gendarme planting a compact electric lamp a couple of feet inside the hole. He flicked a switch and the small lamp radiated an impressively bright aura. He saw her glance and misinterpreted her interest. "The batteries are good for six hours, signorina. Very reliable."

"Great," she said, and turned her attention to the way ahead. All she could distinguish in the slapdash play of flashlights were transitory glimpses of earthen walls and a low ceiling.

She waited, her boots deep in the accumulated dust of ages, as the policeman placed the lamps along the walls, each some three yards apart. They were standing in a small, rectangular room fronting a tunnel similar to the one they had just left. Its dull brown length sloped downward into a blotch of darkness.

She stood, listening to the silence. Time held its breath here.

This place had lain undisturbed, locked from the world, when emperors still ruled in Rome. It had retained its dark and silence when Rome fell, when the Saxons invaded Britain, when Muhammad stormed Mecca, when the Norseman ravaged Europe, when the great abbeys of the High Middle Ages were raised, when Michelangelo sculpted his David. And on, down the succeeding centuries, this tunnel lay hidden, undiscovered.

But as the lamps threw light on the farther reaches of the passageway, all that showed was a dead end. The tunnel seemed to lead nowhere.

She looked questioningly at Chavet but he appeared unperturbed. He stepped forward, beckoning her to follow. She tracked his long paces down the tunnel until the outlines of a wall came into clear focus at the far end. The workman Esposito had gone on ahead and was scraping at the wall with stubby fingers, releasing a cloud of dust. He aimed the flashlight at the spot he'd uncovered and then grinned at the cardinal.

"Plaster," he said. "A partition wall, like the first one."

Chavet released a satisfied breath. "We're almost there." He stared at the wall as though mesmerized. "Can you feel it?"

She was about to inquire "feel what?" but then realized she knew perfectly well. Since her first sight of the Transitus wall, it was there. Below her current anxieties, her hope of survival and fear of extinction, it was there.

It was holy awe, or dread. Perhaps the two were the same.

She reached out to touch the wall. Then drew back her hand, leaving it untouched.

Chapter 50

Inch by inch, the tall door of San Callisto grated inward with the prolonged complaint of a low groan. The church door halted when a vertical slice of darkness, scarcely a foot wide, invited entrance. Dominic peered inside but saw nothing but blackness.

"Thomas Chen?" he inquired in a whisper.

"Come in," replied an equally hushed voice. "Quickly."

He edged sideways through the door and was left in pitch black to the accompaniment of a heavy bolt sliding in its groove. The silence that succeeded it was as palpable as the dust motes brushing his skin. He shuddered, and wondered if apprehension was getting to him, then realized the cold in the church outmatched the cold outside.

"It's best not to show a light," said a voice with a distinct Yorkshire accent. "I know the way in the dark."

Fingers touched Dominic's shoulder, then slid down to take a firm grip of his forearm. The hand exerted a mild tug and he followed the prompt, shuffling over the stony floor.

After a dozen paces his guide whispered in his ear. "No need to inch along quite so slowly. We're going down the middle of the right aisle."

"Whatever you say. But what's wrong with a flashlight?"

"People might be watching." The tone was matter-of-fact. "There are cracks in the bricked-up windows."

The hand pulled back on his arm and he stopped in mid-stride. He waited, feeling the presence of the cold black spaces and unseen statues around him.

"We're here," informed the voice from the dark. "The well of St. Callixtus. There's a Dacron line dangling into it. Just kneel and feel for it, then slide down. It's not too far. I'll go first. Wait until I call out before you follow— I don't want you landing on top of my head."

"Is this the same well that Pope Callixtus was thrown down?"

"According to legend, yes."

Dominic listened to the sounds of soft shuffling and the occasional strained gasp, followed by the faint whisper of a body sliding down a cord. Then a muffled scraping.

After a minute's silence a voiced echoed out the well. "Come down. The well's quite dry."

He fished for the cord, then slipped his leg into what felt like a rough circular opening and slid slowly down the line, periodically brushing the wall with his toecaps. He soon alighted on what he guessed was a pile of powdered debris.

"*Fiat lux.*"

As Thomas spoke a faint light appeared and waxed in illumination until Dominic could form a hazy impression of his surroundings. Standing little more than a hand's length distance was a chubby, elderly Chinese wearing the clerical garb of black suit and Roman collar. His rounded, amiable features, sporting wire-framed glasses, were underlit by a flashlight attached to his lapel.

"Good to put a face to the voice, Father Thomas."

"Good to meet you, Dominic." The priest grinned. "And it's plain Thomas. I'm not one for patriarchal titles."

"Fine by me. Uh— are you leaving the grappling line where it is?"

"For tonight, yes. My niece usually pulls it back up. However, after tonight, it won't matter anymore."

The priest pushed hard at a floor-level section of the brickwork that started to grate inward, then, at another push, swung to one side.

"This way," Thomas instructed, forcing his ample frame into the square breach. "It's a tight squeeze."

Once Thomas was through he followed his lead, scratching both shoulders on stonework as he wriggled through into open space and stood up on what felt like level paving. Breathing heavily, Thomas started to push the wall section back into place. Dominic instantly lent his own weight, glancing at the complicated hinge system that allowed access.

"Old habits die hard," the priest admitted as the stone slotted into place. "By tomorrow it won't matter if anyone looks down the well and sees a hole but... old habits die hard."

"That's some Heath Robinson contraption you've got there," Dominic observed, indicating the complex network of brackets and hinges.

"Took me a while." Thomas turned around and pointed the flashlight past Dominic's shoulder. The beam picked out a flight of narrow stone steps angling upward. "We're in what was once a wine-cellar. The Shrine's above us. The original meeting place was called the House of Prophecies until the Virgin Mary's sarcophagus was brought here from Ephesus in 227."

"Why was it relocated to the Vatican?"

"For the Collyridians, Mary belonged at the center of power. After Constantine ordered a basilica to be constructed over St. Peter tomb, Mary's devotees secreted her tomb in the necropolis before it was filled in to provide the basilica's foundations." Thomas began to shuffle to the steps. "This way. Almost there."

He followed Thomas up the stairway, the priest's shape silhouetted in pallid light as he climbed toward a door almost denuded of paint.

Almost there.

Thomas's casual remark struck Dominic with inappropriate force. In the headlong rush of events since Carson stormed into the Long Woman's Grave, he'd been cut adrift and carried along on wild currents, going with the racing flow. But now he was close to landfall.

That hard fact brought him down to earth with a thump, dwarfed by the daunting scale of this latter-day Roman epic he'd fallen into.

My life's grown larger. I'll grow to fit it.

He halted as Thomas opened the door, then took a few tentative steps into the dark. The tap of stone under his feet was replaced by the soft thud of floorboards.

A click sounded to his left and the lights stuttered on. He'd expected to blink in the sudden illumination but the solitary low-wattage light bulb dangling from the ceiling in the short hallway merely replaced darkness with murk.

Thomas sat down on a stool and slowly, carefully, removed his shoes, his features tightened in a pronounced wince. Free of shoes, the priest reached under the stool and produced a pair of slippers with pink pom-poms. As he slipped them on, he glanced up at Dominic with a resigned heave of his stocky shoulders.

"Present from my niece," he chuckled semi-apologetically. "She has a sense of humor, God bless her."

Thomas stood and shuffled to the door at the right-hand end of the corridor. Dominic noted the priest's hobbling gait, which he'd put down to negotiating a path through darkness. "Foot problems?"

"Gout," Thomas responded with a grin that was uncomfortably close to a grimace. "Feel free to laugh. I have an affliction best suited to a nineteenth-century port-drinking British colonel in India with his foot propped on a cushion and a punkah-wallah at his side."

"A couple of my friends have gout. I know it's no joke."

They entered a room of bare floorboards containing nothing but two wooden chairs, a couple of portable lamps, a laptop resting on a folding table and a sturdy wooden crate up against a bare wall.

Thomas subsided into a chair. "Please take a seat." He viewed the state of Dominic's jacket. "Are those stains what I think they are?"

Dominic sat and faced him. "Blood. Two of Jones's men tried to kill me— and my uncle. I was lucky to get the better of them." He paused. "They're both dead."

The priest cast him an understanding glance. "We do what we must. Leave it at that. I gather Monsignor Martin's plans have gone awry."

"They have. I've been thinking perhaps I should head for the necropolis. Chavet may have taken Rachel there."

"Up to you. But nothing will happen until after ten p.m., according to Doctor Verecchia— he's the director of the archeological team. He owes me some favors so he keeps me informed." He sucked in a breath. "On a quite different matter, your uncle called me with news of Martha. She's alive."

Dominic stared, and stared some more. Slowly broke into a wide smile. Then the smile faltered. "She can't be. I saw a photo..."

"I heard about that. She was hanged. But she survived, somehow."

"She's alive? She *survived*?" He felt like jumping out of his chair and punching the air. "That *is* good news. That's— *great* news."

"Yes, great news indeed." The priest's tone sobered. "Normally we'd be celebrating the glad tidings, but this is not the moment."

"Any other time, I'd be racing to Martha's bedside. But— as you say, this isn't the moment."

"There's little time and a lot to tell, but first let me give you something." He leaned down to the crate beside his chair, rummaged inside for several seconds. "Ah, here's one. Keep it as a reminder." The priest lifted up a crucifix, some four inches in length, and handed it to Dominic.

Dominic held the crucifix in his palm. It was identical to the one Hypatia wore, a cross bearing the Virgin Mary nailed to the wood, crowned with roses and thorns.

"I've seen this before. Hypatia said there was a legend that she suffered the stigmata of Christ's crucifixion in the last moments of her life."

"Indeed. That was recorded in the Apocryphon Mariæ. Also, there was a wound in her breast as though a sword had been driven into her heart. There are many legends surrounding Mary. Hers is a strange story."

"I heard some of it but missed the post-mortem epilogue."

"More than an epilogue. You could say it's the end of the beginning. Have you heard of the Indwelling— aside from what Martha and Martin may have mentioned?"

Dominic considered a moment. "I think so, in connection with an indwelling spirit, the presence of God in Christ."

"I was thinking more of the Holy Spirit's presence in the Virgin Mary. Even John Paul II made a reference to 'a special and privileged indwelling in Mary.' But for Silentium, Mary was not so much a vessel of an indwelling spirit, she *was* the indwelling spirit. And those in whom she dwelled were known as amphorae." The priest smiled awkwardly. "What I have to tell you is a wild story and gets tangled up with weird science and ancient visions."

Dominic leaned back in his chair. "Go ahead. I'm listening."

Chapter 51

The street was a riot of flashing lights in the enfolding fog.

Jones and Deacon stood at the back of a crescent of onlookers, the gawkers held at bay by four gum-chewing policemen on motorbikes, allowing plenty of space for the squad cars parked close to two partially fused corpses. Jones peered up at the shattered window at the top of the tenement, a smudge of light in the mist, then back down at his former soldiers. There was nothing to show who'd hurled Carson and Calabrese to their deaths, but Jones had a name, a name carved in marble, as in tombstone.

"*Quinn.*"

When he'd driven the car from the Lungotevere Farnesina into Trastevere, he'd sighted strobing lights and shadowy activity. And something told him Quinn was involved. But he hadn't reckoned on two of his men as victims.

Jones prided himself on being above anger. No one since childhood had made Jones angry. But Quinn was getting under his skin, and he didn't want anyone within even touching distance. He tried to mute the shrill, silly tone of rage inside him. The voice that shrieked: Quinn *dares* to challenge me? Challenge *me?* The voice threatened to well up in his throat.

Deacon sidled up to him and muttered, "There were ten of us this morning. There are seven of us this evening."

Jones turned on his heel, his mind focused on San Callisto. "I can count."

Dominic slipped the Virgin crucifix into his jacket pocket as he waited for Thomas to begin his account of the Indwelling and the mysterious epilogue to Mary's life. The priest had closed his eyes, brow creased in concentration, as if rehearsing the story in his mind.

His eyes opened, and he began:

"We planned on weeks for you to absorb all this, not a few minutes, but— here goes. According to what I've reconstructed from the Ephesian *Transitus Mariæ* analecta, Mary died alone in a sea cave, facing the straits between the Ephesian shore and the island of Samos. Her body was discovered slumped over a chair in the cave mouth. Simon Magus then arranged for Mary to be interred in a sarcophagus placed inside the cave. Days later Mary appeared to Miriam— Mary Magdalene— in a dream and told her that she'd never died. On waking, Miriam summoned Mary's followers and together they opened the sarcophagus. Of those that looked in the tomb, most saw nothing and concluded the body had been moved. A few, however, perceived an inconstant image of Mary that flickered in and out of view— the Greek text is obscure here. Miriam and Simon were among those who glimpsed that elusive image. Helena of Tyre saw nothing— an empty sarcophagus.

"About Helena... three years earlier Mary rescued a fourteen-year-old Helena from a brothel in Tyre. The girl, who'd been hideously abused since the age of ten, became devoted to her savior. When Mary left Mount Carmel for Ephesus, Helena was among her followers. When the unexpected hope of a miraculous resurrection was dashed at the sight of an empty tomb it appears Helena suffered a complete mental collapse. She was on the verge of suicide. And that's when it happened. Mary came. Or rather, Helena became Mary, their souls enjoined. She was filled with Mary's spirit, her suffering transmuted to joy. Simon Magus, probably inspired by a water and wine ritual at the feast of Cana, declared that she was an amphora filled with sacred wine. In later years Helena composed a poem. I'll quote a few lines:

'I was sent forth from the power,
and I have come to those who reflect upon me,
and have been found among those who seek after me...
For I am the first and the last.
I am the honored one and the scorned one.
I am the whore and the holy one.
I am the wife and the virgin.
I am the mother and the daughter.'"

"I know that poem," Dominic exclaimed. "'Thunder, Perfect Mind.' And you're claiming Helena of Tyre wrote it?"

"I am. She did. And it was in those two inexplicable events, Mary's apotheosis and Helena's redemption, that the Marian religion was born. Simon Magus, who was in love with Mary, now switched his adoration to Helena, extolling her as the Virgin Mother incarnate, one in whom the spirit of Mary indwelt. Simon preached his gospel of Mary and effectively founded the religion later known as Silentium. Adapting his message to the Greek and Roman world, he proclaimed that Helena was Sophia, the divine spirit of Wisdom come to earth. A frequent visitor to the Library of Alexandria, he also contributed to the compilation of the Apocryphon Mariæ. But it was Helena, not Simon, who wrote most of the early sections of the apocryphon, inspired by Mary's indwelling spirit. Thus we can never be entirely sure which of the apocryphon's passages are written by the living Mary and which are by Helena."

Dominic studied the priest's apparently reasonable expression. "Frankly, the sarcophagus sounds like a pious variant on Christ's resurrection story. And, benign possession?"

Thomas carefully adjusted his glasses. "What you call possession, we call the Indwelling. By whatever strange pathways of thought and time, Mary is said to have entered people's dreams and healed troubled minds from within. The historian Sozomen, writing of the early fifth-century Anastasia church in

Constantinople, stated that the Mother of God had manifested herself there in visions and dreams, a divine healing power. The answer, Dominic, lies not in possession, but the nature of time. To be precise, what we now call the mathematical block conception of time."

"Martha mentioned block time on the way to Rome. Time is a book and consciousness resides outside the book, reading the contents an infinite number of times."

Thomas nodded vigorously. "Correct. But Mary wasn't starting from a blank slate: Parmenides of Elea, a Greek metaphysician who lived five centuries before the Christian era, was at least one influence. Mary developed Parmenides' ideas, no doubt supplemented by other scientific works in the Alexandrian Library that are long lost. The apocryphon contains the first recorded analogy of time as a book. The reader— so to speak— can skip back to earlier pages with full knowledge of what succeeded them."

"But wouldn't that alter time?" Dominic queried. "If my consciousness returned to the age of, say, ten, with the knowledge I possess now, I'd instantaneously change the past. I'd be a ten-year-old with an adult mind. Create a new timeline, in fact."

"Yes, and that new timeline would be an alternative reality, an alternative universe. The first line of the very first extract we possess from the Apocryphon Mariæ reads: 'We are alone in the universe, but the universe is not alone.' That is, we are probably the only conscious beings in this universe, but there exists an infinity of universes containing an infinity of beings. What can exist does exist— a loose translation from Parmenides."

"The Everett-Wheeler Many Worlds hypothesis," Dominic noted. "The multiverse. Controversial in scientific circles back in the 1950s, now pretty much mainstream. But— it makes my head spin when I speculate on what all that means. In a different timeline, Rachel and I are happily married and living on Cape Cod. In another, we never met. Here, now, Martha barely survived death. And out there— somewhere in an infinity of worlds— she did die. For that matter, in an alternative universe, I'm sitting where you are and you're sitting where I am with me trying to convince you of the truth of the Apocryphon Mariæ."

Thomas gave a quick nod. "Indeed. And let's hope you're making a better job of it than I am." His hand strayed to the laptop on the table. "On that note, let's return to the Indwelling"

Dominic shrugged. "Mary's possession of Helena... that sounds like a case of dissociative identity disorder, even if benevolent."

The priest looked down at the interlaced fingers of his clasped hands. "The diagnosis of multiple personality is a valid inference, I grant you, but it doesn't tally with my own experience." He flipped open the laptop, tapped the touchpad, and swerved the screen toward Dominic. "I suggest you look at this. It's just a few edited mpegs I collected from various people."

Dominic experienced a touch of apprehension. Over the last few days he'd been confronted with images of a mother he never knew he had, of an old friend being brutalized, and a new friend hung from a bridge. Now what?

The screen, however, displayed the innocuous scene of a derelict chapel. A shaft of light speared through an arched window and bisected the mismatched image of a jigsaw angel. Kneeling beside the botched and incomplete jigsaw was a young woman in a stained overcoat, her tangled hair hanging in ragged tails over her face. She held a jigsaw piece in one hand, brow furrowed, lips pursed as if attempting to puzzle out where to place the next piece in the pattern. The camera zoomed in and revealed that the puzzle was a small child's jigsaw, no more than twenty pieces.

"That was taken almost a year ago," Thomas informed. "She was a nineteen-year-old with the mind of a two-year-old. Some people were very cruel to her: they called her the Imbecile Madonna."

The image was replaced by the same woman in a small courtyard, again stooped over the unfinished jigsaw. The identical theme was played out in swift, succeeding locations, a couple identifiably Roman.

Then the scene switched to the Piazza of Santa Maria in Trastevere. The woman was sitting on the steps of the fountain. She looked up as Father Thomas approached and knelt at her side.

The screen went blank for a couple of seconds. The next location was a small area of ancient paving stones, illuminated by candlelight. This time she was hunched over her bungled puzzle. Then her face lifted to witness something he couldn't see. Whatever she saw, it transfigured her. He barely caught her whisper: "*Maria rimane.*" Mary abides.

She looked down at the puzzle, her mouth big with a smile. "Gabriel."

A momentary blackness, then the following clip showed the jigsaw close up, laid out flat on the archaic paving, each piece slotted into place, the picture complete.

A jigsaw angel spread its wings, poised to fly.

The screen turned black as the videos concluded.

Dominic closed the lid and stared across the table at the priest. "She resembles a woman I saw when the fog descended. Maria."

Thomas looked down at the interlaced fingers of his clasped hands. "Yes, that was Maria. I gave her that puzzle a year ago, then I lost track of her for several weeks until I came across her, here in Trastevere. I took her in, and a month later, she was transformed, right in front of me. Now she jokingly calls me her Chinese uncle. Not much of an uncle, but then, her father was less than a father. Her disorder wasn't neurological, but a defensive measure: her mind had retreated inside her body. Mary's grace descended upon her and Maria was healed from within." The priest observed Dominic with a shrewd look. "You're thinking— dissociative identity."

Dominic shifted in his chair. Never mind that he didn't know what to think, he wasn't sure he even knew *how* to think about the revelations. "I— don't know. And I shouldn't take any more of your time. Maybe I should move on to the Dormition chamber..."

Thomas nodded assent, then checked his watch. "It's well past nine. You should indeed head down there. After that you may go to the Vatican necropolis if you wish. Whatever the Monsignor said or didn't say, the choice is up to you."

"There's no choice involved." Dominic stretched his sore, stiffening muscles. The damage he'd received from the long fall was sending him a stark message in block capitals. "If my uncle doesn't get help from Il Gesù, I have to go to the Vatican. I figure Rachel may be there." He straightened up in the chair. "If you're done, I'll go visit this Dormition chamber. Best stay where you are— your feet must hurt like hell."

"In fact, you *should* go alone. The solitary pilgrim." Thomas took out a torn sheet of A4 and started sketching a rough map. "One last thought. Besides moving consciously within one's own timeline, the apocryphon suggests that it's possible, at the point of death, to read other people's books. It's a crude analogy, I admit. The best way I can express it is— ah— the awakened soul can share other people's timelines, people from the current era, or the distant past, or the remote future. Mary, at the measureless instant of death, transcended time. Mary's spirit can reach down twenty centuries from that sea cave south of Ephesus and affect the present."

"That's— quite a statement." Dominic stood up. "Any other time I'd be happy to discuss metaphysics to the wee small hours. But, you know..."

"I know." The map completed, the Jesuit handed it over. "You should find your way to the chamber from that."

Dominic hesitated before leaving the room. "The Monsignor claimed the Shrine's heart was haunted. By something more than a ghost."

Thomas's mouth bent in an enigmatic smile. "When you know what you're missing, you know what to look for. Fare forward, voyager."

Chapter 52

Shadows in the fog.

Deacon looked around at the figures strung out in a crescent in front of the church of San Callisto. Alice had sighted Quinn entering this old church a short while ago. Sooner or later he'd have to emerge.

He glanced at Jones and that unnerving woman, Alice, who he'd learned was Jones's sidekick from way back. They stood at the center of the crescent with D'Aloisio, Calabrese's cousin and near-lookalike, on the far side. His own men, the Londoners Craig and Wright, waited to his left.

There were ten of us this morning. There are seven of us this evening.

And standing in wait for Quinn, just six. Racciatti had been assigned the near-futile watch on the old sealed entrance to the Shrine in the Via Venezian.

He returned his attention to Jones. Cold, emotionless. There was a legend that Jones was born in a gun battle at the height of a drug war. Kind of far-fetched, but standing beside this living legend, a man both more and less than human, it was almost believable. Deacon's confidence, shaken by the mangled corpses of Carson and Calabrese, was quickly restored. He almost laughed at his brief lapse of nerve.

Jones was invincible.

And he was just one of six waiting for Quinn.

Six to one.

The Transitus wall had tumbled within twenty minutes. The concrete core partition at the end of the tunnel was taking longer to penetrate. The delay, however, seemed to leave Cardinal Chavet unmoved. He stood with the patience of a desert saint as if turned to stone.

Rachel kept her eyes on the demolition. That way she didn't have to look at Belucci molding the malleable plastique into natural hollows in the tufa rock.

She *knew* plastique could be kneaded like dough and not react. She *knew* plastique was harmless without blasting caps. But her treacherous mind still conjured up images of her head ending up twenty yards from her feet.

She glanced at Chavet. "Why the rush with the explosives?"

"No rush. A dozen bricks of plastique are more than enough for the tunnel. The remaining twenty are for the chamber."

"If there is a chamber."

He kept his gaze on the widening hole. "There's a chamber." A semblance of a smile. "Patience, Rachel, patience. You have already shown considerable courage and resilience in resisting Jones and Deacon."

She glanced sharply at Chavet. "The coin and the hammer—that test was yours?"

"The objective was mine. The details I left to Jones. He—overstepped."

She controlled a surge of anger. She wanted nothing more than to kick him in his shrunken stomach. "How can you, a priest, betray your own faith by sanctioning something like that?"

That got through, that punctured his sang-froid, less than a sword thrust, but more than a pinprick.

He tightened his shoulders, closing in on himself. "I do what I must."

The declaration was succeeded by a crash. She sprang back instinctively, arms shielding her eyes. But all she received was a fine cloud of dust.

The wall had collapsed inward, presenting a sizeable aperture, an open invitation. Chavet dispensed with patience and rushed forward, ignoring the workmen's warning that the air may not yet be breathable. With resigned shrugs they followed him into the gap, flashlights stabbing the dark.

Officer Belucci, prompt to action, left off from attaching the plastique and brushed by Rachel, a batch of lamps in his arms. After a moment's hesitation she tracked Belucci's steps, treading carefully as she negotiated the pile of rubble at the entrance and slowing her pace further as the darkness moved in.

Flashlight beams crossed, recrossed and crisscrossed, revealing little of detail but conveying the size of the chamber, at least fifteen yards in length and ten in breadth under a barrel-vaulted roof.

Then a lamp was switched on. And another. And another. The interior gradually disclosed its secrets as Belucci set up a row of lights at the center of the chamber. Gradually, the lamps revealed the walls as dull brown surfaces, similar to the tunnel although much smoother. The floor was paved, the gray stone visible beneath the omnipresent dust.

And in the middle of the floor was a rectangular shape. A rectangular recess in the ground, maybe two yards long by one yard wide. Aside from that shallow recess, the chamber was featureless. Whatever had lain at the center of the vault, it lay there no longer.

The cardinal stood motionless beside the empty rectangle, blank gaze fixed on its vacancy. "Nothing," he murmured, barely audible. Then, more distinctly: "Nothing."

He backed away, his gaunt frame trembling, then swung round, his glare sweeping the chamber.

"Where is it?" he growled.

The growl expanded to a tormented roar.

"Where is it?"

Chapter 53

If the Shrine had originally been a House of Prophecies, as Father Thomas professed, it wasn't in prophetic vein tonight.

Dominic explored the basement rooms with the aid of Thomas's rudimentary map. He passed through one drab, empty room after another, revealed in the lackluster illumination of grimy light bulbs. Aside from a denuded kitchen and bathroom, each room was like every other room. Bare light bulbs. Bare walls. Scuffed floor tiles. Quiet dust.

There were no eschatological glimpses in the glum haloes of the lights. No voice of thunder prophesying doom resounded in the acoustics of the old building. The sole touch of ethereal theatricality was the occasional soft sift of dust that twirled as wraith dancers and stunted djinns in fluke drafts that leaked from under doors and cracks in the wall. As yet, no psychic creepy-crawlies had made a steeplechase of his spine.

He headed down a passage to where the map indicated a stairway and made his way up to a long, narrow corridor whose ceiling bulb was privileged to wear a shade. Aside from the solitary lampshade there was scant evidence anyone had ever lived here. Which made it all the harder to imagine that, somewhere in this building, maybe in one of the rooms on this floor, Sarah Maitland had given birth to him over three decades ago, not long before the occupants moved out and the emptiness moved in.

Angling down another passage, broader but more poorly lit, he reached a marble staircase, wide enough for four men to climb abreast. He could faintly descry a landing at the top of the first flight. The way up to the Dormition chapel, had to be. He set off up the marble steps, slowing as he moved out of the feeble light and into dense dark. Pausing on the landing, he peered up at the second flight. A solid slab of darkness.

Scaling the stairs, step by careful step, he suddenly had the mordant image of mounting a scaffold blindfolded. Where the steps ended he reached out and his fingertips contacted smooth wood. The pressure of his hand on the door increased as he leaned forward. And the door swung open to the creak of old, tired hinges.

He stepped through the doorway and stopped in his tracks, staring at the chapel.

Where once there would have been a congregation of worshipers there was a small congregation of candles, none less than a foot in height, ranged along the walls of the rib-vaulted chapel and on a low, stone altar at the far end of the nave, fronted by a solitary pew.

And, an inconstant image in the flutter of candles, the Virgin Mary, nailed to a cross, hung high above her altar, flanked and overhung with shadows.

He took a pace forward, then another, feeling like an intruder on a sacrosanct space. It wasn't that a sacred presence haunted the chapel, but more a faint echo, a dim memory. The memory was redolent of the shadowy interior of Santa Maria in Trastevere but with a breath of fear that he could almost inhale. With slowing steps he approached the altar, his gaze gradually ascending as he neared the more-than-life-size image.

Just short of the altar he halted and peered up at the Virgin Crucifix, suspended by a thick chain from the curved ceiling.

The Virgin's features, portrayed in the chiaroscuro of candlelight, were extraordinarily beautiful, if such a timeworn word could be applied to the individual paradox of that face, beatific and sorrowful, young but suggestive of epochs of experience. An embodied enigma, crowned with roses and thorns.

Maybe Martha was right. Maybe Mary could renew the Church with a sense of wonder and mystery and help redeem a darkening world. In the Middle Ages her cult flourished among serfs and soldiers. She was the popular choice, the champion of the common people, willing to cheat the divine justice system by rescuing her devotees from hell itself. In one medieval tale, Satan sent a deputation of devils to the throne of God to complain that Mary was breaking the rules.

It was nineteenth-century piety that tamed Mary. The medieval Madonna was no meek maiden but more like a young Eleanor of Aquitaine, a bright queen fiercely protective of her vassals.

"You were always on our side."

He stepped back and took in the general features of the interior, wondering whether Thomas or the "niece" he mentioned, Maria, had set out the candles. To his right, high on the wall, ranged a row of arched windows, sealed with brick and plaster. To his left, a small door led to what his map described as the dormitory area.

And behind the altar was a narrow, arched door barely his own height. According to the map, a door to a stairway. The way down to the erstwhile Dormition chamber, site of the tomb of Mary in the third century. He noticed a couple of small, used candles lying discarded on the altar, mere stubs of wax. He took the longer of the two and lit it from one of the altar candles in case he had need of light on the stair.

Before entering the arched door he took out his phone to call the Monsignor before the signal was lost underground. And saw that the phone was buckled. Hardly a surprise considering the impact from the long fall. It was a minor miracle he wasn't in similar shape. He tried the power. Nada.

With a shrug he pocketed the phone and circled the altar. The stairway door opened at the turn of a latch, revealing a flagstone floor under a low-wattage light bulb. And, a few strides away, the metallic handrail of a spiral staircase that descended through a hole in the floor. He started down its rusted metal steps into a darkness relieved minimally by the light of the candle stub, his shoulder constantly brushing the stone wall. The descent continued, a dozen steps extended to a hundred and he began to feel that he was spinning on the spot.

Eventually he reached ground and stood on what appeared to be compacted soil under a layer of dust, a stout door in front of him. A turn of the latch and the door swung open.

He entered a roughly hewn tunnel and set off down the passage. At the far end shone a lambent glow that softened the uneven walls.

As he drew nearer to the mellow light he realized that he must be travelling parallel to the Via San Callisto, aiming directly for the Santa Maria church. The Monsignor had mentioned that the former site of Mary's tomb was underneath the crypt of Santa Maria in Trastevere. He was approaching the original Chamber of the Dormition.

Nearing the end of the tunnel, he entered a candlelit dawn. He stood at the threshold of a vaulted chamber some fifteen yards in span. The interior was illuminated by a score of tall candles, each set in a silver stand on the paved floor. Apart from the intermittent sputter of flames, the silence was a solemn weight in the chamber. He blew out his candle and spared a moment for it to cool as he surveyed the vault's expanse.

The compact, bumpy paving stones had a distinct archaic appearance: they could easily have dated back to the third century. And they were identical to the paving in the final video clips on Thomas's laptop. Maria's transfiguration: this was where it happened.

The only floor space clear of candles was the center of the vault where a low, rectangular depression was visible. The hollow, floored with densely packed gravel, was over six feet in length, more than three feet in width. The appropriate size and shape to accommodate a sarcophagus. Reflecting, grimly, that the word sarcophagus was taken from the Greek for "flesh-eating," he advanced and knelt before the recess, eyes focused on the rectangular outline.

And in the flicker of a candle flame, that single focus became a double focus, one on the sarcophagus hollow, the other on the empty slab in Carlingford's Sepulcher chapel, a slab bereft of the Pietà, the dead Christ in the arms of a mourning Mary.

Now he was confronted by another absence, more momentous than a missing plaster effigy. The absence of the Virgin Mary.

Much as he resisted it, for a moment, just a moment, he teetered on the brink of belief. An absence presupposes the loss of a presence. A negative requires a positive. There were no ghosts here, but in this precise instant Dominic almost believed that the chamber was haunted by the memory of deity.

He rose from his kneeling position and took a step back, vacantly viewing the empty niche. Emptiness. Negative space.

Then, from nowhere came nothing that had a name, and reality was engulfed.

The recess became a black rectangle on the floor, a hole in existence, a gateway to oblivion.

A vacuum, it sucked the soul from him.

This is where you come from. This is where you go.

From Nothing to Nothing.

"No!" he gasped, heart hammering as he stumbled backward. The black trance fled as though exorcised with a word.

Reality returned as quickly as it took flight. The chamber rose strong and solid around him. The recess was— just a recess, a gravel-floored memento mori.

Pulse rate gradually slowing, he stared at the hollow. As his breathing eased, it dawned on him that his recent battering had shaken him more than he realized. The hallucination had been so vivid, its impact harrowing. But, breath by breath, he recovered.

Finally he was even able to summon a thin smile. "I was scared of Nothing."

He looked at the graveled recess, preparing to quit this fool's errand. His gaze slowly ascended from the hollow to the candles fronting the far wall. Their slender flames rose straight and untroubled in the chamber's still air. He watched them for a moment, then cast a final glance at the hollow.

A shadow glided over the hollow's gravel. A human silhouette, head and shoulders.

The shadow elongated, sliding over the floor and up the far wall until it looked down on him from above the candlelight.

Chapter 54

The cardinal stood straight as a lightning rod in the center of the vault, fists clenched, eyes crackling with impotent rage. Rachel kept her distance, back to the wall. If ever a man was ready to detonate, it was the man who stood by the dust-filled recess in the floor.

Chavet's hopes were smashed. But that left her where, exactly? For all the cardinal's assurances, it was a flip of the coin whether he'd let her go now that his mission had failed, or— she tried not to dwell on it— eliminate a hostile witness.

She gave a low sigh and leaned her head against the wall. Seen up close, the wall was scratched under the fine dust. Scratched extensively. In fact, the scratches resembled deliberate marks.

A quick brush at the dust with the edge of her palm and she uncovered a patch of bare wall. The illumination from the lamps was weak in this far corner but the markings were clearly a form of writing. Checking she wasn't observed, Rachel blew softly on the uncovered area and flicked away most of the remaining dust particles, transforming the yellowish-brown surface into a dull black expanse which resembled basalt.

It was no slapdash scrawl on the dark surface, but a formal script, meticulously engraved deep into the rock and arranged in neat horizontal rows. Each inscribed letter was little more than half an inch in height. She couldn't read ancient Greek to save her life, but she recognized Greek letters when she saw them. She was on the verge of exploring further when Chavet's high-pitched exclamation startled her into whirling around like a vandal caught dust-handed in the act.

"What are you doing here?" The cardinal was rigid with indignation, stare fixed on the entrance.

A second later Rachel witnessed the cause of his anger emerge from the shattered wall. A tall, distinguished man in a black overcoat, the white of a Roman collar just visible between the lapels. He was accompanied by an apologetic De Mola.

"He wouldn't stop when I ordered," complained the gendarme. "What was I to do? He wears the Petrus ring."

Chavet simmered down and flicked his hand at the policeman. "Return to your post."

De Mola reacted like a scolded puppy, a puppy with attitude. "What's the point? None of this feels right. I'm leaving— for home."

"I need you here!"

The policeman moved away. "This operation is unsanctioned. I wash my hands of it."

"Go, if you must, but keep your vow of silence," Chavet muttered, turning his ire back on the intruder as De Mola left.

"Auguste," the priest greeted the cardinal, giving the impression that he'd spat out the word like sulfuric acid.

"Aylesbury." Chavet's tone was in marked contrast, soft as an eel on velvet.

She had exchanged barely a dozen words with the Monsignor inside Santa Maria in Aracoeli, but he was Dominic's uncle and his unexpected arrival had to be a good thing. Besides, any enemy of Chavet...

The Monsignor caught sight of her and his patrician face broke into a warm smile, offset by the swelling bruise on his jaw. "Rachel! Delighted to see you again." He caught her hand and kissed it with a courtly gesture. Quite the charmer.

She couldn't resist a smile. "You sound like Alan Rickman; anyone ever tell you that?"

"Several people, including Alan Rickman." He leaned close and whispered. "I'd expected to get you away before the first wall was breached, but I'll do my best. I owe it to you." He pulled back, his voice raised. "Would you excuse me a moment? Urgent business, you understand."

"Our business has come to a dead end," Chavet said, indicating the soil in the rectangular recess. "The sarcophagus has gone."

"I'm not blind, Auguste. First things first, we discuss the position of this delightful young lady— in private." He walked back into the tunnel, beckoning Chavet who, after a momentary hesitation, followed in his steps.

Rachel leaned against the wall and waited, straining and failing to catch a word from the distant murmur as the minutes labored past. Finally the two men returned, the Monsignor's grim expression an open admission of defeat.

"No luck, I'm afraid," he said to her remorsefully. "The man's beyond all reason. Certifiably insane."

Chavet glared at him. "I told you, you can go."

The Monsignor squared his shoulders. "If she stays, I stay."

The cardinal gave a shrug of indifference. Then his gaze lowered to the recess, his expression phasing from resentful to thoughtful, from thoughtful to hopeful. "Perhaps," he murmured. "Perhaps we haven't even scratched the surface." He signaled the workmen. "Fetch shovels from the store. Clear the dirt away from this niche. Let's see what's underneath." As if struck by an afterthought, he called to Belucci. "Check the walls, search for straight hairline cracks."

As the workmen left and Belucci began inspecting the walls, the Monsignor approached the cardinal and stopped within punching distance. "I've decided, belatedly, that the sarcophagus isn't worth a human life, Auguste. Can't you do the same?"

"Don't fool yourself. You want to locate the tomb as much as—"

"Your eminence!" Belucci exclaimed. "This wall has words carved into it."

The two priests turned as one, wearing equally eager expressions, and hastened over to Belucci, who had started scraping away at the stone. One look at the wall and Chavet marched to the entranceway and shouted down the passage. "Bring sweeping brushes with the shovels, long-handled sweeping brushes! And hurry!"

Rachel returned to her corner and sat down on the paving stones, observing the Monsignor's barely suppressed fascination.

The Monsignor and the cardinal may be enemies, but they were enemies with a common purpose. They were almost like a couple, trapped in their own history.

And she was stuck in the middle.

It was surprising how much could be accomplished in ten minutes with sweeping brushes, sturdy muscles, and an abundance of enthusiasm. Considerable expanses of the walls, illuminated by a score of electric lamps, revealed their ancient secrets.

And, Rachel noted from her seated position in the corner, the Monsignor became more animated as the cardinal subsided into sullen disapproval. The recess, for the moment, had been put on hold in the heat of discovery.

Every inch of the exposed walls was inscribed with what the Monsignor identified as Koiné Greek script, and not a single Greek letter was even an inch in height. The engraved writing comprised thousands upon thousands of words.

And, as the Monsignor declared within the first minute, the writing on the wall was the Apocryphon Mariæ, carved painstakingly by Mary's later disciples. The papyrus manuscript was destroyed, but the Collyridians had preserved the secret book in stone.

"Look at this!" the Monsignor exclaimed, not for the first time since the uncovering began. "Mary describes the moment of conception, as though she felt it inside her. We had a mere two lines of this passage in our analecta, and had to reconstruct the context."

He scanned the lines, and commenced to translate in a tone suffused with awe:

"And leaving Nazareth by the path of stones, I looked upon the stars reflected in the Sea of Galilee. There it was that Chokmah, the spirit of Wisdom, came upon me. And, by the Sea of Galilee, I cast off my clothes and swam from the shore. New life stirred in my womb as though it were knowledge, that though born of the flesh, our spirit is from the eternal silence of the All. I, Mary, declare that I conceived the flesh of Jesus that night, but not his spirit. And I was no longer in the Sea of Galilee, but reached to the night above the night and swam through a sea of stars."

Chavet scowled and returned to the center of the chamber, ordering Belucci over with a snap of the fingers. "Back to the main task. Clear the muck from this hollow and see what's beneath."

The Monsignor seemed oblivious of the cardinal's actions. He beckoned Rachel to join him as he moved to a cleared wall space near where she was seated. "Look at this. I know, I know, you shouldn't be here, and I blame myself. But— look at this."

She studied the engravings. "I was about to say it's all Greek to me, but this isn't. It looks kind of familiar."

"It should. Those are Indian numerals, mistakenly called Arabic numerals. The Hindus developed these centuries before Mary's era. According to accepted history, Indian numerals and the decimal system weren't introduced into Europe until the eleventh century. Here, that's the symbol for *Shuunya*, zero. If Mary was familiar with the use of zero as an actual number, that's proof the Library of Alexandria possessed a mathematical sophistication far beyond anything credited to it. Buddhist missionaries were present in Alexandria decades before the birth of Mary. They may well have introduced the mathematical concept of zero to the Greek world."

His gaze wandered the engraved notation, his mind in another world. "Here, perhaps, on these walls, are Mary's proofs, whether her own or collected from earlier scholars, of multidimensional space, an infinity of universes, block time, and the nature of mind and spirit. Even mysteries we haven't yet conceived."

She gave a vague nod, recalling the biblical passage Maria had cited: "Mene, mene, tekel, upharsin." At the Monsignor's startled look, she hastened to explain. "You know— the writing on the wall. And here we are, surrounded by it."

The Monsignor thumped his forehead. "Of course! Jonathan Taylor's message. The writing on the wall was, quite literally, the writing on the wall. Writing on *these* walls. That's what he glimpsed in his vision as he knelt before the Transitus wall."

She was about to respond when the scrape of metal on stone made her turn to witness a grinning Belucci clearing earth from an area of stone at the base of the recess.

A circle of onlookers quickly formed around the hollow and watched as a set of two three-feet-wide slabs were revealed, one slab bearing a rusty iron rung bonded to the stone from centuries of pressure and chemical reaction. Fratta grabbed a hammer and chisel from a toolbox and jumped down beside the gendarme, inserting the chisel under the edge of the iron. Several hefty blows on the chisel loosened the stone's grip on the rung. The two men seized the iron ring and heaved back.

At first the slab refused to budge, defying the men's best efforts. Perspiration was soon in evidence, matched with pained grunting.

Chavet leaned over the hollow. "How is the—" His speech was lost in a grinding sound as the slab came loose. It swung back with such unexpected force that the men sprang aside with the speed of shock.

Flashlights aimed into the open square, disclosing a flight of stone steps leading underground in the direction of the breached wall.

Impatience personified, Chavet had hold of a flashlight and was already descending the steps. "You next, Aylesbury," he ordered. "You and Rachel. I want my men behind you."

The Monsignor graced Rachel with an exaggerated bow. "After you, my dear."

With a fleeting smile at the old world charm, she followed the cardinal and the dancing beam of light down into the darkness. Placing her feet cautiously on the narrow, rough-hewn stairway, she counted sixteen steps before her boots crunched into friable soil.

The cardinal was already some distance ahead in the thin tunnel, his figure a blurry silhouette against the wavering beam of the flashlight. She struggled to keep up, almost tripping on the bumpy floor. Her pace eased as other flashlights from the men at her back picked out more details of the subterranean passage, confirming her impression that the tunnel sloped downward in a gentle incline.

As she progressed down the passageway she noticed that the cardinal was taking long, deliberate strides as he had in the tunnel from the Transitus wall to the empty chamber.

But this walk was proving considerably longer than the previous one. She must have covered at least twice the distance. A few more paces and Chavet's spindly figure pulled to a halt, his flashlight steady, highlighting an unidentifiable obstruction.

She plodded on until she stood alongside the cardinal. Before them was a simple wooden door, buckled with age and bereft of the rusted latch that lay on the ground.

Chavet murmured, as much to himself as to her: "Sixty yards, give or take, from St. Peter's tomb to the chamber we just left. At a rough estimate, that's the distance we've traveled. The tomb of St. Peter, and the basilica's main altar, are directly above whatever is on the other side of this door."

Rachel felt it then. The return of awe. If half the apocryphal stories of Mary were true, she had journeyed into dimensions and worlds that frontier physics had only recently contemplated as realities.

And, above all, there was the doctrine that Mary had never truly died. The Catholic Church hailed it as the assumption; the Orthodox Church, the dormition; the Collyridians, the Indwelling. What would it be like, in reality, to encounter a being who had bypassed death, twenty centuries ago, and moved in unseen worlds?

Chavet, hand trembling, reached out and pushed the door. The ancient hinges squealed in protest but he slowly forced the door ajar.

Four flashlight beams probed the dark beyond the door, darting around a spacious chamber. Then, almost in unison, the beams converged on the center of the vault.

And illuminated a sarcophagus mounted on a stone dais.

Chapter 55

For a frozen moment Dominic stared up at the tall shadow on the chamber wall. The moment unfroze, along with his temporary paralysis. He spun round, nervous system a-jangle.

A tall young woman in a navy blue raincoat adorned with a silver star brooch stood a few paces from him, head leaning slightly to one side, a slanted smile on her lips. Straight black hair hung untidily to her shoulders, framing an oval face.

It was the woman who had stood in the foggy street below Martha's apartment. Maria. But he'd formed only the haziest impression of her face. That face was extraordinary, the soul in it naked and glorious as though the flesh were translucent, and the eyes dark fire. Which made it all the more inexplicable that the young woman radiated a disturbing quality, an indefinable sense of danger.

She raised her hand in greeting. "Hello, Dominic."

He gave an automatic nod. Although she spoke in English, her accent was difficult to distinguish. "Maria. It *is* Maria?"

Maria's leftward-slanting smile became more pronounced. She sauntered up to the rectangular hollow. "Find what you were looking for?"

"Maria— if you don't mind me asking, why are you here?"

"I have a bunk bed in one of the upstairs rooms. Thomas has always been accommodating. Why are *you* here?"

He shrugged, feeling awkward and subtly unsettled by the woman's presence. "No idea. Only found an absence, if that makes any sense. Maybe present absence is proof of past presence. File that under glib."

She nodded toward the recess. "An absence. A void that cries out to be filled."

"It was nothing."

"As you wish." A ghost of a smile touched her mouth. She was silent for a brief space, then spoke in a quiet, haunting voice as she slowly paced around the chamber:

"The absence is loss, the sorrow of mortality, first stamped in cuneiform over four thousand years ago in the Epic of Gilgamesh, fifth king of Uruk in the lands of the Sumerians. Gilgamesh went in quest of immortality, but in the end despaired." A vast past flooded Maria's eyes, oceans deep. "This was the lament of Gilgamesh to his friend Enkidu:

'Who can aspire to heaven?

The gods alone live forever under the sun.

The days of men are numbered,

their deeds are as the wind.'"

She halted, head bowed. In the silence that ensued, Dominic was unable to look anywhere but Maria's face. Finally, he found his voice, compelled to an admission:

"Since I was a child, I've been haunted by death. Not the dying, but the blackness that surrounds our lives. I've begun to wonder— maybe death is the negative space that gives life its shape."

Her mouth curved in a wistful smile. "Life isn't circumscribed by death. The dark around the candle's halo is the shadow of eternity. The candle may seem to blow out, but the flame endures, unseen." The smile deepened. "The night, too, has its radiance."

Feeling that he was losing control, drowning in this woman, he broke eye contact and looked back at the tomb recess. "Do you know why I was sent here?"

"We miss things when they're gone. Often, when the loved one's gone, only then can you see that face, hear the voice once heard. Remembered, they shine."

"If you're referring to the missing sarcophagus, I never knew Mary to miss her."

"Really? Well, you can always dream."

He threw a swift glance at the recess. "If you want the truth, I saw— a void. A meaningless nothing. There was no gentle nostalgia, no mystical insight."

"Yes, that can happen. But no need to be afraid of Nothing. Nothing doesn't exist."

"Easy to say."

Maria studied his face. "Imagine," she said. "Imagine there's a heaven. It's hard, but try. And above us, more than sky."

"Words from the pulpit? Tell me, who do you think you— er, who are you?" *If you tell me you're the Virgin Mary, just where do I go from there...*

"You know my name. As for *who* I am, Thomas may have mentioned me."

"He did. You're his adopted niece. Guess he must have had quite an influence on you. Uh... did he plan for us to meet?"

"It was my decision."

"Right. And— he's talked to you, I guess— about history, the Church, the Virgin Mary, the Indwelling? And you— took it all in?"

Smiling at the implication, she let the silence absorb the question. Hands in pockets, she resumed pacing the chamber. When she spoke it was in a melody of a voice that might have come from the morning of the world: "The Virgin Mary— born to Hannah and Joachim of Bethany in the twentieth year of the reign of Herod, and named Mariam, born in a cave known as the Mouth of Sheol. As a child she walked the Canopic Way of Alexandria. As a woman she swam in the Sea of Galilee as it turned into a sea of stars. She gave birth to the Messiah in the same cave in which she entered the world, taught her son all she had learned, and saw him crucified as King of the Jews. And at the end— she found there was no end."

"Are you quoting Father Thomas? The things he says— they're impossible." He regretted the words the instant they left his mouth. If Maria had a pathological identification with Mary, then perhaps the disease was the cure, her Mary persona serving as a refuge from some past or present trauma.

Maria, however, seemed unfazed. "'What can exist does exist...' Parmenides of Elea, 475 BC."

"'It ain't necessarily so...' Ira Gershwin, 1935 AD."

She laughed appreciatively. "And it ain't necessarily so that it ain't necessarily so. But enough chat. Things to do, places to be. I believe Rachel is in the Vatican necropolis." Maria's pacing had brought her to the chamber entrance. "Speaking of which, you'll gain nothing by hanging around here."

He hadn't the slightest intention of hanging around. Nor of bringing this troubled— troubling?— woman with him. "Listen, I wish you well. But I'm going to the Vatican alone."

"You won't get past the guards. So happens I can." With a flourish, she produced an expensive leather holder. "This comes with a Vatican passport in the name of Sister Gratia. It's an excellent fake. So, are you with me?"

His initial reaction was to refuse but the prospect of not reaching Rachel made him think twice.

"We'll stand a better chance of getting Rachel out if we team up," she persisted. "Your call, soldier boy."

Teetering between yes and no, he eventually gave a shrug. "What do I have to lose?"

Her face lit up. "Excellent. By the way, you were followed here. I saw figures in the fog, grouped around the church door. I'll go out on a limb and say they're not tourists."

"I'll lay odds it's Jones," he hissed softly. "Any other way out of here?"

"I have an idea." She took out a photo from her raincoat pocket and held it up.

He studied the photo. "That's— nice," he said uncertainly. "So..."

Her eyes flicked up to the ceiling. "A gift from Father Thomas. Up in the church."

It took only a second for the other shoe to drop. "Ah, right." Then another thought occurred. "Does this church have a belfry?"

Chapter 56

Unswerving, Jones kept his focus trained on the door of San Callisto. An hour since Alice reported Quinn entering the church. He'd been waiting outside the better part of that hour. They would wait all night if necessary.

A black Ford transit was parked ten yards from the church doorway, ready for Quinn to be bundled inside. Jones had a feeling that would be happening real soon. When paid to do a job, he did the job well. Part of a job well done was style. And the fear it sparked in others. He had risen from the back streets and alleys of his impoverished hometown by the exercise of fear. Now he dominated the wide avenues and boulevards of America and Europe by fear. Executing your targets wasn't enough: their deaths must become the stuff of legend.

Quinn would die as a rat. By rat poison. And a rat trap.

His rat poison of choice was good old-fashioned strychnine in solution: no bleeding heart warfarin or barium carbonate for Quinn. The leather pouch with four hypodermics was tucked into the inside pocket of his jacket. Just a tiny amount of strychnine in three of the hypos, 0.05mg per 1kg, insufficient to kill at first jab. In the last hypo in the row, 0.3mg per 1kg, the death stroke to be dealt only after Quinn hung on to life for days, spine broken under the crossbar of a weight-lifting machine, Jones' own improvised rat trap.

Jones first witnessed the symptoms of strychnine poisoning on a grown man when he was seven, and he was impressed. Twenty minutes after the poison entered the bloodstream, it kicked in, causing severe muscle spasms to head and neck. The convulsions then spread to the rest of the body, becoming more acute, the pain more intense. Death, when it came, was by asphyxiation.

Quinn would join the list of legends in Jones's scrapbook: rat death Quinn.

The rattle of the door latch swept him into instant, fluid action that took him to the doorway. The gap was sufficient to allow a wide-shouldered man access. And not one inch more did it move.

Was he expected to fall for such a simple ruse? Charge blind into the dark?

Then the bell tolled. A long, sonorous note. He glanced up at the church roof, then back at the shoulder-width gap. What the hell was Quinn doing, summoning aid with a bell like some medieval monk? The bell tolled again before the first reverberation died away. And this time he distinguished another sound below the echoing percussion. It struck him as familiar, but he couldn't quite place it.

The sound was drowned in another peal that rang out over Trastevere. He tensed, wondering what trick he was missing. The bell note faded away. And that tauntingly familiar noise was back in redoubled force. Louder, and nearer.

He identified it too late. By the time he'd put a name to the sound, familiar in every street in Rome, a Vespa blasted out of the narrow gap, scraping through by the rubber skin of its handlebars.

Its rider was a black-haired woman in a billowing raincoat, its pillion passenger Dominic Quinn.

The Vespa, exiting at an angle, slammed into the skin-headed Wright and yanked him off his feet at the same moment the church door slammed shut. The Londoner reacted instinctively, seizing hold of the handlebars and wrapping his legs around the front of the speeding scooter. He pulled back his head to deliver a head-butt, not catching on that the Vespa had carried him clean across the tiny square...

...and bang into a wall that met the back of his skull. Jones heard the terminal crack from ten yards away.

Wright dropped, a dead weight, landing face-first on the ground as the jolted scooter's front wheel mounted the wall and then skidded obliquely, tilting the machine sharply to the left. A moment later it was sliding along the street on its side, taking the rider with it. Quinn had tumbled off in the opposite direction on impact, rolling to the right the moment he hit ground.

Jones nearly bit through his lip in fury at the raw fact that Quinn and the unknown woman had outwitted him. Outwitted *him*, in front of his own people.

"Alice! Deacon! Get the woman!" he yelled, racing toward Quinn, his anger further inflamed at the shrill note in his voice. "The rest of you, get Quinn! No, not in the truck! *Run!*"

The one saving grace was that his people were in between Quinn and the rider, who had quickly righted her vehicle. No free ride out for the American. Quinn was already sprinting in the opposite direction, one arm signaling his companion to vamoose. The revving of the scooter and the squeal of tires proved she was taking his advice.

The nearest one to Quinn was D'Aloisio, as hefty as his cousin Calabrese, but no great shakes on the chase. He lumbered rather than sprinted. Quinn, in contrast, was a blur of speed.

By the time Jones had caught up and passed the leaden-footed D'Aloisio, his quarry had disappeared around the corner into the Via della Cisterna. In this fog, in the maze of Trastevere, Quinn would escape them if he wasn't run down in the next few seconds.

Skidding around the street corner, Jones cursed aloud. No sign of Quinn in the thick fog. Receding footsteps, but it was impossible to judge their direction.

A minute later, after traversing half a dozen streets, Jones still saw no sign of Quinn. The bastard had escaped him.

Well, Jones still had five of his people to scour the area. One phone call would send them fanning out.

But the bastard had still escaped him.

He slowed to a halt, panting with exertion, and tasted a pure, distilled hate that was beyond even his experience.

Quinn had given him the slip, for now, but he hadn't gotten clear. He was a rat in a maze. And the exterminators were closing in.

Chapter 57

Yet again, Rachel contemplated taking her chances and running like hell, out of this chamber, out of the necropolis, out of Vatican City.

Yet again, she remembered her family— her mom and dad, hard on the ground rules and heavy on the love; her seven-year-old brother, serious beyond his years, nose stuck in a book; her twelve-year-old sister, a cheeky little miss who'd give you her last candy bar. Four good reasons to stay put.

She sat hunched in a corner of the Testament Chamber, as Chavet had dubbed the chamber bearing the engraved Apocryphon Mariæ, and observed the Monsignor shifting restlessly along the edges of the room, reading the writing on the wall.

After that fleeting glimpse of the sarcophagus in the combined flashlights, the cardinal had ushered them back up the tunnel while the Chamber of the Dormition was being "prepared," whatever that signified. Belucci had stationed himself, arms akimbo, in front of the breached wall as though daring her to escape.

Far more disconcertingly, Belucci had fixed blasting caps to the plastique in the tunnel that sloped up to the Transitus wall. One press of a button on a remote detonator and down would come the tunnel roof. Not a comforting thought while she was on the wrong side of the tunnel.

Intermittently, Esposito and Fratta passed to and fro, carrying lamps and demolition tools down the tunnel. A mounting unease was visible on their faces.

"Rachel!"

The Monsignor's excited exclamation startled her but she rose to the summons, crossing to the far wall where he stood enraptured by whatever he was reading in the inscribed text.

"What is it?"

The Monsignor replied in a hushed tone: "Quantum superposition."

She waited for an elaboration. None came. "Well," she said finally, "that explains everything. Why didn't we see it from the start?"

He swung around, eyebrows arched. "Oh, forgive me. If I read this passage right, Mary or one of her disciples is posing the most fundamental question of human existence: at the instant of death, where does consciousness go? Not into oblivion because oblivion isn't something you can go *into*. It isn't there. The end of the line is, by definition, the end of the line."

Wasn't that merely playing with words? She let it pass. "So, what's the solution?"

"The answer is manifold, and I confess I grasp merely a part of it. The 'inner dark,' that is, the observer, the self, the soul, reverts to the beginning of the line, lives the same life over again. According to that interpretation, we never really die but simply re-enact the same timeline."

"As in, we've been this way before," she said.

"Indeed, an infinite number of times. But that's not the only option. Many lives are, after all, riven with suffering. To avoid that fate, the inner dark can pull back, as it were, and reside in what Mary calls the sea of stars. At first I took that sea to represent the universe but, more fundamentally, it stands for a spiritual ocean which bears some resemblance to current theories of the zero-point field or the earlier concept of the Dirac Sea, a sea of infinite negative particles."

"Monsignor, I almost flunked science at high school. Cut me some slack."

He smiled in apology. "Then I'll come to what the apocryphon calls the 'way of the million worlds.' That's where quantum superposition applies. I'll give you an analogy. Imagine a needle balanced precisely on its point in a vacuum within a constant gravitational field. The needle has the choice of an infinite number of directions in which to fall. In fact, the needle falls in *all* those infinite directions and each of those directions is another universe. We, however, will perceive it to fall in only one direction because we exist in a single four-dimensional space-time."

Rachel winced. "I'm following so far. Barely."

"I'll try to keep it non-technical. After all, I'm no scientist either. So... a God's-eye view of my hypothetical needle would show it as something like an active metal dome, a solid block which is the sum of its infinite fallen arcs. That, in layman-speak, is the needle in a state of quantum superposition. The needle exists in an infinite number of positions simultaneously."

"Okay, so how does this tie in to human immortality?"

"It ties in because at the last instant of consciousness, the end of the fall of a single direction of the needle so to speak, consciousness has the capacity to leave that direction and skip to another. That is, skip to another life."

"Reincarnation?" she suggested tentatively.

"Not in any traditional understanding of the term." He glanced up at the ranks of Greek script. "Mary, as best as I can grasp, aimed to rove through what we'd call superspace— the sum of all possible universes— from the last conscious moment of her life as if that were an abiding point of departure and return." He straightened his back and sighed. "However, it's far more complex than that. The sea of stars comes into it in a way I can't fathom."

"Well," Rachel said, "it so happens I dream regularly about three alternative New Yorks, very different from the one in our world, each internally consistent every time I visit them. Vivid dreams, those."

"And I visit internally consistent Londons and Dublins in my dreams," he said. "According to Mary, certain dreams are glimpses of neighboring universes."

"There's always more than we think," Rachel observed, then winced. "Sorry for the platitude."

"Not at all," he said firmly. "That's it in a nutshell." His awed gaze roved the chamber. "Somewhere, on these walls, is a passage that Silentium preserved from the Apocryphon Mariæ: 'We are alone in the universe, but the universe is not alone.' Mary concluded that we are the only intelligent, conscious inhabitants of the universe. But there are other universes, an infinite number, containing an infinite number of possible beings. And, under rare circumstances, those beings can cross the intangible borders between worlds. When they do, we call them angels, or devils. I believe in both."

She moved away from the wall. "I get that this is important. It's— it's *momentous*. But if you hadn't noticed, the cardinal is about to blow this place to smithereens."

"Chavet will open the sarcophagus before he detonates a single lump of plastique. Trust me on that; I know how he thinks."

His attention strayed past her as she caught the pad of footsteps on stone. She turned to witness Chavet emerge from the recess, followed by Esposito and Fratta.

The cardinal stood to one side of the gap and extended an arm. "Everything's ready. Please enter. Both of you."

Not for the first time in her life, Rachel wished she were Ripley from the Alien movies or, better still, Xena, warrior princess. But she wasn't. Live with it. "Hey, why not," she said casually as she strolled to the square cavity and began descending the steps. "Should be fun."

Then the floor rose out of sight and the murk closed in. Her momentary dash of bravado was quenched with the loss of an audience. She reached the bottom step and started down the low-roofed, narrow tunnel, patchily lit by lamps stationed at ten yard intervals.

As she progressed down the tunnel, hardly conscious of the tracking footsteps, her attention became fixed on the rectangle of subdued light at the end of the passageway. Nothing of the sarcophagus could be distinguished in that light except for the pale brown shape she'd already glimpsed.

Her image of the mild maid of Nazareth had been replaced by a towering figure of mystery, so inspiring that later generations garlanded her image with an abundance of myths and legends. If the stories were true, the source of those myths and legends lay in that sarcophagus.

Nearing the Chamber of the Dormition, Rachel deliberately quickened her pace. Apprehensive though she was, creeping in like a furtive intruder went too much against the grain. She moved a few steps into the vault and studied her surroundings. The workmen hadn't been sparing with the lamps: almost a score of them were ranged around the walls of a room similar in size and construction to the Testament Chamber. The interior was plain and simple, the dull ochre walls unadorned.

In the corner to her right, crowbars, chisels, mallets, sledgehammers and pickaxes were piled in a heap beside a couple of metal boxes. Aside from the tools of the wrecking trade, all that the Chamber of the Dormition contained was the sarcophagus and— what the flashlights had missed at first sweep— a twice-life-size marble sculpture surmounting a pedestal on the far side of the vault.

The sculpture, carved with sublime artistry, was fashioned in the representational Greco-Roman style. It portrayed a woman in a hooded robe, face upraised, arms uplifted straight above her head, aspiring to the heavens.

Rachel lowered her gaze to the sarcophagus in the center of the vault. The tomb, resting on a low dais, was of a dark sandy color that might be brown limestone. The sides were covered in bas-reliefs in which a solar-flared sun, a crescent moon, stars, and stylized waves of water were the dominant themes.

She advanced several paces to view the image on the bulky lid. And withheld a gasp as she saw the engraved image that extended across the surface. She had never seen the image before, but she'd read of it in her research on the Collyridians.

The text, taken from the twelfth chapter of the Book of Revelations, was as engraved in her memory as was the image carved into the sarcophagus lid:

And a great sign appeared in heaven,
A woman clothed with the sun,
With the moon under her feet,

And on her head a crown of twelve stars.

Here was the icon of the exalted Mary, standing on the moon, crowned with stars, her face an exact likeness of the sculpture that loomed near the chamber's far wall.

Before she could marvel further, Chavet's voice broke the spell. "You see, it's true. This is the tomb of Mary."

She spared a glance over her shoulder as the workmen trudged into the vault and stood behind the cardinal. "Yes, it's true. So what happens now?"

"We open the sarcophagus."

Chapter 58

He was somewhere in the Trastevere labyrinth. Other than that his location was anyone's guess. Dominic had taken so many turnings in the past ten minutes he was unable to judge north from south.

Thank God Maria had gotten free of Jones's people: a backward glance before he turned into the thin alleyway had shown her speeding off in front of a blurry figure that might have been Deacon making a futile lunge.

Good for Maria.

It didn't matter whether Maria was an extraordinary case of multiple personality or a singular personality with a bizarre identification with the Madonna: there was no denying her luminous character and astute mind. Besides, how could he not admire a woman who thought nothing of parking her Vespa inside an eighth-century church?

He flinched as he swerved too abruptly around a street corner into a narrow alley. His chest and back muscles were protesting at full screech now that some of the numbness had worn off. Or maybe he'd been on an adrenaline boost since Carson burst into the room. Whatever the reason, his pained muscles were as stiff as his impacted spine.

He turned another corner onto a crooked street and discerned a scrawny woman in the fog, advancing down the thin vicolo. Sighting Dominic, the woman executed the speediest of double takes and fished a phone from her pocket, pressed a button, and spoke in a low, urgent voice. If that weren't sufficient to set alarm bells ringing full blast, it was the same woman who'd blundered into him outside the Ristorante Sabatini, metamorphosed from befuddled tourist to— what sprang to mind was psychotic schoolmarm.

He'd heard Jones yell the name Alice to a barely-glimpsed woman outside San Callisto. And earlier, Carson had taunted:

Anyone tell you about Martha... Alice gave her a good stomach stomping, pulped her insides a treat.

There was a triumphant smirk on her face. She had phoned the message through. They were coming.

He expected her to turn tail and run. Instead, she charged. Shrieking, she hurtled at him, bony fingers extended, a harridan from hell.

Before he could turn she was on him, serrated fingernails reaching for his eyes. He caught her wrists— and simultaneously caught her bony knee in his stomach. Bolts of pain shot through his nervous system.

His mind was telling him one thing— *smash the bitch, get clear before Jones comes*— his instincts another. Not once had he hit a woman. His reactions weren't up to speed. Though she was wide open to a head-butt, he hesitated a fraction. And in that instant she buried her teeth in his neck and hung on like a rabid weasel.

This maniac was determined to keep him here come hell or high heaven. No way could he tear her from his neck without losing a chunk of flesh. She had to be forced to let go. He released her left wrist and threw all he had into an uppercut. Despite the awkward angle, the fist connected with Alice's jaw full force.

A crack of broken jawbone. The deadly grip relented. Pulling back, hand clasping the throat wound, he readied himself to run but instead began to double up. That blow to the stomach had been more serious than he realized.

His legs folded under him.

Damn.

Alice, her slack-jawed face grotesque, was coming for him again full pelt, arms outstretched to embrace, hug tight for as long as it took. Unable to sidestep he dropped to the ground, ducking under her extended arms before he rolled toward the middle of the narrow lane, grimly ignoring the raw pain of his twisting torso.

Alice had overshot her mark and pulled to an abrupt halt, slightly unbalanced. But she was still just within the frame of a shop window, right in front of him.

For the moment, standing upright was out of the question. But, doubled-up, he could charge like a bull, head lowered. Ramming her into a wall would knock some of the stuffing out of her but she would bounce back with a vengeance. He didn't intend for her to bounce back.

As Alice swung round, he was off his knees and charging. Whether it was the distracting pain of a broken jaw or plain stupidity, instead of dodging she rushed to meet him.

The impact as his head rammed her stomach damn near broke his neck. She was launched clean off her feet and sailed backward, one moment seemingly hovering in mid-air, the next blasting through the window in a storm of glass knives.

Dominic sprawled on the ground, then forced his head up and dispassionately observed Alice's predicament. Smash a body hard into a window and they don't bounce back.

There was a reason it was a classic.

Alice's spindly shape convulsed on a set of crushed shelves, flesh pierced by several glass shards. Her legs trailed over the jagged ledge, the right thigh impaled on a glass spike. Her leg wound sprouted a fountain that was painting the shop front a new color.

As she thrashed about and banged her fists on the crumpled shelves, she screeched, over and over:

"He's here! He's here!"

Clutching his stomach with one hand, neck wound stanched with the other, Dominic managed to sway to his feet. He was dazed and he hurt like hell but, mercifully, sensed no symptoms of an impending blackout. For the second time that night, he saw windows swing open all around him, expelling staccato bursts of Italian. He slowly retraced his steps to the corner.

Only to hear the throb of an engine, approaching fast. Odds on it was Jones. His heart plummeted. If he were in any fit condition, the Ford Transit he'd glimpsed outside the church would be next to useless in pursuing him through the tangle of tight lanes. But the best he could achieve was a clumsy trot. He stumbled in the opposite direction to the approaching vehicle, and then noticed an extra note to the engine.

No, not an extra note. Another engine, its noise closer to a buzz than a roar. And the buzzing sound was coming from the direction he was heading, past the howling Alice.

It was the buzz of a scooter. Maria burst out of the fog on her red Vespa, skidding in an arc to stop right in front of him.

She broke into a grin. "I heard breaking glass and screaming. Figured you might be involved."

He climbed onto the passenger seat and held her waist.

"Maria," he said as she revved the scooter and sped down the lane. "I love you."

She glanced over her shoulder, eyebrow lofted. "Shall I quote that to Rachel?"

"Only in context." He looked back and saw the headlights of a vehicle. "I think that's them."

"Don't worry, there's a vicolo up ahead that even the average car couldn't squeeze through."

Her promise was confirmed in under a minute. The headlights receded into invisibility. Maria eased up on the throttle and halted under the cover of a low arch.

"You're a hard man to find," she said. "I've been searching all over Trastevere as well as dodging those goons."

"I could hardly walk around these streets calling out your name, could I?"

"Of course not. Besides, you'd sound like a scene from West Side Story." She swung off the scooter and gave him the once over. "You really have been in the wars. That neck wound will need stitches, just missed the carotid. In the meantime, I have a little cache of those stick-on plasters."

He bent his neck to one side as Maria picked out a small packet from the scooter's storage box. "That's another one I owe you," he acknowledged as she started patching him up.

Soon she moved back and assessed her handiwork. "There, that'll hold, saving any violent neck rotations."

"Maria... thanks."

"All part of the service and— we'd better get going." She gave him a concerned glance. "You look ready to drop."

"Then I look better than I feel."

"That bad? By the way, I got a call from Thomas ten minutes ago. An archeologist at the necropolis excavations just phoned and said they were ejected at eight. Pity he didn't call earlier. Chavet has had the necropolis all to himself for almost two hours."

Animated by the last piece of information, Dominic was back on the pillion seat the instant she finished speaking. "As you said, let's get going."

Maria jumped onto the scooter, fired the engine, and raced off.

He experienced the ride through fog as a blind, suicidal rush, complete with sudden swerves. But he'd come to trust Maria's instincts in the brief time he'd known her. He only marginally feared crashing into a wall or window. The series of tight swerves gradually moderated to a gentle curve and a distinct sensation of travelling uphill. As though reading his mind, Maria shouted back to him:

"We're climbing the Janiculum. Soon be at the Vatican."

In a short while they had crested the hill and descended to what he guessed was the Borgo Santo Spirito. A gateway with a raised barrier materialized and a guard emerged from the gate booth, palm upraised.

Maria pulled up the Vespa and displayed the fake Vatican passport. "We're required for special operations in the necropolis," she announced with a note of authority. "Orders from Cardinal Chavet."

He shouldered the Beretta submachine gun, checked the passport, and nodded as he handed it back. "I heard the cardinal was down there," he said, almost chattily. "We've been forbidden to go anywhere near the necropolis tonight. And there's a large truck parked outside the Scavi office. What's going on?"

She tapped the side of her nose and winked. "Sworn to secrecy. You know how it is."

He scowled. "Don't I just. Go on through. Head past the Holy Office here and—"

"I know the way, thanks." With that she rode the Vespa onto Vatican territory and crossed the courtyard, skirting St. Peter's basilica until a small office came into sight on the building's outer arm.

She stopped in front of the office door beside a large blue truck, turned off the engine, then looked back at Dominic. "The Scavi office. We're here."

Chapter 59

Jones glared through the passenger window of the Ford transit at the locked door of San Callisto. He hadn't said a word for some time. In turn, no one dared speak to him.

Deacon raised a hand to the knot of his silk tie, then thought better of the action and peered over his shoulder at Craig and D'Aloisio sitting in the rear of the truck with two plastic-wrapped corpses laid out on the floor. Jones was a stickler for tidiness.

The silence was becoming unendurable. Deacon hated long silences. With a nod, he indicated the bodies on the van floor. "Where do we dump Alice and Wright?"

"We'll bury Wright outside the city before morning," Jones replied. "As for Alice— I'll dissolve her body in an acid bath." He gazed at the mist beyond the windscreen. "It's what she would have wanted."

Deacon's eyebrows shot up. Was it conceivable Jones was making a joke? Or was Alice even more psychotic than she appeared? Or maybe... Let it remain forever a mystery. "Uh— do we try to get into San Callisto or should I drive— someplace?"

Jones answered in an even flatter monotone than usual. "I figure there's one place Quinn might be. Chavet has some pet project in the necropolis, something that ties all this together. Quinn must be tied into it too."

"So, I drive up someplace near the Vatican?" Deacon fired the engine and steered the van out of the Piazza San Callisto. "We catch Quinn in there before he leaves?"

"If I catch him before he leaves, he'll never leave."

Officer Belucci, arms folded, barred the way out of the Dormition Chamber. He hadn't budged in over ten minutes. The workmen, too, had dropped the congenial masks. If she made a run for it, they'd be on her like a ton of masonry.

Chavet had given his orders. The sarcophagus would be smashed to pieces, by pickaxe, sledgehammer, and even plastique if necessary. Given the size and density of the tomb, a substantial amount of explosive would be required to reduce it to fragments. Those fragments would be hauled out in wheelbarrows to a truck parked outside. But before the vehicle departed the outer tunnel would be blown with explosives, burying both the Testament Chamber and the Chamber of the Dormition.

Rachel watched the men at work, wondering just what was going on in their minds. These men were Catholics; surely they had reservations about the task, despite the cardinal's authority. If so, they showed no sign of it. The workmen Esposito and Fratta were preparing to shift the lid off the sarcophagus. Fratta, wielding a mallet and chisel, was loosening the lid on Rachel's side of the tomb. Esposito was likewise engaged on the far side.

She suppressed a tremor. *Won't be long...*

"Rachel," Chavet summoned. "Approach the tomb, if you would."

The note of anxiety in his tone confirmed a growing suspicion. "Why should I do that? What's the real reason you want me here?"

"There is— a possibility— a possibility the tomb contains..." The sentence ended in an incoherent mutter.

"Contains what?"

"A dark miracle." He took the smallest step away from the sarcophagus. "The possibility is of course remote. Superstition. But— one must be sure."

At first she couldn't place the new expression in the cardinal's face, then it dawned on her. There was dread written into his features, but even deeper, guilt.

"And what's a dark miracle got to do with me?"

He ignored the question and stepped forward as Esposito and Fratta moved back from their work, the lid presumably loosened to their satisfaction.

Hands clasped in prayer, Chavet suppressed whatever demons were in him, raising his eyes to a hidden heaven: "Begin."

The two laborers advanced to the sarcophagus, inserted chisels into slim gaps under the lid, then delivered powerful mallet blows that transmitted a vibration through the chamber floor. She watched as blow after blow hammered into the lid's underside. Collyridian legends aside, she couldn't ignore that this *was* the tomb of Mary, beyond reasonable doubt. A few feet from where she stood was— what? Dust? Bone fragments? An intact skeleton? Or— hadn't she read of an "exceeding great marvel" connected with Mary's mysterious passing...

Her heart skipped as the lid slipped a fraction, the grating sound ominous. Another set of blows in virtual unison and the stone shifted another fraction, leaving an inch-wide gap of darkness.

There was a short hiatus as the workmen replaced chisels with crowbars. They inserted the wedge ends into the breach and gave a simultaneous heave.

The limestone slab shifted with a grinding reverberation.

Chapter 60

The walls closed in and the dry warmth increased as Dominic and Maria descended into the necropolis, passing a striated layer that indicated the foundations of Constantine's original basilica.

A further short flight of steps and they reached the subterranean ground level. Maria led the way at a run down a street of the Roman dead. Dominic forced his legs to keep up with her, ignoring the mounting pain of cracked ribs and damaged muscles. He hardly spared a glance at the tiny funeral houses as he sped by. Swift impressions of brick façades, stucco ornamentation, and faded frescoes flashed past.

She took a sharp left turn and they headed down a plain tunnel, passing through a transparent door wedged ajar. He saw a demolished wall up ahead and knew he was close to his goal. He prayed that Rachel would be there, safe and well.

They ran through the breach and Maria pulled to a halt. He was about to ask why but a sideways step showed exactly what was wrong. In the downward sloping tunnel to another breached barrier, a dozen pale yellow lumps lined the walls, illuminated by electric lamps. From his Ranger days he instantly identified the lumps as C-4 plastique, primed with blasting caps. No wires were visible, which meant a remote detonator. The damn things could go off at any time. Like, now.

"Dominic..."

"I know. I see them."

They instantly set about plucking the metal caps from the ductile explosives. They accomplished the task within two minutes. It felt a lot longer.

"Whoever set this up is an amateur," he observed as they dumped the blasting caps behind a pile of rubble at the original breached entrance. "A single brick of plastique, strategically placed, could bring the tunnel roof down. A dozen bricks, that's over-the-top— and then some."

"Why don't I find that reassuring?' she remarked.

Blasting caps safely hidden, they raced down the tunnel to the second breach. Emerging into a spacious chamber, he instantly spun around, arms raised against attack, rapidly taking in his surroundings.

No enemies, just dark walls inscribed with Greek script. And— despite his haste he had to spare one moment— a surface close by bore what looked like, what *were*, Hindu numerals of the decimal system. He wasted scant seconds before moving to the square aperture in a recess similar to the one in the Shrine. Maria was already disappearing into it and he was fast on her heels, almost tripping on the bumpy steps.

As they descended she spoke without looking back. "Any plan in mind?"

"No," he whispered. "No time for recon. So just charge in and rely on surprise. But keep well behind me."

He slid past her at the bottom of the stairway and started down the passage. And found himself lurching to one side. The floor was at a deceptively steep angle... And the lights were dimming rapidly. Bright sparks disrupted his vision. Red flashes.

Thrown off balance, Dominic had toppled to his knees before the reality hit him: he was close to passing out. The recent punishment he'd received was taking its toll.

Not *now*. Please God, not *now*.

Another minute and he might have wrested Rachel free of her captors. One more wretched minute.

Maria was whispering in his ear: "Don't try to get up. Take a moment, a long moment."

Her words were almost drowned out by the arrhythmic drumming of his rapid heartbeat. But he managed a nod of acceptance as he crumpled against a wall.

He concentrated first in slowing his hyperventilation. Slow the breath and the pounding pulse would follow the lead. Close his eyes and go into the inner dark without losing consciousness. Slow down, but stay conscious.

After a brief rest in the dark, he started the countdown. Ten, nine...

When I reach the count of one, I'll be okay.

Six, five...

Almost ready.

Three, two...

He opened his eyes as the countdown concluded. His surroundings no longer appeared dim and blurred and his heart rate had eased. He still hurt like crazy from head to toe but that was neither here nor there. He was damn lucky he hadn't passed out.

"Rapid recovery," Maria murmured appreciatively as he heaved himself upright. "A trick you learned in the army?"

"No, Brooklyn." He glanced down the passageway. "Let's go."

Maria caught his arm. "Are you okay?"

He took a couple of steps, and managed to stay erect. Shaky, but mobile. "I'll hold up. Stay behind me, but not too close."

He edged down the tunnel, then upped the pace as he neared the blob of light that terminated the passage. Fortunately the floor was thick with dust, his footfalls barely audible. He began to distinguish shapes in the rectangle of light. A pale brown block. Indistinct figures, one in front of the block. He padded down the last stretch and soon identified the nearest figure, at the tunnel exit, as a Vigilanza.

At the last moment the officer sensed something amiss and whirled round. To meet Dominic's fist bang on the jaw. The policeman tottered back, arms wheeling to regain balance, eyes uncomprehending. Then he fell flat on his back, out cold.

And that same moment Dominic saw Rachel. She stared at him in astonishment, her smile wide with happy surprise. The two men flanking her were less happy. They circled the tomb and advanced on him, crowbars brandished.

Then the men stopped, glanced at the prone gendarme, glanced back at Dominic. And dropped the crowbars, hands raised high as they ran for the tunnel, one muttering *"Scusi, scusi."*

It was a welcome anticlimax but Dominic didn't lower his guard. "Wait!" He pointed to the policeman. "Take him. I don't want him."

The two men traded glances, then obeyed, making quick work of grabbing ankles and underarms and carrying the gendarme out of the chamber. Maria followed, calling over her shoulder: "I'll make sure they get well clear. And that they don't raise the alarm."

Dominic turned his full attention on Rachel, who had moved up close. He advanced to meet her in a couple of strides and stifled a gasp of pain as she caught him in a tight hug. The joy of finding Rachel safe outweighed any physical hurt. He basked in the warmth of her embrace, inhaling the unmistakeable scent of her skin and hair.

"Glad you came," she breathed into his ear. "What took you so long?"

"Traffic was a bitch."

"Was that a movie reference?"

"It was."

She examined his face, her gaze lowering to the bloodstained jacket. "You've been in a battle."

"More of a skirmish."

Out the corner of his eye he saw the Monsignor look on benignly while a beanpole of priest that could only be Cardinal Chavet stood quivering with outrage.

The cardinal looked like he was about to snap. And snap he did. He strode toward Dominic as if to throw him out bodily. *"You!"* he shrilled.

"And you," Dominic said, warmth replaced by cold as he reluctantly disengaged from Rachel's embrace, "would be Chavet. Best keep your distance."

Chavet took another step. And another. Dominic responded with a warning fist.

The cardinal stared at the fist, appalled. "Would you dare strike me?"

He swung a punch that rammed the side of Chavet's chin and propelled him backward to thump onto the floor. "I think that answers your question."

Leaving Chavet sprawled and stunned, Dominic approached his uncle. "Get sidetracked on your way to Il Gesù?" He lifted a hand as the Monsignor began to speak. "Save the explanations."

The Monsignor nodded, glancing at the sarcophagus, whose lid had been shifted to present a two-inch-plus gap. "Agreed, explanations will keep. But— we're standing beside the tomb of Mary. By whatever devious route we came, just consider where we are."

Dominic looked at the sarcophagus, noting the engraved Mary of Revelations on its lid. Yes, he did appreciate the significance of this hallowed place, but for now Rachel's safety was paramount. "We should just go," he said.

Rachel nodded. "Sounds right to me." She opened her mouth, then closed it, then opened it again. "Uh, about the tomb... we'll always be wondering 'what if', won't we?"

"Yes," he admitted. "We'll always wonder."

He looked past her to the marble statue. "Could that be a genuine likeness?" he mused. "Strange thing is, she looks familiar."

Rachel's wide eyes of shock, staring past him, made him spin round. Chavet was back on his feet, arm raised, a metallic object in his hand that Dominic guessed was a remote detonator.

"You think you can walk out of here, Quinn?" the cardinal challenged. "*No one* walks out of here. No one leaves. Ever."

To the accompaniment of Rachel's cry of dismay, he double-twisted the detonator's safety switch.

Silence.

Chavet waited a few seconds, then twisted the switch again.

Silence.

The cardinal resorted to pressing frantically. "The batteries..."

Dominic shook his head. "Not the batteries. We removed the caps from the plastique. The only things you've detonated are the blasting caps. Your men must have set them for delay - standard

practise. I'd guess maybe forty seconds since you activated them."
He paused, angling his head to the tunnel.

Several seconds passed. Then a deep *whump* reverberated in
the chamber. "There they go. Delay of about fifty seconds. If the C-
4 had gone off you'd know about it, believe me."

Chavet glared at him, speechless with rage. Then at Dominic's
approach, he whirled around and darted for the tunnel, his
movements hampered by his tightly-buttoned cassock.

That did it. This reverend maniac might well be on the hunt for
more blasting caps and that was not a welcome prospect. Dominic
raced after the cardinal, grabbed him by the collar, yanked his
head back, then banged it hard against the wall. Chavet moaned,
reeled, then tumbled to the ground, his eyes blank.

With Chavet out of action Dominic relieved him of the
detonator and, as an added precaution, laid it on the floor,
grabbed one of the sledgehammers, and brought it down to smash
the device to smithereens.

The Monsignor was studying the prone cardinal. "Did you kill
him?"

"I used to be a soldier, not a murderer. Of course I didn't kill
him." Ignoring the felled Chavet, he gestured toward the
sarcophagus. "So this is where the followers of Silentium
eventually interred her. Is this what kept their religion alive?"

"Not the sarcophagus itself, but the power it signifies. Silentium
struggled to exist, surviving by word of mouth, in out-of-the-way
places, in convents, monasteries, secret houses. The faith dwindled
down through the ages. But Mary's spell couldn't be eradicated.
Why is Christ seen so rarely in visions? Why is Mary the one
witnessed in apparitions from the fifth century to the present day?
She appears in grottoes, on hilltops, above a tree in a hollow,
above a Coptic church in Egypt. Vision or hallucination, it's her
they see. It's Mary herself that perpetuates the ancient faith of the
Collyridians."

Dominic surveyed the engraving of Mary of the Apocalypse on
the sarcophagus lid. "You believe this tomb contains some secret
that will transform Christianity into a Christian-Marian religion."

"I do," came the firm reply. "The modern Church is a hollow shell. Mystery must be restored to it or the Church will shatter." He threw an overt glance at the sarcophagus lid. "Shall we?"

"Before we rush in like fools, maybe we should take a look at the inscriptions in the other chamber back there. A very *quick* look."

"You want to know what's carved into those walls?" the Monsignor said. "The Apocryphon Mariæ, proof incontrovertible that Mary was acquainted with theories of multidimensional space-time and infinite universes. That requires rather more than a quick look."

Dominic relented with a shrug, then moved to the sarcophagus and touched the brown limestone surface. The Monsignor was convinced the spirit or living memory of Mary resided within this stone. His agnostic soul required evidence. Extraordinary claims required extraordinary proofs.

He looked at Rachel. "What do you think?"

She smiled a little shyly. "I'm consumed with curiosity."

"Curiosity killed Schrödinger's cat," Dominic quipped, then flinched at Rachel's raised eyebrow. "Physics joke. Sorry. So you vote yes?"

"I think so, yes."

"Me too." He brushed a sense of misgiving aside. "It's unanimous, unless we wait for Maria to come back."

The Monsignor glanced at the tunnel. "Speaking of whom, here she comes." He looked at Dominic. "Who is she, exactly?"

"A friend of Thomas Chen's. Let's leave it at that."

Maria strolled out of the passageway, observing the faces turned in her direction. "Should my ears be burning?" She pointed to the sarcophagus. "Not opened it yet?"

"We were just about to," Dominic said, grabbing a crowbar.

The room fell silent as the two men inserted the crowbars and gave an initial heave. The slab grated open another inch. Another heave, another inch.

Dominic blinked as his vision began to swim. The vertigo that had threatened a dead faint was spinning his head again. He took a slow breath and subdued the dizziness.

As the gap widened, Dominic's sense of misgiving intensified. The source of apprehension was elusive. The myth of Pandora's box? Maybe. Perhaps the thought experiment of Schrödinger's cat, where the unobserved cat in a box was in the potential state of being both alive *and* dead until the box was opened and the observer collapsed that quantum superposition into a cat that was alive *or* dead. By opening the tomb, were they affecting reality, fools rushing in? But above all, he experienced a subtle dread that the Virgin Mary might actually be in there, in some state of being even frontier physics hadn't imagined.

By concerted effort, the lid shifted, fraction by fraction. Then suddenly slid several inches, as though an obstacle, a resistance, had been overcome. The gap was a foot wide.

Dominic squared his shoulders. *Now we're in for it, whatever it is.*

The Monsignor aimed a flashlight into the sarcophagus. All but Maria bunched close and looked into the tomb.

Dominic hardly heard his own stunned whisper. "It's impossible..."

Chapter 61

Twenty seconds.

Jones had given his men twenty seconds before they emerged from the fog and entered the Vatican barrier gate. That's all the time it took him to deal with the guard. Walk up alone, affecting a limp, tourist map in hand. Grab the guard's gun and jab the man's neck with the weapon's butt.

Twenty seconds after Jones first approached the gate, he'd bundled the policeman back into the booth he emerged from and Deacon, D'Aloisio, and Craig joined him at the barrier and passed through into Vatican City.

Deacon, as usual, was twitchy. "Why didn't you take the gun?"

"You know the score. No weapons. Concentrates the mind."

"But Carson carried a bat... is that a borderline case?"

"You're the borderline case, Deacon."

Phil Craig chuckled at the exchange. "Think I might join up with you, Jones, if there's a vacancy."

"Yeah, I'll have you on the team. That's an invite I'll not give Deacon."

Jones peered ahead at the Scavi office. A red Vespa was parked outside. Vespas were familiar sights on the streets of Rome, not so much in the Vatican.

"He's here."

Empty," the Monsignor mumbled.

Dominic blinked, and then the sarcophagus was empty.

But before, he'd seen. He *knew* he'd seen.

It was impossible, but he'd seen her. The hooded woman, the living image of the sculpture above him, lying with arms crossed at her breast. And with that image came a tumble of disconnected memories that raced by too quickly for him to seize.

He'd *seen*.

Unless— unless he'd programmed himself to see what wasn't there. It didn't help that he was close to passing out. He was wide open to hallucination.

"Empty," the Monsignor repeated, his tone as hollow as the word. He swung away, anguish etched in every line of his features. "It's empty."

Maria observed from a distance, maintaining silence.

Dominic nodded numbly. "Hardly a speck of dust." The moment his uncle had declared the tomb to be empty, the vision had vanished. Perhaps his battered condition was overriding his sanity but he wondered if his earlier quip about Schrödinger's cat might have been close to the mark. Maybe Mary was simultaneously present in *and* absent from the sarcophagus and, for an instant, he saw what might be there until it was banished by a single word. Maybe unbelief was stronger than belief.

He shook his head. "No, that can't be."

Rachel clasped his hand. "What can't be?"

He was tempted to short-change her with a half-truth, but thought better of it. "For a moment I saw what I thought was Mary, lying in the tomb." He glanced up at the marble statue. "She was the living image of that effigy. And also, seeing her as a living person, or someone beyond life and death, I had the feeling I'd seen her before, somewhere."

She studied his face intently. "Do you think you had a— vision?"

Faced with a straight question, common sense reasserted itself. "No," he stated flatly. "It was a hallucination, that's all."

Rachel nodded uncertainly, then pointed to the distraught Monsignor, slumped against the wall on the other side of the statue. After a glance at Maria, who was now peering into the sarcophagus, he moved over to the priest. His uncle was drained of volition, the quintessence of the disillusioned believer, suddenly bereft of the foundations of his faith.

The Monsignor raised his head at Dominic's approach. "Forgive me." His tone was bleak as winter. "Forgive me, both of you. I'm so sorry. It was for nothing. All of it, for nothing."

"There's that word again— nothing." The voice of Maria. "Just a suggestion..." She indicated the partially open tomb. "If you start a job, you should finish it."

The lady had a point. He followed her back to the sarcophagus and the two of them took up their positions, heads low, arms and shoulders ready.

"Okay," Dominic said. "Here goes."

They pushed, and the lid immediately began to move, slowly at first, but gathering momentum. Before anyone started to puff and pant, the slab abruptly tilted and crashed onto the other side of the dais.

Rachel rushed around and inspected the lid. She vented a breath of relief and gave the thumbs-up. "No damage done."

"Thank God for that," Dominic said fervently. "It just shot off at that last heave."

The Monsignor, roused from his dejection, joined them and looked into the tomb, a glint of renewed hope in his expression. "I wonder what would happen if I got inside? It's just possible that might trigger something. Unlikely, but— just possible."

Dominic shrugged. "Unlikely is the word, but maybe I should test the water before you jump in."

He gazed down at the rectangular recess, its profile rounded at the corners. It looked innocuous, no sense of miracles locked in the stone. Slowly, he reached a hand down into the hollow. When his stretched fingers descended a few inches below the rim, he was hindered by a sensation similar to a low electric discharge as if he'd broken through an invisible layer.

His pulse accelerated for a few moments, but the electric sensation ceased. It was nothing— just overwrought nerves. He hesitated, then decided to get it over with and thrust his hand deep into the sarcophagus. His fingertips touched the cool limestone of the base.

The stone was merely— stone.

The anticlimax teased a smile from his lips. He'd let legends of an indwelling power get the better of him.

Ordinary stone, nothing more. He began to withdraw his hand.

Then he fell headlong.

And the world went away.

He fell through night. He fell through light.

It took an instant. An instantaneous eternity.

Directionless now, and now was all there was, he was conscious only of the bare fact of his existence. Nothing was actual, everything potential.

Then, a glimpse of green and gray, seen far off. The sense of direction returned along with a rudimentary sense of identity. He coasted toward a broadening vista of mountains and gray skies and a dull blue stretch of water.

A figure stood in a graveyard, facing the mountains and the lough. As he drew nearer, he perceived that the figure was himself.

Closer now, he could almost view the panorama through the eyes of his earlier self.

The dawn light, filtered through massed clouds, was dove-gray and docile, softening the undulating contours of the Mountains of Mourne on the far side of Carlingford Lough.

He could now feel the faint smile on his former self's lips, could hear those lips reciting the lines of a ballad in a murmur softer than the rain:

"So I'll wait for the wild rose that's waiting for me

Where the Mountains of Mourne sweep down to the sea."

And then he was there, not in spirit, not in memory, but actually *there*.

The smile, slight as it was, vanished.

He looked around in astonishment. He wasn't dreaming. This was real. The mud and gravel under his boots, the gale-borne droplets of rain on his skin. Real.

He was standing in Carlingford Lough at the same spot by his father's grave where he stood four days ago.

He whispered, faintly: "I remember."

This *was* four days ago. He was back, in Carlingford.

No, it's impossible.

As though he'd uttered an incantation, it became impossible. The reality collapsed.

Light. Dark.

Plenum. Vacuum.

He came to with a jolt and found himself springing back from the sarcophagus, hand outstretched. Off-balance momentarily, he felt Rachel's steadying hand slip under his arm.

"Are you all right?" she asked anxiously.

"Uh— I think so." He looked around the chamber, struggling to regain his bearings. "How long was I gone?"

Rachel's brow formed puzzled lines. "You were right here. You put your hand in the sarcophagus and then pulled it back."

"And that's all that happened?" He looked her full in the face. "Rachel, I went back in time."

"What did you see?" the Monsignor inquired eagerly.

"For a second or two I was in Carlingford. Not in memory— actually *there*."

Even as he spoke, the substance of the experience evaporated. It had more substance than a dream at the time, but now seemed less than real. Less real, because nigh impossible to believe.

I remember.

Had he whispered those words four days ago, thoughts full of Rachel, the wild rose, as he recited the Mountains of Mourne ballad?

Ironically, he couldn't remember.

Now that Dominic considered the question, with the reality of the experience slipping away, serious doubts intruded. What was more likely, that he'd journeyed back in time, or that he'd undergone a vivid hallucination, brought on by fatigue and injury? It wouldn't be the first time tonight...

Before he could respond, his uncle's exclamation put all speculations to flight. "Damn!" The priest was glaring in the direction of the tunnel. "Chavet— he's up and gone."

Dominic spun around and saw an empty passageway. "The plastique," he breathed hoarsely. "If there are more blasting caps up there... Oh Christ."

Chapter 62

Jones had located the vault within ten minutes of entering the unguarded necropolis. He observed the ancient writing on the walls with minimal interest. A discovery like this should bring in a truckload of money, but right now he had more immediate concerns.

Chavet had emerged from the aperture in the floor scarcely a minute after Jones's arrival. The cardinal wore a king-size lump on his forehead, which might explain his dulled wits and gabbled speech, but after several minutes' interrogation, the setup became clear. Quinn and company were in a chamber farther underground and someone— Chavet?— had primed plastique to blow after some Crypt job was finished. Jones had his own ideas about that. There could be a lot of wealth in what was written on these walls. If so, he wanted a piece of it. The chamber would stay intact.

D'Aloisio was already gathering blasting caps to replace the detonated ones under the rubble of the first breached wall. Jones had spotted at first glance that the caps had been removed: it was a sure bet Quinn was responsible. If Quinn wanted the tunnel explosives rendered harmless then Jones wanted them primed and the detonator in his hand.

He held out his palm to the cardinal. "Detonator."

The cardinal, gaze unfocused, dribble on his chin, mumbled, "The sarcophagus burns with divine fire... she's rising... Stabat Mater..."

Jones frowned at the man's babbling. Chavet's expression was blank, the look of a man in shock. He was totally out of it, a notch below village idiot.

"Hey! Wake up! Where's the remote detonator?"

"Oh— ah... Quinn destroyed it," Chavet mumbled.

"Backup?"

"Backup? What..."

Jones kept his tone level. "Back-up det-on-at-or."

A little light dawned. The man was coming round. But real slow. "Detonator. Yes. There's one in the metal toolbox. Blue metal toolbox. Down in the Dormition Chamber. But it's locked. The toolbox is locked."

"Blue metal toolbox, right. Got a key?"

Whatever little wits the priest had regained were ebbing away again. "Uh— key... key..."

At a signal from Jones, Deacon and Craig grabbed hold of the prelate and made efficient work of frisking him. Inside ten seconds Deacon held up a Zeiss key and passed it to Jones.

Jones tossed the key in the air and caught it. "We're in business." He walked up to the befuddled Chavet, taking closer note of the swelling bruises on the priest's jaw and forehead. "How many are down there?"

A brief pause. "Four. Two men. Quinn— and Aylesbury." A longer pause. "And a woman, Gurevich. And another woman."

"Weapons?"

"They have no weapons. This is Crypt territory." A hint of lucidity gleamed again in Chavet's eyes. "But— there are tools they could use as weapons."

Jones snorted in derision. "So Quinn has an old man and two women for troops. Too easy." He turned to D'Aloisio. "Start planting the blasting caps in the tunnel." He gestured to Craig. "Go give him a hand. Oh yeah, and make sure the caps are hidden inside the plastique just in case anyone escapes from down there. Let them think the explosives are still unprimed."

Deacon was distinctly jittery. "Why prime the plastique before we go in? Why not wait until we've finished Quinn off and then blow the tunnel when we're outside?"

Jones subjected him to a cold stare. "Two reasons. Reason one, Quinn may still have a trick up his sleeve and we may have to get out fast, so I want the explosives ready to blow. Ready to bury him. And reason two... We're not pussies like you, Deacon."

To the accompaniment of chuckles from D'Aloisio and Craig, Jones knelt and picked up a claw hammer from a small pile of tools collected from the necropolis. "I won't say choose your weapons, but select the right tool for the job. Still within Crypt rules, right, cardinal?"

His mind evidently drifting once more, Chavet muttered, "Stabat Mater... the sarcophagus burns with divine fire... Annunciata...she's rising..."

Jones snorted in contempt. "Stay here, Chavet. The rest of you, get ready."

D'Aloisio and Craig picked up scratch awls with needle-sharp points and Deacon followed Jones's lead by selecting a hammer.

Brandishing an awl, Craig stabbed the air. "Okay if I do the women, Jones? Kinda like to hear 'em squeal like stuck pigs."

"Sure. Get stuck in."

Jones strode over to the hole in the recess and descended the steps. "Remember..." He took out the leather pouch and flipped it open to display the hypodermics. "Quinn's mine. He goes out the hard way."

Standing directly beneath the Testament Chamber, Dominic held his breath. When he identified Jones's voice up above the stairway, he was brought to earth with a thump. And a thud of gravediggers' spades.

He had caught only the occasional phrase but that was enough to tell him that fresh blasting caps had been found and— he cursed himself for his stupidity— he hadn't checked out Chavet for a replacement detonator.

He padded softly back down the tunnel, quickening his pace as he neared the vault.

"Jones," he announced as he entered the vault. "And he's got company." He faced his uncle. "Are you up to taking on one of these men?"

"Out of practice since Amsterdam, but I can at least keep one of them busy while you're fighting the good fight."

"Okay." Dominic's engine was running on the after-scent of fumes and liable to conk out any second. "One question. What are our chances if we take on Jones and his men face to face?"

"With all respect to your Ranger training, near zero," the Monsignor replied soberly. "Jones was once the target of simultaneous attack by five armed marines. He killed them all with his bare hands in eleven seconds. The event was captured on CCTV. One marine had his head twisted around almost 180 degrees. And any man Jones employs is a professional killer. In a fair fight, we'll all die."

Dominic released a slow breath. "So it's a blindsiding attack. Improvised ambush. Okay then... The width of the passage will allow two men to come in abreast. They'll either edge around the corner or rush in. If they edge in, we have an advantage."

He crossed the chamber, collected the pickaxes and chisels, and returned, tossing one of each to his uncle. "You'll have a chance for just one swing, so make it count. It's more likely to disable than kill. But disabling works. If not, it's the chisel unless you can get some distance for another swing."

The Monsignor made a gesture of comprehension and took a stand on the other side of the tunnel entrance, pickaxe hoisted.

Dominic switched his attention to the women. "If they see the two of you chatting around the sarcophagus when they come down the passage it might lull them into overconfidence. One of you needs to stand at the foot or head of the tomb so that the passageway is just visible out the corner of the eye. Whoever takes watch, signal me with the fingers of your right hand to show how many are coming. Use the fingers of your left to let me know whether the vanguard is entering one or two abreast. If you can tell they're about to charge in, close your fists. Got that?"

There was a silence, broken by Rachel. "Run that past me again, and with a little less pressure on the gas."

"It's fine," Maria said. "I've got it. I'll take watch."

The women took up their positions by the tomb and Dominic was touched when he saw Rachel place a handful of pebbles on the tomb ledge, a ceremonial sign of respect from one Jewish woman to another.

Rachel and Maria commenced a loud, breezy exchange about the age of the sarcophagus for the benefit of any intruders. They didn't have long to wait. In minutes the curled fingers of Maria's right hand spread out in a casually contrived gesture. Four fingers were on display.

Four hostiles. He drew gradual breaths, as deep as his damaged ribcage permitted, and eased the pickaxe back for a full swing.

Maria raised her left hand and wagged a finger in mock chiding at Rachel. The enemy was coming in single file. He'd hoped for two abreast. He lifted a forefinger to his uncle and then signaled they attack simultaneously. The Monsignor indicated his understanding. There was a pause. The pause lengthened. And lengthened.

Dominic knew what the enemy was thinking: were the women unaware of their approach, or were they faking? And they would be waiting to catch sight of at least one of the two men in the chamber, presuming Chavet had told them of their numbers. But, in the enemy's mind, the longer Jones and his men waited, the more they risked being discovered.

Maria shifted her left hand on the sarcophagus ledge, two fingers trailing. *Approaching two abreast.*

Then her hands abruptly formed fists. *They're charging.*

Dominic exploded into action.

Praying that his uncle had spotted the two-abreast signal, he swung the pickaxe full force around the tunnel corner. A judder ran up his arms as the metal head rammed home. An instant later a stocky man in pale blue denim tumbled into the chamber, pickaxe lodged in his chest, blood jetting on the paving stones. The awl he'd held fell and skittered across the floor.

At the same moment, a ponytailed hulk blundered past the Monsignor, catching a slashed shoulder from the misdirected axe. His uncle *had* missed the hand signal. Ponytail swerved and, wielding an awl from an outstretched hand, went straight for the Monsignor.

And then came Jones and Deacon.

Dominic hurled the chisel at Ponytail's right arm and was rewarded with a pained grunt as metal connected with bone and the awl fell from the man's grip. Before the awl hit the floor, he moved to put himself between Jones and the women. But Jones and Deacon's onrush had given them a head start. He sprinted to catch up.

And didn't realize his mistake until Jones stopped dead and stuck out a straight leg in Dominic's path. He flew headlong and landed face first.

He hardly had time to glimpse Deacon sidetrack to the pickaxe victim before a searing pain lightning-flashed up his spine. Glancing over his shoulder, he saw Jones retract his heel, ready to stomp down again. Ignoring the pile-driver sensation in his back, he side-rolled and managed to regain his feet before Jones was on him again.

He instinctively raised his knee and Jones ran right into it, getting the full impact in his abdomen. An instant later he jumped back, narrowly avoiding Dominic's attempt at a head-butt.

If Jones experienced any hurt from the knee in the stomach, he didn't show it. If anything, there was a flicker of outrage that someone had landed a blow. With a gesture of contempt he cast aside his claw hammer.

"Quinn," he sneered. "You're a rat in a trap." Then he let loose a flying kick that Dominic barely evaded by ducking low.

Another kick came from nowhere and grazed Dominic's thigh as he leapt backward. There was no respite as more kicks came thick and fast, streaks of light, keeping him permanently on the retreat.

He succeeded in blocking most of the inhumanly rapid kicks from his opponent, but pace after pace he was forced to a side wall. And behind Jones, he saw Deacon yank the pickaxe from the body of the first intruder and head straight for the women.

He made a wild side lunge to stop Deacon but Jones, with uncanny instinct, anticipated the move and drove his toecap into

Dominic's midriff. He doubled-up, eyesight alternately blacking out and sun-flashing as other blows rained down on him. His neck snapped to one side from a kick to the head.

He fought to stay conscious. He *had* to stay conscious. That remained the sole thought in his head, a fixed light.

Another kick to the head.

Then the light shrank to a pixel and blinked out, the last glint of hope gone.

Chapter 63

A storm of impressions. That's all Rachel took in as the chamber was invaded.

Observing Maria's sudden clenching of fists and hearing the rush of feet, she spun around to witness a shaven-headed man with a pickaxe in his chest, already toppling as his bulky partner threw his full weight on the Monsignor, bringing both crashing to the floor.

And Jones and Deacon, pounding in her direction. Jones stopping abruptly, leg outstretched. Dominic falling. Deacon swerving aside and backtracking to the axed body.

Dominic dodging a bewildering flurry of kicks from Jones, the combat too swift to follow. Deacon ripping out the pickaxe from the dead man's ribcage and dispensing with his claw hammer.

So much mayhem crammed into so few seconds.

Then Deacon was coming straight at her, pickaxe raised.

She scooted around the tomb and grabbed the secreted crowbar, exchanging a brief glance with Maria who was similarly occupied, then reared up to confront Deacon, metal bar in her grip.

And instantly ducked as a bloodied pickaxe swung at her skull. She stayed crouched behind the sarcophagus and kept watch on the tomb's right hand corner, gesturing Maria to guard the left. Maria, unaccountably, shook her head in refusal.

Rachel gave a questioning shrug. *What do you mean, no?*

Maria looked upward. And in the same instant Rachel heard the sound of scraped stone. She looked up to see Deacon jump onto the ledge above them, pickaxe already on a downward arc. The wind of its passing stirred her hair as she flung herself back.

The *whish* of a crowbar showed that Maria was swift on the counterattack. But the swing of the bar passed through empty space. Deacon had already leaped off the ledge and landed lightly on the floor. Rachel had underestimated the man. He was one mean athlete.

He swung back the axe. And simultaneously Maria barged into him, head low to ram his stomach. And that was where Deacon betrayed a serious flaw. He'd underestimated the women more than they underestimated him.

Instead of reacting by immediate retreat, he wasted a moment gawping at Maria in astonishment. And then expelled a *whoof* of air as he folded, mouth agape. Rachel seized hold of the pickaxe handle and yanked it from his loosening grip, leaving Maria's fists free to do their worst.

Maria took advantage to pound a succession of punches into Deacon's solar plexus. Rachel joined in by delivering a hefty kick to his crotch. He looked at her in bemusement, then crumpled, eyes glazing.

As he hit the ground Maria straightened up and glanced over the sarcophagus. Her expression became troubled. She met Rachel's eyes. "Can you handle this? The Monsignor..."

Rachel gave a nod. "You go help him."

"Finish Deacon off quickly," Maria urged as she vaulted over the tomb. "Dominic's out cold."

"He's what?" Rachel sprang to her feet and saw Dominic sprawled near a side wall, Jones standing over him.

Then the chamber tilted crazily and the floor came up fast.

Deacon had made a comeback, his hands around her ankles, wrenching her off her feet. She met the paving stones with a jarring thud but managed to kick her legs free. Even as she got loose Deacon reared up, slouched from the punishment he'd received but still a deadly giant from her ground level eye-view.

"Should have ended me while I was down," he chided between gasps. "Silly little girl."

He was drowning in a black river, his name forgotten, his life forgotten.

Then he heard his name called out. *Dominic.* It was Maria, from the other side of the world.

Her voice drew him up and out of the river and he found himself in a barge with white samite sails. It sailed down all the rivers of the world in a moment.

And brought him to a sea of ancient time.

A hooded woman in white sits in a cave, looking out to sea. She has waited there for him. She has waited there for everyone.

Few come.

He stood on a beach in front of the hooded woman in her wheeled throne of iron. She pulled back her hood, revealing the face of Maria. Her voice was a glissando on a lyre:

"There's a storm out at sea."

He nodded. "It was always coming my way."

"Then remember," she said, "I am the Star of the Sea."

She arose from the metal throne and started to wheel it toward the advancing tide. A push sent it rolling into the waves. She turned to him with a smile. "I'm better off without it. I've always been more of a traveler." A tinge of sadness softened her smile. "You can't stay."

"I know." He looked across the waves. "I have a sea to swim."

"It's the wrong sea. You'll sink."

She reached out and touched his hand. "When you need me most, call my name. I always come in the dark hour."

"Is this a dream?" he asked.

As always. Time to wake up. Into the storm."

She lifted her hand and gave him a gentle push. Slight though the pressure, it sent him reeling. He toppled backward. And fell.

And fell.

An instant of blindness.

Gradually, his vision returned and he discerned a barrel-vaulted roof. He became aware that he was lying on his back, and that he was one long throb of pain from head to toe.

Jones's face loomed up close, blocking his view of the ceiling. "Back so soon?" He brandished a hypodermic and grabbed hold of Dominic's hair. "All the better. I want you to see and feel everything."

The needle descended to Dominic's neck, Jones's thumb firmly on the plunger.

"Strychnine. Not enough to kill. That can wait. But enough to give you convulsions, enough for your lungs to gasp for breath, enough for you to suffer the torments of the damned."

As the needle sank in, he struggled to rise but his limbs refused to obey. He fought to twist his neck away from the needle but the grip Jones had on his hair was unyielding. The plunger was depressed and he could feel the strychnine pumping into him.

"The poison will kick in real soon," Jones's thin mouth was close to a smirk. "You've got ten minutes, max. Count on it."

Maria raced to the tunnel mouth where the battered Monsignor lay supine, a granite block of a man straddling his waist and throttling his narrow throat.

In turn, the Monsignor had his hands at the assailant's face, although there was little force behind the action. And he was awash with blood.

She leaped at the attacker and let fly with a kick to his temples that flung him against the wall and damn near broke her toes. As he tumbled over, she saw what the Monsignor had been doing to the man's face when his eye sockets pulled free of the priest's thumbs. A victim of strangulation, the Monsignor had blinded his strangler. And the chisel embedded in the man's chest, spouting blood from its deep wound, showed that the Monsignor had got in an early, fatal stroke. His ponytailed opponent had, at best, mere minutes to live. It was the attacker's blood that covered the priest, not his own.

The mercenary strained to rise, then flopped into a nerveless heap. She knelt at the Monsignor's side, tore off his Roman collar, and checked for injury. The breath rattled in his throat and his pulse was feeble and erratic. And his ribcage was partially crushed. He'd evidently been battered ferociously before the strangulation.

If he weren't in hospital within half an hour, he'd be dead. She glanced across the vault to where Jones, oblivious to all else in the chamber, was engaged in unlocking a blue metal toolbox. He flipped open the toolbox lid and reached inside.

It seemed that Dominic, sprawled near to Jones, was in no danger for the next few seconds.

The cardinal, for reasons best known to himself, had staggered in and dropped to his knees in a corner, immersed in prayer to God knows what cruel god.

She switched her attention to the area beyond the sarcophagus to ensure Rachel was unhurt.

She exhaled sharply. "Oh, hell."

Silly little girl.

Lying on her back with Deacon looming over her, those words burned into Rachel, branded her as the slight thing Deacon declared her to be. She should have been more like him and buried the pickaxe in his skull in the seconds he was out cold.

Except, that was a line she couldn't cross. It just wasn't in her to kill a defenseless man, however rotten his soul. Not silly, just human.

And not a little girl.

She side-rolled from the path of a wayward kick from Deacon and scrambled to her feet, casting about for a weapon. There was none in sight, and she realized she'd ended up with her back to the Virgin Mary statue with no obvious route of escape.

Still dazed, he swayed slightly as he took a step closer.

"I'd like to get to know you a little better before I finish you off," he breathed hoarsely. He stretched out a finger and circled her left breast. "No prizes for guessing what happens next." He drew back a fist. "First a little softening up."

His fist swung at her face. But she ducked quicker than the speed of the fist. His knuckles cracked into the marble of Mary's effigy. Eyes wide with shock, he vented a sharp grunt.

She slipped under his reach and sprang to one side, muscles tensed to strike a blow. He whirled around on her. And she drove her foot into his stomach.

His arms encircled his waist as he bent forward, head lolling, gray silk tie hanging loose. She grabbed the end of the tie in both hands, gave it a twist for extra purchase, then swung the distracted Deacon full tilt at the statue.

His skull bashed into the effigy with a loud, lethal crack, expelling the light from his eyes and the life from his brain.

Slowly, he slid down the marble, transformed from man to corpse.

Rachel stepped back as he dropped and, with a sideways look, sighted Maria rushing up.

"Are you okay?" Maria inquired urgently.

"I'm fine," she replied, then pointed to where Jones stood with his foot on Dominic's chest.

Maria gave a nod. "Keep in mind that Jones isn't Deacon. Jones is— Jones."

Side by side, they sped across the chamber. Dominic's eyes were open although he appeared immobilized. Charged with fury, Rachel flew at Jones. "Leave my man alone, you prick!"

She lashed out a foot to meet Jones squarely in the head. The kick met vacant air. Jones had vanished like a conjurer. Bewildered, she regained her balance. A supercilious smile curving his lips, Jones stood over four yards away.

Huh? How did he *do* that?

Maria was at her side, bending down to examine Dominic. Jones continued to stand and watch, smiling, just as Chavet knelt in prayer in the background. There was a touch of the surreal to the scene. Then, as she was about to join Maria in seeing to

Dominic, Jones extracted a coin from his pocket and flipped it. He caught it with an easy gesture and looked at the upturned side. He threw a glance at Rachel. "You lose."

He fished inside his jacket, pulling out a leather pouch. Its function was revealed when he slid a hypodermic from inside and held it in an outstretched hand.

"I can spare one for you, girl. You can watch what I do to the other bitch while you're convulsing and gasping for air."

Then in a flash he hurtled at them, a blurred streak of deadliness...

...that ran straight into Dominic's leg which had shot out as swiftly as Jones's onrush.

Tripped at full charge, Jones went airborne, arms windmilling. Hypodermic dropping from a vainly clutching hand, Jones performed an involuntary somersault and crashed headfirst on the ground with bone-jolting impact.

Dominic struggled to his feet, glare fixed on the spreadeagled figure of Jones.

"I'm back."

Chapter 64

Dominic's body still throbbed from the hammering Jones had given him on top of all the punishment it had suffered that night. Ligaments felt strained or torn, muscles complained at every movement, joints protested at the weight he put on them. And his brain felt as though hot tar had been poured into it.

And he had, at best, a ten-minute countdown until the strychnine in his veins laid him low. But he was back on his feet and determined to stay that way while he still retained a spark of awareness.

He wouldn't be long on his feet if Jones had any choice in the matter. The impact to the skull on hitting the floor should have resulted in coma or death, but Jones was swaying upright, ready to renew hostilities. The deep indentation in his forehead was evidence of shattered bone thrust into the brain but he was acting as though he'd received a light tap from a rod.

"Is he human?" Rachel whispered.

Dominic launched himself at Jones as she spoke. Human, superhuman, subhuman, Jones was still in the process of recovery, however fast. With an adversary of this caliber he wasn't about to take any chances.

When he reached the spot where Jones stood, the man had vanished. He'd hopped to one side, quick as thought. But Dominic had read the man's style, and delivered a side-kick in mid-leap. It was his luck the kick was aimed in the direction his opponent had dodged.

And a dash more luck that his kick connected with Jones's knee. The crack of a broken kneecap wasn't the most unwelcome sound he'd ever heard.

He spun around on landing and was surprised to see Jones bearing down on him with hardly a sign of a limp. But the man wore a new expression: uncontrolled rage. It was stamped on his face, sheer outrage at suffering injury from a lesser mortal. He might just as well have shouted out: How dare you? How *dare* you?

Dominic's obvious move was to meet the onrush with a kick to head or stomach. He assumed the stance to do just that. And then performed a completely different maneuver, dropping to the floor and sweeping his right foot across Jones's legs, catching the man by surprise as he swerved aside at the last instant, evading the expected kick.

Jones's sheer speed went against him as he flew over Dominic's foot for the second time in a minute. Dominic helped him on his way with an upward hook of his foot, and watched as Jones crashed headlong and received a facefull of floor to the accompaniment of crushed bone.

A moment after Jones hit the ground, Dominic raced to finish him off. Jones spun around on the floor, left leg bent to deliver a snap-kick. His expression, under the mashed bridge of the nose and broken cheekbones, was indomitable: *I always win.*

Dominic's toecap belied that belief as it slammed into Jones's left temple. And slammed in again, and again. Finally, Jones's eyes clouded. His bruised mouth fell slack, revealing broken teeth. He lay inert, still breathing but comatose.

Then Dominic landed a last kick to the sightless head, out of precaution, or sheer bloody-mindedness.

He was about to step back when an absurd but disturbing thought occurred. According to what he'd heard of Jones from the occasional remark by Martha, and what he'd just witnessed, the man was something more and less than human. Maybe he'd fallen for all the boogeyman superstition surrounding Jones but it was hard to believe this slippery rat was finally down and out.

No, that was crazy. His own banged-up state was getting the better of him. He advanced to meet Rachel, who wore the gladdest of grins.

He tried not to wince as she embraced him, tried to hide the bolts of pain shooting out his nerve endings. "Is everyone okay?" he asked, stroking her hair.

She pulled back. "Oh God— your uncle..."

"Yes," Maria said, "your uncle." She indicated the tunnel mouth where the Monsignor lay, motionless. "He's not dead, but if we don't get him into hospital very, very quickly, he will be." She held up a phone. "No signal down here. We'll have to carry him."

He nodded. "You two carry him. I can barely stand. I'll follow on behind." He didn't want to her to know he had at best eight minutes before the strychnine in his body rendered him incapable of anything.

Rachel regarded him warily. "You're following behind... How close behind?"

"I'll be trudging, not marching, but close."

"How close is close?"

Maria, who seemed to grasp his intention, stepped in, her face impressively stern. "Rachel! This is childish! If Dominic's uncle dies because he was too late in ER, I'm holding you responsible. Every second counts and that's no figure of speech. Now *come on!*" She underlined the point by striding to the prone figure of the Monsignor.

Rachel relented, following in her wake. "Okay, but don't play me for dumb." She looked over her shoulder at Dominic. "Whatever you plan to do, do it quick."

"I promise I'll try." He looked at Chavet. "I'd better check him for a remote detonator, just in case Jones was crazy enough to plant fresh blasting caps in the C-4."

Maria grinned. "Already done. He's clean. I frisked him while you were kicking Jones's head in. He pretended to pray throughout the whole thing."

He gave her a nod. "Thanks."

"You're welcome," she responded as she lifted the Monsignor by the underarms and Rachel raised his legs.

"Oh, and Maria,'" he said. "To be ultra cautious, if new blasting caps were put in the plastique, would you give me a shout? I'll come up and disarm them myself– you can't waste precious minutes with my uncle in such a bad way."

"Consider it done."

Dominic watched as the women carried his uncle up the tunnel, Rachel with the occasional backward glance of concern.

"See you soon," he said in a tone that sounded more like a farewell. He gazed at Rachel for a long moment, then wheeled around and approached Jones.

Up close, the man looked dead to the world. No hint of breath, no rise and fall of the chest. Dominic touched the wiry neck and felt for a pulse. He couldn't detect one. He gave it a few more seconds. Nothing. Jones was dead, as so he should be.

He speedily went through the man's pockets. Apart from a leather pouch containing two hypos there was nothing. No detonator. No means for Chavet to turn the tables and bring the roof down. A glance at an open metal toolbox close by– nothing there either.

So, now for the reason he'd stayed behind: Chavet.

He stood up and approached the cardinal, who knelt lost in prayer in a shadowy corner. Standing over the priest, he waited several seconds– precious seconds, considering the strychnine in his bloodstream– then spoke in a quiet voice:

"Do you have something to confess?"

Rachel began to feel the strain of carrying the Monsignor partway up the stairs to the Testament Chamber. Dominic's uncle may have been on the slim side but he made up for it in height. Despite that, not for a moment did she consider him a burden. Whatever his flaws, he'd come through for his friends in the end.

After they had carefully maneuvered the priest through the manhole into the Testament Chamber and she viewed again the dark walls that displayed the mysteries of the Apocryphon Mariæ, she couldn't help but reflect on the truly historic mission that Dominic's uncle had drawn her into. The Testament Chamber. The sarcophagus in the Chamber of the Dormition. Was it all worth it?

Hell, if they all survived, it was worth it a thousand times over. *If we survive, all is forgiven, Monsignor.*

They had passed through the breached wall into the upper passageway and, while taking care to hold the Monsignor as level and steady as possible, she examined the lumps of plastique. No sign of any reinserted blasting caps. Maria was also glancing around, and kept up the examination as they progressed up the tunnel.

"I don't see any caps in the plastique," she said. "Looks life we're safe."

Maria nodded. "Looks that way."

As they headed down the passage Rachel's thoughts returned to Dominic. He was interrogating Chavet, she knew that. She understood why. But she also had an unformed premonition of something bad coming Dominic's way. Something dark as midnight.

The rest of the journey through the necropolis felt painfully slow and the Monsignor's pallor increasingly deathly but at last the steps up to the surface came into sight. But the stairs proved the hard part. Her muscles developed an acute ache as the climb extended interminably.

Finally they scaled the last flight and entered the Scavi office. Maria checked for a signal on her phone, then instantly punched up a number and awaited a response. "I'm calling Salvator Mundi, a Catholic hospital on the Janiculum," she informed Rachel. "It's near, and one of the best hospitals in Europe. And the Crypt also has dealings—" Her tone abruptly switched to relatively formal as someone came on the line. "Hello, Monsignor Martin Aylesbury's assistant here. You know him? Good. Extreme emergency. The Monsignor has suffered critical injuries, external and internal. We're in the Vatican's Scavi office..." An angry frown creased her brow. "Who cares about Vatican sovereign territory? Oh, okay, we'll bring him to the gateway booth by the Holy Office. Now please, *hurry!*"

She turned off the phone and gave Rachel an apologetic shrug. "A little farther."

Maria wedged the office door open and they carried the priest out into the fog and across the courtyard to the entrance booth, which seemed deserted. Inside they discovered it was occupied by an unconscious guard dumped on the floor.

"I see Jones has passed this way," Maria observed. "Shouldn't be long, even in this fog. It's a short drive from Salvator Mundi. You lie down the other side of the Monsignor and keep him warm. And wait."

"What about Dominic?"

Maria sank to the floor and closed her eyes. Her whisper was scarcely audible. "Just wait."

Chapter 65

Dominic gave the kneeling cardinal a light kick on the thigh. "I said— confess what you did."

Chavet remained in the posture of prayer, hands clasped, eyes tight shut, mouth stirring in silent supplication.

He'd posed the same question about his mother's murder in a dozen variations, and a dozen times the prelate had ignored his existence. What was he supposed to do with this obdurate cardinal? Torture him?

Time was running out. By his reckoning the symptoms of strychnine poisoning were due to hit in fewer than five minutes. At least he didn't have to head up and remove blasting caps: he would have heard from Maria by now if that was required.

Now how in hell to get the cardinal to confess? Confirm, beyond any doubt, his guilt?

Then he caught Chavet glancing at the sarcophagus. The look was fleeting, and fearful. He muttered, barely above a breath: "Stabat Mater." Perhaps, in his scrambled wits, he saw something of dread in the tomb. And maybe the prospect of being thrust inside it would shake the truth loose.

He threw Jones's leather pouch aside and unceremoniously hauled the priest to his feet, biting his lip at the pain of the effort. At the brusque intrusion Chavet gave up the pretense of prayer, protesting loudly. "Are you afraid God will answer my prayers?"

"I'm afraid he won't answer mine," he muttered, dragging the priest to the sarcophagus. The exertion of manhandling the priest was wearing him down, his breathing accelerating, his heartbeat soaring into the red zone. Unless his captive cracked soon...

"What are you doing?" Chavet demanded in a shrill tone.

"I have the perfect spot for you to lie down."

Chavet's feet skidded across the paving as he struggled to break free. "No! You're not putting me in there." He voice subsided to a mumble. "Blood streaming from her wrists, crucified on the air."

A tremor ran up Dominic's back muscles. And he realized that over the last minute or so he'd felt increasingly hot, his face and palms perspiring. And his labored breathing, the heart palpitation...

Those weren't the results of injury and exertion. They were the symptoms of strychnine poisoning. Time was almost up.

He slammed the cardinal's back onto the rim of the tomb. "Tell me the truth or in you go."

The cardinal looked down into the recess in stark dread. His emaciated features had the look of a desert ascetic faced with all the devils in hot hell as he recited the words of a hymn:

"Stabat Mater dolorosa
iuxta crucem lacrimosa,
dum pendebat filius.
Cuius animam gementem,
contristatam et dolentem
pertransivit gladius."

Dominic was familiar with the medieval sequence:

Stands the mother of sorrows
Weeping before the cross
On which her son is hung.
Through her sighing spirit,
Compassionate and mourning
Is thrust a sword.

Whatever Chavet saw in the tomb, seismic, it shook the foundations of his soul.

He was on the verge of confessing.

Since surfacing into consciousness, and instantly having the presence of mind to sham insensibility, Jones had quickly registered the extent of his injuries. The damage to his skull was the most critical. A true professional, he had made a study of anatomy, sometimes on living subjects.

He had also practiced control of his autonomic nervous system. With concentration, he was able to slow his heartbeat, reduce his respiration to two breaths a minute. There were times, rare times, when it was best policy to appear weak in order to emerge all the stronger. Or rise from the dead.

It had been a close thing when the American rifled through his pockets. The merest hint that Quinn had guessed he was faking and Jones would have been up and at his throat.

He listened as Quinn became more heated, more involved with Chavet. The voices came from the direction of the sarcophagus. Quinn was ripe. Ripe for the taking. Jones opened his eyes a fraction and observed the two men at the tomb, the American with his back turned. He accelerated his heartbeat, quietly increased his respiration.

Then slipped the detonator from his mouth and back into the jacket pocket that previously held it.

Jones slowly uncoiled, raising his head from the floor.

Chapter 66

Dominic, shaken by another spasm, held Chavet by the throat, forcing his head back into the tomb's recess.

"Confess, Chavet," he gasped, pulse pounding in his ears. "Last chance." Another spasm, the most severe yet, arched his back.

Chavet's fright subsided as he observed the symptoms take hold. "You're poisoned. Jones injected the poison."

"I'm just a little under the weather."

"I don't think so. You're getting weaker."

"Still stronger than you." He twisted Chavet's head, forcing him to look down into the tomb. "Tell me now, last chance."

"No," came the flat response.

Then the cardinal's newfound confidence fell away as quickly as it had risen. His stare, stark with fear, was focused on the tomb's interior. His mouth worked spasmodically, venting an incoherent mumble.

Dominic leaned up close. "What was that?" He was starting to hyperventilate but he forced the words out. "Speak up."

But Chavet wasn't aware of him: his sole attention was on the stony hollow. And whatever he saw or sensed there, it terrified him.

Listening intently to the man's muffled babble, difficult to distinguish through the pounding in his head, Dominic began to identify a few phrases:

"...burning light... Annunciata... go back... *Stabat Mater*... don't look at me... you're dead... *Cuius animam gementem*... Annunciata, I prayed that I sent you to purgatory... I prayed every day... if you're in hell, the guilt is yours... it's not mine, not mine..."

Dominic released the cardinal and staggered back. He had his answer.

I prayed that I sent you to purgatory...

Chavet saw what he feared in the sarcophagus. The ghosts of the past. And one of those ghosts, Dominic's mother.

The cardinal slithered to the floor, hand clasping his pectoral crucifix as though the metal would preserve the shreds of his sanity. Then, unsteadily, Chavet rose to his feet. Either the crucifix was working its magic or breaking contact with the sarcophagus had banished the ghosts. The cardinal wasn't fully sane, if he ever had been, but the storm of madness had abated. He pulled himself erect and stared straight past Dominic. What he saw back there restored his confidence. The priest might have been looking at anything, a gendarme, a Vatican official, a vision of Christ.

But somehow Dominic knew it was Jones. He knew. Jones, risen from the dead.

He kicked Chavet aside and vaulted over the tomb, spinning around as he landed on the far side. And damn near collapsed on the spot from the effort.

Jones's broken face reared up from behind the sarcophagus. An instant later, despite his cracked knee, he landed lightly on the ledge and smiled down at Dominic.

"I heard you like the high ground, Quinn. I've taken it from you. Me topsy, you turvy. And maybe you didn't hear— I've come out of a coma before, real quick. What's inside me— you can't begin to guess at."

"Sure I can. You have hidden shallows."

In response Jones lashed out with a kick. Instead of retreating, Dominic jumped to receive it. The jolt that ran through his shoulder traveled right down to his shoes and up to his scalp. But he was on the ledge, level with Jones.

Flinging his arms around his tormentor, Dominic threw his weight down and to the side. And fell into the recess, Jones caught under him.

After expelling a faint grunt at the impact of the stone on his back, Jones grinned up at him in mockery. "It'll take more than that to finish me, Quinn."

"I know," Dominic gasped, feeling as if his thudding heart was close to bursting.

And Jones was right. The fall into the sarcophagus meant nothing to a man who should be dead twice over. But his adversary's strong suit was his abnormal speed, fleet of foot, virtuoso of the rapid twist and turn. None of which could be employed within a confined space.

Inside the sarcophagus, Dominic had a chance of defeating Jones. Hammer him down into death.

Then he choked at the hands throttling his throat. Jones had moved his arms like a striking snake. In the closest of close combat, he still had tricks up his sleeve.

Dominic returned the favor, circling his fingers around the other's throat and squeezing with his last reservoir of strength. As they strangled each other, it was as much a contest of will as of strength. All down to who would black out first. For a while it was an even contest.

Then he began to lose.

The pressure on his windpipe, already strained from the effects of strychnine, soon took its toll. His pulse thundered in his ears. His eyesight faded.

He started to hallucinate. Bright flashes of the past, evanescent scenes of his life, scarcely glimpsed as they rushed by.

And a strange sensation that the sarcophagus was emitting an unearthly light around him, coming to life.

He was dying.

Dying, but keeping a tight grip on his enemy, a primal instinct.

A kaleidoscope of imagery overwhelmed his vision, spun what remained of his wits.

Through the riot of phantasmagoria, Jones's face emerged, grinning in victory. His voice resounded from a vast distance as the grin widened. "You're finished. Say goodbye."

The grin froze on the last word. That same instant, Dominic felt a coldness seep through him, to the core of bone and the essence of blood.

Although Jones remained visible, nothing else did. The sarcophagus had vanished. In its place was nothing. Black vacancy. No heaven above. No hell below. No earth between.

Everywhere was a nowhere.

In that void, he and Jones hovered, motionless, hands around each other's throats, Jones still wearing that rictus grin, a freeze-frame of a face.

After the descent into disorientation, the sudden clarity of Dominic's thoughts was all the more remarkable. He might have been dead, but he knew he wasn't. He might have been banished to a region of space where stars had died or never been born, but he knew he hadn't.

The gulfs between the stars were brimming with plenitude compared to the nowhere in which he floated. This wasn't even the space-time of a universe devoid of stars. Space expanded forever outward from the loud whisper of its superheated birth. Space curved and stretched. Space was *something*.

But he had fallen into nothing. Negative space. He didn't belong here. He believed in *something*.

But there was nowhere to go, no up, no down, no direction. And there was no one to call out to, even if he had a voice. No one...

Then he remembered. The hooded woman. The sea cave. Dream or reality, they shone in memory. They beckoned.

Maria, he implored.

Maria...

A ripple spread across the blackness. More ripples followed, accompanied by a sound, the plash of an oar. Silver foam stirred from the agitated dark. And a boat drew alongside. In the boat was the hooded woman, her face composed of starlight.

She lowered the oars and reached down a hand. "It's the wrong sea," she said. "You'll drown."

He grasped her hand. She pulled him onboard with an effortless swing of the arm.

"Now fly," she commanded.

And he flew. He soared, and as he soared he watched the image of Jones, with its rictus of a smile shrink into the distance.

An instant later, Dominic was back in the sarcophagus. He was part of the world. Pulse beating, breath heaving.

A convulsion curved his back and he reared up, neck pulling free of Jones's encircling hands. Jones stayed where he was, arms locked in the act of strangulation, eyes vacant, body inert.

He crawled out of the tomb, struggling for breath and scarcely able to stand. Chavet hovered close by but retreated a step at a look from Dominic.

Ignoring the priest, he peered into the sarcophagus. Jones wasn't dead, there was a barely detectable rise and fall of the chest. But nor could he be described as alive. He was back there, in nowhere. Something told him that Jones would always be there. Jones was undead.

Then it hit home what he was telling himself. Undead? Nowhere Man? He shook his head. The poison must have unhinged him. He'd hallucinated on the verge of a blackout, weaving the memory of a hooded woman dream, and Jones had lapsed into a coma. And this time he wouldn't be coming back—ever.

The world was rid of that monster, but one thing was sure, he had no right to lie in the tomb of Mary. Dominic could hear his heart palpitating, feel his legs buckling, but no way would he leave Jones in Mary's resting-place. He took as deep a breath as he could, and summoned what vestige of energy remained.

It was a lung-busting struggle, but he managed to heave the undead body out of the recess and let it drop to the floor. Task accomplished, he confronted Chavet who had watched the whole proceeding in silence.

Senses abruptly see-sawing, Dominic staggered to one side and averted a fall by grabbing the sarcophagus rim. Simultaneously, the priest darted up to Jones and bent over the body, muttering prayers.

Preparing to drag himself out the chamber, Dominic gave a farewell look at the sarcophagus.

And then he saw her, lying in the limestone base.

It was the woman he'd glimpsed on first opening the tomb, but this time she didn't vanish in the blink of an eye. Her body reposed, the essence of stillness, enclosing silence.

He gazed, entranced, not simply by her beauty, but the beauty behind the beauty.

A moment passed, or an age of undiscovered gods, and the sarcophagus base dissolved into a sea. A sea of stars, Mary buoyant upon the waves. That sea was full to the brim, and resonated with silent hymns in starlight communion. It was the soul of all that could be.

It was too good not to be true. And, as he'd always known, always forgotten, it was Home.

Remote but clear, he heard a benediction from a distant shore of time:

Our birth is but a sleep and a forgetting:
The soul that rises with us, our life's star,
Hath had elsewhere its setting,
And cometh from afar...

He took out the stubby candle he'd found in the Shrine and reached out his hand, candle lofted. He held up the candle to a star in the sea.

And lit the candle from a star.

Star of the sea. *Stella Maris*

The light of the candle rose up before him, a living flame of maternal radiance. A maternal maiden.

My mother's younger than me.

Then there was no candle, only the flame. One more star.

He looked down to where Mary reposed on the sea, and reached down to touch her face, the most sacred and sacrilegious act of his life.

His hand contacted nothing but air. The vision vanished: a dream too large for the world.

The sea rolled away. The world turned to stone.

His fingers grasped for the quicksilver of illumination even as it escaped. Beyond his reach.

He stumbled back from the empty sarcophagus, almost remembering, almost... But he was already losing the memory. It was too real to remember. His world couldn't contain it.

Swaying on his feet, he became aware of his surroundings. Back in the world. No— back in *a* world. He looked around as the world rushed in on him. The chamber. Chavet. The poison in his veins. Before the strychnine laid him low he had to walk or crawl his way to the surface. Back to Rachel.

A quick glance at the candle stub in his hand. Unlit. Unhallowed. No star-born flame. But there was— a legacy. What passed for real life was no more than the agitated surface of an infinite sea. That he wouldn't forget.

On the other side of the tomb Chavet continued his garbled prayers, hunched over the undead Jones. It appeared that the cardinal had witnessed nothing out of the ordinary. No visions, no flame of the spirit.

The miracle wasn't in the stone. It was in the presence. The presence was gone, its testament a sense of loss.

Dominic moved to the tunnel. And stifled a cry as a violent spasm sent him reeling, nerves afire. Fighting for breath, he rode out the storm. Fever mounting, he stumbled across the floor, observing the priest from the corner of his eye.

The hard stamp of psychosis was imprinted on Chavet's features. His trembling fingers scrabbled in Jones's jacket. And from the jacket pocket he plucked a small, oval object.

"Oh, God," Dominic groaned. A detonator. "How did you..."

"You were looking at me when Jones took it from his mouth. I was looking at him."

"And the blasting caps?"

"Concealed inside the plastique." Chavet's fingers moved to the safety switch. "Quinn, I must bury this evil. And that means burying us both. It has to be done."

Dominic's heart lurched as Chavet double-switched the detonator. He flinched in anticipation of an almighty explosion.

None came.

An instant of relief, until the truth struck home.

"Of course," he murmured. "Your men used delay caps."

Dominic's thoughts raced in a blur. Judging from the earlier explosion, he had from forty seconds to a minute. And he'd already squandered the best part of ten seconds since the trigger signal was transmitted. At the very most, fifty seconds to get clear.

He *had* to believe he had the full fifty seconds or there wasn't a hope in hell.

With that thought he pushed his reluctant limbs into what was intended a sprint but resulted in an unsteady scramble.

"Stay and pray in these last moments!" Chavet implored.

"Pray for your own soul," Dominic muttered as he stumbled out of the chamber.

From there on it was keep going, keep going, to the background of an undefined countdown. In normal fitness he could probably reach minimal safe distance in forty seconds. The state he was in, heart bashing his ribs, gasping for air, burning up with fever, he had only the ghost of a chance.

He labored up a tunnel that seemed to elongate. By the time he reached the steps the deadly count in his head hit the thirty-seconds-to-go mark, give or take a heartbeat.

But it might blow right now...

That taunting inner voice tracked him all the way.

He clambered up the stairway, cursing aloud as a searing convulsion flung him back down the steps. He damn near bit his lower lip off in his determination to force through the agony, battle against his wracked maze of nerves.

He resumed his ascent and lurched into the Testament Chamber. A spasm hit as he swerved to the breach, beyond which ranged clumps of primed explosives. From here on it was instant death if they detonated.

For a fleeting moment he considered whether he should attempt to extract the blasting caps, then dismissed the idea as crazy. If Chavet weren't obsessed with overdoing the amount of explosives, he might have taken the risk. But by the time he'd extricated a couple of caps the whole area would be blown to glory.

Twenty seconds to go, give or take.

He toiled up the passageway, aware his luck was already stretched to breaking point as his heart was close to bursting.

Seconds later he reached the breached entrance to the necropolis, a vague smudge to his feverish, failing vision.

Another ten seconds and he'd be clear.

As he stumbled through the breach he dredged the last of his reserves and drove himself down the necropolis passageway. Up ahead was the open climate control door. If he could reach it and slam it shut behind him...

But he couldn't see it anymore. He couldn't see anything.

And with the onset of blindness his legs finally gave way. So close, but his ravaged constitution couldn't take him any farther.

The ground came up to meet him. He hardly felt the impact.

So, he'd done his best. His body had performed a minor miracle to take him this far, but a major miracle was required.

He would never see Rachel again. He would never see anyone again.

Goodbye.

After a long second of despair he heard a voice cross an immense distance.

"Dominic. Did you think I'd leave you after the ambulance arrived?" Maria's voice.

"The tunnel's going to blow," he managed to gasp. "Any second..."

A vague sensation of hands grasping his wrists and his body sliding along the ground. When the sliding motion halted his eyesight returned in impressionistic daubs.

Maria, pushing the plexiglass door shut behind them.

Maria, pulling him to his feet.

And suddenly a hard surface slammed into his back and he was airborne, carried on a blistering gust. Ear-shattering thunder blasted in its wake, numbing what was left of his senses. For a while, he imagined himself sailing on the wind and thunder forever.

Then he came to earth with a jolt, enveloped by dense, choking clouds. He lay still for a space, face down. After a few moments he realized there was a weight on his back.

Maria lay prone beside him, her mouth spreading in a smile. "Close call," she said, darting an upward glance. "The door on top of us took the brunt of the blast. Rachel's on her way. Lucky for her she's not too fast on her feet."

He looked up at the debris-strewn tunnel ahead. And heard a blessed voice echo down it.

"Maria!" Rachel's voice was high with alarm. "What happened? How's Dominic?"

Dominic scarcely heard his croak of a reply through the ringing in his ears:

"Never better."

Chapter 67

The hours passed in the Chamber of the Dormition, and with the passing of hours, the lamps went out, one by one.

And the dark moved in, step by step. And so did the fear, breath by breath.

Chavet approached the tomb, overlooked by a marble Virgin Mary. If he looked inside the tomb, and nothing was in there, the fear might go away. So he looked. And there was nothing. He started to smile.

The smile died.

A woman in a hooded robe of rough white wool lay in the sarcophagus.

A blink of the eyes and she was gone. Another had taken her place. Annunciata.

Annunciata looked up and stretched out her hand to the marble image of Mary. Shuddering, he backed away. He was locked in this terrible place with Annunciata, with only one means of escape. God would understand.

He took the hypodermics from Jones' leather pouch and injected them into his arm. Hands clasped in prayer, he waited for the end to come.

When the end came, it was not with grace, or kindness. His body convulsed, the spasms increasing in frequency. Soon he was a gasping fish, floundering, thrashing the floor. A savage convulsion arched him upward, arms outstretched in the pose of crucifixion.

At the end, in his last brutal seizure, lungs bursting from asphyxiation, he toppled against the statue of Mary and collapsed at her feet.

His last breath was a prayer.

"*Ad Jesum per Mariam.*"

Noon sunlight gilded the dome of Peter and slanted across the vast oval of St. Peter's Piazza.

In a bluff, rising wind that presaged a gale, the tourists were out in force, roaming between Bernini's colonnades and pouring in and out of St. Peter's basilica. Some eyes glanced warily at a man and two women standing under one of the massive pillars. The women wore scratches and bruises, along with a few adhesive bandages. The man looked like a walking wounded freshly returned from a war zone with full bandage and plaster outfit and iodine-ethanol makeup.

Dominic met the odd wary look with the occasional weary smile.

Rachel and Maria were at his side and Martha was in the palm of his hand.

Martha's image on the iPhone, her onscreen movements jerky, grinned up at him from her hospital bed.

"So the Monsignor lives to fight another day," she said. "What about you? Was Salvator Mundi so grim you had to get out of there before you could barely walk? Activated charcoal infusions take a while to counteract strychnine. I know about these things."

"I can visit the hospital for the infusions and I've had all the phenobarbital I need. Also I'm clear of the twenty-four-hour danger period. Forty-plus hours' hospital time is plenty for me, even though the staff treated me like nobility. A doctor gave me this phone, gratis."

"That figures. You have friends in Jesuit places. Oh, by the way, Monsignor Ortega here wants you to know you guys are immune from prosecution. Officially, you were never here."

He pocketed the palmtop and glanced at Rachel. "We'll visit her this afternoon."

"And I," said Maria, "must be moving on." She held out a grubby plastic bag. "Parting gifts."

"May I?" asked Rachel, already delving into the bag.

Maria flicked back a strand of hair the wind had blown across her eyes. "Of course."

Rachel extracted two items from the bag, two thick spiral-bound pads, dog-eared and dusty. She flipped through one and glanced up. "It's covered in Greek writing— in blue biro."

Maria, her mouth slanting leftward in a charming, quirky smile, started to move away. "It seems as good a time as any to show it around. I was thinking of putting it on the web." She gave a conspiratorial wink, then backed away, saying goodbye with an upraised hand. "I'll see you in your dreams."

They returned her farewell as Maria swung around and strolled across the piazza, waving a hand over her shoulder without looking back.

His gaze veered from Maria to the writing pads in Rachel's hand. "Greek, you said. As in classical Greek?"

"Uh-huh. As in classical Greek." She lifted an eyebrow. "And yes, I'm thinking what you're thinking."

"I'm not sure I dare think what I'm thinking. So— what's in the other pad?"

She passed it over to him. "Have fun. Check it out."

He opened the first page to discover the writing was in English. A translation of the other book?

The first lines were vivid on the page:

I, Mary of Bethlehem, mother of Jesus, was a witness to the beginning, and will be a witness to the end. We are alone in the universe, but the universe is not alone.

He looked up from the script. Rachel's attention was fixed on ceding figure of Maria, still a dominant presence in the

"And the excavation?"

Her smile became rueful. "It'll stay buried. Keep the secret in the Vatican family. They're putting out a story of 'subsidence' in the necropolis caused by a combination of... Oh, hang on, the doctor wants a word..."

He lowered the phone, gaze wandering the piazza. Study of the Testament Chamber alone might have transformed the world. The loss hit him in the two most painful places— in the heart and in the head.

As for the visions he'd witnessed in the Dormition Chamber, he would never be sure if they were supernatural or delusional. Only he had experienced them, and in an exhausted state susceptible to hallucination. No definitive proof.

But in the end that didn't matter. He had faith now in the unknown, and that opened up a whole world— or worlds. And, in his heart, there was a conviction. The flame of the spirit isn't snuffed out when the dark closes in. In a hierarchy of realms beyond imagining, the flame still burns.

And the divine, the numinous, the visionary gleam— however the inexpressible was clumsily expressed— it wasn't lost for all time. His thoughts drifted back to the beginning, to the coasts of his childhood on the Irish Sea:

...Though inland far we be,
Our souls have sight of that immortal sea
Which brought us hither,
Can in a moment travel thither,
And see the children sport upon the shore
And hear the mighty waters rolling evermore.

"Dominic?"

Reverie dispelled, he returned his attention to the palmtop screen.

Martha gave a sideways nod. "*Il Duce* here tells me I have rest. I'm about to get cut off."

"Well, you take it easy now."

She gave a wink. "Keep the faith."

About the Author

Stephen Marley, the author of eight novels and a designer of video games, was born in Derby, England. He was expelled from one school and left another with virtually no qualifications, then worked as a building site labourer, office worker, shop worker and other uninspiring jobs until he finally made it to university where he earned an MSc in the history of science and almost finished a PhD in ancient Chinese science. He left his academic career to take up writing full time and now lives by a Derbyshire river a short frisbee throw from Augustus Pugin's first church and a javelin throw from the world's oldest factory. He likes Buffy the Vampire Slayer and boxer dogs and describes himself as a Leonard Cohen Catholic.

en.wikipedia.org/wiki/Stephen_Marley_(writer)

www.facebook.com/stephen.marley.543

twitter.com/@Marley_Author

"Dominic," Rachel murmured, "who do you think she is, really?"

He watched Maria enter the far colonnade, blue raincoat flapping as she headed into the face of a mounting gale. "I know who I want her to be."

He raised a hand in salutation as the dark blue figure passed out of sight:

"Ave, Maria."

THE END

Printed in Poland
by Amazon Fulfillment
Poland Sp. z o.o., Wrocław